Easter's Lilly

Judy Serrano

6k Publishing

www.6kPublishing.com

ISBN-13: 978-1544967073

PUBLISHED BY 6K PUBLISHING

www.6kPublishing.com

Printed in the United States of America

Praise for Judy Serrano and the Easter's Lilly Series

""…One of those books that you just cannot put down."
——Melissa Vera, Adventures of Frugal Mom

""Judy Serrano is a great author never leaving a dull moment in the book."
——Rachel Simons, blogger Stressed Rach

""Judy has masterfully written a love story full of so much passion, courage, strength, and oh, the excitement! Easter's Lilly is stuffed full of non-stop action and will leave you falling in love, yearning for more."
——Jodi Baker, Uniquely Moi Books

""I tried to sleep but I found myself thinking of the story too much."
—Gina Butler, www.ginaslibrary.info

""I read this in two nights… It's a love story with a mobster family twist and it moves fast enough to keep you glued to the pages. I enjoy the way Judy Serrano tells a story."
——Lisa E. Taylor, "Lisa @ kssnnikkel"

CONTENTS

Author Notes

About the Author
Other Exciting Reads
Connect with Judy

Author Notes

I would like to thank my family for always being so supportive. My husband Miguel who never complains when I ask him to format, edit, and create covers for my novels, Miguel, Theo, Tad, and Enrique for always giving me encouragement and time to write, and my mother, Barbara O'Brien for always encouraging me to follow my dreams.

I would also like to thank you, my wonderful readers for giving me the opportunity to put out these books. My Easter's Lilly Series is very special to me, and I am grateful that you enjoy reading them as much as I enjoy writing them.

CHAPTER 1

The Discovery

I opened my eyes to unfamiliar surroundings. The air had a stench of old cigarettes and stale beer. My eyes caught notice of my skirt draped over my purse on a chair, by the door. This startled me as I reached down to feel what I was wearing. I had on a pair of sweatpants, which fit me rather well and I was grateful I was still wearing the same shirt from last night. I pulled myself up a bit; just to notice the three half-smoked cigarettes in the ashtray beside me on the nightstand and a bong in desperate need of cleaning next to it. There were four beer cans by the ashtray, empty and crushed in the middle. I had discovered the source of the smell. Just then I heard the door crack open and a head popped into the doorway. I was startled and jumped a little as he said, "Good, you're awake." He had long stringy brown hair and some facial hair on his chin that I was sure he thought was a goatee. His mustache was pencil thin and looked as though it had been painted on his face. He was wearing a hat that was worn back in the old days in gangster movies. He looked about my age, twenty-something, and was very thin. I guessed that it was his sweatpants I was wearing after I got a good look at him. "How do you feel?"

"I'm fine," I said. "I have a bit of a headache, though. Who are you?"

He approached me at that point and I jerked back. He had on red sneakers and clothing that matched only to the blind. I assumed Good Will was his department store of choice. "I'm Johnny Malone," he answered. "I already know you're Lilly O'Hara. We met at the party last night."

My heart leapt into my mouth, which I was sure was filled with cotton. I was shocked and speechless. Finally, after an awkward pause I managed to squeak out, "Did we…?"

"No, no…" he answered quickly. "I'm nothing if not a gentleman." I breathed out a sigh of relief.

"Darla, my roommate Patrick's girlfriend, helped you change your clothes last night."

But I'm in your bed, aren't I?" I asked.

"I slept on the couch." He gave me a crooked smile when I said that. It was kind of charming.

"Thank you for that." I was so embarrassed. "Was I drugged? What am I doing here?"

"I got a tip last night that the cops were on their way to the party. I ran out there to tell Rudy so he could flush the drugs and get everyone out of the house." He paused. "Rudy, being Rudy, refused and is now spending a little time jail."

I had to think for a minute. I remembered meeting Rudy last night at the club down the hill from my house. He invited me to a party at his house. Then I remembered him inviting me into a back room. I could feel my face flush. It felt like rushing hot water. There was a mountain of white powder on the mirror in the back room. I looked at Johnny and said, "Oh my gosh, I do remember."

"You were the only person at the party I didn't know, so I tried to get you out of there. You came home with me pretty easily. You were very friendly." He smiled. "I drove your car here and you passed out in the front seat. Pat and Darla drove the other car home." I was stunned. This was very out of character for me. I don't do drugs, get drunk or go home with unidentified men. "We poured you into bed and let you sleep it off. You're Mick's daughter, right?"

"How do you know my dad?"

"Chief of police, right?"

"Don't tell me how you know. I don't think I want to know." I laid my head back down on the pillow.

"It's not like that," he snickered. "Trust me, Mick would have been furious if he found you there."

"I guess I owe you an apology and a thank you," I answered. "You're right, my dad would've freaked."

"How about some breakfast," he offered. "I work at the Grey Willow here in town. I'm an excellent cook."

"If you don't say so yourself," I answered. I began to find his eccentricities a little alluring.

"Really," he said. "I'm the assistant chef at the restaurant."

"Breakfast sounds great," I answered. "I'm sold."

I stumbled out of bed as he left me to go cook breakfast. I found his presence oddly comforting. I made the bed, opened the door to the bedroom and looked around for the kitchen. I could smell the garlic and onions mixed with the aroma of the coffee. It drew me like a child to danger. He presented me with a cheese omelet with potatoes incomparable to anything I had ever tasted before. When it was time to go, I carried my heels and skirt and walked barefooted on his pebbled driveway to my car. All I could think about was how I was going to sneak into the house unnoticed. Fortunately, my room had a back entrance and when I got home, I slipped into bed and closed my eyes. I noticed my mother's red head look in and out of the door. I glance at the clock and it was already nine thirty in the morning.

"I told you she was here," I heard my mother whisper to my dad. "She must have gotten home late."

"She wasn't here," he answered.

"How would you know?" she asked in an agitated voice. "You worked all night."

"That's how I know." I didn't hear any more words after that.

I was never more grateful to a stranger. I slept for another hour or so and took a shower. I couldn't stop thinking about Johnny. From where did he get a tip about the police going to the party? Is there a leak in the police department that I needed to tell my dad about? If I did tell him, he would know where I was last night and that couldn't happen.

I tossed Johnny's sweatpants in the washing machine with some of my other clothes, looking for a reason to see him again. I finished with the laundry and headed into the living room where my father was sitting. "Lilly?" he asked.

"Yes, dad, it's me," I answered in dismay. I poured myself a cup of my father's coffee and headed into the living room.

"Let's go outside onto the patio and enjoy the view." I followed him outside and we sat on the very uncomfortable wicker furniture admiring the mountains. "Lilly, I worry about you."

"Dad, I'm fine. What are you worried about?" I answered, knowing that somehow, he knew that I had spent the night at Johnny's.

I heard you were at the club last night. Meet anyone?"

I paused and wondered what would be an acceptable answer. "I don't know; a few people."

"Lilly, stay away from there," he answered.

"Why?" I asked. His face was beginning to acquire worry lines as we talked.

"I already know you spent the night out there with Rudy and Johnny." He got up and started to walk around the patio.

"I'm not sure what the problem is," I answered. I knew what the problem was but wasn't sure what to say.

"Did you sleep with him, Lilly?"

"Who?" I answered back. I was having trouble swallowing at this point, terrified of being discovered.

"Okay, let's stop playing games." He continued to walk around nervously. "John… did you sleep with John?"

"No dad, I just met him."

"You spent the whole damn night at his house. How can you explain that?"

"Dad, I don't need to." I stood up and became very defensive. "What's wrong with you? I'm 23 years old and he's just a guy."

"That's just it, Lilly, he's not just a guy."

"What are you talking about? He's a cook at the Grey Willow."

"Just stay away, Lilly. Promise me…"

"Fine. I'll stay away." I said it but had no intention of standing behind my words.

"Good." He smiled. "Have you given any thought to getting a job?" That came out of left field but I shouldn't have been surprised. I quit college and was drifting along senselessly for quite a while. "Maybe you could try to find a new place to sing." I spent a lot of time singing locally before we moved to Sedona, Arizona. "How about finding a job?"

"Fine, I'll find a job somewhere." I got up and went back into the kitchen. I was desperate to see Johnny again and threw the sweatpants into the dryer. It was about a half-hour before they were done and I folded them up and drove as fast as I could to Johnny's house.

When I pulled into the driveway, my heart was racing. I could feel my knees weakening, as I got closer to the door. I rang the doorbell in unexplainable anticipation. A woman with frizzy blond hair answered the door. She was wearing a bathrobe that obviously did not belong to her and she had a cigarette hanging out of her mouth. She had that "just woke up" look about her. "Yeah?" she asked. It took me a few minutes to remember how to speak. I could see Darla on the couch, so I knew this woman was not there with Pat.

"Is Johnny home?" I asked. I was so hoping for a, "Nope, not here," answer.

"John!" she screamed. I began to feel like I was in the middle of a bad movie. He came to the door with a towel wrapped around his waist. I was breathless and afraid that my look of shock was not disguised very well. "Here," I said, pushing the sweats into his stomach as I tried to make a quick, discreet getaway.

"Wait!" he yelled to me.

I turned and looked at him. "Thanks for your help the other night. I'm so sorry I interrupted." I could barely feel my legs anymore as I briskly walked to my car. I could hear his low voice calling my name as I stumbled into the car and flew out of the driveway. It took me a few minutes to maintain a steady heartbeat after I got a safe distance from the house. It was at this defining moment that I realized I would have to find a life for myself that was independent of any man, and that included Johnny and my father.

Since finding a job singing was unlikely in this tiny town, I decided to go back to my old standby: Waitressing. I drove down to the main highway and noticed a French bistro off the beaten path cradled in the red rocks. I drove down the small windy road and parked in the strangely inconvenient parking lot. As I approached the restaurant, I noticed a tall, well-built man in a tuxedo at the front door. "One for lunch?" he asked.

"No sir," I answered. "I was wondering if you were looking to hire a waitress."

He looked at me curiously. "Go ahead and ask the bartender for an application." He was still sizing me up a bit. He was flamboyantly homosexual. "I don't like to hire girls. Men are more professional." He said it with a hint of superiority. I tried not to comment and headed towards the bartender. I knew at this point that my good looks were not going to get me this job. The bartender looked at me very much the same way the guy at the door did.

What do you want?" He had a thick French accent.

"An application please," I answered.

"Any experience waiting tables?" I looked behind me only to find a man in a chef's uniform standing there. He was a very handsome man with an enticing French accent. "I said, any experience, beautiful lady?"

"Yes," I answered. I looked at him trying to figure out if he too, was more interested in men than women.

He took my hand and kissed it. "Pierre." He smiled, thinking himself to be very seductive.

"Lilly," I responded. "About five years."

"I would have guessed Marilyn." He looked up at my face and I could see his brown eyes well with delight.

"Marilyn?" I asked curiously. "Who's she?"

"You look just like Marilyn Monroe," he answered, rather pleased with himself.

"Sure I do." I started to think that maybe my good looks would land me this job.

"It appears that I have embarrassed you," he replied. "You're hired." He laughed a bit. "I'm sorry, but I have to have a woman in here somewhere before I go crazy."

"No girls?" I looked around suspiciously.

"No girls," he answered with disappointment in his tone. "I have a breakfast and lunch shift open. Be here at 5:30 in the morning."

"Seriously?" I asked.

"Is this going to be a problem?" He smiled a serious smile at me that was almost irresistible.

"No, no problem." I was very unhappy with the hours but knew at this point that I had no choice. It was important for me to establish an independent life and this was going to be the beginning.

"5:30 then, Marilyn. Don't be late."

When 5:30 arrived, it was not a happy moment for me. I had to wake up at 4:30 just to arrive on time. I had never thought of myself as a morning person. As a matter of fact, when I was younger, my dad used to tease me about being a vampire. He said I never opened my eyes until it was almost dark. When I got to the restaurant, Pierre

was singing and very energetically preparing the food for the breakfast rush. His handsome body was distracting. I must admit that the accent was ridiculously sexy. He continuously referred to me as Marilyn, which I found annoying. But as time went on, I got used to it.

When 6:00 came around they opened the doors and the very first customers were Johnny and Rudy. I was shocked that he had found me when I never told him about my new job. Before I even had a moment to meet his eyes; the owner, Jim, confronted him aggressively. Jim put his hand on Johnny's chest and pushed him outside. "Do not show up here." Jim put out as masculine a voice as he could muster.

"I'm not leaving until I see her," Johnny said, intentionally antagonizing him. I peeked around the doorway and saw Johnny's face right up against Jim's.

"I'll call Mick and have you arrested. I have a restraining order and you know that."

"I won't cause trouble, Jim. Just let me see her."

"This is why I don't hire women. They're always trouble. Besides she and Pierre have a thing. Get lost!"

Johnny and Rudy hesitated before they walked away. Rudy put his hand on Johnny's shoulder. "Look man, a relationship is out of the question anyway. Let it go."

"Pierre and Lilly? I won't have it," Johnny sputtered as they disappeared from view out the door.

Jim walked up to me and grabbed my arm. "Since you were eavesdropping, I won't mince words." His grip began to sting. "I suppose I have you to thank for this."

"I didn't ask him to come."

"I have spent years keeping him away. Don't invite him here." He walked away angrily.

I ran after him. "Wait Jim!" I finally caught up with him in the kitchen. Pierre and the other cooks had their eyes on both of us. "What is it about Johnny that everyone is telling me to keep away from?"

The room got very quiet. Jim grabbed me again by the arms and shook me. "He's a drug addict and a dealer. He's dangerous. He buys his supplies from some crazy guy in Mexico. They call this guy

Satan or the beast! People around him die." He walked off leaving me standing there with red marks on my forearms. I could barely catch my breath. This "drug addict" saved me from a possible arrest. He was a perfect gentleman. How could he be so bad?

I ran after him again and cried out, "Jim, I don't know how he found me. I promise, I didn't invite him."

Jim laughed almost uncontrollably when I said that. "He has eyes and ears everywhere. I hope for your sake, you're not involved with him. He's like a disease, you know. An incurable one." He left me there, speechless wondering what had just happened. I couldn't move or breathe. Pierre came up behind me and put his hands on my shoulders. "Marilyn, get back to work." And I did just that.

I hung up my apron and left the building. As I approached my car I saw a tall, lanky figure with a hat by my car. As I got closer I thought to myself, "Oh my gosh… it's Johnny." My heart was filled with panic and I wasn't sure how to react. I looked back to see if anyone in the restaurant was looking. Pierre was on the front porch, smoking a cigarette, watching us. "What are you doing here?" I asked in a horrified whisper.

"Just open the door and let me in," he said. "You don't want good ol' Pierre reporting you to Jim, do you?"

I quickly opened the door and shoved him inside the car. "Doesn't your girlfriend mind your hanging around me?" I asked.

"I don't do the girlfriend thing," he answered. "I don't commit and safe is no fun."

"Fine," I answered. "What do you want?"

"I have a special place I'd like to take you." I smiled and all the anxiety I was feeling seemed to wash away like unnecessary tears. We headed out to the Red Rock Crossing. He led me down a long windy road and took me through the mountains and by a creek. We pulled off the road into the parking lot. "This is where I go when I want to be alone." He pointed to the water. "I bring my guitar here and soak up the beauty." I was mystified. We walked around the rocks and laughed together. The sunlight danced along the rocks and the water sang sweetly as the waves crashed against the cliffs. We traveled quite a ways through the clearing. I was in heaven looking around to see how far we had gone from the road. As I looked from side to side, I noticed three figures following behind us. One of these figures was Rudy. The other two were Hispanic men, not much older than Johnny. I had never seen them before. He noticed my distraction and looked over his shoulder to see the men approaching. "Lilly," he said impatiently, "you need to get out of sight. Go over to the clearing and do not come out." He pointed to a wooded area and I complied without a word. I had recognized that what everyone had said was probably true. With panic flowing through veins like ice water, I sat in the woods in hiding. They all saw me and I saw one of the men point to me. I could hear them talk in Spanish and this concerned me. I was thinking about how Jim mentioned something about Johnny buying drugs from a man in Mexico. I heard my father's name mentioned a few times.

"What are you doing with her?" Rudy asked.

"I tell you what to do!" Johnny answered. "Don't make another mistake like that."

"Seriously…" Rudy looked back over at me. "Stop seeing her. You're just asking for trouble."

"Business, boys," one of the men reminded them. "Get rid of her," Rudy said, one last time. They walked off and I was too frightened to move. Johnny went to where I was sitting and sat beside me.

"Are you okay?" I couldn't speak. I looked at him with fear in my eyes. He put his hands on both sides of my face and kissed me. I felt a warm tingling spread through my body. I responded to him, much to my surprise. He began to lose control and I stood up suddenly. "What's happening, John?"

"Okay, you're right, we have to leave. Let's go." We walked in silence back to the car. When we got back to Johnny's house he grabbed my hand and kissed it. "I have about an hour. Come inside?"

I was so taken with him that I agreed. He moved towards me and kissed my lips. There was something about him that reached a part of me that had never been reached before. I was helpless in his arms. We got out of the car and he opened his front door. A woman with long brown hair in trashy, revealing clothes ran to him and hugged him. She reached for his face and kissed him passionately while I watched. "Who's the kid?" the woman asked.

"I do not believe this!" I yelled at him. "Do you have some kind of illness?"

"I told you," he answered. "I don't do commitments."

I turned and walked out, heading for my car. I could hear him behind me as I struggled with my keys. He grabbed me, turned me around and kissed me but I pushed him backwards. I could hear the woman in the background screaming, "Come on, John. Forget her!"

"I'm not going to share you with all these women." I couldn't believe that I had to explain that.

"We're not in a committed relationship," he answered. "We're not sleeping together yet." I almost threw up.

"I'll never have sex with a man who has so many partners. So, if you want me, you had better make a decision." I pushed him away again. He backed up lifting both his hands in the air as if to indicate that he was not going to stop me. I unlocked the car and got inside. He backed up farther away and then went back to the girl who was eagerly waiting for him.

I couldn't help but wonder why he came for me in the first place when he had all those women. Was he selling them drugs? Does he have some kind of self-esteem issue? I had to fight the tears that were forming in my eyes. I felt so foolish. This would not happen again.

I drove home and my father was waiting for me in the driveway. I knew he had someone watching me. It was pretty obvious at this point. I got out of the car and my father grabbed me and hugged me. "What is it, dad?" I asked.

"Why, Lilly? Why can't you stay away from him?"

"I won't be seeing him anymore, dad. I'm done with that egomaniac."

"Lilly, he's clever. Keep your guard up at all times."

"He has some kind of problem. I'm done." My father seemed satisfied with that answer and we went inside the house together. As I shut the front door, I noticed that there was a black sedan parked outside of the house.

CHAPTER 2

Addicted

When I got out of work the next day, I noticed Johnny standing outside my car. He was casually leaning on the hood with a smug smile on his face. Grateful that the parking lot was so far from the restaurant, I briskly ran to the car and scolded him. "For goodness sakes, Johnny, would you just go away."

"I'm afraid I can't do that," he answered. "Let's head back out to the crossing. I'm not expecting company today."

"Are you sick?" I was shocked at his shameless behavior. "I'll never sleep with you. So, if that's the plan, make a new one."

"You'd better hurry up and let me in." He pointed to the restaurant and Pierre was watching us again.

"Are you trying to get me fired?" I was furious.

"He's all talk. He won't fire you." He leaned in closer to me. I backed up.

"Please Johnny." I tried to calm my voice so he would see that I was serious. "Please stop coming here."

"Still watching…" He pointed to Pierre, who by this time had taken a seat and was watching us while smoking his cigarette. He was looking at us like we were today's entertainment.

I hurried over and let him in. "Crossing?" he asked me.

"I'm taking you home," I answered. He was still smiling. I don't think he quite accepted defeat yet.

"Home?" He reached for my hand as I started the car. I looked over at him.

"John, I can't keep doing this." I pulled my hand away. "I will never be what you want me to be in your life. I'm taking you home. Just leave me alone."

I hadn't put the car in gear yet as he leaned into me and pulled me close. I swallowed hard. He was starting to make me uncomfortable. He put his face up close to mine. His breath was warm against my ear. He touched my cheek with his. My dad was right; he was clever. I must admit the logical side of me was still standing in the parking lot outside of the car. There was something about him… I couldn't explain it. I pushed his chest back away from me but it took all of my strength to do it.

"Fine!" I gave in.

"You know you're sexy when you're mad." He was still pretty pleased with himself.

"Don't push it." I tried not to smile back but it was hard. I could feel the sides of my mouth begin to turn up but I fought it.

I drove out there against my better judgment and we walked back to our original spot. He stopped by the rushing waters and took both my hands in his. He pulled them tightly around his waist and put his hands around the back of my chest. He pulled me close into him. I was sure he was going to kiss me. My heart was beating loud enough for him to hear it. He pulled back for a moment. "Lilly, let's go for a little hike." I wasn't sure if he was messing with me or looking for a place to be alone.

"I'm in my waitress uniform," I answered.

"Okay, maybe next time." He smiled as he let me go. The water was crashing in the background against the rocks. I could smell the spray as it gently touched my skin.

"I don't get you," I started. "Why are you pursuing me?"

"I like you. We don't have to be exclusive to date." He was pretty sure of himself.

"We can hang out now and then," I continued. "But we'll never be more than friends. Not unless you clean out your bedroom." He laughed and took my hand.

"Can I kiss you?" He didn't wait for a response when he began pulling me to him.

"Can I stop you?" I braced myself for his touch. I needed to stay strong.

"Probably not." He stared into my eyes with excessive longing. He had me in such a lock that it frightened me. It was like a car accident you happen to see on the street. You know you shouldn't look but you can't keep your eyes off of it.

He placed his lips ever so gently on mine and drove himself closer and closer into my body. When he kissed me, I melted like the wax of a candle under a hot flame. He stopped there this time. He didn't lose control. He didn't try to push. I was almost disappointed.

I drove him home and he asked me if I wanted to go inside. "I'm not that stupid," I answered. "I'm sure that someone is in there waiting for you."

"You may be right," he answered. "After all, I am the candy man."

"So you're selling drugs to these girls?" I asked, almost astonished that he admitted it so freely.

"I don't know what you're talking about." He smiled mischievously. "I just mean that I'm so very sweet."

"Get out." I pushed him out the door and he stumbled. "I'm sure I'll see you soon." He went to his front door and the blond was there waiting for him. Diana was what he said her name was. He waved to me and I drove away from the house. I could feel the tears well up in my eyes. It was clear that if I didn't sleep with him, this kind of behavior would continue. But on the other side was always the question of whether or not he would stop even if I did sleep with him. Would he just add me to the list? I parked the car in my driveway and noticed the black sedan was still outside my house. I got out of the car and walked inside.

My dad was pacing back and forth with his arms crossed. Being Irish probably accounted for his bad temper. His fair skin was red with anger. "Why Lilly? Why do you lie to me?"

"Hi daddy." I began to try to pass him and go to my room.

"Get back here NOW!" He was pretty upset. He grabbed my forearm and pulled me backwards. I stopped, almost shocked at his tone. "You obviously don't see the severity of the situation."

"What situation, dad?"

"Stay away from John, Rudy and all the other delinquents that are involved with him." He was so angry. I thought the vein in his forehead was going to burst.

"No problem dad. But really, is having me followed necessary?"

"I guess so," he answered. He was still pacing.

"So you are having me followed?" He stopped pacing and sighed.

"Okay Lilly, go sit down." He had a defeated tone in his voice. I went to the couch and my dad sat beside me. "Johnny is a drug dealer who gets his supplies from a man we're trying to find, probably in Mexico. Many women in Johnny's life have turned up as lifeless bodies along the creek." This startled me and I shuddered. "I know he takes you there. I'm really afraid, Lilly."

"How do you know he sells? I mean, are you sure?" I could feel myself beginning to panic. It was getting hard for me to breathe.

"There's something about that man that women find irresistible. But you're going to have to trust me."

"I won't see him anymore," I lied.

"He has a multitude of women that he is with constantly. Don't embarrass yourself any further."

"No problem there," I answered. Okay, now I was worried.

Every day after that day, Johnny met me in the parking lot and we hiked out at the crossing. I began to bring a change of clothes and hiking boots to work with me to change into before we met. It was like we had known each other forever, and I never saw Rudy at the crossing again. I knew that I could never leave him. I was addicted. I could not let go of whatever that magnetic pull was he seemed to have over me. Pierre watched us leave together every day. I knew at some point he would want to collect on the fact that he never reported me to Jim.

"Marilyn?" Pierre asked. "Would you go to dinner with me tonight?"

"Pierre, every day you ask me out and every day I say no. When are you going to quit doing this to yourself?" He seemed to ignore my comment.

"This new seafood restaurant on the mountain just opened and all the chefs in the area are invited. I would like you to be my guest." He stood before me almost demanding a "yes" from me.

"Well…" I thought about it for a second. It could be interesting. "All right," I decided. "But just as friends."

"You'll be my date," he insisted. "Come on, Lilly. You never go out."

"Sure, why not," I answered. "Besides, you called me Lilly. You remembered my name. I guess that deserves a small reward." I walked away trying to figure out what to do. I guess I had no choice or I would lose my job for sure. I began to think that this might not be so bad. He was handsome and rich. Johnny never took me out in public. Maybe I should consider this as an option.

When I got to my car, Johnny was waiting for me as he always did. "Sorry Johnny, not today. But I'll drive you home."

"Why, what's wrong?"

"I have a date. Yes, out to a restaurant." He looked stunned, as though I had just punched him in the stomach and he got the wind knocked out of him. He must have known that this day would come. "We're not in a committed relationship," I reminded him.

"Who?" he asked. "You and me or you and him?"

I laughed. "Neither," I answered. "Look, you were the one who said that you do not want to commit. So, I guess I don't commit either." He was still staring at me in utter surprise. "Safe is no fun." When I said that it just fueled the fire. He began to get a little angry and I could see the blood drain from his face. He turned away from me and said, "Just take me home."

When we got to his house he got out of the car and slammed the car door behind him. He said not one word to me as he walked straight for his front door and it appeared that there was no one there to greet him. Suddenly I felt a little empty inside. I knew his rules were simply unacceptable yet I continued to play by them. It was time for a reality check. So, I drove home and prepared for my date with Pierre.

CHAPTER 3

Is That a Yes?

As I was putting on my eyeliner, my dad stopped at the bathroom door. "So, Pierre now, is it?"

"Yes, daddy," I answered. "This should make you very happy."

"It does, it does." He smiled. "He's a good man who makes a good living." I laughed inside. If he only knew about all the harassment I got from Pierre at work, he wouldn't be saying that. I only accepted this date to make Johnny jealous. I knew if I became less available, Johnny would want me more.

"Where's he taking you?"

"Some new restaurant called The Lobster Bisque. It's a local chef gathering." I answered.

He smirked. "Is Johnny going to be there? Isn't he a chef at The Grey Willow?"

"I'm sure if he were going he would have told me," I answered. "Don't worry."

He didn't look satisfied with my answer. "I'll let you know when he gets here," he said, walking towards the living room. I didn't give any previous thought to whether or not Johnny was going to be there. I put on a form fitting red dress with a low cut neck. The dress came just below the knee and had a slit down the side. When I walked out into the living room my dad whistled. "Does John ever take you out?"

"No, he doesn't. But I'm going out now, okay dad?" I was a little embarrassed that Johnny never did take me anywhere. "Oh and by the way, he calls me Marilyn." My dad laughed at that.

"Marilyn Monroe? I see the resemblance."

"Not funny."

"It is a huge compliment, baby. She was very beautiful and most desired."

"I guess." I began to adjust my dress in the mirror in the hallway. I was not used to being all dressed up anymore.

"It's about time you met someone who respects you."

Just then the doorbell rang and it was Pierre. He shook my dad's hand and they made small talk for a while. Then he put his arm out for me to take it and said, "Shall we go?" I took his arm and we walked out the door. I thought my dad was going to explode with joy.

"Wow! You look incredible," he said. "Johnny's a lucky man."

"Thanks," I answered. "But no more use of the J word. I'm all yours tonight." He smiled at that last comment and opened the door to his Jaguar for me to get inside the passenger's seat. I realized at this point that Johnny doesn't even own a car. I drive him everywhere. What is my attraction to that man?

"Marilyn," he started. "You are worth more than I could ever give you." He shut the car door and got into the driver's side. I was puzzled. What was he up to?

We pulled into the parking lot and it was packed. There were tons of very expensive cars parked in the parking lot and I suddenly felt very privileged to be invited. He valet parked the car and we walked in arm in arm. I carefully scanned the faces looking for anyone familiar. Okay, so maybe I was looking for one face in particular. I noticed a man with brown hair, wearing a ponytail. He had a suit jacket on and was wearing a black, old-fashioned hat. When he turned and looked at me, my heart sank into my stomach. It was Johnny. He was with a tall, thin brunette in a tight, short black dress. I could almost see her bare chest coming out of that dress. She looked cheap and bought. She was all over him like a wet T-shirt. He nodded to me. He was the king of unspoken acknowledgement. I nodded back, as though I thought this would go unnoticed by Pierre. "Is this going to be a problem?" he asked, obviously disappointed in me.

"N-no," I answered. "I'm sorry. You have my full attention." I was still watching Johnny from the corner of my eye.

Although he did not appear to believe me, we walked around a bit and socialized. We intentionally stayed away from Johnny and his date. We were finally seated at a table for two. He ordered us a bottle of Chardonnay and took my hands. "Lilly," he paused for a minute. "Tell me something about yourself that I don't know."

"I don't know," I answered. "Like what?" I was unsuccessfully searching the room to see where Johnny had settled.

"Like maybe how Johnny meets you outside the restaurant every day after work and Jim has a restraining order against him."

My mouth hung open. I suppose now was the time he was going to use this against me. I knew it was coming. I just didn't know when.

I don't know what you're talking about," I answered. I pulled my hands out of his.

"You do know that Jim would probably have John arrested and you fired, if he knew about your little secret."

"What do you want, Pierre?" I asked. This dinner had suddenly taken a turn for the worst. I noticed Johnny and his date were seated in a convenient location. They were sitting fairly close to us and Johnny's eyes were on me.

"You should be a little more discrete," he answered. "He's been watching us since we got here." He looked at Johnny and shot him a nasty glare. "It appears that you are having a hard time detaching from him as well."

"We're not dating," I answered. "We're just friends."

"Why didn't he invite you here?" he asked.

I must admit that I thought that was a pretty good question. Somehow, he seemed to always know where I was. "I'm guessing he wasn't originally planning on attending."

"Somehow?" he asked. "Do you know who he is?"

"Can we talk about something else please?" I asked.

He reached into his pocket and pulled out a small box. It looked like a ring box. My heart began to palpitate. He opened the box and there sat the largest diamond I had ever seen. I looked over at Johnny and his face had turned a deep shade of red. I thought Johnny was going to have a stroke or pull out a gun or something. Pierre got down on one knee and held the ring up for me to view. "Lilly, will you do me the honor of becoming my wife?"

I quickly reached over and closed the ring box. "What's wrong with you?" I asked. "Put that away before anyone else sees you."

"I think it's a little too late for that." He looked over at Johnny. He was blatantly staring at us.

"Well, at least you got my name right," I answered. "Why would I marry you Pierre? This is our first date." I was hoping this was some kind of ridiculous joke. But he seemed pretty serious and he never smiled.

"Is that a yes?" he asked.

"No," I answered sarcastically. "That is a NO."

"I suggest you reconsider," he responded. "My work visa expired and if you don't marry me, I may have to go public with your little affair."

"Fraud is against the law," I replied. "And besides…" I paused and looked over at Johnny who was still glaring at us. Then I whispered, "There is no affair."

"Take some time to think about it." It became obvious that he wasn't kidding. He was going to blackmail me into marrying him. "I have a lot of information on your friend, as you like to call him."

The meals arrived and I picked at my steak for a few minutes. "I'll think about it," I answered. I needed to figure this out.

Dinner was great but Pierre was sure he could have done better. We both ordered coffee at the end of our meal. "So, I understand that you sing," he said unexpectedly.

"Yes, I do," I answered, making every attempt to be cordial.

How about I take you to Redneck's after dinner? It's a little country bar down the road and the band always invites people on stage."

"Rednecks?" I asked. "I don't know if I like the name."

"It's a very close knit group of people. You'll like it," he continued.

He paid the bill and we headed out. I half expected Johnny to follow us, but he didn't. I watched him watch us leave.

CHAPTER 4

Cheating Heart

We pulled up to a small little building with loud music pounding into the parking lot from inside. Pierre held the door open and I walked inside. All eyes were on us as we were terribly overdressed. The room smelled very much like Johnny's bedroom. Cigarette smoke held like smog over the dance floor and stale beer was the prominent stench. We sat at a little table by the band. I pulled a tissue out of my purse to wipe the liquid off of the table… whatever it was. The lead singer was finishing up an old George Jones song and the crowd was clapping enthusiastically. "We have a guest singer tonight," he announced. "My brother Bobby would like to sing a song he wrote. Give it up for Bobby!"

The crowd roared as a very handsome man in cowboy attire got onto the stage. He had a small ponytail behind his cowboy hat, cleaner and neater than Johnny's. I must admit that my heart skipped a beat when I first laid eyes on him. He had dark hair and dark eyes. He was thin, like Johnny but much better looking. Good looks were not Johnny's appeal. At this point a waitress came over and dropped off the beers that Pierre had ordered when we first walked into the bar. His voice was smooth and alluring. I was entranced by his performance. He must have noticed my swooning because as soon as he finished, he looked and me and said, "Aren't we a little over dressed?" I could feel the blood rushing to my face. The pounding in my ears made me think Pierre could hear it. "Do you sing?" he asked.

"She does," Pierre answered as he gave me a nudge to get up.

"Great!" he replied. "Your name?"

"Lilly," I answered. I was hoping the floor would open beneath me and swallow me whole.

"Like the flower." He smiled. "Let's hear it for Lilly!" I got on the stage and he handed me the microphone. Everyone was clapping madly.

"Forgive my attire," I started. Someone in the back whistled. "I'll remember to bring my boots next time." The crowd laughed and clapped louder. "How about some Cheatin' Heart, boys?" I directed my question to the band and they began to play. Just then Rudy walked in with a girl and they sat at a small table by the door. He started to clap loudly and disorderly, which made me miss my cue. Everyone looked at him and the band stopped playing. Rudy had an intimidating appearance. He was blond with spiked hair and always wore a black leather jacket. His cigarette was hanging casually out of his mouth.

"Oh don't mind me," he shouted, pulling the cigarette away from his lips. "Cheating Heart is a great song for you."

Bobby signaled the band to start playing again and I sang trying not to look at Rudy. He walked over to Pierre and put his arm around him. I could see them exchanging words, and then Rudy walked back to his seat. When I finished, everyone clapped and I sat down with Pierre. Pierre took my hand and quietly whispered, "Let's go."

"What?" I was surprised. "Why? What did he say to you?"

He yanked me out of my chair and I stumbled to my feet. Bobby took notice as Pierre hurried me towards the door. As we walked briskly passed Rudy he grabbed my arm and stopped us. He whispered, "I'll tell Johnny you send your love." I looked at him curiously as Pierre pulled me in the other direction, out the door.

"What on earth is wrong with you?" I asked.

"Are you and Johnny married or something?"

"Don't be ridiculous," I answered.

"Are you together?"

"No, I already told you that." I was starting to get impatient. "What did Rudy say to you?"

"Nothing," he answered. "Don't worry about it." We drove in silence to my house. "Thanks for dinner," I said. The energy between us had become strained.

"Anytime." He attempted a weak smile. "Think about what I said."

I walked into the house and my mom and dad were in the living room pretending to read. "How was your date?" my dad asked looking up from his reading glasses.

"It was fun." I was still preoccupied with how tight my dress was and couldn't help but readjust it. "He proposed, you know."

"What?" My dad leapt to his feet. "Why would he do that?"

"He said he loves me," I answered. "Crazy, right?"

"Please tell me you turned him down," he groaned as he sat back down.

"Of course I did." I smiled. "My heart belongs to another." He smirked at me.

"I mean it, Lilly. Stay away from Malone."

"Yes sir," I said in a militant tone. I excused myself and went to bed.

For the next few days there was no Johnny. I was missing him and started to feel a void inside. Pierre continued to propose, day after day, but since Johnny was no longer waiting for me, I figured there was no hurry.

I hung up my apron and walked to my car. The spot John had always waited for me was deserted. I got into my car and drove to Rednecks. Bobby was at the bar talking to his brother. They were drinking draft beers and when I walked in they stopped talking and called me over. "Can I buy you a beer?" Bobby asked.

"Please," I answered. He was signaling the bartender and ordered me a draft. Just then a Hispanic man walked through the door. He was dressed in cowboy attire from his hat down to his boots. His eyes were black and they caught mine immediately. He sat in the corner and ordered a beer. He looked completely out of place. He talked to no one and seemed to be watching me. "Thanks," I said, a little distracted when the beer arrived.

"So, what brings you here to our humble, little watering hole?" Bobby asked.

"I was bored," I answered. "No one to play with."

"The band is getting back up there in a few minutes. Would you like to sing a duet?" He smiled a captivating smile at me. I was glad I went.

"I would love to," I answered.

We were up there for only a few seconds when Rudy came in. He sat with the Hispanic guy and watched us. I was beginning to feel a little frightened. Why did Johnny disappear and why are his friends following me? I saw him slip something to the man and head for the door. "You have a lovely voice," Bobby said to me. "Do you play anything?"

Still distracted I answered, "I play guitar." I watched Rudy leave. His eyes never left mine as he disappeared into the darkness.

"Bring it next time," he replied, noticing my preoccupation.

"Maybe," I answered. I was having trouble concentrating. "We'll see." I smiled and headed out. As I put the key in the ignition I saw the Hispanic man walking out the door. Okay, I thought. Now I know he's watching me. All this meant to me was that although Johnny was keeping away, he was having me watched for some reason.

The next day I followed the same routine. Bobby and I danced and sang and his brother Joe and I became fast friends. I was slowly becoming one of the regulars. Instead of going to The Crossing with Johnny, I was hanging out with Bobby at Rednecks. I was starting to wonder if I would ever see the cinnamon colors of the rocks being teased by the water's edge again. At least not with Johnny by my side. Maybe it was time to let go.

I got to work at 5:30 as I always did. Jim was waiting for me at the front door. This was bad; I knew Pierre had ratted me out. I took a deep breath and got ready to face the consequences of my actions. "Hi Jim," I said as casually as I could.

"Pierre is gone," he said to me. "What did you have to do with that?" His arms were crossed over his chest and he was tapping his foot impatiently.

"Gone?" I asked. "What do you mean, gone?"

"He was deported after you left yesterday." His face was disturbingly distorted.

"Oh no," I answered. "He did say that his work visa had expired."

"Look, Lilly, I'm going to level with you." He looked very serious. "He left me a note telling me everything. I'm not happy with you."

"What exactly did he tell you?" I wasn't sure how much to admit to just yet.

"I called Mick and told him that you and John have been meeting after work." I gasped. "It's for your own good. You can't see him anymore, he's trouble."

"When did you call my dad?" I asked.

"A few minutes ago. He's going to talk to you. I'm not going to fire you. I don't need any trouble. Just keep him away from here, do you understand?"

"I haven't seen him in weeks," I answered. I realized that I sounded disappointed.

"He must be off somewhere picking up a shipment," he answered. "He'll be back, he always is. When he gets here, you tell him to stay away."

"Yes sir," I answered. I was sincere this time.

"If you keep allowing him to come here, I will fire you and he will go to jail." He walked away in a huff. I wondered if Johnny reported Pierre to the INS, but at the same time, I wasn't sure I really wanted to know.

I walked into the kitchen to meet our new daytime chef. "I'm Lilly," I told him.

"I know," he answered. "I'm Roberto." He turned to look at me and smiled. I got the creeps. He was Mexican. I found that to be unusual for a French Bistro.

I went through my day as usual and Jim didn't say one word. I walked to my car only to find no Johnny waiting for me. I missed him so much that I ached inside. I felt the tears well up in my eyes as I got into my car. Off to Rednecks I went hoping to find Bobby there. When I got to the bar, I noticed Bobby sitting by himself talking to the bartender. "Hey beautiful." He turned to look at me. Behind me walked the Hispanic cowboy. The bartender cried out, "Hey Ray, how's it going?" Ray waved, walked to the bar and sat a few stools away from Bobby. At least I knew his name now. He ordered a beer and subtly watched Bobby and me interact. As we casually exchanged pleasantries, I felt a tap on my shoulder. Before I turned around I noticed Ray stand up from his stool. This sent a shot of alarm through my spine. I turned around to see a blond headed woman, about 15 years older than Bobby, standing right in my face. She was so close that I could feel her breath on me.

"Listen, little girl," she started. "He's taken, so beat it!"

I looked at Bobby for some kind of defense. He just shrugged his shoulders and said, "It's not my fight."

She grabbed my arm and started pulling me towards the door. "We'll settle this outside." I couldn't believe she really thought I would fight her. Without warning, Ray who was watching me, grabbed her. She let me go and shouted, "OUCH! Get off of me!"

"Is there a problem here?" he asked me.

"Not anymore," I replied. "Thanks." He tipped his hat like a cowboy might do.

She pushed him aside and said, "We're not finished yet!"

He grabbed both her arms and in a rough manner sat her down in a nearby chair. "You are done. Are we clear?"

She said nothing. She was finally intimidated. I could see the beads of sweat forming on her forehead. She swallowed hard and looked at Bobby for support. Still, Bobby sat idly by, doing nothing. "May I walk you to your car, Lilly?" Ray asked me. I grabbed my purse and we took off out the door.

"Who are you?" I asked. "Oh, and thank you." I smiled.

"You're welcome," he answered. "Let's just say I'm a friend of a friend." He smiled like he had some kind of naughty secret. "Stay away from here for a while. Give her some cooling down time."

"Not going to be a problem," I told him. "I think I've worn out my welcome."

I unlocked my car door and he opened it for me. "I'll see you around." He closed the door and headed to his own car… a black sedan. I could see him on his cell phone and he talked for a few minutes, probably checking in with whoever sent him here in the first place. Then it dawned on me. I was alone. The tears flowed from my eyes. I couldn't see well enough to drive. I started wiping my face and looked out the window to see if anyone was watching. My heart sank and I gasped with excitement. It was Johnny. He was standing beside my car. He pulled open my door and I leapt into his arms.

"You know," he said, "there's a reason they call this place Redneck's." We both laughed. My tears were all over his shirt.

"Who was that guy?"

"What guy?" he asked. Pulling me back a little so that he could see my face.

"The Mexican guy from the bar. Ray, I think his name is."

His face broke out in an unexpected smile. "Oh… Ray." He pulled me close again. "When you're with someone like me…" He paused. "I'll explain that part later. But let's just say Ray is your health insurance." I did not like the sound of that at all and he was aware of my discomfort. He promptly changed the subject. "I bought a car." He pointed to the red convertible in the parking lot. "Let me drive you, for a change."

"I've got to get my car out of here," I told him. "Let me follow you to your house." I began to relax a little.

"Now we're talking." He smiled and stroked my hair. "Follow me." He briskly walked to his car and I followed his cherry red convertible to his house. When I got out of the car I asked him, "Are we alone?"

"You bet," he answered. "Come on inside." I was trembling with excitement. He let me in and latched the door behind us. I could feel my anxiety rise when he did that. He took my hands and said, "You're shaking." I was shaking. I was scared. I needed him tonight in a way that was not familiar to me.

"It's been a long day," I answered.

"Lilly," he led me to the couch, "we need to talk."

"Uh-oh…"

He laughed and brushed my hair from my face. He ran his hand down my cheek. "I never want to be without you for that long again." I could feel my heartbeat accelerate. "Lilly, I need you with me."

I couldn't speak. I was afraid I would forget to breathe. Although his physical beauty was not outstanding, the electrical charge between us was undeniable. "I hear you have been busy while I was away. Did you say yes?"

He threw me off guard with that question. "Say yes?" I asked. "Say yes to what?"

"Pierre," he answered. "That was a nice ring he offered you." He was smirking a little. I could tell he knew that Pierre was gone.

"Oh that," I replied in a nonchalant tone. "No, silly, why would I say yes?"

"I heard he was blackmailing you," he answered. It was then I knew it was him. He called the INS. But I didn't ask. I couldn't and didn't really want to know for sure.

"He's gone now," I answered. "So, it doesn't matter anymore. But Jim…" I hesitated.

"I know, I know…" he interrupted. "Stay away from La Papillion… old story, same song."

"He said he'd fire me."

"You don't need to work," he replied. "I have plenty of money."

I laughed. "Please Johnny. It won't kill you to stay away."

He put both hands on either side of my face and looked hard into my eyes. "I don't know, it might." Just then he pressed his lips most gently against mine. I couldn't breathe. I couldn't move. I was terrified of the feelings that were wildly stirring within me. He let me go and said, "I love you, Lilly. I'm ready to commit to you. You're all I think about." He hesitated. "Am I too late?"

"God help me," I answered. "But I love you too." I felt like I was home in his arms. He pulled me close and continued to kiss me until he laid me down beneath him on the couch. I could feel my will power diminishing as he overtook me with his eagerness.

At that moment he pulled back from me. "Lilly, are you ready for this?" I couldn't speak. My body and mind were no longer communicating. I reached out and touched his cheek. I could feel his breath on my face and I could not move.

"I love you," I answered. "Yes, I'm ready." He put his lips on mine and I had lost all control of what was happening to my body. Then, like the sunsets into the horizon, we were as one.

CHAPTER 5

BANG!

I woke in the morning feeling like a different person. When I got out of bed, I could smell the bacon and hear the coffee brewing. "Good morning, sleepy head," a familiar voice whispered in my ear. He leaned over me with his lips almost against my ear.

"You're up early," I answered. He was already up, dressed and cooking breakfast.

"Too beautiful a day to sleep it away," he responded. "Eggs?"

I sat up and grabbed my clothes. We had slept on the couch all night. I put them back on and I sat down at the table. He put before me an omelet with bacon and coffee. "I could get used to this." I smiled. He was so at home in the kitchen. He whistled as he cooked and moved like music.

"Lilly?" he asked. "Why didn't you tell me this was your first time?"

A feeling of alarm went through my body. He was so experienced; I was reluctant to reveal such a secret. "I was afraid you might change your mind if you knew." I could feel my face blushing. "Did I do something wrong?" I began to get concerned. He smiled at me in a comforting way. "How did you know?"

"Of course I knew." He grabbed my hands. "I could just tell that you hadn't done anything like that before. It was a nice change for me."

"I'll bet," I said sarcastically. "Were you disappointed?"

"Disappointed?" He pulled me up out of my chair. "I couldn't be happier." He pulled me close and let his lips graze mine as I felt myself collapsing in his arms. "I'm so in love with you," he said as he released me and let me sit back down. He poured me some more coffee. "Still want me to stay away from the restaurant?" He laughed a little.

"I swear, if you get me fired…."

"Now, now…" He sat down in front of me. "I'm just playing with you. I'll stay away." I smiled and felt like I had gotten my point across.

A little time had passed and I looked at my watch. The unthinkable moment had approached. "I think it's time we realize that I have to go home." I finished my eggs and he took my plate away from me.

"What can I do to make you stay?" He looked over his shoulder from the sink, where he was washing the dishes.

"You know I have to go see my father sometime."

"I know," he agreed. "Do you want me to come with you?" I couldn't believe he asked me that question.

"Death wish?" I asked. "He carries a gun, you know."

"So do I," he answered. Suddenly, he became very serious. "Your dad is just worried about your safety. I would be worried too if my daughter was dating someone like me." I grimaced. "Seriously, I tried to stay away," he continued. "But when I heard Bobby and Pierre were making moves on you…" He hesitated. "I lost control and came back."

"No need to be jealous." I thought that was so funny. If he only knew how tortured I felt without him. "Bobby was using me to make his mother… I mean his girlfriend jealous." Johnny laughed. "Whatever she was."

"Mother, huh? I don't know," he said. "Maybe this guy meant something to you."

"No," I answered, "nothing."

"Pierre had a ring," he said sarcastically.

"Okay," I replied. "Enough about Pierre." I really didn't want him to tell me he had him deported. "I think I need to go."

He took my hands and kissed them. "I love when you do that," I told him.

Go ahead and face the music. I'll miss you." I took a deep breath, kissed him lightly and turned for the door. "Lilly?" he called to me. I turned to look at him. He grabbed my hand and pulled me towards him. His arms went around my back pulling my body into his as he pulled my hands around his waist. He moved one hand to my cheek and ran one through my hair. "I just can't let you go yet." He said it so sorrowfully that I believed him. "Come and see me at the restaurant?" He smiled like he just remembered something. "You do know it's Easter Sunday?"

I hadn't thought about it. I can't believe I forgot the holiest holiday of the year. He kissed me deeply and then his phone rang. We ignored it. He finally pulled it off his belt and said, "What Rudy." He sounded annoyed. "Stop using them, Rudy, and just move them. Got it! I'm busy." He shut the phone and put his body up against mine like before. His passion continuously consumed me like a fire suffocating a forest with its blaze. I was helplessly under his spell. "Okay," he sighed, releasing me. For a moment I thought I might lose my balance and fall. "Good luck. I'll see you later."

"I'll try to come by but Easter is a pretty big deal at my house." I stopped and looked at the pout on his face.

"You're my Easter Lilly, aren't you." He smiled again.

"I love you," I said before I left.

"I love you more," he replied. I walked to my car and he followed behind. He opened my door and let me in. "Be safe," he said, "And always remember that I love you more." I put the keys in the ignition and the car purred. I blew him a kiss as I drove off and he pretended to catch it.

As I drove away I noticed a black sedan following behind me. It was Ray, the man who had been watching me in the bar. Johnny must have sent him to keep an eye on me. This was starting to become a way of life. I wasn't sure I liked it.

I pulled into my driveway and walked to the front door. The sedan was parked across the street. I breathed in deeply, remembering the events of the evening for my strength. Then, I pushed open the door.

"Lillian Margaret O'Hara!" my father shouted. "Where in the bleeding hell have you been?" My father's face was a new shade of red. He was standing with his hands folded and my mom was sitting on the couch, equally annoyed.

"Dad, I'm a grown woman!" I shouted in anticipation of the upcoming argument.

"Are you kidding me?" he asked. "Grown women don't stay out all night."

"I'm fine," I insisted. "I was with some friends."

Suddenly his face changed. "Oh no, no not him!" He began pacing back and forth like a mad man. "Are you sleeping with him, Lilly? Are you part of his harem now?"

I was shocked and mortified that he assumed I would allow myself to be part of a string of women. "It's not like that, dad."

"Oh no!" he kept saying. "It's worse than I thought." He was still pacing. My mother got up from the couch and stood beside him.

"Do you love him?" she asked.

"He's a skinny, little drug dealer, of course she doesn't love him," my father barked.

"I do love him, dad." I moved slightly away from him. "I can't help it, I need him." My father continued to pace. If it were possible, steam would be coming out of his ears.

"I know this guy, Lil. He has a different girl every night. I know his friends personally. I have arrested all of them at least once but we can't seem to catch John."

"Maybe you're wrong about him!" I shouted. "He's with me now, dad. Only me."

"Lilly, why are you being so naive? He sells drugs to kids."

I didn't quite know how to win this one. Of course, I was suspicious that he was involved in illegal activities. He wouldn't have people watching me if he wasn't. But I never asked and he never told. It was just kind of understood that I didn't want to know. He carried a gun; that much I did knew. He was the first person I had ever known to carry a gun that wasn't a police officer.

"Have you noticed the Hispanic population growing around you?" he asked. "Roberto and Ray, just to name a few."

"So what?" I asked.

"John's superior is a Latino somewhere. We're trying to find him. He's having you protected for some reason, Lil. This means you have a purpose. I don't like it."

"Purpose?" I asked in surprise. "I don't have anything they would want."

"You are now his Achilles' heel. They'll keep you safe until they need leverage." He said that last part very slowly as if to make his warning clear. I began to feel a little sick to my stomach. This was too much for me and my head was beginning to spin.

"Lilly, I may have to move you," he said. Then there was a pounding on the door.

"Is he coming over here today?" he asked.

"It's Easter." I too was surprised. "He works on Easter at the restaurant. I'm not expecting anyone."

My dad reached for the doorknob and pulled the door open. It was Rudy. He had sweat dripping from his face and his hands were shaking. He pointed a gun at my father and said, "Sorry Mick. Wrong place, wrong time." We heard a loud BANG! My father dropped to the floor and the vase behind me shattered. His icy blue eyes were blood red. My mother ran into the kitchen screaming. He turned and pointed the gun at me. "You should've picked me, Lilly. But they always go for John. It could've been different. I would've protected you."

I am sure I had that "deer in the headlights" look as he stood there pointing his gun at me. His sweat was covering the gun as his hands shook involuntarily. I began to think my relationship with Johnny might have been a mistake. How many times was I warned? Why did I continue to see him?

"At first you were just something new to play with. But then you became like an obsession and he couldn't put you down. You're now nothing more than a unnecessary distraction." I bit my bottom lip as I watched him get ready to shoot me. "Goodbye Lilly." Before I had a chance to move, I heard another loud BANG!

CHAPTER 6

Just One More Night

I woke up in a hospital room and Johnny was sitting next to me holding my hand. The smell of antiseptic and old people tickled my nose causing me some nausea. Then I remembered. "My dad!" I shouted. "Oh my gosh, my dad!" Johnny jumped up as though I had awakened him.

"Your dad is fine. The bullet went right through his shoulder, that's why the vase behind you shattered."

"Was I shot?" I began to check my body for holes.

"No baby, you're fine." I looked around to evaluate the situation. "Then why does my head hurt?"

"You fainted. You're good." I looked at him and he seemed almost amused. "You have a few cuts on your arms from the glass and a bump on the head but that's about it."

"Johnny, what happened?" A nurse walked in and looked over at us suspiciously. Johnny gave her a nod and she left the room.

"Ray saved your life," he answered. "After you fainted, Ray shot Rudy."

"I thought Rudy shot me."

"No, that second shot you heard came from Ray's gun."

I was astonished. "Oh no." I was still trying to understand this. "Is Rudy …" I tried to catch my breath, "dead?"

"Yes, Rudy is gone," he answered. "Better him than you."

"You seem pretty okay with this," I pointed out to him, a little bewildered. I wondered why he wasn't more upset.

"He was eating up too much of my profits anyway." He smiled. "Okay, I'll try to be more sensitive." He started stroking my hair. "It's time to go, baby. I have to move you." I remembered my father saying that to me just before Rudy shot him.

"I need to see my dad." I started to get up when my mother appeared in the door.

"That young man at the door with the gun… he worked for you?" She had her arms crossed in front her body.

Johnny said nothing. "Lilly, we warned you time and time again; stay away, stay away. Well if you can't stay away, I guess it's up to me then." She uncrossed her arms and her eyes changed. "Get the hell out of my house and don't come back until you lose this piece of trash!" She stormed out of the room.

"Johnny, I'm sorry."

"I've been called worse. But seriously Lilly, you need to get out of here for a while."

"John, I don't feel so good. I think this is just too much for me." I started to feel overwhelmed and things started getting cloudy in my head. "I don't want to leave you."

"I have a friend who works in Las Vegas as a leasing manger. She said she would find you a job leasing and hook you up with an apartment. Just until things settle down here. I don't think you're made for this kind of life, Lilly."

"Johnny, I know nothing about leasing apartments, and I don't want to leave you." I grabbed his hand and put it on my cheek.

"She's a really good teacher." He smiled. "Time to get going." He pulled his hand away and started handing me my clothes.

We went back to the house and started packing. "Johnny, I can't do this. How long will I be without you?"

"Only a few months," he answered. "Just long enough to make people think we're no longer involved. Do you see why I don't commit?" I gave him a look but yes, I got it. He wanted to keep me safe and now I wasn't.

He kept me at his house for about a month and then he moved me to Las Vegas. I guess he had to wait for a job to become available. I wasn't feeling very well. At first Johnny thought it might be stress but as it got worse he began to get worried that I might be pregnant. We didn't use protection that first time and I couldn't keep anything down. I refused to take a test because… well… I didn't want to know. We walked into the apartment leasing office and it was very busy. I was so nauseous; I could barely stand. A blond-haired woman in her 50s ran over to Johnny and threw her arms around him. She was very attractive and dressed well. I did not like that. "Johnny, Johnny, is it really you?"

"Yes, mom, it's me," he answered. I was comforted that it was his mother.

"Your mother?" I asked. "You could have mentioned in passing that she was your mom, you know."

"Don't take offense, dear." She took my hands and smiled. "He doesn't tell anyone that we're related." She looked a little embarrassed.

"Seriously, Johnny," I said.

"She is lovely, dear. I'm so pleased that you've entrusted her to me."

"I had nowhere else to go mom. Don't let me down." He gave her a serious look and then he winked. She smiled.

"Lilly, this is Cammy, my mom." She smiled a very pleasing smile at me.

Just then a handsome, Hispanic man, maybe about thirty years old, walked in. Johnny was definitely upset with the expression on my face. I tried not to stare but… wow! He was dark skinned with bright green eyes. His body was solid and he stood about six foot tall. It was all I could do to take my eyes off of him. "What are you doing here?" Johnny asked, obviously not pleased to see him.

"It's just as big a surprise to me, John, as it is to you," Cammy acknowledged. "Diego got transferred here last night."

"Really?" Johnny asked. "What a coincidence." Diego walked over to me and took my hand. Johnny pushed him back and stood in front of me.

"Boys…" Cammy pleaded. "Play nice, there's a lady present." Diego shoved Johnny away and grabbed my hand again.

"Forgive him for his rudeness," he said. He had a thick, and very sexy, Spanish accent. "I am Diego." I was almost sweating from the steam coming off of his body.

"It's a pleasure to meet you," I replied.

The pleasure is all mine." He kissed my hand never disconnecting his eyes from my gaze.

"Get off of her," Johnny responded. He pulled me away from him. "I can't believe you're here."

"I've missed you too, John," he answered. The two of them bickered back and forth until Cammy assigned me an apartment number and then they fought over who got to take me there. She finally intervened. "Johnny, apartment 346. Just take her." Diego gave her a very unfriendly look. She turned her eyes away and handed Johnny the keys. As we left, I saw in the reflection of the window, Diego grab her arm and the two struggle a bit.

"Do we need to worry about her?" I asked.

"If there's one thing I can tell you about Cammy, it's that she can definitely take care of herself." We walked into the modestly furnished room and I began to unpack my bags. I didn't like the moldy smell or the hotel-like appearance of the room. "I don't know, Johnny," I said. "Can you stay with me tonight?" I was a little afraid to be alone.

"No," he answered. "I need to get going."

"Why?" I asked. "Just one more night… please… please John."

"Well…" He paused. "Rudy was right about one thing." He put his arms around my waist. "You do make me weak." He laid me down on the bed and we made love. When I awoke and found him gone; I was devastated.

I walked into the leasing office, just to discover white lilies all over the room. "What's wrong?" Cammy asked. "I'm guessing these are for you. You should be smiling." She pointed towards all the flowers that were everywhere around the room.

"I woke up and he was gone without a trace," I answered. "I don't know, I felt kind of abandoned." I had to fight back to urge to cry but my voice was cracking and I'm sure she could hear it.

"Johnny does that 'disappearing without a trace' thing, well," she admitted. I looked down, trying to hide my face. "He left a note." She handed me a card that was stuck to one of the flower arrangements. I took it out of the envelope and read it. You'll always be my Easter Lilly. I'll be back for you. I put it back in the envelope and I cried a little more. Cammy hugged me until we saw Diego walk into the office with a grim expression on his face. Cammy seemed to be analyzing his look and then out of nowhere cried, "Oh no! Do not tell me what I think you're gonna tell me."

He came over to me and said, "I need you ladies to go into the back office with me for a minute."

"NO!" Cammy shouted. "NO! You didn't!" He looked at her a little surprised.

I followed him into the office and Cammy followed behind. "Johnny was in an accident on his way home."

"Where is he?" I asked breathlessly. "I need to be with him."

"I'm sorry Lilly," he answered.

Cammy started screaming and punching him in the chest. "No! No! I don't believe you!" He held her back and I sat there frozen. I ran into the bathroom in the back and threw up. When I came out, she was calmer and I sat down feeling disoriented. "I'm really all alone, now," I said. "What am I going to do?"

"Lilly, go back to your apartment," Cammy told me. "I'll meet you there in a few minutes. Let Diego take you." I think I walked on my own but I felt as though I was in a dream. He drove me in his golf cart and he unlocked the door for me with his master key. He walked around looking at my things as though he was looking for something specific. "Is this your dad?" he asked, as he picked up Mick's picture.

"Yeah," I said. "That's him."

I could not believe all the changes that had taken place in such a short period of time. I think I was happy for a minute. Just for one brief minute and then it was all over.

A little time went by, I'm not sure how much and Cammy came barreling in with a paper bag in her hand. "What's that?" I asked.

"Johnny told me before you got here that he thought you might be pregnant."

I grabbed the bag from her and threw it on the floor. "I'm not taking that."

"Lilly," Diego got on one knee in front of me. I was sitting on the couch, motionless. He took my hands and said, "You are not alone." I could not make eye contact with him. I looked at the floor. "I have a lot of money. I could take care of you. You can have your own room..." He paused for a minute. "I will ask nothing of you, but I could take care of you and your baby."

"Why… why would you do that?" I asked.

"Cammy and I go way back. Let me do this for you." I got up feeling like a zombie, picked the bag up off of the floor and went into the bathroom.

I could hear the two of them arguing outside. I waited for the stick to give me an answer. My life changing decision was riding on a plus or a negative sign. After the test was complete I stayed in the bathroom a little longer. They were having some kind of heated argument out there and Cammy was definitely blaming Diego for Johnny's death. I wasn't sure if I wanted to re-enter the room just yet. When I came back they got quiet and waited for me to say something. I looked over at Diego. He looked so sincere and he was so very beautiful. But still… I took a deep breath and finally found the courage to speak. "Well Diego…" I started. "It looks like we're going to have a baby."

CHAPTER 7

Family?

He took me home with him. Needless to say, I was very depressed. He had a million servants and lived in some ridiculously huge mansion. How a maintenance supervisor in an apartment community could afford to live here, I had no idea. He said his brother would be in the kitchen doing some work and to ignore him if he was rude. When we arrived, that is where we found him. He was in the kitchen crunching numbers. There were wads of paper all over the floor. He was as handsome as Diego, if not more so. He was light-skinned however and Diego was bronze. His eyes were icy blue and to my surprise he was blond. He was sitting at the table in a button-down shirt, which was hanging open. I could smell the coffee that was still in the air from breakfast mixed in with delicately flavored cologne. It was strange. He never looked up at me.

"Max?" Diego tried to get his attention. "Max, this is Lilly." He looked up at that point but didn't smile. "Lilly and I are getting married next week," he continued.

"Why?" he asked. Then he looked at me. "You knocked her up? Know what a condom is bro?" He was very sarcastic. I didn't like him. Diego smacked him in the back of the head.

"Ouch!" Max yelled.

"Respect, Max, show some respect."

"Pregnant?" he asked me. I nodded but said nothing.

"Loud mouth too…" he continued. "You hit the jackpot." He smacked him again in the back of the head.

"Stop hitting me!" he shouted.

"Behave," Diego insisted. "She's moving in here with us. Have Leticia get her a room."

"Not your room?" he asked.

"Mind your own business," Diego answered.

"Not your baby," he said with certainty. "Didn't think you'd be that irresponsible," he added. "If not yours, then whose? And why you?"

"We'll talk later, Max," he answered. "Too many questions." Diego and Max both looked at me at that point and I sat in a chair awkwardly at the table with Max. "Max will be your bodyguard," Diego continued. "You'll need someone to watch you and I trust him."

"Bodyguard?" Max asked. "Oooo, this sounds way more fun than my usual gig."

"Can you keep an eye on her for me, Max?" Diego asked. "Seriously, if you won't, you'll have to assign someone for me."

"No, no… I'll gladly do it," he answered.

"Max is in charge of…" he paused, "security."

Max looked at me and winked. "Don't worry, Lilly. I'll take good care of you."

"Not that good," Diego replied. "Try to remember she's marrying me."

"She looks worried," he said. "I was just trying to reassure her." I began to understand where the big house came from. He and Johnny were in the same business and that's how he knew Johnny was killed. Max got on the radio and called to Leticia and said a few words in Spanish. "She'll have something for you in a few minutes," Max told me. "In the meantime, let me tell you the rules." He looked at Diego. "She does talk, right?"

"Yes, I talk," I answered sarcastically.

"Whew," he said. "Lovely voice too."

"Max…" Diego warned.

"You cannot leave the house without me," he continued. "And when you're in the house, I need to know where you are."

"Okay," I agreed.

"And…" he paused, "I think it might be important that you tell me who the father is." He paused again. "Come on Diego, what if he shows up here?"

"He won't," he answered. I looked at the floor.

"Okay then. We're clear, Lilly?"

"Yes sir," I answered.

"Oh no way!" He looked at Diego and laughed a little. "You can call me anything but that. Max or Maxwell is fine. Whatever you're most comfortable with."

"Okay Max," I answered and I winked back at him.

"I like her," he said to Diego. "Where'd you find her?"

"At the apartment community." Max got a look of revelation in his eyes and looked back at me. "No… she's not…"

Diego nodded. "That's her."

"What's up with that skinny little drug addict?" Max looked at me. "How does he get so many women?"

A voice came in on Max's radio and said something in Spanish. Max smiled and said to Diego, "Her room is ready. Want me to take her there?"

"Yeah thanks. I have to get back to the property." He hesitated for a moment. "Behave, Max." Max smiled mischievously. "And button up, will you? We've got a lady in the house now."

He stood up to button up his shirt. He was a little shorter than Diego but not by much. I couldn't keep my eyes off of the well-maintained six-pack on his stomach that was exposed when he stood. He watched me watch him intently. Our eyes were locked and I couldn't pull away. I couldn't help but wonder if Diego looked like that under his shirt. "Yes," he said as though he was reading my thoughts. "Diego looks something like this too."

I could see Diego smile and look at us peripherally. "Mine is better," he said and laughed a little. I was so embarrassed that I was busted.

"When are you going to show her what you've got?" Max asked him. I was starting to get a little nervous.

"That's not part of the deal," he answered. "I told her I'd take care of her. And I will."

"Can I have her?" Max asked. I think he was kidding.

Diego looked at him with a silly smirk on his face. "No, you can't have her. She's not a Barbie doll."

"Well, someone's got to have her, why can't it be me?"

"She'll be my wife, Max, keep that in mind." He was still smiling.

"Can I take her out and play with her once in a while?" He finished buttoning his shirt, still staring at me. I knew my face had to be red by now.

"Forgive my brother," Diego answered. "He's a little... quirky sometimes." Then he looked at Max and said, "Clothes on at all times, got it?"

Max saluted him, "Clothes on… got it." They both laughed and Diego shook his head in comedic disbelief. Then Max said something disconcerting. "You may change your mind later right? And… well… you know."

Diego walked over to me and kissed my hand. "I promise, you'll be safe here." He left the two of us alone, still shaking his head as he walked out the door, muttering something in Spanish. I looked at Max and he went back to playing with his calculator. I tried to break the tension in the air. "What do you do, Max?" I asked.

"Unspeakable things, Lilly, unspeakable things." He still did not look up. "But I like my new job. It sounds like it could be fun. Follow me, I'll help you get settled." He took my bags and we climbed a flight of stairs. He pointed out Diego's room and mine was two doors down. "Mine is next to yours." He smiled. "You know, in case you get scared or just need something." I could tell he was embarrassed that I might have thought he was hitting on me for real this time. He was very sweet and I think under that entire 'bad boy' image, a little shy. His humor was obviously what he used to cover up that fact. He brought in my bags and quickly got out of the room. "If you need me, I'll be downstairs," he said. "One more rule." He looked at me quite seriously.

"Yes Max, anything," I answered.

"You're not allowed to be afraid of me. I'm here to keep you safe. If you need me, you find me." He handed me a radio. "Push this button and call me. It's quick and easy. Like Johnny," he continued.

I made a face.

"I was just making a joke," he said. "Sorry… too soon." I walked over to him, hugged him and kissed his cheek. He backed away. "Thank you." I could feel the tears welling up in my eyes. "I'm all alone now, you know."

He took both my hands and brought them up to his lips. He kissed them but never took his eyes off of mine. "You'll never be alone again," he said, softly after releasing my hands. Then he walked off.

After I finished unpacking I went downstairs to the kitchen. Max was cleaning up whatever it is he was doing with the calculator. "So, are you the pretty one, or the smart one?" I asked. He smiled.

"Most people think I'm the pretty one," he answered. "But I actually do have a degree." I was very surprised by that.

"A degree?" I asked. "In accounting?"

"Yes," he replied. "Numbers are my thing." He started cleaning up his papers. "But Diego's pretty too," he answered, laughing a little to himself. "So, you must be the pretty one," he added sarcastically.

"Why, because I'm single and pregnant and marrying a man I barely know?"

"Yeah, something like that," he answered. "You really need someone to explain the whole, 'how you get pregnant thing,' to you." I looked at the floor, embarrassed.

"I'm sorry," he said. "I have no idea who you are and have no right to judge."

"He was my first," I answered. "I trusted him."

"That piece of..." He stopped himself.

"It's my fault too," I replied. "He didn't know. But I did trust him to know what to do."

"It was his job to protect you," he answered. "Whether he knew or not." He paused. "But seriously, Lilly, with all the girls Johnny has had, he probably knew as soon as he started to undress you that it was your first time." He reached out and took my hand. "I would have protected you." He made my knees weak. "How long did you know him?"

"Not long," I answered. "I'm not sure I even liked it. I just liked the closeness." His expression didn't change.

"Men are selfish, Lilly." He didn't even look surprised at my comment. "If they think they can get away with getting you into bed with the smallest amount of work..." he shook his head and closed his eyes for a second. "Well, that's the road they'll take."

"What about you?" I asked, trying to embarrass him for a change. "Are you selfish?"

"Maybe someday, you'll find out." He smiled and winked at me. "But until then..." He reflected for a moment. "It looks like you are stuck with me as your bodyguard." He took my hand and led me out of the kitchen. "And soon, you'll be stuck with my brother as your husband, which would complicate the first part." He was silly and playful. I was actually starting to feel happy.

"Where are we going?" I asked.

"I thought I might take you for a walk on the grounds." We began to walk out the back door. "Diego and I have a beautiful property. Our father left it to us when he died. I think he thought it would bond us or something. You should see it for yourself."

It was HUGE! There were trees and ponds among hills and flowers. I had never seen the likes of such a property up-close. "How can you afford to take care of all of this?" I asked him.

"We sell drugs to children," he said, quite casually. "I thought you were up to speed on all that."

I was a little stunned by his candor. He obviously does not feel good about what he does or he wouldn't have said it like that. "What?" I asked.

"You heard me," he replied.

"Why didn't you get a different kind of job?" I asked. "You seem capable."

"I ask myself that every day," he answered. "But now I know why." He smiled at me. "Someone had to be here to take care of you." He was still holding my hand and we were walking together like lovers through a meadow. It felt good and safe. He walked me to the back of the property by a creek. It was breathtaking. We sat on a couple of large rocks by the water and he let go of my hand. I felt a little sad when he did that. "I come here a lot," he told me. "Sometimes just to talk to God and be with Him."

"You believe in God?" I asked.

"Why so surprised?" He gave me a boyish grin that tickled a little.

"Aren't you a hit-man?" I asked.

"Enforcer," he said in a drawn out tone. "I prefer enforcer."

We both laughed a little. He put his arm over my shoulder and pulled me close. "It's going to be all right, Lilly." I put my head on his shoulder.

"Have you ever been a bodyguard before?" I asked.

"No," he answered. "But I do watch Diego's back all the time. So, I guess I'm his bodyguard." He picked up my chin with his fingers. "He's a very powerful man, you know." Actually, I didn't know. I had no idea what I had gotten myself into. "So, be careful with him." I put my head back down on his shoulder and he held me for a while.

"Are you going to keep me safe?" I asked. I was worried now, about his brother.

"I will put my life down for you." He pulled me even closer and rocked me a little. I never felt so secure before. You could smell the water as it cascaded into the rocks and made a swishing sound. It was heaven to me.

"Does Diego ever come out here?" I asked.

"I don't think he remembers it's here," he answered. He gave me a knowing look. It was like this was going to be our spot.

CHAPTER 8

What was the Most Important Rule Again?

Months had gone by, and I had my baby in late November. Max was the only one with me when I went into labor and Diego didn't even come to see me in the hospital after the baby was born. Diego insisted on naming him Diego Jr., so we did. He treated me like a guest in his home and never seemed to notice the inappropriateness of my relationship with his brother. Max called me "baby girl" and often referred to himself as "daddy." I never even saw Diego look up from his coffee when we were playing inappropriately at the breakfast table. In all these months Diego had never laid a hand on me, nor did he ask to. Max and I were totally platonic, although I must admit that I was crazy about him. The line was very clearly drawn. Whatever feelings we may have had or not had, Diego was my husband and Max was my bodyguard and best friend.

Time went on. I had been living there almost three years and never heard a word from my parents. Johnny had become a distant memory. With the baby named Diego I hardly gave Johnny a second thought. We ended up calling him Dieguito, which means little Diego. It became very confusing with two Diego's in the house. Max kept me busy for the most part. My baby called him Uncle Max and Leticia was very helpful. Max cooked me breakfast every morning and the cook made dinner every night. We spend hours upon hours at the creek. Max read me poetry by the water at night. I put my head in his lap and he would stroke my hair as he read. Yeats, Keats, Marvell and Donne, to name a few of the poets he shared with me. Every day I grew closer and closer to my husband's brother.

It was two days before Easter when I got the phone call from Sedona. My mom had been shot in her own living room and the funeral was Easter Sunday. Everything always seemed to happen on Easter. We left the baby with his nanny, Leticia, and Diego, Max and I headed for Arizona. The anticipation was overwhelming. I hadn't seen or heard from my dad in years. I assumed he knew I had married the high profile criminal but he never sent a note, a gift or any recognition at all of the blessed event. When we got to the house, my dad didn't even acknowledge Diego. "Max," was all he said.

"I'm sorry sir, for your loss," Max said as he hugged him. Diego went to hug him and my dad rudely walked away.

"I'm sorry, Diego, he's just devastated," I said as I tried to make excuses. Diego said nothing and headed into the kitchen. Max poured my dad some Irish whiskey and the two of them went outside onto the patio together. It was weird. We sat through the funeral and went to the gravesite. My mom and I did not speak for the last few years of her life, so I was a little uncomfortable. I wasn't asked to speak, so I didn't.

I looked over in the distance and saw in the fog a hooded figure walking through the trees. At first I thought I was hallucinating, but then I realized that it was a man. I could see long brown hair falling around the hood and I realized… Oh my gosh! Could it be Johnny? The figure disappeared and I looked around to see if anyone else had seen him. Max looked at me and shook his head in disapproval. So I remained where I was and we went back to the house. I knew Max saw the hooded figure. Could Johnny still be alive?

My old friend Candy showed up for the reception. She used to work for Johnny and we lost touch after his death. "I came as soon as I could," she said. "Let's help out your dad and go to the store for some more food." She kissed my dad on the cheek and told him where we were going.

"Sure," I said. We headed out the door. We passed the supermarket and I looked at her curiously. "Where are we going?"

"You'll see," she answered. She drove us straight to John's old house. "What are you doing?" I asked. She pulled into the driveway. My heart was pounding. She opened the door and Johnny was standing in the kitchen wearing a black hooded sweatshirt.

"Johnny!" I shouted. "I thought you were dead!" I ran over to him in the kitchen and hugged him.

"You have one hour," Candy said as she left and closed the front door behind her.

"It's been three years." I backed up and looked at him. "Why didn't you tell me you were alive? We have a baby, you know."

"It's a long story, Lilly and we only have an hour." He pulled me close and tried to kiss me. I pushed him back. "What is it?" he asked.

"It's been a long time, John."

"John?" he asked sadly. "I don't think you've ever called me that before?"

"Johnny," I said, correcting myself, "I'm married now."

"To Max or Diego?" he asked. My face flushed and totally gave me away.

"What?" I started to wonder if this was some kind of set up.

"I have people too, you know. I hear you and Max are always together. Holding hands, touching…" He stopped. "Are you and Max… together?"

"He's my bodyguard," I answered. "Why were you having me watched?"

"Because I love you, Lilly. My Easter Lilly." He stroked my hair back away from my now sweaty face. "Make love to me. I've missed you." He moved to kiss me and he held me close. I couldn't break free.

"Stop!" I said. "Let go!"

Just then the door flew open and Max was standing there at the door with a gun pointed at Johnny. "Lilly, you broke my most important rule!"

"I know," I said. I pushed John away and ran to Max. "Don't leave the house without telling you."

"No sex with Johnny!" he shouted. Johnny laughed.

"Calm down, Max. Nothing happened that she didn't want to happen."

"This is a huge mistake," I said. "Candy brought me here and dropped me off. I thought we were going to the store." I was breathless and desperate for him to believe me.

"Tell her why I've been dead all this time, Max." Max never took his eyes off of John, pointing the gun right at him. You could see it was a struggle for him not to just shoot him.

"Lilly, he's married." Max glanced at me for a second. "He knocked you up, dropped you off on our doorstep and married Diana."

I couldn't believe it. I put my hands over my mouth and stared Johnny down. "How could you? You really are a pig, aren't you?"

"Diego said if I tried to contact you or the baby, he'd have you both killed!" Johnny blurted. "He made me marry Diana so I wouldn't be able to come after you." He looked at Max who was still pointing a gun at him. "Come on Max tell her!" Max began to lower the gun. "We don't live in God's world, do we Max. We live in Diego's world. He is in control." Max picked up the gun again. Beads of sweat began to form on his brow.

"I should just blow a hole through you and put you out of your misery."

"Max!" I cried. "Stop!"

"I bet you want her too, don't you? But you're going to hand her over to him, just like I did." Johnny was pretty smug for a man with a gun pointed at him.

"She's not mine to give," Max replied.

"But she could be, right Lilly?" Johnny asked. "You want her so bad…" He paused and smiled as though he knew what he was going to say would destroy Max. "You can almost taste her." Max's eyes changed when he said that. "And I don't mean just her lips," he continued. Max shot a hole through the wall inches from Johnny's face. "I think I hit a nerve."

"Shut up, you idiot!" I screamed. "Max, is Diego on his way?"

He put the gun away and grabbed my hand. "Watch your mouth with my brother," Max said to John. "He's on his way and he's not in a good mood."

"You know, I'm right, Maxwell!" he yelled after us. Max opened the car door for me and we took off.

"Is what he said true?" I asked.

"Lilly, you need to promise me that you will do everything I tell you until Diego has calmed down."

"Okay Max, whatever you say."

"I don't care what Diego says to you, you cannot leave my side."

"I can do that," I said playfully.

"I'm being serious, Lilly. He's going to think you slept with John and after he's done with John, he's probably going to think you slept with me." I began to panic. "Baby girl," he continued. I loved when he called me that. "I will protect you. Just don't leave me." He grabbed my hand and squeezed it.

"You didn't tell me if what Johnny said was true," I reminded him.

He was quiet for a minute. "Yes Lilly, every word." We pulled into the driveway of my father's house. Then he took my face into his hands and put his face close to mine. His breath on my face was warm. "Yes Lilly, sometimes I can almost taste you." He let me go and my stomach leapt through the air. I never wanted him more. "Come on," he said. "I need to see your dad."

We walked inside and my father was in the kitchen. "Mick!" he shouted. "Mick, send some men to Candy's house."

"She brought her to John's house, didn't she?" he asked.

"It's probably too late," Max said. "But try anyway." I started getting scared. My dad called the station but when they got to Candy's house she was gone. "Too late?" Max asked.

"You?" my dad asked.

"I don't do women or children," Max answered.

"Great, a hit man with a conscience," he snickered.

"Would I tell you about it, if I did it myself?"

"Okay, I guess not," he answered. I wasn't sure if they were kidding or serious.

"Call Ray," Max suggested. "He and Candy go out together."

My dad called the station and had them pick up Ray.

"What the hell were you doing there?" my dad yelled at me. "After all these years, you still can't stay away from him?"

"Don't worry," Max answered. "When I got there she was pushing him away."

"Did he…"

"No, I got there before anything happened," Max answered. I loved how they were carrying on this conversation as though I was not in the room. "Mick?" he started.

"Go ahead."

"When Diego gets here, you're gonna have to trust me."

"Meaning?" he asked. His face had alarm written all over it.

"I'm the only one who can handle him. If you pull your gun on me when I'm trying to control him, he could take her."

"I don't like the sound of this," he said.

"I'm afraid he'll take her, hurt her, lock her up…" He paused. "They're legally married, you know. So please let me handle him."

"All right," he agreed. "Why can't she just leave him?"

"No one leaves Diego," he answered. "Unless it's in a body bag." He hesitated. "We'd both be dead before we got out the front door." I wrapped my arms around Max and he held me close. "Daddy's here, baby girl," he said. My dad looked at him strangely. Max sat on the couch and put a pillow in his lap and motioned for me to lie down. I laid my head in his lap and he stroked my hair. I always felt so safe with him. He was reciting some poetry to me from memory, obviously trying to calm me.

"I don't get it, Max." My father looked at us perplexed by our inappropriate relationship. Max was quiet for a minute. "Just leave him, Lilly and marry Max." Max laughed a little and I looked up at him. "You'd make a great cop," my father suggested. They both laughed.

"I'm the bad guy, Mick, remember?" Max looked at me with sadness in his eyes.

The phone rang and my father talked for a few minutes and hung up. "Ray said he and Candy had a fight and she left town."

"She's dead," Max said casually.

"Max, who did it?" my father asked. "Diego?"

"I can't tell you, Mick. I have to protect myself to keep an eye on Lilly, you know that."

"Don't they call you the iron man?" my father asked. Max laughed. "You know, the one no one can kill?"

"Let's hope it stays that way," he answered. Then he turned my face to him.

"Lilly, this is going to push Diego into overdrive and I want you to be prepared."

"Overdrive?" I asked. "You don't mean…"

"Just be prepared, Lilly." He looked very sad when he said it. "He may want to… put his claim on you."

"No, no, no…." I said. "That can't happen."

"Come on Max, take her and run," my father suggested.

"Just don't leave with him tonight." I turned back over and Max held me. My father watched us for a little while and left the room.

"Sleep with him?" I looked at Max for some kind of comfort.

"It'll be okay," he answered. "He's not selfish."

"I can't do that, Max." It was totally unspoken between us but it was the elephant in the room.

"I can't take you yet. I have to stay focused."

"Is there something going on?" I asked.

"I'll talk to him, first." His eyes filled with water and he turned away. "I'll talk to him first," he said again, almost under his breath.

He was quiet for a minute. Then he turned my face to his and smiled. "Look at it this way. By the time you get to me, you'll have saved the best for last." He tried to make light of a really ugly situation.

"I'm scared, Max."

"I know," he said. "My only fear is that you might fall in love with my brother." He paused for a few seconds. "He'll treat you right." He ran his fingers through my hair. "Sexually, I mean." Then he said, "Sometimes I wish he was a little more like Johnny."

"Don't worry," my father said, coming back into the room. "If she falls in love with him, I'll kill him myself." Max gave up a halfhearted smile but the tears were still there. I reached up and touched his face. "Do you two know that you're in love?" he asked us. "Seriously, is it that you just don't know?" Max and I smiled at each other. I rolled over in his lap and I think we both fell asleep. Next thing I knew, I was awakened by my husband who was dragging me by the arm across the floor off of Max's lap.

CHAPTER 9

Not Tonight

I hit my head against the coffee table and there was blood everywhere. Max leapt to his feet and stood in front of me. He pulled his gun out and cocked it before he threw it in Diego's face. "Seriously Maxwell. You're going to shoot me?" he asked.

"Diego, not tonight."

"Are you sleeping with my wife too?" he asked.

"No one is sleeping with your wife," he answered.

"I'm about to change that," Diego answered. "Now give me my wife."

"Not tonight, Diego." My father had his hand on his gun but did not pull it out. Max reached down to pick me up off of the floor and pushed me behind him without once taking his eyes off of Diego.

"Johnny says you're sleeping with her too."

"John didn't get to first base with her," Max answered. "I opened the door and he was forcing himself on her. She did not respond."

"And you? Why was she in your lap?"

"I was comforting her, that's all," he answered. "I think we fell asleep waiting for you." Diego made a face showing disbelief. "Candy took her out there. She didn't know where they were going."

Diego seemed to be calming down. "Give her to me."

"Not tonight." Max stood firm with me behind him. He was clearly not going to let me go. "Go take a walk, and let me clean her up."

"Max, she does not belong to you." He reached out his hand for me. Blood was spilling down my face and into my eyes.

"Don't make me chose between you," Max answered. "You won't win this time."

Diego walked out the door and slammed it behind him. "Thanks for not interfering Mick," Max said. I was shaking uncontrollably, wiping blood from my eyes.

"I'm telling you Max, if you ever change your mind, I'll get you a job." As soon as the tension had ceased Max's hit man exterior fell to the floor like a ceramic mask. He turned to me and pulled me close. "Baby girl, are you all right?" I had blood all over my face and hands. It had dripped all over my clothes and the floor. There was a gash in my head. He brought me to the kitchen and started looking for antiseptic. My dad got him a first-aid kit and he started wiping the blood from my face.

"Does she need stitches?" he asked Max.

"Even a small gash on the head, will spill a lot of blood," he answered. My dad gave him a disapproving look. "Just a little something I learned over the years," he said smiling. He put a band-aide on my head and kissed it.

"Careful," my dad said cautiously. "He'll be back any minute."

He grabbed a towel and started cleaning up the blood. I was shaking too hard to do it myself. "We're going to head back tonight, Mick." Max grabbed my hand. "I'm afraid to leave her in a room with him tonight. I won't have any control."

"That's fine," he answered. "You'd better take care of her, Max." He got suddenly very serious. "I'm trusting you." Their familiarity with each other confused me. I wasn't sure if Max used to live out here or what, but my dad really liked him. We heard the door open and Max stood in front of me again. Diego walked in. "I'm sorry, Lilly." I couldn't believe my ears. "Now, can I have my wife?" Diego looked at Max.

"We're leaving in a few minutes," Max answered. "I meant it when I said, not tonight."

"Fine," he conceded. "Let's get out of here. The sooner we get home, the sooner I get my wife back." He walked out of the kitchen and my father and Max gave each other an unfavorable look. "Max…" I said. I was shivering.

He kissed my hands. "I can't believe how hard this is," he replied. "But we have to go."

We said goodbye to my dad and the three of us got into the car. Diego drove and Max and I sat in the back together. I had my head on his shoulder and he had his arms around me. "When we get home," Diego started, "this thing you two have is over." We didn't move apart. I didn't want to be away from him. I knew what was going to happen when I got home and was trying as hard as I could not to think about it.

For the first few days, Diego ignored me. Max continued to make breakfast for us every morning, like he always did and he and Diego talked business like they always have. Then one day, the thing I dreaded more than anything else in the world happened. Diego came into my bedroom after dinner. I was reading a book on my bed and when I saw him, I shuddered. "I'm not going to hurt you," he said. "You don't need to be afraid of me." He started taking off his shirt. I never noticed how beautiful his body was before. He had rippling muscles on his stomach and his arms were huge. He walked over and sat on the bed beside me. I don't know what I was thinking but I reached out and touched his stomach. "It's okay, Lilly, you're allowed to touch me." I quickly pulled my hand back. "I had a long talk with Max," he started. "He told me Johnny was your first, and only lover." I could feel my face turning red. "Don't be embarrassed," he said. "That explains a lot." I still didn't say anything. "Max asked me to be gentle with you." He seemed genuinely sincere. "He asked me to protect you and make it a pleasant experience for you. I understand that Johnny didn't do that." I was so embarrassed I wanted to crawl into a hole and die. "But there are a few things we need to talk about," he continued. "You can't let Maxwell call you baby girl anymore." I could feel tears well up in my eyes. He reached up and dried them. "You can never have him, Lilly. He would never betray me like that." I looked up and met his eyes. "And you can't call him daddy anymore." I laughed.

"I don't call him that," I answered. "He calls himself that." We both laughed.

"He's quite a character, isn't he." He looked kind of serious. "Lilly, I'm not going to take you against your will. I don't want this to be rape. I want you to give me a real chance. I want us to make love." I swallowed hard. I was never so scared in my life. This was the only thing Max could not protect me from.

"Okay," was all I could offer. He took my face into his hands and kissed me. He was very gentle but my hands were still shaking.

"Lilly, are you scared of me?" he asked.

"I've only done this a few times," I answered.

"If I were Max, would you be so nervous?"

I swallowed back the tears I was feeling. "I don't know," I answered honestly. He kissed me again, a little harder this time and he pushed me down on the bed. I closed my eyes and tried to think of Max, but eventually I realized that this was definitely not Max.

He started removing my clothes and I thought I might throw up. There was one article of clothing left between me and having an intimate relationship with him. He slipped them off and I am sure that I gasped a little. He removed the rest of his own clothing as he was kissing my neck. It actually felt nice. I started to relax a little. He worked his way down and things started to change. My heart rate started to accelerate and my body started to tingle. He put me on top of him and securely grabbed hold of me. As he moved me forward something started to happen. Something I couldn't control. "Diego!" I yelled. "Stop, stop…" But he didn't. He rolled me over and climbed on top of me. He whispered in my ear, "Hold on tight, Lilly and let go of all your fears." So I wrapped my arms around him and closed my eyes. My body disconnected from my mind and as soon as that happened I let out a yell of pleasure that I wished I could have taken back as soon as it escaped my lips. "Diego, oh my God!" I screamed it over and over again. My body shuddered and the feelings that were going through me were new and unfamiliar. He looked at me with a proud smile and called my name out just a few moments later. When it was all over, he collapsed beside me.

I was almost afraid to ask, but I had to know. "Was that supposed to happen?" I asked breathlessly.

"Every time," he smiled. "At least once."

"More than once?" I asked. "Really?"

My innocence amused him. "Johnny is a selfish dog," he added. Then he picked up my chin with his fingers so that I was looking right at him and said, "The more I get to know you, Lilly, the better it will feel." I wrapped my arms around him and put my head on his chest. He stroked my hair. "I'm not so bad now, am I?" he asked.

"No," I answered. "I didn't expect to like it so much," I told him. And boy did I mean that. I was sick to my stomach that I enjoyed it the way I did. I just wanted to be with Max, that's all. We slept in each other's arms and made love a few more times that night.

In the morning Max had breakfast made as usual and he was sitting at the table with his calculator like always. When he acknowledged our presence he winked at me. He was trying to be strong, I could tell, but his eyes were empty. "He was here last night," Max said to Diego.

"Who?" he asked. "Jorge?"

"No," he answered. He was obviously trying to keep something from me. "You know, tonight's the meeting."

"Yes, of course," he answered. Then they had a moment of understanding between them and Diego started to laugh. "Lilly, maybe you could excuse us for a minute."

"No," I said. "Who was here?"

"Johnny." Diego answered.

"Oh my God!" I cried.

"Yeah, that's about what we heard when he was here." Max couldn't make eye contact with me when he said that. I know my face flushed because I got suddenly over-heated. "You're gonna take her with you to the meeting, right? Cause if you're not, I need to stay here with her."

"Okay Max, spill," Diego replied. "Tell me what happened."

"In front of Lilly?" He looked at me then with concern in his eyes.

"Yes," I said sarcastically. "In front of Lilly."

He looked up at Diego and he gave him a nod to go ahead. "He came in with his delivery and said, 'finally Diego has a woman. I was starting to worry about him.' I didn't say anything," Max continued, "but he pushed me."

"Go on…" Diego responded.

"Then he said, 'wow, sounds like a wild one. Who's he got up there?'"

Diego began to laugh and said, "You didn't…"

"Yeah, I did," Max replied. "I said, 'Well, I guess you never made her scream like that before, or you would've recognized her voice.' Then he threw his envelope on the table and said, 'Is that my Lilly?'"

"What'd you say?" I asked.

"It sounds to me like she's Diego's Lilly now." Diego high fived Max and said, "I couldn't have planned that better myself." Max's face dropped a little.

"Well, now we have a little problem," Max confessed. "If you don't take her with you, John will show up here before the meeting. He ran out of here like his ponytail was on fire. He was pissed."

"Okay," Diego agreed. "I'll take her."

"What meeting, Diego, and why do I have to worry about Johnny? We've been over for a long time now."

"I'm afraid he may try to force his way back into your life," Max answered. "I don't want to take any chances with you." He looked at me in earnest. I wanted to touch him so badly.

"You know how I go to a business meeting once a month, baby?" Diego asked me. Max twinged when he called me that.

"Yes, of course," I answered.

"They are really territory meetings. Jorge is in charge of the entire organization and I am the number two. We hold cocktail parties in a hotel and invite the territory leaders and their enforcers. They all bring their wives, girlfriends or significant others with them. After the party, the men have dinner together; have their meeting, and the women have dinner together. It bonds the women and we get to talk business and have a nice meal."

"I think I'm hurt," I answered. "Why haven't you taken me before?"

"I didn't want you to see Johnny," he answered. "But the cat's out of the bag now, so you may as well come with me." Max had his eyes fixed on me. It was very uncomfortable.

"Besides," Diego continued. "We weren't really husband and wife, like we are now. I think you'll have a good time." I could hear Max swallow loudly.

"Sure," I said. "Sounds like fun."

"I'll order you a dress and some shoes. They'll be here in about an hour. Then get dressed for me, okay?"

"Yes, of course," I answered. He took my face into his hands and kissed me. "I can't wait to see you later," he said and he left the room. "Max, I'll be back in an hour!" We heard the door slam. Max and I looked at each other as soon as he was gone. We simultaneously got up and ran into each other's arms. He hugged me and I started crying uncontrollably. "You didn't have to like it that much," he said, trying to make light of this most uncomfortable situation. He picked up my chin the same way Diego had done and looked at me. "It'll get easier, Lilly." His eyes were full of tears and I reached up and brushed them away.

Why couldn't it be you?" I asked. "I will never be Diego's Lilly," I said. Just then his brother Hector burst into the kitchen and Max in his shock pushed me back quickly. "Oh, it's just you," he said and he held me again.

"Careful," Hector said, "Jorge isn't far behind. What's wrong with her?"

"She had sex with Diego last night," Max answered.

Hector laughed, "Yeah, I'd be crying too." He reached over and pulled me away from Max. "Look you two, knock it off. Jorge can't see this." Max let me go and turned his face away and I grabbed a napkin and wiped my eyes. "Remember Max, stay focused. This doesn't look focused to me." He went to the door of the kitchen looking out for Jorge. Hector was the second youngest brother. Max was the baby. He was Jorge's enforcer and looked very similar to Max. He was blond and light skinned and very handsome. He had the same icy blue eyes that Max did. He was acting very nervous.

"Here he comes. Lilly, you okay?" Hector asked me.

Yeah," I said. "I'm good."

"Good, because your life depends on it," Hector said and in walked Jorge and his gorgeous wife. Olivia was slight in build. She was Latina, had long dark hair, and a face that was dark and smooth. Jorge looked a little like Diego but the two were not as similar as the younger brothers. He was very dark, darker than Diego with those same green eyes. He was tall like Diego, I think a little taller, but his face was what was different. He had craters in his face that I understand occur from excessive drug use. He also had a long scar on the side of his forehead, just over his eye. He was scary to look at, not pleasing at all. I could feel evil all over him when he entered the room.

"This is Lilly," Max said to Jorge. "Lilly, this is Jorge, Olivia and Hector." I smiled and said, "Mucho gusto."

"Very good," Jorge answered. "But I'm betting that is all you know."

"Yes sir," I added.

"His ego is big enough, please don't call him sir," Olivia added. "Will you be joining us tonight?"

"Yes." I smiled. "I'm looking forward to it."

"Why don't you go and get ready," Max asked, obviously trying to get rid of me. "I'm sure your dress will be here soon."

"I'll help." Olivia took my hand. "I hate business talk anyway." We left the room and the conversation in the other room turned to Spanish.

"You'll get used to that," she assured me. Then the doorbell rang and it was my dress. We grabbed it and ran upstairs. I was actually kind of excited. Olivia and I ran up the steps and she helped me prepare.

CHAPTER 10

The Party

I came down the stairs in the flowing white gown Diego had bought for me to wear. It was incredible. When I got downstairs all the men were in very expensive suits the likes of which I had never seen before. They all looked amazing, especially Max. He took my breath away. "You are stunning," Diego said as he put his arm out for me to take.

"Yes, truly breath taking," Max added, smiling at me. Olivia came down the steps next and Jorge and Hector followed suit with compliments. We all got into a stretch limo and went to the party together. When we walked in the door the room swarmed over Diego and Jorge. They let go of our hands almost immediately and left us with Hector and Max. Olivia grabbed my hand and we wandered into the crowd. Hector and Max parked themselves in the back of the room with their eyes locked on the two of us. "So, how long has it been?" Olivia asked me.

"How long has what been?" I asked.

"You and Max." She smiled. "How long?"

"Oh, no…" I answered. "There's no Max and me."

"The sexual tension between you is not only obvious but a little painful." As she said that I noticed Hector wink at her. She smiled and looked at the floor.

"No…!" I said to her. I leaned closer to her ear and whispered, "You and Hector?"

She smiled again and squeezed my hand tighter before she let it go. "He is everything to me," she answered. "If it wasn't for him, I couldn't get through a day."

"Wow, that's something," I answered. "He didn't say anything." Then I thought about how serious he was about Max staying focused and staying away from me. What was that all about?

"He wouldn't ever say anything," she said. "It's been about three years." I was stunned. I mean, really stunned.

"How do you keep it from Jorge?" I asked, hoping for some help in that area.

"Looking for tips?" she asked.

"We're not sleeping together," I confessed. "He won't."

"Ah ha…" she said. "So I was right."

"Well?" I asked. "Does Jorge know?"

"He only married me as a business deal," she continued. "My father is a very important politician in Mexico. He marries me and they mutually benefit each other."

"So the older ones marry and the younger ones get a little side dish?" I asked. "What would Jorge do if he found out?"

"I don't think he cares. Seriously, we've been married a long time." Max walked over to us at that point, obviously concerned about what we were talking about.

"Hello ladies." He smiled that boyish grin that took me to my knees. "What are we talking about?"

"Hector looks sharp tonight," she said smiling. "Don't you think so?"

"Easy girl." He put his hand on her shoulder. "Your husband is around here somewhere."

"Max, why are you playing hard to get?" She playfully grabbed his hand and laughed.

"Lilly?" He was shocked that I told her.

"She said nothing," Olivia responded. "But you just confirmed it for me." He pulled his hand away from hers and reached down and squeezed my hand. Olivia separated us. "Careful, Max," she warned.

"It's too dangerous, Olivia." He leaned close to my hair as if he were taking in my fragrance.

"Yeah, you're real discreet," she said. "Max, if you give in to each other," she leaned in to his ear and whispered, "it won't be as obvious."

"They're together all the time, Olivia, I don't think I could take it. What if she slips?"

"First of all," she answered. "It's new for them. And the fact that it is obviously tearing you apart, I'm sure is an added bonus for him." He nodded in agreement.

"I've been sleeping with Jorge for 15 years, he's probably glad I don't want it from him so much." Max laughed. "For all I know, he's having his own affairs."

"Oh, I would love it if Diego would have an affair." It slipped out of my mouth before I realized it was out. They both laughed.

"He'll leave her alone after they've been together for a while. And trust me…" She looked over at Hector who shot her a very sexy smile. She leaned over to him so no one would hear her. "It will be different with you. She will always know who she's with." He smiled and blushed a little. I never saw him blush before.

"Thanks Olivia," he said and he kissed her cheek. "I just want to keep her safe."

"Think about it Max," she said. "If you would let go, her life would be more bearable. You don't know what it's like for us." Hector walked over and whispered something in Olivia's ear. She laughed a little and he put his hand on her back. "What's all the chit chat about?" he asked.

"I have a better question for you." I looked at Hector with what I'm sure was an unattractive smirk.

"Uh-oh, she knows…" slipped out of his mouth.

"Why is it all right for you but not for Max?" I asked.

"Max is a mess," he answered. "This whole thing with Diego and you is torturing him."

"I am not a mess," he said, a little annoyed with that description.

"You're both a mess," Hector continued. "You need to put the reality into the situation." He looked around for Diego and Jorge but they were nowhere to be found. "She's married to our brother. You can have her from time to time. That's it."

"I don't think I can talk about this anymore," Max said. He reached from my hand again and breathed me in. "You smell like paradise." I got chills when he said that and shuddered.

"Seriously, Max. How long can the two of you go on like this?" Olivia asked.

"Not much longer," Max answered. "I need a drink." He let go of my hand and walked to the bar.

"Can I get you ladies something?" Hector asked.

"Please Hector, champagne for both of us," she answered. He walked away.

"Thanks Olivia," I told her. "I think you may have gotten to him this time." The boys came back each with a champagne glass for both of us. "I promise, Olivia, I'll give your suggestion some real thought."

"Where are the men?" she asked.

"They're around here somewhere," Max answered. Let's not talk about them. We're here with the people we want to be here with. Let's enjoy it while we can." We held up our glasses and toasted to our temporary freedom.

Every month was a new party. I was lucky enough to get a new dress, shoes and a handbag for each one. Sometimes, if I behaved as Diego preferred, I even got diamonds. Time was passing and Diego and I were a real married couple. He watched Max and me more closely now. When Diego was working we would try to steal a moment by the creek but more often than not, Diego would take his work home with him. There were no more evenings of romantic poetry. No more playing around like children. I could see that it was starting to take its toll on Max. His sense of humor had dwindled. I wasn't sure how much more he could take.

I put on my newest white, lace gown with diamonds dripping from my neck like icicles on the outside of a house. Diego preferred to see me in white. As I slowly walked down the spiral staircase, Max was waiting at the bottom. "Wow!" he said. "I always knew you were an angel."

"Maxwell, I have missed you." I walked slowly to him as to not tear my dress. I looked around for company and saw no one, so I kissed his cheek. He sighed.

"Sometimes, it just hurts," he said. "I'm really starting to need you." Just after he said that Diego came from around the corner with Jorge and Olivia. We weren't sure if they heard.

"Are you all right Max? You look a little sad. So unlike you." Diego knew what was wrong and was being sarcastic.

"I'm fine," he said. "Let's go."

It was the usual routine. Diego and Jorge being treated like kings and Olivia and I being discarded like coats headed for the cloakroom. Max and Hector were always left to watch us. That was the only part of the night I liked.

The men went to their meeting as soon as Diego and Jorge came back inside from whatever it is they were doing and the women all had dinner together. "It's weird," Olivia said. "When he's not around, it hurts."

"Max was just saying that," I told her. "I feel the same way. I ache for him," I answered. "If he were to leave, I would die." Olivia smiled.

"I'm so glad we have each other now," she said. "We're not alone anymore." Only we were alone. Every time Diego or Jorge closed that bedroom door behind us, we were alone. I was vulnerable to whatever he wanted and he gave me no say. Every night that I had to be with him, I prayed that he would die or find someone else. When our dinner was over the men came out of the back room and Diego and Jorge came to claim their respective wives. Max and Hector were sent back to our house while they kept us there in hotel rooms for their pleasure. As Diego was shoving me into the room, I watched Max watch me go. Hector reluctantly pulled him down the hall by the back of his collar but Max watched me until I could no longer see him. When Diego closed the door behind him I was scared. Max was never this far away before. "What is it, Lilly?" he asked. "You look a little more frightened than usual." I didn't like his tone. I was afraid he may be speeding, but I wasn't sure. "Come on Lilly, what is it?" he asked me again.

"Nothing, Diego, I'm fine. The party was fun." I was trying so hard to act normal but with Max gone, I was terrified.

"It seems that you and Olivia have a lot in common." He got close to me. I could just tell what was coming. Obviously, Jorge knows about Hector, and Diego thinks he knows something about Max. I was sorry that I hadn't been with Max. I really thought he was going to kill me.

"She's very nice," I answered with a lack of something clever to say.

"Isn't she, though," he responded. "I think a little too nice sometimes." He was watching me and his eyes looked dark.

"Let's go to sleep, Diego, it's late," I answered. I tried to step away from him. I was praying he would want to leave me alone tonight but I knew he had a plan if he kept me there.

He put his hand behind my neck and grabbed my hair. I was startled for a second and then he kissed me pulling my head back. He threw me on the bed and began to take off his pants. I was thinking to myself, "If I could just get through this, I could see Max tomorrow." But he had his way with me and then smacked me in the face as I went flying onto the floor. He picked me up again and threw me against the wall with another slap. "This is your last warning," he said. "Stay out of my brother's bed!" He reached down to the floor picked me up as he pulled me back onto the bed. I was crying by now, not sure if I was going to live through this. He put himself on top of me and rolled over. He passed out suddenly. I grabbed my clothes and ran out the door. I called a taxi and went home. When I got there, I quickly headed upstairs and changed into shorts and a T-shirt and ran to find Max. I got to his door and prayed he was alone. "Max," I whispered and I peeked inside. He was laying in his bed in nothing more than boxer shorts staring at the ceiling with his hands behind his head. He was so beautiful. He sat up and looked at me.

"Oh no, Lilly." I walked inside and he locked the door behind me. He picked me up and put me in his bed and lay down next to me after he covered us in his blanket. "Dear God, Lilly, he beat you."

"Max, if you don't make love to me tonight, I swear I'll steal your gun and kill myself. I mean it!"

"Lilly, did he rape you?"

"Yes!" I cried and he pulled me close to him.

"Lilly, I am not going to make love to you right after you've been raped, forget it." But he sat up a little and took my battered face into his hands. Then he kissed me. He finally kissed me. I lost all feeling in my legs and collapsed in his arms. "Oh Max," I cried.

"You have no idea, how long I've waited to hear that." He put his cheek on my wounded one.

"I love you, Max. I need a reason to keep on going." He dried my tears with his fingers and kissed me again. We lay in each other's arms for what felt like forever, kissing and touching. "Max, please don't leave me," I cried. "I don't think I can do this anymore."

"Lilly, you are my whole world. I love you with everything I am, that's what makes it so hard not to just put a bullet in his head." He kissed me again and said, "I don't know if I can stay away anymore."

"I thought you said you don't use drugs." When I said that his face changed and he sat up startled. "What are you talking about?" he asked.

"Diego was speeding on something," I answered. "I think coke, but I'm not sure."

"You're kidding me," he answered. "Now he's using?"

"I think so Max. He looked weird and accused me of sleeping with you."

"I am such a fool," he replied and lay back down next to me. "Everyone thinks we're having an affair." I smiled. "We may as well be having an affair."

"He told me to stay out of his brother's bed." Ironically, this was the first time I had actually been in his brother's bed.

"This is why I stayed away from you in the first place," he replied. "Lilly, I am going to take some pictures of your face with my phone, okay?"

"No police, Max. He'll kill me." I was terrified.

"No police." He started photographing my face. "I will talk to him tomorrow and tell him we are not sleeping together." He stroked my bruise with his fingers. "But after tomorrow, we will be sleeping together." I reached out and touched his bare chest. "We need each other," he said. I knew he was right. We both knew Olivia was right.

"Does Jorge beat Olivia?" I asked.

"Sometimes," he answered. "Usually if he has too much to drink or… something else."

"What does Hector do?" I asked.

"As soon as we get involved, we open up an area of flying bullets. We have to be sure neither one of you gets hurt. He's stopped Jorge from killing her before, as I did for you the night I found you at John's house. But when we get involved in the bedroom, that confirms our involvement with you."

"You're saying if he rapes me in our bedroom, you can't help me?" I asked.

"After I get done with him tomorrow, he won't." He seemed pretty certain. "I'll have a substance abuse conversation with him again." He put his cheek against mine. "He can't eat up the profits… that kind of thing."

"So, no love?" I asked.

He smiled. "You can spend the night here," he answered. "He'll probably crash hard and come back in the afternoon."

"I can sleep with you?" I was really excited.

"You are so cute," he answered. "Yes, baby girl, you can spend the night in daddy's arms." And I did. It was the best night I had ever had. He was right, Diego did not come home in the morning and we took a shower and ate breakfast together before we heard the angry bear slam open the door screaming my name like a crazy person. I gasped and Max put me behind him as he often did and pulled out his gun.

"Where is she Max?" Then he saw me and reached for me but Max cocked his revolver.

"I have no problem killing you right now," Max said. "You raped her and beat her, you bastard!" For a minute, I really thought he was going to shoot him. There was a small part of me that was hoping he would. "We're not together," Max said. "I'm in love with her, but she won't have me." I couldn't believe he said that.

"What?" Diego asked. "Are you serious?"

"She's in love with you, Diego, or she was until last night." I was shocked, confused and sick to my stomach. Diego calmed right down after that. He backed up and sat at the table in the kitchen.

"How stupid do you think I am?" he asked. "She's not in love with me."

"You have to cut this out, Diego. Stop beating her up. If you're angry take it out on me. I can take it. She's a little girl."

Diego appeared to think about it for a minute. "Lilly, I'm so sorry," he said. Max put the gun down and stepped aside. He put his head in his hands and said, "I'm so sorry."

"No more eating the profits," Max said. "You know you can't use and sell, Diego."

"Come here, Lilly." He put his hand out for me and Max gave me an approving nod. He put me on his lap and kissed me. Then he looked at my bruise and kissed it. "Forgive me, please."

"I already have," I lied with tears in my eyes. He hugged me and then pushed me up so that he could get up out of the chair. "I have to go to work today, Max." He started to walk away. "Keep an eye on her. I'll be back in a few hours." As he walked off I opened my mouth to scream at him but he shushed me. Then I whispered, "In love with him? Are you crazy?"

"I had to defuse this," he said. "He gave in way too soon. He's up to something."

We waited about fifteen minutes after he left and he did not come back. We made idle chatter and had some coffee while we waited for the call from the guard confirming Diego had officially left the property. The call finally came in. Max's face lit up like a kid on Christmas morning. "Lilly?" He did not have to say another word. I knew what was on his mind. "If you feel up to it…" He paused and smiled at me. "Say something, baby girl, I 'm going crazy here."

I smiled at him and said, "Did you just ask me that out loud?" I had been begging him for months to break his own rules. "Of course I'm ready."

"Are you sure?" he asked. "Are you sure this is what you want?"

CHAPTER 11

Oh Brother

We started up the stairs and hurried into Max's room. He and I lay on the bed for what I think was one second, before Hector came flying through the door. "Am I wearing a tracking device, or something?" Max asked.

Hurry, Jorge just pulled up." Hector was out of breath and obviously frightened.

Max jumped up and said, "I'm going to go first, and you follow. Something's not right." He ran out the door after Hector and I waited before following. When I got downstairs Jorge and Hector were in each other's faces and Max was trying to break them up. Olivia was bleeding and bruised and sitting in a corner on the floor in the kitchen, rocking back and forth.

Find my brother!" Jorge yelled at me. I grabbed my cell and called Diego. "Come home now, Diego!" I said over the phone.

"What is it, Lilly?" he asked, knowing I would never call him requesting his presence.

"It's Jorge. Olivia's bleeding," I said. "Hector and Jorge…"

"I'm on my way," he replied. "Find Max."

"He's here but it's not good," I said. He hung up the phone and I said, "He's on his way." Jorge backed down from Hector.

"Jorge?" I asked. "May I please clean her up a bit?"

"Take her," Jorge answered. "I don't want her anymore."

I took her to the bathroom in my bedroom where we could have some privacy. She was crying and her face was badly bruised. "What happened, Olivia?" I asked.

"I'm pregnant," she answered.

"Pregnant?" I asked. "Why is Jorge so upset about that?"

"Jorge can't have children," she answered. "He's sterile."

"Oh, no…" was my clever response. "How does Jorge know it's Hector's?"

"I told him. I had to." She put her hand to her bruised face.

"Didn't you protect yourselves?" I asked, feeling very hypocritical about that question.

"Yes of course," she answered. "I just can't believe this."

"So, what's happening down there?"

"Jorge is throwing me out and leaving me here, I think," she said. "I hope he didn't' kill the baby, when he beat me up this morning." I was mortified. What have we gotten ourselves into? I cleaned her up and bandaged her cuts. He really threw her around. She wasn't more than 100 pounds soaking wet. She hugged me and sobbed. "Lilly, I think he's going to kill me," she continued as she cried.

"He came here for help," I answered. "Let him talk to Diego." I walked her back down to the kitchen and Diego had arrived. "Thank you, Lilly," Diego said. "You did the right thing by calling me."

"You take her," Jorge said. "I'm done." Diego didn't know what to make of this. Obviously both the younger men took their wives and he was obviously puzzled by the whole thing.

"Why?" He looked at Hector. "Why?" He glared at Max. "You half-breeds come into our world and you steal from us. Why do you do it?"

"Look Diego," Max explained. "When Lilly came here you barely noticed she was alive. You ignored her and she was pregnant and alone. It was easy for me to slide in there and become close with her. It was easy. We have been close for more than three years. You didn't decide to pee all over her until we found her with Johnny. Then all of a sudden, it was real important for you to sleep with her. You're too late."

Everyone looked at Max like he was out of his mind. Jorge took out his gun and pointed it at Max. Diego pushed it down and said, "He's right, Jorge."

"What the hell is wrong with you?" Jorge sputtered. His face was full of hate and I was afraid. I'm sure I wasn't the only one wishing I were a hundred miles away from here.

"Lilly and I have only been intimate for a few weeks. Max and Lilly, even if they really aren't intimate yet, have been close for years."

"She is your wife," Jorge responded.

"Yes but in name only, for a long time." He paused. "I've been watching their improper relationship for many years now, and I never said a thing."

"Just put him out of his misery," Jorge answered.

"Put it away Jorge," he said. "Maybe instead of teaching them how to obey us, we need to teach them to love us." He looked at me and put his fingers on my bruised face. "Maybe instead of beating them and forcing ourselves on them…" He paused and looked at Jorge. "I don't think we're teaching them to want us." Max sat down on one of the chairs and his face changed. He suddenly looked very defeated. "Let's you, me, Olivia and Hector, sit together in the living room and fix this." Then he looked at Max and me. "I'm going back to work after this, but the three of us need to have the same kind of talk later." He put both his hands on my face and I could see Max move towards me from the corner of my eye. "I won't ever raise my hand to you again. I will fix this. Maybe it's time we started our own family." He kissed me, softly and let me go. "I'll be back by 6," he told Max, and the four of them walked off into the living room.

Max looked at me with a hollow expression. I had never seen him look so distant before. "I'm going to lose you," he said. "He's going to try to get you to fall in love with him. It's over and I never got the chance to…" He looked at me with tears in his eyes. "I waited too long."

By this time I was sick of people talking about me like I was property. I took Max's hand and said, "It's time, Max." He was so defeated. He sat in his chair and looked at me with empty eyes. I sat on his lap and wrapped my legs around him. "It's time Max." I kissed him and ran my fingers through his hair. He instantly responded and I could feel him getting aroused. "Come on…" I insisted. We walked into the hall and could hear them all talking in the living room. We went up the stairs and opened the door to Max's bedroom. "I don't care if we get caught," I told him. "I love you, and I need you to take me and make me your own." He said nothing. He picked me up and put me in his bed. He kissed me in places I had never been kissed and awakened parts of my body that I didn't know were asleep. He reached for protection and I knocked it out of his hands.

"Do you want to end up like Olivia?" he asked me.

"Yes," I said. "I want to always be yours," I answered. "I can't have his baby, Max. Please don't make me go there."

He didn't say another word. He became enflamed with passion and ripped off my clothes. He brought me to the place only known by Diego over and over again for hours. I tried to be quiet, so I wouldn't draw any attention to us but I whispered his name in his ear. "I've only dreamed about this day," he said. I wrapped my legs around him and he put his lips on mine to keep me quiet. By the time it was over, we were both spent and exhausted.

"You weren't kidding," I said with a smile.

"How's that?" he asked.

"Definitely the best for last," I answered. My body felt rejuvenated.

"Querida." He pulled me onto his chest. "I need a promise from you."

"Anything daddy," I answered. He smiled. "You know I can't resist you when you call me that."

"Anything daddy," I said again.

"Please marry me when we get you out of this." he said. "I need to know, that whatever Diego says to us…" He stopped for a second and sighed. "Whatever he says to us that you are still mine."

"I need you to promise me something," I added.

"Anything querida," he answered.

"You will never leave me." He put his fingers under my chin and kissed me.

"Is that a yes?" he asked.

I'd marry you now, if I could," I answered. "How exactly are you and Hector going to fix this?" I asked.

"Just know that he is as trustworthy as I am." He smiled. "In case you ever need him and I am not around."

"I'm ovulating, you know," I said to him. He looked a little panicked.

"Lilly," he said with a smile. "I haven't been with a woman in three years."

"Three years? You mean…."

"Yes," he said. "Since you arrived." He sat up a little and looked at me. "If you were trying to play Russian roulette with getting pregnant, now was not the time. If you're ovulating, you're probably already pregnant."

"I want to be yours and only yours," I told him. "I hope I'm pregnant. I hope I have your baby." He pulled me close to him and kissed my forehead. "Querida," he started, "I have to go check on Hector."

"I know," I answered. "Are we okay?"

"No matter what Diego asks you, you agree, do you understand?"

"Are we going to tell him?" I asked.

"Hell no!" he answered. "But if he tells you to stop seeing me, you agree. Whatever stops the abuse."

"Does that mean you won't touch me anymore?" I asked. I could feel the panic in my uneven heartbeat.

"No matter what we agree to," he started, "you are the love of my life. I cannot leave you alone."

We went downstairs to the kitchen and Hector was sitting at the table by himself. "Right under his nose, you're with his wife. Right under his nose. I go for three years without being discovered and she turns up pregnant."

"Did he ask where we were?" he asked. Hector was tapping his fingers on the kitchen table.

"He just told me to tell you he'll be home between 5 and 6." I shuddered. Hector grabbed my arm and said, "He also told me to tell you not to be afraid. That he would never hurt you again. Oh and he is not sending Max away." Max and I looked at each other in surprise.

"I'm sorry, what?" I asked.

"It's like he had a religious conversion or something, Max. He wants to… talk. Are you going to tell him you're banging his wife?"

"Please don't say that," Max answered. "And NO!"

"He thinks you've been having an affair all this time," he told us. "You probably should've been."

"Definitely." Max took my hand and smiled. "We really should've been."

"I tried but you wouldn't have me," I answered. "This is your fault, daddy."

"Oh yuck!" I think Hector had had enough of us. "Way too much information."

"Sorry Hector," I said blushing. Max was still smiling like he used to.

"You know you have to have humor in this business." Hector laughed. "I hope you're prepared to face the music."

"Remember what I said, Lilly," Max said to me. "Whatever you have to do to end the abuse." He looked at Hector. "Where's Olivia?"

"He took her and left me here." Max patted him on the back. "I'm sorry, man."

"It's my baby, Max." He looked at me. "I don't know what to do now."

"What did Diego say?" he asked.

"You mean besides telling us that he and Lilly were going to try to have a baby?" My legs fell from under me and I collapsed onto the floor. Max ran over to me and picked up my head. "Lilly, Lilly…" I looked up at him. "Please Max, just kill me." He kissed my lips and sat on the floor beside me. He lifted me into his lap and rocked me. "It's going to be my baby," he said.

"No…" Hector said. "No Max, you didn't."

"I did," he said. "I'm so in love with her, Hector." He kissed my cheek. "How did we get so personally involved? Wasn't this nothing more than a job five years ago?"

Hector came up behind him and hugged him. "Yes, brother, just a job." We all sat there on the floor holding each other. It was strange to have no control over our own destiny. Diego's world, that's where we lived. When the clock struck 5:30, the three of us were together in the living room. We had agreed to watch each other's backs and try to stay strong.

CHAPTER 12

All's fair in love and war, isn't it?

Diego walked into the room and we all looked up at him. "Hector, excuse us please," he said.

"If it's all the same to you, Diego, I'd like my half-breed brother to stay here with me." Max was already annoyed.

"I'm sorry I said that," Diego responded.

"What does that mean?" I asked.

"Different mothers," they all said together. "Our mother was white," Hector added.

"Our mother was Mexican," Diego replied.

"You didn't grow up in the same house?" I asked.

"Not for very long, anyway," Diego answered.

"This is all becoming very clear to me now," I said.

"Well, you're right Lilly, we have not been behaving like brothers." He sat down across from Max and me. "Max was the one you turned to. He cared for you for more than three years. Then I decided I wanted a physical relationship with you and you already had one with him."

"I don't," I said. "I know it looks that way, but we are just close." He didn't buy that, even a little.

"Where were you when I left today?" he asked. "I'm not judging; this is my fault."

Hector looked at Max as though he thought it was time to come clean. But Max continued to deny it. "I am her bodyguard," he responded. "Where she goes, I go. Seriously Diego, it's been that way for years."

"I want us to be honest," Diego said. "This won't do us any good if we don't talk about it."

"What do you want, Diego?" Max asked.

"I want my wife back." Max and I looked at each other, which was a stupid move. "Tell me you're not in love," he continued. "I saw that look."

"So, you come in here and say, 'I want my wife back.'" Max got up and started walking around. "What does that mean exactly?"

Diego got up and got right up to Max's face. He grabbed his arms and Hector stood up. "Just stop making love to her," he demanded. "Just stop and let me win her heart." Max pulled away from him. I was shaking. "I won't send you away. I won't take her away. No violence. Just please let me try to win her back."

The room got very quiet. I wanted to scream, "NO, I LOVE MAX!" But Max told me to agree with whatever Diego wanted to do. Diego sat down in front of me and got on one knee. I saw Max and Hector exchange looks. "Please Lilly, take this ring and let's start a family." He held out a huge diamond. I picked it up and put it on my finger.

"Okay Diego, I'll give you a chance."

Then Max said, "What if she doesn't fall in love with you, then what?"

"She will," he said. "You were just a place holder." Max's face turned bright red. He reached for his gun but Hector stopped him.

"Does this mean, I'll have a choice?" My eyes filled up with tears and I ran out of the room. I could hear them arguing while I was gone and I threw up in the bathroom. I really didn't want to sleep with him anymore. Max warned me that once we were together this would be a problem.

I came back out and Diego stood up. He reached for my hands and said, "I will never force myself on you again. I want you to have a choice. I will be more like Maxwell, I promise."

The thought of his hands on my body made me physically sick. I couldn't imagine going through this anymore. But I dried my eyes and took a deep breath. "Okay," I said. "But you do need to know that you were wrong."

"Wrong?"

"All this time that you thought I had been visiting your brother's bed…" I paused. "You were wrong."

He looked into my eyes. "We'll see," he said. "Even if you weren't making love in the physical sense," he continued, "there is no doubt in my mind that you are making love right now in your minds."

He walked off and left the three of us there. "A baby, Max," I said. "A baby."

"We'll be okay, Lilly. Just hang on for me." He looked at Hector. "How much longer is this going to take?"

"Not much longer."

"Still not going to tell me?" I asked.

"Just trust me, baby girl," and he smiled.

After my brief encounter with Max, Diego didn't lay a finger on me for a little more than three weeks. If I did show up pregnant, there would be enough time to figure out who the father was. When Diego did finally show some interest in me, I had to comply. When I woke up in the morning, I got sick again. Diego was concerned because there was no way I could have been pregnant. "Are you sick, Lilly?" he asked. "Is being with me that horrible for you?" I couldn't tell him being intimate with him was killing me, so I just told him I wasn't feeling well.

We went down stairs to share the wonderful breakfast that Max always had for us but there was no breakfast and no Max. "Where's Max?" I asked.

"I was just going to ask you the same thing," he answered.

"I'm not really hungry anyway," I told him.

"Okay then." He took me into his arms and kissed me. "I'll see you later." Before Diego's footsteps were even cold from the kitchen I ran out the back door to the creek. There he was sitting on a rock staring out at the water. I walked up beside him and sat down.

"Querida," he grabbed my hand, "you look pale, are you not feeling well?"

"I was sick this morning," I answered. He reached over and hugged me.

"What happened?" he asked. He looked like he already knew.

"Why don't you tell me what you're doing out here first," I added.

"Oh God, I can't stand being in the same house as you when I know…" He put his head in his hands.

"That's why I got sick," I answered. He kissed my lips and I lay down in his lap. "I need you Max, please don't leave me."

"Never," he answered. "I'll stop being such a baby." He smiled. "Did he hurt you?" he asked. He suddenly got a very serious look on his face.

"No, no…" I answered. "It's just that it's not you."

"It didn't used to be like that," he remembered. I hit him in the arm.

"That was before you," I added. "Max, how much longer?"

"Oh querida," he paused, "if I could run away with you today, I would." He looked thoughtfully for a moment. "Could you be pregnant?" he asked. "Maybe you're carrying my baby." He put his hand on my stomach. "Too soon?"

"I don't know," I said. "But you didn't make me breakfast and I'm mad at you." We hugged and kissed for a while out there before deciding to come back inside. We saw Hector coming up the path.

"How do you always know where I am?" Max asked.

"Diego's back," he answered. "He wants you to come with him."

"Of course he does," he replied. "I guess it's going to be like this for a while."

We went back to the house and Diego gave us an unfavorable glance. "Come on Max, I actually have work for you to do." Diego kissed me goodbye and Max moved towards me but Diego reached and pulled him back by the shirt. "Did you almost kiss her?" he asked.

Max laughed. "No, of course not." Diego dragged him out of the house and Max blew me a kiss.

"He's a clown, sometimes," Hector added. "It's gonna get him in trouble someday." Hector walked out the front door and I headed into the living room.

I turned to grab the television remote when someone came up from behind me and covered my mouth. I screamed and struggled but I couldn't get free. He forced me to the floor and I looked up and saw Johnny. My eyes opened wide and he removed his hand from my mouth. "What the hell are you doing?" I asked.

"I promised I'd come back for you," he answered. "Now I'm here." He was on top of me with his knees holding my arms down.

"John, we're over now. I'm married to Diego." I looked into his eyes and did not see my Johnny there anymore. His eyes were vacant and all I saw was desperation.

"Don't you mean you're in love with Maxwell?" He started unbuttoning my blouse.

"No, no…no…" I protested. "You don't want to do this. They'll kill you."

"I'm willing to risk it."

I started screaming and before I knew what was happening, I heard the sound of guns cocking. Diego was on one side of him, Max on the other and Hector behind Max. "Let go of my wife," Diego said calmly.

He slowly stood up and Max looked at Hector, "You got him for me?"

Hector put his gun right up at Johnny's temple. Max grabbed me and pulled me out from under him. "Button up," he said. I ran out the door of the living room and re-fastened my blouse. My heart was beating so fast, I thought I would have a heart attack. I went back in and asked, "How did you know to come back?"

"Max noticed a car nearby that isn't usually here," Diego answered. "We came back, just in case." Max and Hector lead Johnny out of the house by gunpoint and Diego and I stood together in the living room. "Are you all right?" he asked.

"Talk about timing," I answered. Then I went to him and hugged him. He was stroking my hair with one hand and had another hand on the small of my back. We heard a shuffling and he pushed me away from him. I turned to the door and there were men everywhere with guns and I heard a BANG! Diego went down. I screamed for Max and Hector and two of the men grabbed me and started dragging me towards the back door. Before I knew what was happening Max and Hector came rushing in with a gun in each hand shooting the men down like a video game. There were bodies all over the floor and Max looked down and saw the puddle of blood next to Diego get bigger and bigger. "Oh my God!" he said, "Lilly call 911!"

Hector said, "I'll look around back," and Max tossed him the radio. Hector started talking on the radio in Spanish and I called 911. I watched Max open his wallet and take out a credit card and press it on Diego's wound, which was in his stomach. Diego let out a shout. "Sorry, brother," he said. "Don't get a big head about this though. Just because I won't let you bleed to death, doesn't mean I won't still fight you for the girl." Diego made an attempt at a smile.

"Get her out of here," Diego whispered. "How many…?" He was having trouble speaking.

"We're not leaving you," he said. I grabbed his hand.

Lilly," he gasped. "I love you." I squeezed his hand and looked at Max.

Still giving me a hard time," Max added with his usual attempt at levity.

Hector came back. "I got them all, and they're down." Then Diego said, "Lilly… Max, Lilly…" Max and Hector looked at me.

"Oh no!" Hector blurted. "She's bleeding."

Max looked up, and I saw blood coming from my side. Hector reached over and grabbed the credit card that Max had pressed against Diego and Max took off his shirt and pushed it up against my side. "Where's that ambulance!" Max yelled. We heard sirens shortly after that and I think that is when I lost consciousness. All I knew was life was never going to be the same after that day.

Chapter 13

The baby?

When I opened my eyes Max and Hector were asleep on separate chairs in my hospital room. "Max?" I said in a weak tone. He looked up at me and smiled a calm smile. He walked over and took my hand. "Well querida, I have good news and bad news, which do you want first?"

"Good," I said, "always good."

"You didn't lose the baby." He took my hands and kissed them.

"Baby?" I asked. "There's a baby?" Tears came to my eyes, as he looked at me so contented.

"Please tell me you haven't been with Diego in the three weeks after we made love." He was almost holding his breath.

"No daddy, just you," I answered. "I was only with him the morning he got shot," I continued. "That was the only time." He bent down and hugged me.

"We're going to have a baby." He was very excited.

"Half-breeds two, Mexicans zero," Hector added.

"What's the bad news?" I asked.

"That son of a gun is still alive and kicking," he answered.

"You were grazed by the bullet on your side before it hit him," he continued. I looked at my side. "You probably saved his life by slowing down the bullet." He smiled playfully.

"I think it was you trying to stop him from bleeding to death," I answered. "Why did you save his life?" I asked. "That was confusing to me."

"I have come too far Lilly, he is not going to die on me now." Hector laughed.

"The truth is that they have a weird relationship," Hector confessed. "You think they hate each other with all the gun pulling and the competition but there is some real devotion there."

"Well, they are brothers," I added. "I can see how you wouldn't want him to die."

"It was weird," Max, added. "I was running on instinct. I didn't even think."

"What is up with the credit card?" I asked.

Let's just say that wasn't our first rodeo," Hector answered.

"We've been down that road before," Max clarified. "A baby…" he said again.

"Max, you can't tell Diego." I began to panic. "Is the nurse going to tell him?"

"I already talked to the staff and told them that these are your records and your business." He smiled wide. "I also told them that your husband has a bad temper and might hurt you if he found out about it."

"So basically you told the nurse that the baby wasn't his," I added.

"Well…" Max said. "It seemed to get the point across." He looked around the room and bent over to kiss me.

"Careful brother," Hector said. "The beast is in the waiting room."

"Jorge?" I asked.

"Jorge," he answered.

"Watch your step, baby. If he wants you to try to have a baby with him, just agree." I made a face. "If he thinks the baby is his, you guarantee your safety."

"Fine," I answered. "I always do what you tell me," I said in a defeated tone.

"I wish Olivia was more like you," Hector added. "She never does what I ask her to do." Just then Jorge walked in. We all got quiet and you could feel the tension in the room.

"Get away from my brother's wife," he said to Maxwell. "I hate that every time I walk into a room, the two of you are together."

"She was shot, Jorge." Max replied. "Try to have some sympathy."

"Diego is awake and he wants to talk to you," he said to Max. "I think he wants to thank you, or something." Max looked at Hector and Hector nodded.

"I'll be right back," he said to me. When he left Jorge said, "Hector, go find something to do,"

"No," Hector replied and quite abruptly. "Whatever you have to say to her, you can say in front of me."

"Come on, Hector. What am I going to do to her in a hospital?" He looked over at him with pleading eyes but Hector didn't budge.

He looked at me with an angry face. I felt as though I was staring down the devil. It didn't take him long to switch moods. "How long have you been sleeping with Max?" he asked.

"We don't have a physical relationship," I answered. Hector had a watchful eye on Jorge.

"Diego only believes that because he doesn't want to admit to himself that his wife is a whore." I was startled and sat up a little. Hector stood up and walked over to my bed.

"Get the hell out of here," he told him. "You can't talk to her like that. Diego wouldn't want you to."

"I'm taking him," Jorge told me. "After Hector and Max take care of Johnny, your other lover, I'm taking Max with me to Mexico."

I didn't say anything. I needed to process the information. Obviously Max doesn't know of Jorge's plans. If I fight him, I will give us away.

"Did you hear me, Lilly?" he asked. "I'm taking him." I still said nothing. I looked at Hector for a cue.

"He's too soft for Mexico, you know that," Hector added. "He'll get killed in the first few weeks."

"You're staying here and he's coming with me. You should have thought about that before the two of you set your sights on our wives." He continued. "Max is mine now. Have you found Johnny yet?"

"No, he's in hiding," Hector responded. "We'll find him. I have all kinds of men looking for him."

"See that you do and fast," Jorge answered. "I am ready to go home."

"And we're ready for you to leave," Hector added. Jorge left the room. "Good job," he told me.

I gasped. "Max can't leave me, I'll die!" I grabbed Hector's shirt in panic. Max walked in right then, pulled my grip off of Hector and hugged me.

"Why would I leave you?" he asked. "We're having a baby," he said, happy as a little boy with a new toy.

"Max, we need to find Johnny," Hector said. "Jorge wants to take you back to Mexico."

"What?" he asked. "I can't go to Mexico."

"I think he's serious," he said. "He wants to switch us out."

"This will slow us down," Max answered. "I'd better make a phone call."

He pulled out his phone and hit the speed dial. "Hey," he said. "Lilly's fine and Diego's still alive. It'll take more than a bullet to take that guy out," he continued. "Listen, Diego will be out of the hospital tomorrow. Can you be here sometime after noon? Where's Johnny?" He laughed and said, "This is so perfect, and I can't believe how well this is going to work out." He looked at Hector, and Hector looked at him curiously. "Hey listen, you may have to stay in touch with Hector for a while. You have his number, right? Jorge wants to take me to Mexico and they'll probably take away my cell phone so that I can't call Lilly. I'll be fine. Hector and I will just switch gears, that's all. I'll make sure he keeps an eye on Lilly. Okay, see ya later, bye."

"What's up?" Hector asked.

"I'll tell you later. I don't want her to have to lie for us," he added.

"Okay, who was that?" I asked.

"I love you, Lilly," he answered. He and Hector sat with me until a doctor came in to check on me. The doctor cleared me to go home and the boys checked me out. I went to see Diego before I left.

He looked surprisingly well for a man who was just shot in the stomach. He smiled when he saw me and reached out his hand. "You're all right?" he asked.

"Just a graze." I answered.

"I was so scared that something had happened to you." He took my hands and put them to his face. "Go home, Lilly and get some rest. I will see you tomorrow." I kissed him as a dutiful wife is supposed to do and he was pleased. "Max, you and Hector wait to go after Johnny. I want you to stay with Lilly until I can be there myself. Just in case." We knew he was serious since the last thing he would ever do would be to ask Max to 'watch me' for him. "And thanks again Max, I owe you one."

"You sure do," Max answered. "When I get shot I expect the same act of kindness." They both laughed. Leave it to Max to make a joke like that.

"Don't say that," Diego answered. "I may hate your guts sometimes, but I don't want you dead." The three of us left and Jorge and Olivia stayed with Diego. I was relieved. Jorge made me very nervous. Jorge and Olivia spent the night in our house, I am sure to insure our faithfulness for the evening. I was disappointed that I didn't get to spend the night in Max's arms.

In the morning Jorge knocked on my door. It was about 8:00 and I was still sleeping. I opened the door and he said, "Let's go pick up my brother from the hospital."

"I don't think he's even ready to go yet," I answered. "It's too early."

He grabbed my arm and said, "Get dressed, your boyfriend can't help you now."

"Let go!" I cried. "I'll be down in a while, I have to get dressed."

"I'll be waiting right here for you," he told me. I took a shower and got dressed and when I opened my door he was standing there. It was creepy. He grabbed my arm and started hurrying me down the stairs. When we got to the door Hector and Max were sitting on the floor in front of it. "What the hell…?" Jorge started.

"Did you think we would let you take her in a car alone with you?" Max asked. "We're going too."

"Do you think Diego wants to see you at all?" he asked Max.

"Hey, I saved his miserable life. He'll see me." We all got into a limo and headed out to the hospital. When we got there Diego looked well and happy to see us.

"Max, bring me my beautiful wife." Max put his hand on my back and walked me over to him. He was standing up putting on his shirt. He hugged me and put his hands on my face. "I have missed this," and then he kissed me. Max turned away and the four of them started speaking in Spanish. I always hated that.

The drive home was awkward. We sat in the limo as Diego put his arm around me and held my hand. I was very uncomfortable. When we got home we headed for the kitchen and as usual, Max started preparing food. The doorbell rang and Hector said, "Wait here, I'll check it out." A few minutes later we heard, "Diego, it's Lilly's dad."

"My dad?" I asked in great surprise. "What's he doing here?" We all went out into the foyer except for Jorge. "Dad," I said and I ran to hug him. "What are you doing here?"

"I came to try to talk your husband into turning over states evidence."

"I run a property management company Mick, what are you talking about?" Diego said with a smug look on his face.

"Come on Diego, roll over on your brother and I'll keep you out of it."

"I have no reason to roll over on anyone," he said again. "And even if I did…" he paused, "my loyalty lies with him first."

"Johnny is rolling over on you," my dad continued. "He's in witness protection right now, in case you've been looking for him."

"That little drug addict is nothing but a little pain in the ass," Diego said. "What exactly does he think he has?"

"Enough to put you all away," he answered. "Think about it Diego." He started to walk away. "You too, Max."

After he left Max said to Hector, "That's why we couldn't find him. I'll bet I know where he is now."

"I thought he said he was in witness protection?" I asked, getting a little confused at this point.

"Witness protection is for amateurs," Hector added. "Pack a bag Max, let's go get him."

"I want you to do it," Jorge said to Max. "I want him dead, you hear me?"

"Not more than I do," Max answered. "Let's go pack." He and Hector walked off and headed upstairs to pack a bag. I was shocked at Max's 'hit-man' attitude, but I guess that is who he was before I met him. He probably just kept it away from me. "I'm not leaving until they get back," Jorge said to Diego. "Then I'm taking Max with me." Diego didn't say anything and Jorge walked out the front door. I looked at Diego for some kind of confirmation that he wasn't taking Max but he said nothing. Finally he took my hand and we went into the kitchen.

CHAPTER 14

You do hate me.

"Lilly, let's talk about having a baby." I looked at him trying to find the strength to look positive about this. "You did promise to love and obey me and you're not doing a very good job." He was half kidding but looked a little serious.

"Now?" I asked. "You want to try now?"

"Why not?" he answered.

"Have they left yet?" I asked. He seemed disturbed by my question. He picked up the radio and said something in Spanish over it.

"They'll call me when they go," he answered. He walked away for a few minutes and my stomach began to feel sick. When he came back in, someone on the radio said, "Max and Hector have left the property." They said it in English, which surprised me. I have never heard Max or Hector speak in English on the radio. He took my hand and walked me to his bedroom. Our bedroom.

He put me on the bed and undressed me rather quickly. He got on top of me and started kissing my neck. He was calling my name out when the door opened and I heard Max say, "Diego, what is so important, I have to go…" He looked up and saw us and I screamed bloody murder.

I grabbed a blanket and shouted, "Oh my God Max, I'm so sorry!" I tried to push Diego off of me but he wouldn't free me.

"You pig!" Max said to him and looked away from us. "I should have left you on the floor bleeding."

"But you're not that kind of man Max," Diego replied. "She'll be pregnant by the time you get back. So, don't even think she'll be waiting for you."

"Don't you have any respect for her?" He shook his head. "I have to go."

His head was still looking away from us when he said, "Lilly this doesn't change anything between us." Then he looked up at me for a second and in a weak voice said, "I love you," and he closed the door.

I could hear his footsteps walking away from our bedroom in the hall when Diego got violent with me and started pinning me down. I began to scream and I could hear Max's footsteps coming back. I know he said he would never get involved in the bedroom but I think he was changing his mind. "Diego, stop!" I said. "Diego don't! You promised!" He stopped immediately and collapsed beside me on the bed.

"You're right," he agreed, "I did promise. I always keep my word. It just makes me so mad when I hear him tell you he loves you. You are my wife."

He turned to me and took a deep breath. Then he wiped the hair from my face and kissed me. "If we're going to have a baby together, there's only one way to do it you know," he said with a smile.

"You didn't have to do that," I scolded. "You didn't have to call him in like that."

"I want him to have that image in his head while he's away." He started stroking my hair. "I want him to move on and get over you."

"Please don't do that again," I asked. "Please, if you want me to treat you like a husband, you have to treat me like a wife."

"Is sleeping with my brother, treating me like a husband?" he asked.

"Is smacking me around, treating me like a wife?" I asked.

"I guess it depends on whose wife," he answered with a smirk. Then he got serious and said, "You're right. But Lilly, once you're pregnant you're mine and it's over with him."

"I know," I said. "I know." He was much more gentle with me when we finally started to touch and I heard Max's footsteps go away from the door. It was breaking my heart and I was in absolute pain knowing he would be gone for three days. I still couldn't believe he was going to kill someone. This whole life was unbelievable sometimes.

We made love so many times in those three days that I was sick all the time. He wanted to be absolutely sure that I was pregnant before Max got back. I was supposed to be ovulating during those days, so he was pretty confident. When the three days were over Diego, Jorge and I were waiting in the kitchen for their eminent return. They walked in and Jorge said, "Is it done?"

Hector replied, "Done."

"Did he suffer?" Jorge asked.

"That son of bitch, got what he deserved," Max answered.

"Yeah, Max was not in a good mood, to say the least," Hector told them. Diego smiled. Max pulled a beer out of the fridge and walked out the back door without even a glance at me. The three brothers started talking in Spanish and I slipped out the side door and tried to catch up with him. It was dark and the property was large. The stars were shining brightly and the sky was lit by the full moon. "Max," I called. "Max!" He slowed down and looked back at me. He smiled and held his hand out for me to take it. "I'm sorry querida," he answered. "I just wanted to spend some time by the creek before I was banished."

"Without me?" I asked. "You do hate me," I continued. I could feel the tears forming in my eyes and my heart rate accelerate.

He stopped walking and put his free hand on the side of my face. "Baby girl, you are my whole world. I don't hate you because of Diego." He took my hand back into his and we walked to the creek side. "I'm going to miss you," he said. I threw my arms around his neck and kissed him. He put his beer down on the rocks and picked me up into his arms. He carried me to a wooded area and put me in the grass as he lay down beside me. He pushed me underneath him, put one hand under my hair behind my neck and one on my back as he pulled me close. We kissed like it would be our last time. He moved his lips slowly down my body and rested them on parts never touched by Diego. I moaned in pleasure, which only inspired him more. He continued to caress me with his lips and I prayed that the moment would go on forever. He traced his lips down my body undressing me as he moved being careful not to miss a spot. As his lips reached the inside of my thighs, I shivered with excitement. He made me feel things I didn't think possible and he made love to me right there in the dark, under the stars. He brought me to heights over and over and I held onto him with my last breath. He covered my mouth with his to keep me quiet but it was to no avail. I had never reached the places he took me before that night. I was so overwhelmed with emotion that there were tears running down my face. When he was done loving me he helped me get dressed again. It was hard to do. We knew he was leaving soon. We saw three figures in the dark as Max was getting himself dressed. "Oh no!" He grabbed my hand and pulled out his gun with the other. "I'm sorry Lilly." He put me behind him. It was Jorge, Diego and Hector.

"Do you think they saw us?" I asked.

"I think they heard us," was his reply. He smiled and kissed me one last time. "Lilly if they shoot me, let Hector take care of you."

"Max," I whispered, "don't say that."

It wasn't long before they were right there upon us. Jorge pulled out a gun and pointed it at Max. "In the air, half-breed!" Max pointed his gun right back at Jorge. "Diego, a gun?" Max asked. "Come on…"

"Making love to my wife five minutes after you get here. I can't believe the nerve you half-breeds have," he responded.

"How long were you standing there?" I asked.

"Long enough that he paid me back," Diego answered. "Lilly, when you're having an affair, silence is a virtue." He tried to walk around Max to grab me but Max moved me out of reach.

"Look," Diego said. "Jorge, they're faster than us and we can't beat them."

Jorge continued to hold the gun up at Max. Max still unwavering with his gun pointed at Jorge.

"Come on boys," Diego continued. "We all have guns here. Lilly is probably pregnant with someone's baby. She'll end up being the one who gets hurt. Drop the guns." Jorge lowered his weapon. Max did the same.

"Did you use protection?" he asked Max. Max said nothing. "Did you use protection? I have a right to know." Max still said nothing. "I have to send you away, Max." He looked a little disappointed. "I don't want to kill you, so Mexico is the only way. We can't live together anymore."

I think I lost my sanity for a minute. I threw myself at Diego's feet and began to beg. "Please Diego, please don't send him away. Please… I'll do whatever you want. I won't ever see him again. Please…"

Max started to approach me when Diego said, "No, take him to the house." Jorge pulled Max by the arm and shoved him in the direction of the house. Diego tried to pick me up off the ground but I kept pleading with him. Hector scooped me up off of the ground; I put my arms around his neck and buried my face in his chest. Diego led us back to the house. Hector let me back down and we were standing behind Diego. Jorge put his gun up to Max's temple and cocked it. Max closed his eyes. I think he was giving up. Hector pulled his gun out so fast I didn't see his hand move. "I swear to God if you kill him, I will drop you before he hits the ground!"

"Boys, put the guns away," Diego ordered. But no one listened. I had to do something. I remembered that Max kept his gun in his waistband in the back of his pants. I wondered if Diego did the same. I reached in front of me and grabbed for Diego's gun and that is exactly where it was. I held it up and pointed it at Diego. Hector and Jorge instantly lowered their weapons.

If I had known that pointing a gun at the favorite brother would have such an effect, I would have done it a long time ago," I said.

Then at the same time Hector and Max both spouted, "He's not my favorite brother."

"This is not funny!" I screamed. "I am trapped in this house and I have no choices!"

"Lilly," Max said. "Don't shoot Diego, shoot Jorge." I continued to point the gun at Diego. Although I had always found Max's humor charming, right now, I was not laughing. Jorge hit Max in the back of the head when he said that and I shouted, "Don't tempt me Jorge, I'd rather see you dead than anyone else here!"

"Max, get the gun," Diego said calmly.

"I can't do this anymore," I continued. "I don't want to have sex with my husband and make love with my lover anymore. I can't do it!" My hands began to shake. "You can't take him from me! I need him! You can't take him from me!"

"Max," Diego said, "do something."

"I don't want to live anymore," I told them, and I moved the gun from Diego and pointed it at my temple. I heard all four men gasp and say, "No, no, no…"

"Oh my God," Hector gasped. "I think you two have pushed her as far as she can go. Max, get the gun."

"Lilly…" Max walked over to me and had a very calm tone in his voice. "Remember, you might be pregnant. We're talking about a baby."

"I don't want to have Diego's baby!" I shouted. I started to feel overwhelmed and confused. I had been with Diego so many times over past few days; I was feeling disoriented, trapped and desperate.

"Am I pregnant?" I asked him.

"Lilly, hand me the gun," he said.

"Am I pregnant!" I began to lose control of my voice.

"Baby girl. If you hurt yourself, you could hurt the baby." He took a step closer. "Now, don't move and I'll take the gun."

"NO!" I screamed. "I want to die, Max."

"Lilly please…" His eyes began to fill with water. "Please do what I say and give me the gun."

"He's making you leave me," I reminded him. "You'll have to move on with another woman and I'll still be here, pregnant with Diego's baby. I don't know how you watch him touch me over and over again. I can't watch you marry someone else." I was losing control, I was aware of that. My emotional pain became physical.

"Max…" Hector was beginning to panic. "Max, what's happening?"

"Lilly, there's no one else. There will never be anyone else."

"That's what Johnny said," I answered. "That's just what he said."

"Lilly, he will have to find someone else, he isn't coming back," Diego started and I cocked the gun.

"Shut up you idiot!" Max shouted at Diego.

"Max!" Hector said in a desperate tone.

"I know," Max replied, "I heard it." He reached for the gun but I moved and he stopped. "Lilly, I'm not Johnny. You're my everything."

"No," I said, "I can't live like this anymore. You're leaving me here and I'm pregnant with Diego's baby. I can't do this without you." I put my finger on the trigger. "It's over Max."

"Diego, tell her she can have a few minutes with me before I go," Max pleaded. Diego said nothing. "Tell her!" he shouted.

"Lilly, you can have as much time as you need with him before he leaves." Diego was scared; I could hear it in his voice.

"Lilly…" Max's voice was very calm and his hand was gently pushing the gun to the floor. "I'm going to take the gun away. Don't move, Lilly." He pulled the gun away and slipped it into Diego's hand, who was standing behind him. "Good girl," he said. There were deep sighs all through the room. "Come with me into the living room."

"No," I said. "No, it's over." The truth was that I couldn't move my legs. He picked me up into his arms and carried me into the living room. He sat on the couch and put me in his lap. Then he put his hands on my face and kissed me over and over until he thought I might be coherent again. I could see Diego, Hector and Jorge watching from the kitchen. Max lifted up my chin so I would be looking at him. "Lilly, whose baby are you carrying?" He said it almost in a whisper.

"I don't know," I answered. "It's him, then you, it's him, then you…" I put my hands over my face. "I don't remember." I started sobbing.

"Lilly, look at me." I turned my face so I could see his eyes. "It's my baby. You're carrying my baby."

"How can you be sure?" I asked.

"I'm very sure." He reached up and brushed my hair from my sweaty brow.

"Thank God," I responded and I threw my arms around his neck.

"You can't fall apart on me, baby girl. You have to stay strong."

"I'm sorry, Max, but I know I'll never see you again."

"I want you to pack a bag for you and one for the baby." He kissed me and turned his head away so the men in the kitchen couldn't see what he was saying. "I will be back in two months and we will have little time to get out, so you must be ready." He continued, "If Diego sees the bag, you tell him it's a pregnancy emergency bag, okay?"

"Yes sir," I answered. "I pack a bag for me and Dieguito and have it ready for when you return in two months."

"Good girl," he said and he gently brushed my cheek with his fingers. "Whose baby are you carrying?"

"Yours," I answered. "I'm a little over two months now, right."

"I think so," he replied. "You're coming back to me now, that's good."

"I'm okay, Max," I answered. "I just can't imagine being without you for so long."

"Hector will take care of you." He smiled. "But don't get too attached. I know how you get with your bodyguards." I laughed. "Oh and one more thing," he added. "You'll have to stop seeing Diego when I get back. I'll be done sharing at that time, got it." I laughed a little more. "Okay Lilly, who's the father of your baby?"

I smiled. "I'm all right Max. It's you and only you."

"Am I coming back?" he asked.

"Yes, in two months," I answered.

"Stay strong querida." He took my face into his hands and kissed me.

"If you don't come back, I will end my life," I told him, "after our baby is born."

"I'll be back, I promise." Tears started falling from his eyes. "Please promise me…" He paused. "No suicide." He grabbed me and kissed me hard and pulled me close. I almost lost control. "Promise me Lilly, promise me."

"I'll wait for you, Max," I promised.

"I'll be thinking of nothing else," he added. "When this is all over, we'll get married and make it legal." I kissed him again and Diego came out.

"Okay, that's enough," he said.

Jorge came out and pulled his gun and pointed it at Max. "Let's go, half-breed."

"No guns," Diego told him. He pushed the gun to the floor much like Max did to me. "No guns, he'll go."

"I'll go," he agreed. He kissed me one more time and got up. "Remember what I said." He blew me a kiss as Jorge shoved him out the door. Hector and Diego stared at me with not a clue of what to do next. I sat on the couch feeling empty and cold.

"Do you want me to handle this?" Hector asked.

"She's my wife, I'll handle her." Diego began to approach me.

"I want Hector," I said with little emotion in my voice.

"Lilly let's go," Diego said calmly as he put out his hand.

"I want Hector!" I yelled.

Hector looked at Diego for a minute and said, "Let me take care of her tonight. You can trust me with her."

Diego backed up and said something to Hector in Spanish. Then Hector put his hand out for me to take it. "Come on Lilly." I stood up and took his hand. "You can sleep in my room and I'll sleep on the floor." I realized that Diego had probably suggested the sleeping arrangement in Spanish.

"That's fine," I agreed. "I don't want to be alone." We walked passed Diego who was watching me like he thought I might break. We walked in silence to Hector's bedroom and he led me to his bed. I sat there motionless. He took out some covers and a pillow from the closet and laid them on the floor. Then he took off his pants right in front of me and slipped on some sweats. I was a little surprised that he was okay with my seeing him in his underwear but he seemed so at home with me just sitting there. Then he took off his shirt and revealed his marble-like chest. He put on a tee shirt and smiled. "What?"

"How did you get to be so modest?" I asked sarcastically.

"Sorry," he said. "You've seen Diego and Max undress… what's the difference?"

"The difference is that I don't get naked with you." He laughed and threw me a pair of sweatpants that looked to be my size. "My emergency, girl pair," he said with a chuckle. "Here's a tee shirt. Get comfortable, I'll be right back." He walked out. I changed quickly so as not to get caught undressed and slid under the covers. He was oddly neat and clean like Maxwell. Everything in its place. The room almost smelled sterile. When he came back he had a pillow with him. "Here." He put it under my head and moved the other to the side. "It's Max's." I smelled it first thing and he smiled. Then he got himself set up on the floor.

"Hector?" I asked.

"Yes Lilly."

"Will you do something for me?"

"Yes Lilly, anything."

"Will you hold me?" He looked at me for a minute, not sure what to say.

"In there?" he asked, pointing to the bed.

"Please Hector. I really want you to put your arms around me. Make me feel safe?" He thought about it for another minute. He stood up and locked the door.

"If anyone asks, I slept on the floor… alone." He crawled into bed with me and spooned me. He wrapped his arms tightly around my waist and I let out a sigh. "Is this what you want?" he asked.

"Yes," I answered. "Thank you."

"This so has to stay between us, Lilly. My brother… you know the one… the psycho Iron Man?" I laughed. "He will shoot me first and ask you about it later. This is between us, okay?"

"Between us," I agreed. I closed my eyes and drifted off to sleep.

When I woke up Hector was staring at the ceiling with his hands behind his head and I was wrapped around him with my head on his chest. "So totally inappropriate," he said nervously. "If Max knew what I had wrapped around me right now, he would totally kill me."

"I'm sorry, Hector, but I feel so safe with you." I tightened my grip around his chest.

"You feel nice," he said. "I'm starting to see why they are both so desperate to have you."

"Am I arousing you?" I asked in a joking tone.

"No Lilly, it's just morning." He laughed a little. "And keep your eyes up here." He pointed to his eyes. I snuggled closer into his chest. I put my hand under his tee shirt for a second. I simply had to feel that chest. He grabbed my hand and moved it back to the outside of his shirt.

"Lilly?" He put his fingers under my chin and pointed my face up. "Are you trying to seduce me?"

"Sorry," I answered. "It won't happen again."

"I'm sure Max and the bronze God have just as hard a chest as I do."

"I don't know," I said. "You won't let me touch it." He laughed.

"No, you can't touch it." He stroked my hair. "I'm only a man, you know. I'm strong, but let's not see how strong."

I moved my hand back to where it was before so that I was wrapped around him. I sighed a little as I pressed my head back down on his chest. "He'll be back for you, you know," he told me. "It's not over."

"I know that's what he said," I answered. "But they all say they'll come back but they don't." I was trying to discretely feel his muscles from over his tee shirt. He suddenly rolled over on top of me and put his hands behind my back. He pulled me into him and pressed his cheek against mine. I could feel his breath in my ear and it was shockingly stimulating. I moaned slightly and when I did, he pulled away quickly and repositioned me back on his chest. I was breathless. He was smiling.

"What was that?" I asked in shock. This was not something Hector and I would ever do. I was just messing around with him but learned better after that.

"That, little girl is what you do not want to happen. So… watch your hands." I was still breathless. "Did I get to you?" he asked.

"Yes," I answered bashfully. "It was both terrifying and exciting at the same time." He peered down at me almost proud of himself. "I'll bet you're good at that."

"I'm sure I'm no better than Max," he replied, reminding me not to get any ideas.

"I'm just saying…" I paused. "Wow!"

"Lilly, that is a part of me that I will never share with you." He touched my face for a second. "At least I'm not planning on it."

"Well, if you don't want to share that part of yourself with me, don't do that again," I said. He was red in the face and laughing.

"You're adorable." He went back to stroking my hair. "This just feels very comfortable."

"I told you," I replied. "I promise, I'll behave. I just wanted to feel your chest." He put his other hand on my back under my shirt. He slid his fingers up, between my shoulder blades and securely grabbed onto the back of my bra. I quivered a little. "What are you doing?" I asked.

"If I let you touch mine, will you let me touch yours?" He had the most mischievous smile on his face.

"Okay, okay… Max's rule… no touching."

"That's what I thought you'd say." He let go and removed his hand.

"Hector?" I looked up at him.

"Yes Lilly, anything." I smiled.

"Thank you for making me feel safe."

"You're welcome, anytime." We lay there for a while saying nothing. He ran his fingers through my hair and I remained wrapped around him like a vine. "I think it's time for me to deliver you to your husband." My eyes filled with water. "I will be here for you." He still didn't let me go. "If you need me to hold you, I guess I can suffer through it." He stopped stroking my hair and sat up. "I'll get dressed in the bathroom this time." He smiled. I pulled the covers over my head. I heard the bathroom door close and I quickly slipped back on yesterday's clothes. He came out, took my hand and said, "Time to go."

He walked me down the hall to Diego's room and knocked on the door. Diego opened it and Hector said, "She feels better now. Thanks for letting me take care of her."

"Where'd you sleep?" he asked.

"He slept on the floor," I quickly answered.

"Thank you, Hector," he continued. "I owe you one."

"I did it for Max," he said. "I did it for Lilly." He turned and walked away. I suddenly felt very alone. Diego closed the door behind me and said, "I'm going to go make you some breakfast. Why don't you take a shower and get dressed."

"You don't want to…" I stopped myself.

"You need a little time. That's okay. Go clean up. I'll see you in a few." He walked out and I sat down on the bed in shock.

Diego didn't try to get intimate with me for at least a week. But I wouldn't respond to him as I did before and the emptiness became almost unbearable. I grew very depressed.

I decided to go to the creek, where Max and I last made love. I walked to the rocks and noticed that his beer bottle was still sitting there. I picked it up and Hector came up beside me. I jumped a little. "Sorry," he said, "but I'm supposed to be watching you."

It's not mine," I told him, holding up the beer bottle. "It was Max's last time he was here."

"If you want, I'll leave you alone but I have to be able to see you. I'll give you your privacy, though," he suggested.

"No," I answered. "It's all right. I could use the company." We sat down on the rocks and looked out at the water. "How is he?" I asked. "My eyes filled up with tears as soon as I asked him. He put his arm around me and said, "Only seven more weeks," and he smiled.

"Can I talk to him?" I asked.

"Lilly, I think that will make it worse." He paused for a moment. "Try to get used to him being gone. I started to cry and put my head in my hands. He pulled out a handkerchief and handed it to me. "Did he ever tell you about Darla?"

"Darla?" I asked. "Johnny's roommate's girlfriend?"

"Johnny's brother's girlfriend," he answered. "Patrick was Johnny's brother."

"What is up with that guy?" I asked. "He lied to me about everything."

"It appears that way," he answered. "Pat started out as John's enforcer until he started dipping his hand in the candy jar. Then he became Johnny's permanent houseguest.

"Darla? Max and Darla?" I asked in surprise.

"It was before you got here. They met at one of those territory meetings."

"Okay, I can see that," I blurted.

"They started… fooling around, I guess we'll call it."

"Max?" I asked. "How, out of character."

"Yeah, real out of character," he said sarcastically. "What's he doing with you?"

"He waited almost four years," I answered.

"Well, he didn't with her." He looked down. "They snuck around for a while and I think that's when Pat started using."

"So, I was hanging around John when all this was going on?"

"Yes, you were. I think it ended a day or two before you got here."

"What happened?" I was saturated with curiosity.

"Pat caught Max and Darla together." He cleared his throat. "He vowed revenge and came after Darla when Max was gone."

"I don't like where this is headed," I answered.

"Long story short, Max found Patrick after he had beaten and raped Darla and he was on top of her on the floor." I gasped. "Max shot him without a second thought and Patrick fell dead on the floor beside her."

"Self-defense, right?" I asked.

"Darla reached over, pulled Patrick's gun out from his waistband and blew her brains out."

"Oh my God!" I shouted. "Right in front of him?"

"Right in front of him." He took my hand. "So, when you got here, he wasn't just helping you out…"

"I was helping him heal too," I finished.

"Please don't doubt that his love is true. He has grown very attached to you." I smiled. "And no more 'gun to the head' thing, okay?"

"I can't believe I did that," I answered.

"It's our world, Lilly." He picked the beer bottle out of my hand and dumped the contents out onto the grass. "It's dark, its ugly and it often destroys the women we choose to let into it."

"Why didn't he share that with me?" I asked.

"I think he's a little ashamed," he answered. "For starters, he took a woman that didn't belong to him and in the end, he couldn't protect her." I started to see the similarities to our situations. "That's why it's important that I watch you," he continued. "He trusts me."

"It's just hard without him," I added.

"Lilly, right now I'm your safest relationship."

"And how's that?" I asked.

"I'll never ask you for sex and you can tell me anything and I won't turn you in." He laughed.

"Turn me in?" I asked.

"I won't tell your husband, or your boyfriend." He put the bottle down on the grass beside him.

"My husband or my boyfriend," I repeated. "Never thought those words would be in my vocabulary."

"The good news is, with Max out of the picture, Diego won't be so… demanding." He smiled. I was a little embarrassed but I knew to what he was referring.

"Do you think so?" I asked with a glimmer of hope.

"I think he was just trying to wear you out to keep Max at bay," he answered. "Not that anything could keep Max at bay," and he laughed to himself.

"Cut it out," I said and I hit him playfully on the shoulder. We both laughed.

"Look a smile," he said. "That's good."

"I hope you're right," I added. "I only want to be with Max."

"That's not what you said last night." He looked up at me with a vague memory of our one night of closeness in his eyes.

"Shut up!" I yelled and smacked him in the arm again. This time I think I hurt my hand and I shook it in pain. He shook his head at me. "You wouldn't have… if I…" I was too embarrassed to finish the sentence.

"Sometimes I think you're a little too curious for your own good." He took my hand and kissed it.

"You haven't answered my question," I reminded him.

"Soon," he said, "he'll be back very soon."

We went back to the house and Diego was fixing himself a sandwich in the kitchen. "Tell me I don't have to worry about you too, Hector," he said in a half angry tone.

"That's just gross," Hector replied.

"Gross?" I asked. "Now I'm gross?"

Diego and Hector started cracking up together. "No baby, he didn't mean you were gross," Diego commented. "He meant that he would never be number 3."

"Okay," I said. "What?"

"You're fine with number two, though, aren't ya Hector?" Diego said sarcastically.

"Two's okay," he answered, "but three is just sloppy left-overs from what one and two didn't finish."

"What's so good about being number two?" I asked.

"Number two is usually the one the girl wishes was number one but number three is just the guy who can't find his own girl."

"You know you guys are crazy," I added.

"Hector, I think she's smiling today," Diego added.

"It's my charm and wit," he offered. "Much like my brother's." Diego made and face and Hector winked at me. "She'll be okay," he replied. "Just keep doin' what you're doin'." I knew what he was implying and I just smiled and kissed Hector on the cheek.

CHAPTER 15

Tell me again what it does to you when I call you that.

Hector was right. As time went by, things got easier. Diego was not nearly as demanding as he used to be and I could feel Max's baby growing inside of me. Hector wouldn't allow me contact with Max and Diego became very comfortable with my relationship with Hector. One night Diego was working late and I snuck over to Hector's room and knocked on the door. He opened the door and looked at me. "Is everything all right, Lilly?"

"Would you hold me?" I asked.

"Lilly," he took my hands, "I can't have that kind of relationship with you." He was serious.

"You idiot!" I shouted. "I just want to be here when Max calls."

"You're becoming way too much like him," he added. "I thought you were coming on to me." He smiled. "I think I'm disappointed."

"Shut up and let me in," I demanded.

"Hell no!" he answered. "If I get caught with you in my bedroom, I am such a dead man!"

"Diego's still out. Let me stay, please…"

He stepped outside the door and looked around. "Fine," he agreed, "come in. Let me get a shirt on."

I went inside and said, "Please put a shirt on, I can't control myself."

He laughed. "I wouldn't want you to start feeling me up again."

"I'm going to hurt you," I replied, still obviously amusing him.

"Oh, so much like Max," he said, and the phone rang.

"Hey, what's up?" he asked. My heart started pounding excessively. I could feel my face flush as I waited to speak with him.

"Before you say anything," he told him, "Lilly is here waiting to talk to you." He laughed. "No man, that's gross," he blurted.

"Would you stop calling me that!" I shouted.

"She just came to my room to talk to you. I swear she's not in my bed." I grabbed the phone from him.

"Daddy, I miss you," I whispered. His voice was like honey dripping down the phone lines.

"Baby girl," he answered. "What are you doing in Hector's room?"

"Waiting for your phone call," I replied. "Seriously Max, you're not jealous?"

"Should I be?" he asked.

"I just needed to hear your voice." I paused. "Do you still love me?"

"Madly and completely," he answered. I felt relief run through my body. "I love you so much." I started to cry.

"I'll be back to get you on Easter." I think he was trying to calm me. "I want there to be one good Easter in your life." I got a bad feeling when he said that. Everything bad happens on Easter Sunday.

"That's two days from now," I added. "You'll be home in two days?"

"Two days, baby girl." He paused. "Hang on for me, okay?"

"I can't wait to see you," I told him.

"Me either. Stay strong for me querida, and get out of Hector's room." I smiled and handed the phone back to Hector.

"Now that's a smile I haven't seen for a while," he said to Max. Then a call on the radio came into Hector. "Diego's home, get out of my bedroom before he finds you here." Hector grabbed me and pushed me out the door. I kissed his cheek and ran back to my bedroom. I couldn't believe I got to hear his voice. Two more days.

When that day came, I woke up full of joy. I looked into the mirror and looked at my little tummy. I wasn't showing much, but I could tell that my jeans were getting tight. I was four months pregnant now, but if Diego makes me get a test, I will have to tell him three. I came down the stairs to find Jorge, Hector, Elena and Diego all in the kitchen. I knew this wasn't good. "What are you all doing here?" I asked.

Diego handed me a pregnancy test. "Take it, Lilly."

"You invited your family here to watch me pee on a stick?" I asked.

"Just take it. Even though we won't know for sure who the father is." He put his hands over his face for a minute. Elena hugged him from behind and shot me an angry glare. "I need to know for sure that you're pregnant. Then it's really over for the two of you."

He gave me the test and I looked at Hector for some kind of confirmation. He winked at me and gave me a reassuring nod. He and I both already knew I was pregnant. I went into the bathroom and took the test, came outside and handed it to Diego. He put it on top of a napkin on the counter and set a timer. Hector's expression was grave. "Where's Max?" I asked. No one said a word. I sat down on an empty chair next to Hector. He squeezed my hand under the table. The timer rang and Jorge went over to the test and smiled. "Congratulations, my brother!" He hugged Diego and Hector kissed me on the cheek. Then I got that bad feeling again.

"We have to tell her," Hector sighed.

"Tell me what?" I asked. "Oh no, MAX!" I screamed.

"He's not dead!" Hector said quickly. "But it's bad, Lilly."

"Is this some kind of joke?" I asked. "Easter Sunday and something happens to Max?"

"He was shot in Mexico," Diego started. "I'm having him flown out here for surgery." He shot a look at Jorge that was not friendly.

"Shot?" I screamed. "Who shot him? Where was he shot?" I started to feel off balance and Diego got up and grabbed me.

"Three times," Hector said. "I think it was a hit. He was shot in the stomach and once in the chest."

"Please Diego, please…" I was crying and begging. "Let me see him."

"You're mine now, Lilly." He was very sobering. "You are pregnant with my baby, so I will make a few allowances." He picked up my chin as he often did when he was trying to make a point. "Even if Max is the biological father…" He looked at Jorge, who nodded at him. "This is my baby. Do you understand? And that is what you will tell Max."

"Yes sir." I didn't care. I just wanted to see Maxwell.

"I will look the other way and you do whatever you have to do to get him to fight, do you understand? Whatever you have to do."

"Yes sir," I answered again.

"But when he lives through this," he paused, "and damn it, he will live through this, you have to end it with him. Are we clear?"

"Yes Diego. Whatever you need me to do, I'll do."

"You are weak," Jorge said. "You should have let him die."

"I keep my word, "he replied. "I made him a promise."

I remembered that day when the promise was made. Max saved Diego's life and Diego said if anything ever happened to Max he would do the same. They had the strangest relationship. But I was simply grateful that he was going to save him. We got into the limo and headed for the hospital. "Where's Olivia?" I asked.

"She's riding in the plane with Max," Diego answered. "She didn't want him to be alone. She was right there when he was shot."

"Strange how she walked away without a scratch," Hector responded. "How did anyone get passed your guards, Jorge? Your house is like Fort Knox."

"I guess every now and then, someone slips by," he answered. Hector and Diego shot each other looks of disbelief.

By the time we got to the hospital, no one was speaking to Jorge at all. I think they blamed him for it somehow. We rushed inside and the nurse told us he should be here in another few minutes. "He's still conscious," she told us. "Apparently he still has his sense of humor and is asking for someone named Lilly. Is that you?" she asked me.

"Yes," I gasped. "He's still making jokes?" I asked.

"He's in good spirits," she continued.

"He's happy because he's coming back here," Diego explained. "Remember our deal."

"Yes sir," I answered. "I will do as you ask. Thank you."

The paramedics came pushing him in on a gurney and Olivia came running in behind him. Diego and I got up and ran to him. "Max, it's us, we're here," Diego told him. He reached his hand out and put in on my belly. Then he grabbed my hand. Diego did not like that. He had an oxygen mask on and looked pale and weak.

"Lilly?" he said under his mask. I pulled the mask away for a minute and leaned over to kiss him when I remembered that Diego was standing next to me. Diego caught my eyes and turned his head away from us. I kissed Max on the lips and he kissed me back. I put the mask back on him. "I love you, daddy."

He lifted up his mask and said; "You know what that does to me, when you call me that."

"If you wanted to come back, all you had to do was say so," I replied. He smiled at me and squeezed my hand. "Diego had you flown here from Mexico," I added.

"Gracias, mi hermano," he said to Diego.

"You'd do the same for me," he answered.

"I'll be here when you wake up," I told him. Then he said something to me in Spanish that I did not understand. "Are you his wife?" the nurse asked.

"Yes," I blurted. What was I thinking?

"Sister-in-law," Diego said to her. "It's all right, they're close."

"We have to take him now," she said.

I squeezed his hand and let it go. He kept talking in Spanish. He was obviously woozy from something they gave him. "What did he say?" I asked Diego, hoping he would tell me the truth.

He sighed, took my hands and brought them to his face. "Lovely one, I live for you and you alone." He looked very sad. "That's what he said."

Chapter 16

"I don't know Lilly, would it have made a difference?"

We walked to the cafeteria and Diego got me a glass of water. "We need to talk, Lilly," he started.

"I will forever be in your debt for bringing him back here," I offered. "You really do love him on some level, don't you."

"Yeah, I guess so," he answered. "We used to be very close."

"What happened?" I asked. His face got very grave. He took my hands and kissed them. "You happened, Lilly."

"Max says you would kill us both if I left you," I added. Then I saw him pull out a small book from his pocket. "Is that a…" I paused, "Bible?"

"You bet I would," he said. "I'm not proud of it, but that is who I am. And now you're carrying my baby, so we are connected."

"Then what the hell are you doing with a Bible?" I asked angrily.

"I don't know, Lilly. Maybe I need to be a better person." He started flipping through the pages. "I'm going to take Max back," he added. "And I'm keeping Hector but there have to be some ground rules." I was so excited that my heart almost beat right out of my chest.

"Okay," I responded. "What kind of rules?"

"Hector will continue to be your bodyguard, since I'm pretty sure he won't ever want to change your relationship."

"I'm gross, remember?" I answered. He smiled.

"That's what I mean," he replied. "He could never be with someone Max has been with."

"What else?" I asked.

"Max will go back to doing my numbers and… the other things he did for me that you do not want to know about," he explained. "But you have to break it off."

"I understand," I answered.

"Lilly, I mean it. No sex. If I find the two of you in any compromising positions, he's gone." He was very serious.

"I understand," I said again. "I will leave him alone."

"You can see him at the house and be friendly towards each other but that's it." He looked down at his little book. "I like it when he's around, because you smile more."

"Does Jorge know you're taking him back?" I asked.

"Here's the thing, Lilly." He took a deep breath and held my hands. "I think Jorge put the hit out on Max. I think Max lived because of you. If I send Hector or Max back with him, he will have them killed. It's just a matter of time."

"Why?" I asked. "Why would he do that?"

"You and Max, Hector and Olivia… the betrayal." I looked down towards the table. I suppose there is nothing more horrible than what we did to him. "But I don't want them dead. Our world is full of murder and blood." He paused. "We have to keep each other alive."

"I respect you so much for what you're doing," I added. "Diego, I wish you had given me the opportunity to know you when I first came to your home."

"I don't know Lilly, would it have made a difference? Wouldn't you have fallen in love with him anyway?"

"We'll never know now, will we," I answered. "I think Max would have kept away if you paid attention to me."

"I think you're right," he answered. "But you have such a strong connection. I'm not sure it would have changed anything." We sat quietly for a few minutes. Both of us thinking the same thing… That he should just let me go… but he wouldn't do that.

"You must be mindful of Jorge," he finally admitted. "I'll call Hector over in a minute. He'll need to be with you all the time. I'm really afraid of what he's going to do next. He may come after me once I keep the boys here."

"You mean, come after me, don't you," I asked.

"He has no boundaries," he answered. "Women, children… unborn children… brothers… he doesn't care." He squeezed my hands. "Please do not be alone with him."

"No problem there," I said. "I do not like him." Diego laughed.

"One brother I don't have to worry about." We both laughed and then he picked up his phone and called Hector to meet with us.

Hector showed up right away. "Still no news," he told him. "But he's still holding his own." I breathed a sigh of relief and Hector took my hand. "Thank you for being here," he said.

"Like I'd be anywhere else." Then I looked at Diego and thought about that pregnancy test he made me take. "Diego, if I wasn't pregnant, would you have let me come?"

"No," he answered. "See, I need to be a better person." He picked up his Bible. Hector took it out of his hands.

"You're kidding, right? What are you going to do with this?"

"I don't know," he confessed as he grabbed it back. "I think I should read it." They were both quiet for a minute. Not sure what to say, Diego went back to our previous conversation. "Hector, I'm keeping you and Max with me. You will be Lilly's bodyguard and Max will go back to being… Max." Hector smiled.

"Thank you Diego," he said. "Thank you for reading that book."

"I think Jorge put a hit out on him," Diego continued. "He'll kill both of you if he gets the chance. I can't let that happen."

"I've been in his house for years. No one has ever gotten onto his property uninvited, let alone into his house." Hector shook his head. "And how did the intruder let Olivia live to tell the story? She knows the shooter," he continued.

"That's what I think," Diego conceded. "Look how bruised her face is. What the hell is he doing to her?"

"I know," Hector agreed. "I feel responsible. I thought we were careful."

"Just stay with me for a while and keep a sharp eye on Lilly. I suspect you are my safest bet right now." He laughed and shot me a look.

"I swear if you call me gross one more time, I will slap you," I said to him.

Do not and I repeat, do not leave her alone with Jorge." Diego was quite serious.

"I already have a strict policy about that," he answered. "Thanks Diego."

"I think he picked Easter to send a message," Diego went on to say. He looked at me. "Easter's Lilly and all."

"There's no doubt about that," Hector said. "That's why you think he might go after her next?"

"I think he's going to go after you next." Diego's cell phone rang and he looked at it. "The doctor wants to see us."

We quickly got up from the table and went back to the waiting room. The doctor sat down in front of Diego and Diego grabbed my hand. "How is he?" I asked.

"He's pretty tough," the doctor said. "He must have a lot to live for." Diego looked at me and shook his head. "He was strong and the surgery went well. He's in recovery right now but I expect him to be out and about in a few days." I jumped up off of the chair and jumped up and down. Hector got up and hugged me twirling me in the air. When he put me down Diego stood up and hugged me.

"Thank you, Lilly." He kissed my lips and pulled me close to him in a warm embrace. "Thank you for giving him a reason."

We all went home together that night except for Diego. He was afraid to leave Max alone, so he stayed all night. Hector was glued to me. He even slept in a sleeping bag on my floor at night. Diego wouldn't let me see Max again at the hospital. He went every day to see him and when it was time to take him home I had to stay home and wait. I was warned to keep it friendly but not too friendly before he left to get him. Hector stayed behind for safety purposes.

I really liked Hector. He was silly like Max but smart and serious when he needed to be. He always seemed to know what the right thing to do was and he took very good care of me. "Hector?" I asked. "What would you do if you were Max?"

He smiled at me for a minute and said, "If I were shot or in love with you?"

"If it was you instead of Max. Would you stay here like we did?"

"It doesn't matter what I would do, Lilly." He walked over to where I was sitting on the couch and sat beside me.

"I'm not allowed to touch him anymore. I have to stay with Diego." I looked at the floor and he picked up my chin with his fingers.

"I would have taken you out of here a long time ago," he answered. "Once you told me you were ready to leave Diego…" he paused, "you would have been mine." I got a shiver down my spine and it seemed to amuse him. "I'm sorry, did I get to you, Lilly?"

"A little," I answered. "Every once in a while you do that to me."

"Why do you care what I think, anyway?" he asked.

"I was just wondering," I answered. I smiled back at him thinking thoughts I knew I shouldn't be thinking. "Do you think if you had met me first…?" I paused out of embarrassment. "Never mind." I stopped myself.

"Maybe," he answered. "I don't really know."

The family finally arrived, and I got up and ran to Max. He opened his arms but Diego got in front of him and pushed me in the other direction, gently. "Can I get you something, sir?" I asked Max.

"Come on Diego, you can't be serious." He walked over to me and gave me a hug and let me go. "And do NOT call me sir," he continued. "Yes, Lilly, I would love a cup of coffee, please." He walked into the kitchen and sat down. "I promised I wouldn't have another affair with her, but you can't make us ignore each other. That's just going to be weird."

"You're right," he responded. "It just feels strange having you back."

"You'll get used to me," he laughed. "I bet you miss my cooking."

"Hey!" Hector said. "What's wrong with my cooking?"

"Nothing Hector, you're a wonderful cook," I said sarcastically.

"I heard Hector thinks your gross," Max said laughing.

"I did not say that," he replied.

"I can't believe you called my…" He stopped himself. "Diego's wife gross… really Hector."

"Lilly is lovely, you both know that," he answered. "She's just not my type, that's all." He shot me a look and he winked. I knew I could be his type if he let me.

"I thought your type meant that she had to be married to your brother," Diego added.

Hector made a face and Max laughed. "Ouch, that hurts." He reached for his stomach and we all stood up.

"I'm not an invalid, I'll be fine." he assured us. "When is the next meeting, Diego?"

"Sunday," he answered. "I was trying to miss Easter. Funny how that backfired. You're not going, are you?" Diego asked.

"I thought I was your enforcer," he answered.

"Not with a bunch of holes in your chest. Hector can come; you stay here."

"Fine whatever," he said. "Besides," Diego added. "I'll be taking Lilly with me."

"Oh and Max you need to know something." I took a deep breath before I continued. Diego looked at me and sent me a reassuring smile. "The baby is Diego's." It was part of our deal that I tell Max that. I wanted Diego to feel like he could trust me. "We had a test done and you're not the father." I couldn't help but wonder if he believed me or not.

"I see," he said thoughtfully. He looked at Diego and sighed. "Half-breeds, zero, Mexicans one. Congratulations brother. It's probably better this way anyway."

"Don't say that Max. But yes, it is definitely better this way."

"It's not like he's going to sleep with her anymore," Hector stated. "Sleeping with someone who is pregnant with another man's baby is disgusting."

"You did not just call her disgusting," Max snickered.

"I'm just saying… yuck!"

"That's enough," Diego interrupted. "Stop talking about her like she's today's special. She's coming with me and that's all I'm going to say about that."

"I owe you my life, Diego, you know that," Max told him.

"I think we're about even now," Diego answered. "I have to go to work and make arrangements for the meeting. Keep your eyes open, boys. Look for unfamiliar faces. If Jorge shows up early, call me." He kissed me and left. Max and I looked at each other saying nothing.

The radio went off informing Hector that Diego was gone. Max looked at Hector. "No!" Hector started. "Let's stay focused. Stay away from her. It's only three more days."

Max was still staring at me and he reached for my hand and I took it. "Oh…" he said, "I am feeling warm inside." His eyes were filled with desire. "My body has been cold without yours."

"Max, Diego made me say that," I said quickly. "It's yours, you know that, right?"

"Of course I do," he answered. "I was there when the nurse told me you were three weeks along. You did what you were supposed to do. I'm a big boy, don't worry about me."

Hector separated our hands and said, "Okay Max, we need a plan. I won't be here; I'm going to have to go to the meeting. That means I will be in on it and they will make me right away."

"Maybe after I make the call, you can slip out and I can pick you up," Max suggested. "I don't want to risk, Jorge shooting you just before it's over."

"Okay, you can pick me up by the service entrance. I have a key," Hector said. "We have to call Mick today and let him know we'll be coming and to expect Olivia."

"Why won't you give me the details?" I asked. "We're leaving Sunday and you are doing something terrible to your brothers. That much I got."

"I promise that we will all come clean when we are safely out of Vegas," Max answered. "I'm afraid Jorge will try to kill one of us before the meeting, so we have to stick close together."

"What about me?" I asked. "I will be at the meeting with Hector?" Hector and Max looked at each other.

"Oh, that's right," Max remembered. "I guess you're going to have to get a severe case of morning sickness."

"I can do that," I said and smiled. "He won't want anything to do with me by the time he's ready to go."

We were set and Sunday seemed to take a very long time to get here. I was not allowed to kiss or touch Max and it was killing me, but Hector was afraid that there might be hidden cameras and he didn't want to risk Max getting thrown out of the house before Sunday. When Saturday night rolled around, the radio went off announcing Jorge's arrival. "He's early," Max, said in an alarming tone. Hector picked up the phone and called Diego, while Max grabbed the radio off of Hector's belt. "Miguel, get pictures of all the men who arrive with Jorge on your phone and then send them to me," Max insisted. "Be discreet but I need to know how many he brought with him and who you don't recognize."

"You got it, Max," Miguel's voice replied.

"Brilliant little brother," Hector noted.

"In-coming," Max said and he and Hector started looking at the pictures.

"Wait." Hector pointed at two of the pictures. "I don't know who these guys are." "Miguel," Max called. "The two on the right, who are they?"

"Don't know, Max. Never seen them before."

"Anything different about them?" he asked.

"They don't speak any English," he answered. Max and Hector looked at each other with concern. "He brought hit men with him," Max surmised.

My heart fell into my stomach. Diego walked into the kitchen and said, "Lilly, you look like you've seen a ghost." Max and Hector looked at him. "Oh no," Diego said, "He didn't."

"The beast has been unleashed," Max stated. "He brought hit men with him." He showed Diego the pictures.

"Wait…" Diego held up his hand for pause. "I know that guy." He thought for a few seconds. "This isn't good, Max."

"Who is he?"

"He killed Olivia's first bodyguard about 8 years ago."

"Why?" Hector asked, concerned.

"Why do you think?" Diego answered.

"Oh my God," Hector blurted.

"They can't stay here, Diego, you have to do something!" I cried.

"Let me think," Diego said. "Hector, Max, take Lilly to the creek, let me handle this."

"Are you sure?" Hector asked. "I can stay with you."

"He doesn't want to kill me," he answered. "Now get her out of here."

We left out the back door quickly. I was terrified. I was even afraid to leave Diego alone with him. "Max, what are we going to do?"

"We may be sleeping with one eye open tonight," he answered.

"We may be sleeping in their room with them," Hector added. Max started laughing. "I'm not joking," he continued.

"I know," he said. "I'm just laughing at the irony."

CHAPTER 17

I don't know about this.

We were sitting on the rocks talking and the boys were trying to make me laugh. We could see Diego coming towards us in the distance. "Here goes nothing," Hector said.

"What's up?" Max asked.

"He said he just hired two new guys to replace you two." Max shook his head.

"I don't know Max, but I can't take a chance. Lilly's pregnant and I don't want a stray bullet flying in her direction."

"Hello…" Hector said. "What about us?" He pointed to himself and Max. Max laughed. "Seriously, what if they try to kill us in our sleep? Are you going to sleep with your gun on your chest?"

"You two will stay with us tonight," Diego offered. "We need to stay close until we are sure of what Jorge is up to, Hector's right. What if we wake up and everyone is dead."

"We'll stay with you but…" Max looked at me. "No, inappropriate behavior while I am in your room." He shook his head. "I'm sorry Diego but I'm not ready for that yet."

"I thought we were passed that, Max." Diego stroked my hair. "Nothing inappropriate, I promise." He took my hand. "I want her safe more than I want to prove anything to you."

"Me too," Max agreed. "Me too."

"I'm going to put two men outside the door as well," Hector said. "Miguel and Felix are our two best shooters."

"That'll work," Max agreed.

"I'm scared," I said, and I looked up at Diego. "I'm really scared."

"Between Max and me, do you think anything could ever happen to you?" He asked.

"And me," Hector said sarcastically.

"Well, we don't think she's gross," Max said laughing.

We all loved Max's sense of humor. He was always funny when things were looking bleak. When we went back to the house, Jorge was in the kitchen with his two new enforcers. Diego introduced them to Max and Hector and Jorge introduced them to me. "This is the beautiful Lilly," he said. They went to shake my hand but Diego pushed me behind him and said something to them in Spanish. "They don't speak English Jorge, why introduce her in English?"

"How do you know they don't speak English?" Jorge replied.

"How long have you been working for Jorge?" Max asked them. They said nothing.

"Okay, so maybe they only know a few words," Jorge continued. "Why protect Lilly from them?"

"She doesn't need to know them," Diego answered.

He said something in Spanish to Hector and Hector took my arm and led me away. We went into the living room and I asked, "What's going on?"

"He doesn't want them to get too familiar with you." He looked back to see how close they were. "Rape is always a scary thing when we have unknown hit men in our house."

My eyes opened wide. "Rape?" I freaked out. "Oh no, Hector!"

"Shhh…" he said. "I get a bad vibe from these guys. Promise me you will behave and stay close, Okay?"

"No problem there," I agreed. I began to feel sick. "Hector," I said. "Do you want to come with me to the bathroom?"

He smiled. "No, but I will." We went to the bathroom and he actually held my hair while I threw up. "You do this on purpose, don't you?" he asked smiling.

"Yeah, sure I do," I answered. I sat on the floor of the bathroom. "Hector are we going to make it through the night?" I was feeling so helpless.

"Definitely," he answered. "Max and I are the best in the business." Then he picked up my chin and I looked into his eyes. "Lilly, they are both crazy in love with you. Any one of us would put our lives on the line for you." My eyes welled up with tears. "Any one of us," he repeated. Then he helped me up off the floor and he hugged me. "You are very important to me too," he said. "You're my brother's girl and you're carrying his baby. I love you for that all by itself."

"Thanks Hector." I hugged him back. "What do you think they're talking about?"

"I think Max and Diego are feeling them out," he answered. "We'll be fine, I promise." We walked back into the living room. "Have I been wrong yet?" he asked.

"No," I answered. "Not yet."

Night soon fell and Max and Hector checked the house with guns drawn for intruders. Miguel and Felix were stationed outside the bedroom door and Max and Hector put blankets and pillows on the floor with guns ready to go by their sides. Diego and I lay down in the bed and he put his arms around me, in protection mode. "Diego," Max looked over at us, "if we hear something outside, push Lilly behind the bed and get in front of her."

Diego reached behind him and showed Max his gun. "I'm as ready as you are." "I don't think there is any danger of my sleeping tonight," I told them.

"Remember what I said, Lilly," Hector reminded me. "Any one of us."

"I'm okay Hector, I remember." I smiled at him as he winked at me.

"I'm going to take the first shift," Hector said, checking his gun. "Max you need the rest."

"Yeah right," Max said. "Like I'm going to go to sleep with her in here." Hector and Diego laughed at that. My face turned red, I'm sure. I hid it under the covers. We sat and waited for sounds. It was grueling. Hours went by before we heard anything. Suddenly there were voices outside the door speaking in Spanish. Diego did exactly what Max told him to do and translated for me as the conversations went on in a whisper. Max and Hector both drew their guns, as did Diego. I was never so scared. Diego whispered, "Max and Hector are missing, we need to see Diego." That is what the men outside the door were saying to Miguel and Felix. Then he said, "Jorge ordered a hit on the boys."

Then Diego said, "Miguel is telling them not to disturb me and my wife while we are in bed. The men are saying Jorge ordered them to find me. Miguel is telling them that they don't work for Jorge. One of them just pulled their gun."

Hector moved towards the door and looked at Max. "Not yet." Max motioned for Hector to wait. "Miguel can hold his own. Wait a few more minutes." We heard a loud BANG and a thud and then again, a BANG and a thud. Max opened the door slightly and Miguel walked into the bedroom. Everyone lowered their guns and breathed a sigh of relief. "Here's something new," Miguel said. He held up a needle. "This is what he was going to kill you with."

Max picked it up and looked at it. "How do you know?" he asked.

"He held it up and tried to stick me with it," Miguel answered. "But Felix shot him."

Diego was helping me up and asked me if I was all right. "How'd the last guy die?"

"Same way," Miguel said. "Went after Felix with a needle and I dropped him."

"Good job boys." Max patted Miguel on the back. Diego walked outside the room and I ran to the bathroom to throw up. I was lying on the floor when Miguel walked in. "Should I get Max for you?" he asked. That surprised me. Why would he say that?

"No," I answered. "Diego will be back soon."

Max walked in and nodded at Miguel. "Thanks, but I'll take it from here." He pulled me off the floor and got on his knees beside me. He put me in his lap in front of the toilet and held back my hair. "It's okay baby girl, I'm here now." I threw up in the toilet and Diego walked in.

"Don't worry," Max said. "No sex, just morning sickness."

Diego made a face and said, "Yeah, thanks Max," and walked out.

Max laughed as I puked my brains out. Then I lay back on the floor. "What a devoted husband," I mentioned.

"I told you," he reminded me. "Just throw up and you're all mine." I laughed as he lifted me up off of the floor and put me into bed. "I so want to lay with you," he told me. "I so want to taste you."

"You are a crazy man," I said smiling. "I am sick as a dog."

"You are glowing with beauty," he told me. He reached under my nightgown and glided his hand over my thigh and then removed it quickly. I sat up. "What are you doing?" I asked.

"I just wanted to feel you," he answered. "One more day is an eternity." He looked around the room and kissed me slowly on the lips. "Oh Max," I whispered. "I was just sick a minute ago."

"Oh Lilly," he whispered back. "You taste like honey." I started to get a little excited. But as luck would have it, Hector came back in and dragged Max out of the bedroom.

"Good night Lilly," Hector said smiling. "Say goodnight, Max." He blew me a kiss and they left me. Diego was back in a minute but made no attempt at intimacy. I think my vomiting made him a little sick.

"We're okay now Lilly," he told me. "At least for a while." We slept in each other's arms until Sunday morning. And when I awoke, Diego was gone.

CHAPTER 18

It's time to tell Olivia

The house smelled like chorizo, a Mexican sausage they often cooked. Diego and Hector had already gone and Max and I were alone. "As much as I would love to take advantage of you right now, we have to eat and get moving."

I smiled. "Leave it to you to feed me first," I replied.

"Hey, you're pregnant. Food is important." I laughed. "Besides," he said. "I am waiting for Leticia. She will be coming with us to watch little Diego."

"Why Leticia?" I asked.

"She's a cop," he answered. I sat down almost impulsively when he said that. "What?" I asked.

"She's a cop and I need her watching the baby as we get the hell out of here."

"I think you have a lot of explaining to do," I told him.

"Yes, Lucy, I do." He laughed. "Please trust me, baby girl." He put eggs and some chorizo in a tortilla and put it in front of me. "You need to keep up your strength."

We ate, got dressed and got our bags together. Max put me in the car and put blankets over Leticia, the baby and me as we drove off of the property. He told the guards at the gate that he was going to the meeting after all and had left Miguel with me. Miguel was waiting in the house to give us time to get away. When we got a safe distance from the house, he called Miguel to let him know. We stopped the car at the Flamingo hotel and picked Hector up by the service entrance. "How'd you get out?" he asked.

"Bathroom." He smiled. "The men are all in the back room and the women are having dinner," he told us. As we drove away I could see huge amounts of black sedans and men dressed in black shirts that said, "FBI" on them. They were running into the hotel.

"Step on it!" Hector shouted and Max peeled out of the parking lot onto the highway. My hands were shaking as I strapped Dieguito into his car seat. "They are already at your house," Hector said. "Miguel called and said they had arrested everyone."

"Okay, what the heck is happening?" I asked frantically. "Max, what's going on?"

"Max, you haven't told her?" Leticia asked.

"I didn't want her to lie for us. I was afraid Diego might try to beat it out of her if he got suspicious," he answered. "But I guess it's time now."

Hector pulled his wallet out of his back pocket and handed it to me. "Look inside," he told me. I opened the wallet and saw some identification that said, "Hector Montiago, FBI."

"No way! Are you kidding me?" I asked. "Seriously, you too Max?"

"Yes baby, me too." He turned his head and looked at me for a reaction. "I'm sorry, please don't be angry with me."

"You had your reasons," I answered. "You do love me, don't you? Was that part real?"

He turned his head again. "That part was real," he answered. "It was all real, baby girl."

"If you are FBI, how did you get away with killing Johnny?" I asked. Leticia laughed.

"He's not dead," Hector answered. "We put him in the Witness Protection Program. That's why we were gone for so long."

"But when you came back, Max was all weirded out," I answered.

"We've been infiltrating their organization for five years, now." Hector paused. "We know what kind of behavior they expect from us after certain jobs get done."

"So, John is going to testify against Jorge and Diego?" I asked.

"That's how it works," Leticia responded. Then she showed me her FBI identification.

"One more question," I asked.

"Baby, you have earned the right to ask me as many questions as you want," Max answered.

"Why?" I paused. "Why turn in your brothers like that?"

Max sighed. "They had our mother killed."

"Papi was married to their mother first, obviously I guess, and got our mother pregnant with me," Hector started. "He eventually left Elena for our mom."

"Then they had me," Max continued. "Everything was fine until Hector turned about 12 and I was 10." He took a breath. "Diego was 17 at the time. That would make Jorge 23. They killed our mom, Amelia, in order for their mom to get Papi back into her … good graces."

"Oh no," I replied. I put my hands over my mouth in absolute shock.

"They had her brutally raped and murdered. Then our dad re-married Elena and we had to live with them until we went off to college. Our mom's family put money away for us and we decided to see justice done when we graduated."

"So that's what this is about? Revenge?" I asked.

"After we grew up a bit, we realized that we had to stop the organization from expanding. They sell drugs to kids and Jorge is a brilliant businessman. The organization is beyond huge. It became more about ethics after a while."

"How did they ever let you in?" I asked.

"Long story short," Hector finished. "We played dumb about our mom's murder and they were never caught. We got out of school, went for FBI training and went to our brothers and begged for work. They took us in and the rest is history."

"Aren't you afraid that they are going to kill us when they figure this whole thing out?" I asked.

"Lilly, they would have killed you eventually if you had stayed there. He would have found someone younger and paid her with drugs to sleep with him and you would have been in the way," Max continued. "I had to get you out of there."

"I know, Max." I corrected myself quickly. "I couldn't have stayed in that marriage any longer than I had to."

"For goodness sakes you were threatening to kill yourself." He looked at me again. "We had to speed things up."

"If you hadn't fallen in love with me, would you have left me there?" I asked.

"I was in love with you within the first five minutes I saw you," he answered. "From the moment your pretty eyes met mine. We were locked in, remember?"

"Of course I do." I smiled. "I saw your… yes I remember."

He laughed a little. "So, there's no doubt, you were destined to be stuck with me." I reached over the seat and grabbed his hand. "I would never say stuck," I answered. "I can't wait to…" I paused. "Be alone again."

"Still in the car," Hector said. "Leticia and I are still here."

"I can't wait either," Max responded. "But it's a long drive to Arizona." Hector picked up the phone and called, of all people, my dad. "Mick, is Olivia there yet?" Let me talk to her." He began a long conversation in Spanish and then started talking to my dad again. "It went just like you wanted. We're clear and we've got Lilly, the baby and Leticia." He hung up the phone.

"Okay, not my dad," I said. "He's the chief of police for Sedona."

"Yes he is," Max answered. "He is also in charge of narcotics for the FBI. You're going to find this very amusing, I'm sure," Max continued. "But he's our boss." I was floored. "I have to say that I'm a little mad at him for not introducing me to you sooner," Max continued. "Didn't he know what a great couple we'd be?"

"Your boss?" I was still in shock. "So many things are starting to make sense now," I said. "Like when my mom died and my dad sort of turned to you. I always thought that was strange."

"Hey," Max said in his usual smart mouthed tone, "I am quite charming."

"Always the clown," Hector added. "Always the clown."

When we got to Sedona, Dieguito and I were sound asleep in the back of the car. Leticia carried the baby inside and when I opened my eyes, Max was trying to carry me out of the car. "You're so cute," I said. "You could just wake me."

"You are too beautiful when you sleep to disturb." He helped me out of the car and we started for the front door. My dad opened it and hugged me first and then Max. Hector was already in an embrace with Olivia inside the living room. My dad put his hand on my stomach. "Oh no… why didn't you tell me what that filthy dog did to my baby?"

"No, no, Mick. The baby's mine," Max confessed. "I hope you're okay with that."

"Are you sure?" he asked. "I mean, really sure?"

"I'm pretty sure that you don't want the details, so let me just say, yes I am very sure," Max answered. He hugged Max and kissed me and said, "I am so happy for you. What a wonderful day!"

"You don't mind that I'm having a baby with a man who I'm not married to?" I asked.

"This is just a temporary situation," my dad stated. "Right Max?"

"I'd marry her today if Diego wasn't an issue. Lilly is everything to me."

"I know that," my dad answered. "I'm just messing with you." He patted Max on the back. "I think I knew you were in love before you did."

"Not possible," he responded. "I fell in love with her from the first moment I met her."

"It's time to tell Olivia," Dad said. "She doesn't know." He looked at Max. "Does Lilly know?"

"We told her in the car," he answered. "The FBI in the parking lot tipped her off." He laughed.

"Are you angry, sweetheart?" he asked me.

"No, dad, I'm not angry." I thought about it for a minute. "Maybe at you for keeping this a secret for so many years."

"I know, I am truly sorry." He took my hands. "Keeping you safe has always been a priority." He sighed. "Then you got all mixed up with Johnny and here we all are."

"I'll take care of her, Mick." Max looked very sincere. "She'll be fine." We all sat down in the living room and Olivia looked at me curiously. "What's going on?" she asked. "What are you not telling me?"

Hector pulled out his badge and showed it to her. She got up and smacked him across the face. "How dare you!" she shouted. "How could you not tell me something so important? I had no idea you were having them all arrested."

"I knew bringing her here was a mistake," my dad added. "She's not on our side."

"You're damn right, I'm not," she answered. "I have to be loyal to my husband and Diego."

"What?" Hector asked. "Since when?"

"Since you threw them both in jail," she replied. "You had them arrested tonight, didn't you? It was you!"

Just then my dad's phone rang. He picked it up and went into the kitchen so he could be out of earshot. When he came back in, he sat down. Then Olivia's phone rang. "It's done?" Max asked him.

"Done," he repeated. "They are asking for their wives." My cell phone began to ring just after Olivia's.

"Don't answer it," Max told me. But Olivia picked up hers. She walked off with it but Hector followed her, to make sure she didn't give them up just yet. My phone rang and then beeped that there was a message. I looked at it as though it was going to burn me if I picked it up. "Go ahead," Max, said. "Check the message." I put the phone on speakerphone and hit messages. "Lilly," he said. "Someone ratted us out to the FBI and Jorge and I are in jail. I need you to call my lawyer. The number is in the top drawer by the coffee maker." He paused. "Make sure you call Max and Hector and let them know. All the leaders are in custody. It doesn't look good. I love you." Max closed the phone.

"They don't know what happened yet." He looked over as Hector and Olivia walked back into the room. "It's just a matter of time."

"She gave us up," Hector blurted. "She wants to leave."

"I'll call her a cab," my dad answered. "They were going to find out eventually. I was just hoping it wouldn't be from one of you."

"How could you, Lilly?" she asked me. "Diego is your husband."

"What about Hector?" I asked her. "Aren't you carrying his baby?"

Max and I sat on the couch together while my dad went to call a cab. Hector and Olivia were standing by the door face to face. "It's not even your baby, Hector."

"What?" he asked. "Of course it is." Max and I looked at each other in shock.

"No, it's not." she repeated. "I was hoping I wouldn't have to tell you."

"Was there someone else?" he asked.

"The baby belongs to Max," she answered.

Hector and I looked at him and my dad walked back into the room and said, "It better not be."

"It certainly is NOT!" Max spouted. "Olivia, why would you even say something like that? You and I have never slept together."

"Come on Max, it's time to come clean." She walked towards him and he quickly stood up and walked behind the couch away from her.

"That is not my baby." He looked at Hector. "Brother, you don't doubt me, do you?"

"No, I know you wouldn't…" he paused, "didn't." He stopped. "Olivia, what are you doing?"

"How does it feel to be lied to and betrayed?" She looked at me. "Now, you'll never be sure if I'm telling the truth or not, will you Lilly?"

"I'm sure," I answered. "You're a liar."

"Look, I don't do casual sex, you know that," Max blurted.

"What about Darla?" she asked. "That was pretty casual." He stepped back and swallowed hard as he looked at me for a reaction.

"That's why I don't have casual sex anymore," he said in a defeated tone.

"What's Lilly?" she asked.

"Everything," he replied. "She is my everything."

"The baby's Diego's," she sputtered, suddenly changing her story.

"Diego's?" Hector asked. Now we were all really confused.

"Diego's?" I asked. "When did he have time?"

"Doesn't feel good to be cheated on, does it little white girl." I was stunned. It was hard to watch her flip out like that. The cab came and she pushed Hector back. "Don't follow me, policeman. We're done!" She slapped him across the face a second time and walked out the door. Hector looked at Max and said, "What the hell was that?"

"I don't know," Max answered. "Maybe she is sleeping with Diego. I just don't know." We watched her from the window get into the cab and then we heard machine gun fire. Max grabbed me and threw me to the ground before he got on top of me and covered my face. My dad and Hector also hit the floor. When the shooting stopped Hector screamed out Olivia's name and ran out the door. "Hector, no!" Max shouted.

"I've got Lilly, you go after him," my dad demanded.

"No," Max said, "I'm not leaving her."

"She's my daughter, for God's sake, go after him!" My dad came over and sat on the couch beside where I was on the floor and Max went after his brother. "Stay down a little longer," he said. "I want to make sure it's over." We waited and then he picked me up and sat me on the couch. "Are you two all right?" he asked.

"Fine, dad, we're fine." After a few minutes Max walked back into the house covered in blood. His hands, his face and his shirt were saturated. It was obvious that he had been hugging his brother trying to get him out of the blood filled cab.

"She's gone," he said. "Olivia… the baby…" he paused, "my brother is holding her body… he's devastated."

"Lilly," my dad said. "Go clean him up."

"Yes sir," I answered.

"I'll go get your brother." He left us and walked out the door. I took Max into the kitchen and sat him on a stool. I grabbed a towel, wet it and started cleaning the blood off of his hands. Then I put it up to his face and cleaned the blood off of his cheek and forehead. I put the towel down and started unbuttoning his shirt. I pulled it off and started cleaning off his chest. He put my face into his hands and kissed me. I kissed him back and he pulled me close. I had never seen him like this before. I was afraid he was going to try to make love with me right there on the kitchen floor.

"Lilly," he said. "Show me your old bedroom."

"Now?" I asked in surprise.

"Right now," he said without hesitation. I took his hand and walked him to my bedroom. I could see a certain amount of vulnerability in his eyes. He walked me in and locked the door behind me. Then he wasted no time in getting my clothes off and making love to me. Every time I called out his name, he seemed more motivated to make me do it again. When the loving was over he collapsed beside me and we were both out of breath. "Are you all right?" I asked him.

"We just never know," he said, still trying to catch his breath, "how much time we have." He kissed me. "I wanted to make sure that I was with you… one more time."

I kissed him and pushed myself into his arms. "This was not the last time," I told him. "We will be forever." We held each other for a few minutes. I think this was the only time we made love in less than two hours.

He kissed me and pulled me up off of the bed. "I'm sorry it's so fast," he said. "But your dad will not be happy with me. Let's go check on Hector."

We walked out of the bedroom and my dad was just closing the bathroom door. We could hear the shower going, so we knew Hector was cleaning up.

"I apologize, sir," Max started. "I mean no disrespect to you or your daughter." My dad looked at him with a look of assurance. "I guess I just…" He stopped for a minute. "I think I just lost control."

My dad patted him on the back. "It's okay son." He shot him a smile. "I have lost control so many times." He took a few minutes to collect his thoughts. "I have come back from a job where someone was senselessly murdered and came home only to take Bobby into my arms and make love to her all night."

"Too much information!" I told him.

"Then hold your ears," he said to me. "Sometimes you think to yourself, 'how much time do I have left?' I get that."

"Thank you, sir," Max replied.

We heard the shower go off and my dad said, "Come on, let's get to the kitchen. I don't want him to feel self-conscious. Give him his privacy."

When Hector finally joined us, Max poured him bourbon and I wrapped my arms around his neck from behind. He grabbed my hands and said, "I'm sorry about that Lilly."

"Sorry about what?" I asked.

"You don't think he slept with her, do you? Because I really have no doubts."

"No, Hector, I know better," I assured him. "He loves me."

Hector turned around and kissed my cheek. "I wish we had what you do. But now I'm not sure what we had."

"I am so sorry about the baby," I told him.

"Yeah, me too," he said. "I'm not even sure it was mine."

"They will check the DNA when they examine her," my dad reminded him. "We need to know who might have put the hit out… Diego or Jorge."

"Isn't it the same thing?" I asked.

"Well," dad said. "I'm not sure anymore. What if Olivia and Diego were lovers? Isn't this going to affect his relationship with his brother?"

"It would affect mine," Max added. Hector laughed.

"Maybe Jorge put the hit out on Olivia, thinking the baby was Hector's. Obviously she didn't know you were having them both arrested."

"I should've told her what was going on," Hector said in retrospect.

"No, you shouldn't have even brought her here," my dad reiterated. "Just think about what would have happened if you told her the truth. One or all of you would be dead."

"I need to know," Hector said. "I really need to know."

I'll call and put a rush on the results," dad said. "Maybe we'll know in a few days."

My phone rang just after that. It was an unknown number from Las Vegas. "I think it's the jail," I told them. "What should I do?"

"Go ahead," dad said. "See what he wants." I picked it up and said, "Hello?"

"Put me on speakerphone, baby," was all I heard. I hit speakerphone and put the phone down on the kitchen table. "Max, you're looking good these days." It was definitely Diego. "Lilly, I always thought you looked lovely in white." Max began to look around. He and Hector started checking the furniture for bugs or cameras. "My beautiful Olivia did a very thorough job. You will never find them all. I even planted some in Lilly's bedroom."

I sat down and covered my face. "Diego that is disgusting, even for you."

"I see the two of you couldn't keep your hands off each other long enough to peel Hector away from his dead mistress." Max grabbed my hand. And stood in front of me.

"I think it's sweet Max, that you are still so protective of my wife. But don't worry; there are no guns. I want the baby alive and well when I take it from you."

"Olivia planted the bugs?" Hector asked. "How'd you pull that off?"

"I discovered that she was going out there to be with you. I chose not to tell Jorge if she would choose to plant the cameras."

"Were you sleeping with her?" Max asked.

"Were you?" Diego asked.

"No," he answered calmly. "Were you lovers, Diego?"

"I hear the baby may have been mine," Diego continued. "That was an unfortunate consequence."

"I have to know, Diego," Hector asked. "Did you take it from her or did she give it to you?"

"She gave it to me whenever I asked for it. She was most generous," he continued. "I did not order the hit and we both assumed the baby was yours."

"Great job," Hector said sarcastically.

"I guess that makes you brother number three," Diego said, laughing like a mad man. "I won't let Lilly go, so please return her intact. Oh and keep your hands off her."

"I'll never go back to you, you bastard!" I screamed.

"Sure you will," he replied. "When I kill your lover and steal your baby, you'll be begging me to take you back. Begging…"

"Diego?" Max asked calmly. "Where are you?"

"Right where you left me, bro." He paused. "I can kill you from here, but I won't. Not yet."

"Still in prison, making a phone call and watching us on camera… I don't believe you."

"I'm a powerful man, mi hermano. Jorge is even more powerful than I."

"Just go away and leave us alone," I cried.

"Now what fun would that be?" he continued. "I think I may play with my little brother for a little while longer and then… I'll come back for you. Don't we all tell you that, Lilly? We'll come back for you?" I lost all feeling in my legs; I could not stand or breathe. "Aren't you our Easter Lilly?" Max looked at me for a reaction. "You still belong to me," he continued. "Oh and Hector… watch your back." Then he hung up the phone.

"What the hell was that?" Max asked. "Olivia, cameras, death threats… I think he's finally gone mad."

"I'm scared, Max. What are we going to do?" My hands were shaking and tears were falling out of my eyes. Hector came up behind me and hugged me. "We are the best there is, he doesn't stand a chance." Max and my dad had their heads together in the corner.

"What about Olivia?" I asked. "That could have easily been me!"

"She didn't listen to me," he answered. "If she had just listened to me and stayed here, she would still be alive."

"Oh crap," he said. "Guys!" He called to my dad and Max. "We need to sweep the house for bugs." They turned and looked at him. "Seriously Mick, we need to do it now."

"You're right," he agreed. Then my dad took his cell phone and walked out the door making the call. Max walked over to me and picked me up off of the chair so that I was standing in front of him. "Do you trust me querida?"

"Of course I do," I answered.

"We will keep you safe," he replied. "Do you believe me?"

My knees were weak. All he had to do was touch me and I was useless. He put his lips against mine and I let out a moan. "Gross!" Hector said as he walked out of the kitchen. We stood in there kissing until my dad came back into the room.

"Trying to piss him off?" dad asked.

"Maybe," Max answered. "Maybe he should get what he pays for."

My dad made a face. "Maybe you two should stay apart until we sweep the house," he suggested. Max laughed.

"I'm not going to let him see her, don't worry. We waited almost four years, we can wait a few more days." He kissed me. "Kissing is allowed though, right?" Max laughed, knowing very well the answer to that question. His smile could light up a room.

"Kissing is fine if you must," he answered. "But seriously, try to refrain." Hector walked back in. "When will they be here?" he asked.

"In a few hours," dad replied.

"Thank goodness," I said, unaware that I said it out loud. Max gave me a knowing look of why I wanted those bugs cleared.

"In the meantime," Hector said. "Let's go out for a while."

"Aren't you afraid someone will come after us out in public like that?" I asked.

"Lilly," Hector smiled. "You're with Max and me. Even with four FBI agents standing behind us at the restaurant, you wouldn't be safer than with the two of us."

"Especially me," Max added.

"If he doesn't say so himself," Hector replied.

"I'm a sharp shooter," Max reminded me. I remembered all the times I had seen Max and Hector decimate gunmen before. "I have uncanny reaction time."

"He means no reaction time," Hector corrected him. "You know when you watch TV and some guy grabs and girl and puts a gun to her temple?"

"Yeah," I answered, waiting in anticipation.

"All the people in the room hand over their guns in fear that he will shoot her." He took a breath. "Then the crazy guy makes off with the girl?"

"Yes, of course," I answered.

"Max is the guy who blows his head off before he actually has the girl."

"Thanks for the mental image," I replied. It was actually a little disturbing.

"Hector's the guy who sweeps the cars and defuses the bombs," Max added. "But don't sell him short. Hector is an amazing sharp shooter too. I have never met anyone better than we are."

"Long story short," my dad interrupted. "These egomaniacs are very good at what they do. You will be very well protected."

I grabbed my purse and dad took us out for dinner. It was nice to feel safe, even if it was only for a few minutes.

CHAPTER 19

"Right," Max said. "Focus…"

"I'm just going to say what everyone is thinking," Hector said. "How do we know for sure that it's really your baby in there?" He looked at Max.

"Not in front of her father," Max answered.

"Hector's right," dad said. "We should get a test done or something."

"I'm sure it's Max's baby. I'm sure!" I was starting to get a little mad.

"How can you be sure?" dad asked. "I don't mean to hit on delicate territory but weren't you with both men continuously?"

"Oh God," I said, turning different colors of purple. "I can't have this conversation with you."

"I can," Max, said. "Are you sure you want details, Mick?"

"Yes, I'm sure," he said. "Wait, I don't know." He stopped again. "Keep it simple," he finally concluded.

I sat there looking at Max but he was just having way too much fun with this. "Lilly and I waited… almost four years," he said. "Really, no kidding."

"That's a long time, Max." he replied.

"One day Diego made this huge speech about how he wasn't going to force himself on her anymore and that they were going to make a baby together." My dad made a face and put his head into his hands.

"At that point I realized that I had waited too long. She might fall in love with him and I had never…." He stopped. "Well… you know," he continued.

"Get to the point," dad said, obviously embarrassed.

"I hadn't been with a woman since I met your beautiful daughter," he went on. "So, I knew I would get her pregnant right away. After that day, he didn't touch her for a little over three weeks."

"Did you use protection?" he whispered.

"Mick it was either his baby or mine… be happy she chose me or things would be much worse."

"Okay," he said. "Go on…"

"He slept with her the day they were both shot. You remember; I called you?"

"Of course," he answered.

"The doctor discovered at that time that she was three weeks pregnant. Sorry you asked?" he said with a chuckle.

"A little," he answered. "But what about the times Diego and she were together before that day?"

"We always used protection," I said.

"Still, Lilly, there is no guarantee." I started to realize that he might be right. Max sensed my panic and grabbed my hand. "Even if it isn't mine, which it is." He looked over at my dad, and then he looked back at me. "I will love it and care for it as though it were my own." Tears formed in my eyes.

"That is so sweet," Hector said, pretending to cry.

"Shut up," I blurted, hitting him in the arm.

"Anyway, test… soon…." Hector said. "Okay Max?"

"I'll call the doctor tomorrow," dad agreed. "Both of you go with her and Max do not leave her side." He looked at me. "Even during the test, he stays."

"Yes, sir." I answered.

"I need to know how you got her to say 'sir' when you give her an order," my dad asked laughing. "Good job, boys." I was so embarrassed. But I was also very nervous. What if we were wrong and I was already pregnant when I slept with Max. I couldn't think about that now. We were out and having fun and I didn't want to ruin it. Besides as soon as we got back to the house, we would have to make sure there were no more bugs or cameras. I was very nervous about that too.

When we got home the FBI was not there yet. We went inside and my dad said, "Just keep it casual until the house is clean." Max grabbed me and kissed me. "You've got to stop that, he's just going to get angrier."

"I don't care," he said. "He wanted to watch, let him watch." He put his arms around me and looked into my eyes. "You are my whole world," he whispered. Just then the TV popped on and Diego's face was looking at us. I screamed and Max looked at my dad for some kind of confirmation.

"What exactly is happening here?" Hector yelled.

"Hi boys," he said. "Lilly, you're looking lovely."

"How did you do that?" Max asked. "Diego what's going on?"

"Keep your hands off of my wife," he said. "You're just making it worse for yourself."

"Mick, what is this?" Max asked again. "You can't possibly see us through the TV."

"Cameras, cameras everywhere," he laughed. "You have to wonder Max, don't you?"

"What?" he asked.

"Maybe Hector's a traitor. Maybe it's Mick. Maybe Olivia wasn't acting alone." The men all looked at each other. "Maybe Max is the one on the wrong side." Max went to the Television and tried to turn it off but nothing happened. Then he unplugged it. Diego's face was gone and we were sitting in a sea of doubt. My dad motioned for us all to go outside. Max took my hand and the four of us went to the end of the driveway.

"Come on boys," dad said. "We can't let him do this to us."

"Mick is right," Max said to Hector. "We need to stick together."

The FBI arrived and swept the house for bugs, cameras and anything else that might have been planted illegally. We were pretty sure we were secure. We went to bed that night a little weary but Max and Hector re-checked the house after they left and found nothing. When we got into bed, Max was all excited. "I can't believe we are finally alone," he started. He began to kiss me and I melted into him like ice to fire. Then my TV popped on and I jumped. Max looked up, covered me up and said, "Diego, cut it out, man."

"Haven't you learned that I am everywhere?" and his face went black. Max got up, put his clothes back on and started searching the room. He found a bug that he had never seen before just over my bed. "Oh God!" I said. "How humiliating."

"It's Okay," Max assured me. I'm going to put it in the kitchen with a note on it for Mick. We need to check this out." He dropped it off in the kitchen and came back to check the rest of the room. "I'm sorry, baby, but I need to wake Hector so we can re-check."

I got dressed and the two of them went through the room with a fine toothcomb. "It looks like that was it," Hector told us.

"Thanks, bud, I appreciate it."

"You two need to chill for a few days." Hector laughed.

"I can't leave her alone," he said. "I just can't."

Hector laughed and said, "Goodnight, Lilly." We slept in each other's arms and quietly made love under the covers.

In the morning we went into the kitchen and the bug was gone. "Did you see the bug?" Max asked my dad.

"What bug?" he answered.

Hector and Max looked at each other in disbelief. "So, someone was here last night and …" Max paused, "stole it?"

"What are you talking about?" dad asked.

"I found a bug," Max said. "It was strange looking. I left it for you, right here on the table."

"I didn't see it," he answered. Then he handed Max directions to the doctor's office. "Leave them a DNA sample so they can match yours with the baby's."

Max and Hector walked out with me and we got into the car to go to the hospital. "What do you think, Max?" Hector asked.

"I think he's still controlling him," Max answered. "Lilly, I need you to make sure your dad does not find out the results of the test."

"Yes sir," I answered. "You want him to think the baby is Diego's. Why?"

"You're not supposed to ask why?" Max said laughing. "You're just supposed to say, 'Yes sir.'" He and Hector both continued laughing.

"Max, you don't think it's my dad?"

"Let's get the test done and worry about the rest later," he said, getting a little more serious. "Promise me Lilly, you'll make sure Mick's name isn't on the chart."

"I promise," I replied. "Max, why does he need to think you're not the father?"

"Your being pregnant with Diego's baby is what will keep you alive, for now."

We got to the hospital and Max came with me into the exam room. The nurse put an ultrasound on my belly and we could see the baby moving around. "You're about four months along, now." She said. Max took my hand. "Would you like to know the sex?" she asked.

"I think I see the sex," Max answered. She laughed. "It's a boy!"

I could see how proud Max was. She stuck the needle in my belly and took out the fluid. "How long for the results?" Max asked.

"A few days," she answered. He pulled out his ID and said, "How about a few hours?"

This startled her. "Yes, sir, a few hours." Then she picked up the file. "I have here Mick O'Hara is the contact."

"Please erase that," I asked. "Now," I said, a little louder. She erased it looking at us like we were out of our minds. "I will put you down, Mrs. Montiago, as the only contact."

"Thank you," I added. "Please get his DNA and compare it to the baby's." She looked at us in a disapproving fashion.

"I know how this looks," Max started. "But her husband is a very dangerous man and he cannot find out that I might be the father."

She paused for a second. "Wait a minute…" She looked us both up and down. "Aren't you the wife of that Diego Montiago who was arrested in Las Vegas last week?"

"That's me," I answered.

"He's a hottie!" she sputtered.

"Yeah, we'll call him that," I said sarcastically.

"Are you saying he's better looking than I am?" Max asked, being his humorous, little self.

"You are both very handsome," she answered. "You're a lucky girl."

"Not so lucky," I said. "He'll kill us both if the information leaks, so please…" I didn't say any more. She smiled. She swabbed the inside of his mouth and put it in a baggie.

"I will rush the results. You can wait or go out for a bit."

"We're not going anywhere until the results are back," he told her. We went out to the waiting room and Max asked Hector if he checked on the paternity of Olivia's baby.

"You know," he said. "I need to do that."

We went to the desk and he asked for the results. "I'm sorry," she said. "It is an FBI investigation and I can't give out the results." Hector and Max pulled out their ID's.

"Oh, I apologize," she said. "I'll go get the file."

"I love doing that," Max started.

The nurse came back and said, "I'm sorry sir, but you are not the father."

Hector looked at Max. "I will take a DNA test right now if you are doubting me," Max told him.

"Don't be silly," he said. "I know you'd never sleep with her."

"Then what?" he asked.

"Who is?" he asked. "It's not Jorge, it's not me, it's not you…" They looked at each other. "Lilly?" Max asked. "Do you have anything with you that might have Diego's DNA on it?"

"Why would I have taken anything like that with me?" I asked.

"I'm going to call Miguel," Max decided. "He can get his hair brush or toothbrush or something from the house and mail it to me."

"Keep the file open until further notice," Hector ordered.

"Yes sir," she giggled. "Is there anything else that I can do for you?" Hector smiled a flirty smile at her. "No thanks," he answered. "But I'll let you know if I change my mind." She brushed against him as she disappeared down the hallway. Hector watched her walk away.

"Easy boy," Max jested. "Remember, stay focused."

"You're seriously talking about staying focused?" he asked.

"Yeah okay, you're right," he agreed. They were a charming pair, those two.

We waited for the amnio results impatiently, but Max was too afraid that someone might tamper with the test, so we stayed until she finally came to us with the test results. I held my breath as she approached. "I would like to talk privately if that's all right?" she asked us. The three of us followed her into an exam room.

"I'm not sure if this is good news or not, but I'm afraid you are without a doubt, the father of her baby." I jumped in the air and threw my arms around him. I couldn't stop crying. "Good news?" she asked.

"The best," Max answered. "Please remember this has to stay confidential." Hector patted Max on the back. "Congratulations, man."

"It's a boy," Max said. "We're having a boy!"

"You guys are going to have to look sadder than that if you're going to fool Mick."

"Thank you," I said to the nurse, and she left.

CHAPTER 20

He had zero reaction time

"Why are we hiding this from my dad?" I asked. "I'm telling you, he is not working with my husband." They stayed quiet. "Max?" I asked.

"Well, it's not one of us," Max assured me.

I looked at Hector. "Oh… that hurts, Lilly." He put his hand over his heart like he was wounded.

"It's not Hector," Max said. "I think your dad is a reluctant traitor."

"He would never put a camera in my bedroom," I said, defending him. "He is my father, after all."

"He might if Diego was still using you as a bargaining chip," Max answered. "You know he has been working Mick for years."

I looked at him in disbelief. "I simply do not buy that he would hurt us like that."

"Lilly…" Max looked at Hector with a questioning gaze.

"You'd better tell her, Max," Hector added.

"Diego married you to use you as leverage with your dad. He continued to allow drug trafficking as long as you lived a prominent life style and stayed…well… breathing."

"You knew about this the whole time, didn't you?" I asked.

"I'm sorry, but yes. That's why I was not afraid to get close to you. I knew that was not his initial goal." He pulled me close. "The more I tell you, the less you trust me, no?"

"I trust you. I know you didn't want me to have to lie for you. I still love you."

"Just tell him the baby's Diego's. We can tell the truth when the baby is born." He took my hand. "I want you alive, baby girl."

"I will obey, as always," I said. "I am getting tired of being the obedient mistress." I crossed my arms and turned away.

"You were never my mistress," he added. "You were always the love of my life."

"I'll say the baby is his, but I hate it."

"I'm sorry, Lilly. When this is all over, you won't have to 'obey' me anymore, okay? Just right now it is important that you let me keep your heart beating." He put his hand over my heart and Hector looked away.

"You two really need a room," he added.

"Sorry," Max responded. "I'm a little giddy." He and Hector high fived each other.

"A boy," Max said. "I can't believe it."

"It's not over, Max." Hector reminded us. "We have to put Diego and Jorge in jail. We need to make this happen before she delivers."

"Right," Max said. "Focus…"

We went home and dad was waiting for us. "Are you all right, baby?"

"Fine daddy," I answered.

"How long until the results come in?" he asked.

"A day or so," Max quickly answered. "We're excited."

"I'm glad it's done." He walked away and Max and Hector looked at each other with that mischievous glance they get before they are going to do something bad. Max walked outside the kitchen and looked around. Then the two of them started feeling around for cameras and bugs and it took them no time to find the first camera. Max stepped on it and it broke into pieces on the floor. I put my hands over my mouth in shock. It had to be my dad. There was no one else. Or was there?

We walked outside to the end of the driveway. "I told you," Max started.

"What about Leticia?" I asked. "It could be her, you know. Diego is handsome and she's the right age."

"Did you hear that little brother?" Hector said laughing. "Your woman thinks Diego's handsome."

"How handsome?" Max asked me.

"Would you two cut it out!" I yelled. "Seriously, what about Leticia?"

"That is something to be considered," Hector agreed.

"Okay, we need a plan." Max responded. "I'll start following her around," Max said and looked at me for a reaction.

"How about Hector takes Leticia and you take my dad."

"I'm just kidding, querida," he said smiling. "Yes, that's what we'll do."

"I won't mind following her around," Hector added. "How focused do I need to be?"

"I'm going to kill you both myself," I scolded. "Now get serious and find the leak."

"Yes, ma'am," they both said simultaneously and saluted me. I could see my dad from the front door. He walked out to us. "What are we doing outside?" he asked. "I had the house swept, it's clean."

"You can never be too careful," Max answered.

"What are you talking about that is so private?" he asked.

"Lilly's amnio," Max answered. "She's a little anxious."

"They should call me with the results as soon as they're in," dad said. "It'll be a relief, Lilly, really."

"I asked them to call me, dad. I'll let you know when they do." He didn't like that. His face turned cold when he heard that he was not in control of my results and I began to think that the boys were right.

"I'm going to Las Vegas tomorrow to find out why Diego is wandering around like a free man out there," dad revealed. "You'll call with the results?"

"Of course, daddy," I said and I kissed him on the cheek. We went back inside but were weary of our conversations. Max and Hector spotted bugs all over the house so we knew it was one of them.

After he left in the morning Hector and Max swept the house again. Hector said he didn't see anything unusual about Leticia. I think they were convinced it was my father.

"Go ahead and call him with the results," Max suggested. "Let him tell Diego while he's there."

I called my dad and gave him the news. "You were right, daddy. I was already pregnant when I slept with Max."

"The baby's Diego's then?" he asked. "You're sure?"

"Yes," I answered, trying to sound like I was crying.

"Did he leave you?" he asked.

"No, daddy, he knows and he's still here."

"Good man," he continued. "You're very lucky."

"I know," I said. "I know."

"When are you coming home?" I asked.

"Soon," he answered. "I'll let you know." He was quiet for a minute. "I'm sorry, baby." He hung up.

Max came in with the mail. "It's here. Diego's DNA is in my hands."

"Let's go," Hector started.

"He asked me if you left me," I said, a little surprised.

"I would never do that. I told you, baby girl," he answered.

"You're sure we're doing the right thing?"

"Very sure," he told me. Leticia came into the living room with the baby. "Max we need to talk for a minute."

"Go ahead," he answered. "I have time."

"Can you come with me for a minute?" she asked.

"Okay," he answered reluctantly. "Are you sure you don't want Hector?" he asked as he winked in my direction.

"Very sure," she answered. "I have to show you something."

She and Max walked down the hall and left little Diego with Hector and me. "I'm going to put him to bed," I said. "He looks tired."

I left Hector and laid Dieguito down in his bed. He grabbed his teddy bear and drifted right off to sleep. I came back out and Hector was looking out the window. "Lilly," he whispered. "Come to me." I recognized the tone. It was urgency. I walked to him and he hugged me. "How long has he been in there?"

"Too long," I answered.

"Stay close," he continued. He pulled his gun and looked out the window while hiding behind the wall. "Did you hear that?" he asked. I didn't hear anything but he was definitely scaring me. "Max!" he shouted. "Max, get out here!" Max came running down the hall with his gun drawn.

"Did you hear that?" Max asked.

"Yes, what the hell were you two doing?" Hector asked.

"I can't help that I am devastatingly handsome," he answered.

"We were set up," Hector said. "Whoever set this up, thinks Lilly and I are alone in here and you are…" He paused. "Naked."

"Funny," Max replied.

"Seriously," Hector went on. "What the hell were you doing in there?"

"I was peeling her off of me," he answered.

"I knew you were in there too long." They were both checking out the house.

"She was trying to handcuff me to…" He stopped and glanced at me. "Something in there so that I wouldn't be able to come back out. She was definitely trying to keep me out of the living room."

"Handcuff you to the…" Hector laughed. "To the what?"

Max looked at me again. "To the bedpost," he admitted. "Yeah, go ahead and laugh."

"I can't believe she chose you over me. I'm the pretty one," Hector teased.

"You idiot," Max said laughing. "You know they're going to try to grab Lilly." I was so scared; I couldn't believe how they were making jokes.

I heard a gun cock and someone came behind me and grabbed my neck. That, however, was not the scary part. I was right behind Max, as I always was when there was danger. He had zero reaction time. With one hand he pushed her gun in the air and with the other he shot her in the head. She fell to the ground behind me and I was covered with blood. We turned when we heard a shot and Hector fell against the wall. Max picked up Leticia's gun and began to shoot at the men with both guns. I had never seen anything like this except for in the movies but Hector got up. He grabbed his gun and started shooting like nothing had happened. There were five men and Leticia and they were all down. "My baby!" I screamed and little Diego came running down the hall crying. I grabbed him and hugged him. Max was checking the men to make sure they were all dead or unarmed. "Max, your brother."

He ran to Hector and Hector said, "I'm fine Max, really." Max grabbed his hand and picked him up while I called 911. "Uncle Max… Uncle Max…" Dieguito called. Max went to him and sat him on the couch. "Do not move, little man, you hear me?"

"Yes sir!" he said, proud to be part of the group. I ran to Hector and started unbuttoning his shirt. When I opened it, I must have made a face. Max said to me, "Watch it now, he's my brother remember."

"She thinks I'm pretty," Hector said laughing.

"Prettier than me?" he asked me.

"Of course not," I answered. Then I winked at Hector.

"Knock it off, you two."

"He's getting suspicious, Lilly, tone it down," Hector jested.

"How do you two joke at times like these?" I asked.

"Who's joking?" Hector answered.

"If I wasn't trying to save your life right now, I'd smack you." Max reached into his wallet and pulled out a credit card. He pressed it against Hector and Hector let out a yell. "Now she thinks you're pretty, and a girl," Max said laughing.

"You know I'm too stubborn to die," he reminded him. "I can't leave you alone."

"You're not going anywhere," Max replied. We heard the sirens. "Stay with me, man." Max said. Hector starting coughing up blood and Max started to panic.

The person in charge of the FBI came inside; they called him Luke. He walked over to Max and said, "So, Mick's dirty?"

"Yeah," Max told him. "I think Diego has something on him. I don't think it's malicious intent." He never took his eyes off of Hector as the paramedics began to take care of him.

"Would you like to hang around and watch the shop for me?" he asked.

"You mean run the police department?" Max asked.

"I need FBI on it," he continued. "Come on, Max. Help me out with this."

"We're going home as soon as Hector's okay," he told him.

They finally got him ready to take to the hospital. There were FBI and police in our living room when someone ran in and said, "Luke, turn on the TV. Channel 8." We turned it on.

"Diego and Jorge Montiago have escaped the federal penitentiary in Nevada," the broadcaster said. "It is believed that Michael O'Hara, chief of police in Sedona, Arizona is responsible for signing them out illegally."

Max sat down on the couch like the wind had just been knocked out of him. He looked at me and grabbed my hand. I sat beside him.

"What do you say, Max?" Luke asked.

"Yeah, why not," he agreed. "I'll stick around. I'm not taking her back there with those madmen running around loose."

"We are going to hide you in plain sight," Luke continued.

"How's that?"

"We found you a three bedroom house in the city. Right in the middle of everything."

"Okay," Max agreed. "Less hiding in the trees, I suppose."

"Unless you are sick of Hector already," Luke suggested.

"No, we need him," Max said. "I need him."

Max got up and grabbed an envelope that was sent by Miguel in Las Vegas and said, "Look, I'll answer all your questions but please let me go be with Hector."

"Go," he said. "Then you can tell me how Leticia got that big hole in her head."

Max paused. "Where's her purse?"

Luke reached down onto the floor and handed it to Max. He opened it and pulled out a bunch of ID's and passports. "Lilly would have been Amelia Montiago." He looked at me with sadness in his eyes.

"They would have killed you after the baby was born," he surmised. "Giving you my dead mother's identification was a message to me."

He opened the next one. "So, Diego was Max and Jorge was Hector." Max looked at Luke. "They were going to take her and leave the country."

We need to find them," Luke exclaimed. "Go to your brother. I'll be by later to check on him and give you your new address and keys."

"Thanks, Luke," was all he offered. We ran at high speed out the door and Max put a police light on his car as we sped to the hospital. He got to the desk and said, "I need to talk to someone about the Olivia Montiago case." He flashed his badge and she asked, "What do you need?"

"Please do a DNA check on this guy," he told her. Compare it with the baby's DNA. All the information is in the envelope."

"Yes, sir," she answered. "I'll take care of it personally." She brushed up against him as she walked away.

Max smiled at me. "Don't worry, baby." He kissed my hands. "I only have eyes for you." Then we asked about Hector and they said they were prepping him for surgery. "I need to see him," he insisted.

"Come with me, sir." She led us down the hall.

We went to his room and he was lying in a bed with an oxygen mask on. "Hey, bro," Max started. "We'll be waiting for you, so hold on for me."

"Listen up, Hector," I said. "You can't take a bullet for me and not let me pay you back."

He lifted up his oxygen mask and said, "I want you to care for me when I am well."

"I will, I promise," I told him. Max looked at us uncomfortably. "Reach down inside, Hector. Max would be lost without you."

"And I without him," he assured me. They wheeled him off and Max hugged me as tears fell from his eyes.

"He'll be okay, Max, I promise," I said, hoping I could keep that promise. Hector looked bad. We sat in the waiting room for what felt like forever. "Mr. Montiago?" A nurse came to us from down the hall.

"Yes," he answered.

"I have the DNA results." She handed the file to Max. He looked up at me. "How is this possible?"

"What? Who's the father?"

"I can't believe it," he continued. "How did he sleep with her and keep you so busy?" he asked. "What a damn pig!"

"No!" I said. "Diego is the father?"

"I'm going to start calling him superman," he said. "How is this possible?"

I sat down in shock. "I think I hate him even more."

"It may have been a onetime thing," he suggested. "But there is no doubt… he's the dad." He handed her back the file and thanked her. She flirted with him a bit and walked off. He grabbed me and pulled me close. "I'm sorry, baby girl."

"For what?" I asked.

"That this business has swallowed you up," he continued. "My brother cheated on you while keeping you from me."

"I guess so," I answered. I was still trying to wrap my mind around the whole thing.

"I am forever yours," he said. "Forever." He hugged me tightly. "I think he loved you as much as he was capable of loving anyone."

"I wouldn't call that love," I replied. "Definitely not love."

A nurse came out of the operating room, "Maxwell Montiago?"

"That's me," he answered. "Hector?"

"He is a strong man," she told him. "No complications, he will be fine." Max let out a sigh and hugged me. "Oh thank God!" He started talking in Spanish and looking up at the ceiling. "When can I see him?"

"He'll be in recovery for about two hours," she answered. "Why don't you go home and I'll call you."

"I can't leave," he answered. "We'll be in the hospital." He wrote his cell phone number down on the file. "Please call me when I can see him." She smiled and agreed.

"It's funny how you are acting with Hector right now."

"What about it?" He looked surprised.

"Diego did just the same with you." He looked away.

"Maybe he just had a good day. I was lying in bed with holes in my chest, after all."

"It wasn't like that." I walked around him so that he was looking at me. "He was reading a Bible."

"He was not!" he said in disbelief.

"I'm not kidding, a Bible."

"He must have misplaced it," he said. He looked down at his watch.

"You are all strong," I said, trying to be reassuring. "He'll be fine."

"Thank God," he replied. "I don't know what I'd do without him." Then his face changed and I could see worry in his expression. "Although not happy about the closeness you two seem to have."

"You're not serious."

"I know he wouldn't pursue you on purpose," he added. "But what if he falls in love with you, like I did?"

"Max…" I grabbed his hand and put it on my stomach. "We're having a baby. He smiled. "Hector is totally not attracted to me. He's just being silly like you are and milking the fact that I…" I paused. "That I may have noticed the eight pack on his stomach."

"See," Max said. "You even remember it was an eight pack."

"You've got one too," I reminded him. "A better one." He smiled and kissed me.

"Mine is only a six," he said in a sad, silly voice. "I'm being stupid, aren't I?"

"A little," I answered. "He's just trying to embarrass me. He seems to get a kick out of that."

"I know," he added. "It's part of our charm."

"Let him have fun with it," I said. "His girl was just murdered and he is about to find out that Diego slept with her. I promise, Max, I saved the best for last."

"So, you don't wonder about him?" he asked.

"I wonder about how his mind works sometimes, but never his body," I lied. I felt a little guilty saying that to him. There were many times when I had admired him from afar. There was even that one time when he wasn't too far at all.

"It's just that…" He took a deep breath. "When we kid like that, we are putting it out there."

"Putting it out there?" I repeated. I really wasn't sure what he meant.

"Testing the waters." He looked pensive for a moment. "Sometimes I think he just wants to see how you will react."

"I am absolutely sure you are misreading him," I answered. "There is no sexual attraction there. We are brother and sister in the purest sense."

He seemed satisfied with my answer. We waited for Hector as the news played in the background about the disappearance of the Montiagos and my dad. The whole hospital staff was eying us. Finally the nurse came and said, "He hasn't awakened from the anesthesia yet."

"What does that mean?" Max asked.

"He needs to wake up within the next 24 hours." Her face looked grave.

"Or what?" Max asked again. He was beginning to get impatient.

"Or he may slip into a comma." She paused. "He had serious internal injuries but he is strong."

"Can we see him?" he asked.

"Yes, but you can't bring the little boy with you," she told us.

"I'll watch him," a young nurse said to us. "He looks just like you," she said to Max. We smiled at each other.

"Thanks," he said, flirting with her a little. "You're very kind." We went to see him.

He looked very pale. We went to his bedside. Max sat in a chair by his bed and put his face in his hands. I was stroking Hector's hair. His body felt warm.

"I'm afraid visiting hours will be over in an hour." The nurse was walking around Hector hooking fluids up to him. "You will have to leave soon."

"I'm not leaving," he said. He opened his wallet and showed her his ID. "I have to stay with him and make sure someone doesn't show up to finish the job."

"Is this your wife?" she asked.

"Yes," he answered. She did not believe him.

"May I see your identification please?" I showed her my wallet. We had the same last name but she was still not convinced. "Wait a minute." She looked me over carefully. "Aren't you Diego Montiago's wife?"

"She's my wife," Max insisted. "She can sleep on the recliner and I will sleep in the chair. The little boy in the hall will have to stay with us."

"That will be fine," she said, walking off in a huff.

Little Diego slept beside me all night and when we awoke, Max was sitting beside Hector again. The news was on, playing softly in the background. I carefully slipped little Diego off of me and left him on the chair as I headed for Hector and Max. I stroked his hair again and watched Max's desperate face gradually lose hope. Before too long I noticed something different about Maxwell… he was… crying. I had never actually seen him lose control before. "Max," I said soothingly. I put my arms around him from behind his chair and touched my cheek to his. "He's going to be all right. It's Hector we're talking about."

"Now who looks like a girl…?" we heard a voice say. When we looked up it was Hector. "And Lilly, can you keep doing that thing you were doing with your hand? It really felt nice."

Max went to hug him but stopped himself. "Can I hug you or are you too fragile?"

"You'd better hug me after all those tears I saw." Max hugged him and got up quickly. He turned his face away from us as he started drying his eyes. I pushed the "call nurse" button. Max turned back around. "How long were you awake, Hector?" I asked.

"Your fingers on my hair just felt so good. So warm." He smiled. I think he was serious.

"Save your strength, Romeo," I said. "The nurse will be here in a second."

Two nurses came running in. "Hector, it seems that you have finally decided to grace us with your presence."

"I love this place," he said to Max, who had finally sufficiently regained control of himself.

"Mr. Montiago!" The younger, pretty nurse yelled. "I would appreciate it if you would keep your hands to yourself and concentrate on getting better."

"Hector, behave yourself!" Max said in disapproval.

"I'm sorry," he said. "But it's been a really long time."

"I apologize for my brother's behavior," Max added.

"Mrs. Montiago, are you going to be staying tonight too?"

"Oh no," Hector said. "She's not my Mrs. Montiago. She belongs to him." He pointed at Max and Max laughed as he hugged me.

"Thank God," I answered.

"I'm very single," he continued.

The pretty nurse looked at him and said sarcastically, "I can't imagine why."

"Seriously," Hector said. "I apologize for my behavior. I will be good." Both nurses left the room.

"Max, we need to talk." His face got suddenly grave.

"We'll talk tomorrow, Hector, right now you need to heal for me." Max pulled up a chair and motioned for me to sit down beside his bed.

"Diego, and Jorge… the news," he blurted, a little more seriously. "We have to go find them."

"NO!" I said. "Absolutely not!"

"Hector, tomorrow," Max repeated.

"We'll leave her with Johnny," Hector said.

"I don't think so, Max," I said. "We need to talk."

"We can find them," Hector continued. "Before they get to her."

Max took his hand. "I love you, hermano," he said. "Get well and we will talk tomorrow, I promise."

"We can find them," Hector repeated.

"How do you feel?" I asked, desperately trying to change the subject. I stroked his hair back again trying to calm him. He closed his eyes in pleasure.

"I feel great, now that you're here." He smiled and lifted his hand to my face. "I'll try to keep my shirt on from now on." I pulled my face away and Max laughed.

"Don't push your luck," Max said.

"Don't worry, Hector," I warned. "Max has already made me forget." Max grabbed my hand and squeezed it. "We'll sit with you for a while. Just rest for now." He closed his eyes and Max and I sat on a small couch on the side of the room.

"He's right, you know," Max reminded me. "We have to find them."

"No, you are not leaving me again."

"I will give John and call," he said.

"Are you forgetting that he tried to rape me the last time I saw him?" I asked.

"He's on a different page now," Max answered. "Besides he is heavily monitored by FBI so he doesn't mysteriously disappear."

"No, you can't leave me with him," I argued. "You're worried about Hector but not Johnny?" I asked.

"Nope, not Johnny," he answered. I made a face.

"Too late, baby girl, your secret about his… abilities is out."

"Aren't you worried that he might fall back in love with me?" I asked.

"Of course," he answered. "Am I worried that you will fall back in love with him? Not so much."

"I see I shouldn't have given you so much information."

"You'll be perfectly safe with him. He knows how to use a gun and he still cares for you," he continued.

"I can't believe you would leave me alone with my first lover," I said again in surprise. "How can you do that with such confidence?"

"Well," he said. "Did he make your body quiver with excitement?" I started to feel warm inside. I didn't say a word. "I can tell by the way you're looking at me that the answer is no."

"Aren't we over confidant?" I was starting to get mad that he wasn't even a little jealous.

"Always," he answered.

"I want to talk to him before you drop me off there," I warned. "You remember right, that Dieguito is his baby?"

"I see the irony," he smiled.

"Who took care of me, Max, when I had John's baby?"

"I can't talk about this anymore." He took my hands and pressed them against his cheeks. "We have to find them and you have to go to John. That is the way it will have to be." He was very forceful and I realize that I was supposed to say, "Yes sir," but I was too frustrated. Leaving me with Johnny was not an acceptable answer.

CHAPTER 21

Does anyone else see the irony in this?

"You know you're going to have to tell Hector who the baby's father was." I told him.

"I know," he said." I just keep thinking about how I would feel if your baby wasn't mine."

"I thought you said you would love it like it was your own?" I reminded him.

"Of course I would have," he said, taking me into his arms. "But I really wanted it to be mine." He smiled. "Hector will certainly feel the fool when I tell him."

"I hate to say this out loud," I responded. "But did you ever think that maybe he and Jorge raped her and Jorge already knew who the father was?"

"That has occurred to me," he answered. "I'm a little surprised it occurred to you."

"Jorge has expressed an interest in sleeping with me before," I told him. "I wonder if they don't share from time to time."

"He did what?" Max asked. "And you never told me before because…"

"He never did anything about it." I said. "But he did make insinuations from time to time. I wondered if Diego would be okay with that."

"You never told your husband?" he asked.

"As far as I was concerned, Max," I put my hand on his face, "you were always my husband."

"So, you never told me?"

"I was afraid!" I answered. "He's a scary guy." I backed away for a minute. "He's creepy, you know. It's like looking into the eyes of the devil."

He pulled me close and hugged me. "I'll be sure to mention that possibility to Hector. It might help… I'm not sure," he said. "Would I feel better if they gang raped you or if you freely gave yourself?" he asked. "Probably if you gave it up." He paused. "It would hurt that you betrayed me but I think it would hurt more that they took it from you."

"Okay, I do not want to talk about this anymore. If you call Johnny, I'm talking to him."

He laughed. "I promise, baby girl. I would not leave you with a madman."

Hector took a few more days to heal than we had expected. Max decided to get me out of town. He was too worried about the fact that they were missing and no one seemed to be able to find them. He went to see Hector in the hospital one more time before we left. "Hey man, what you doing still laying around here?" Max asked.

"I feel fine," Hector assured him. "I think it's a plot to let our crazy brothers find me and kill me."

"I doubled the guards in front of your room," he whispered to Hector. Then he leaned over and quietly said, "I'm taking her to Johnny. Then you and I will meet up and find those bastards together."

"I still don't like it," I said. "I thought I was supposed to take care of Hector while he was healing." I was trying to get them to reconsider.

"Max is too jealous," Hector added. "Anything to keep us from being alone, baby."

He laughed and Max said, "Not funny anymore, brother."

"Okay, I'll quit," he said. "She's just so easy to embarrass."

"Yeah, yeah," Max responded. "It's bad enough that I have to leave her with her former lover. Let's not make this any worse than it already is."

"I don't know what you're worried about," Hector said. "She never got an…" He looked at me. "I wouldn't worry about it."

"Shut up you two!" I shouted. "This is personal and a little humiliating."

"Not for you, baby girl," Max added. "Only for him."

"Anyway," I continued. "We will miss you, Hector."

"I'll meet up with you when they let me out. Stay in touch." Max leaned over and hugged him.

"I'll be in touch every day. Stay safe." Then Max, little Diego and I walked out and headed on our way to Johnny's.

"Why didn't you call him first?" I asked. "Don't you think he'll want to know you're coming?"

"Probably not," Max answered. "I personally prefer the element of surprise."

When we got there, we had been traveling non-stop for a long time. "Where are we?" I asked.

"Taos, New Mexico," he answered. "We are officially in the middle of nowhere."

We got out of the car and looked around. There were a few trees and a small house almost alone in the street. There was another house similar in size not too far away, beside it. I grabbed my son's hand and we headed towards the door. My hands were sweaty; I suppose I may have been a little nervous. We knocked on the door and Johnny opened it. His face glowed with joy. "What are you doing here?" he asked. He grabbed Diego's hand and brought him inside. "Can I give him some cookies and some milk, Lilly?" he asked.

"Sure," I said. "He'd love that." He started getting cookies out of his pantry. I noticed he was not nearly as skinny as he used to be. He appeared to have been working out and had gained some weight. I was assuming it was due to the fact that he was clean now. He had to be with FBI everywhere. "This is Johnny, baby," I said to Dieguito. "He is an old friend of mommy's."

"It's nice to meet you, little man." John reached over and shook his tiny hand. "He's about four and a half now, right?"

"Yes," I said. "He'll be five in…"

"A few months," John said. "I know." Then he turned to Max. "To what do I owe this honor?"

"I know you are considered a flight risk, so I'm guessing that the little house beside this one, is the FBI station."

"Yeah," he said unfavorably. "Those are my jailors. Why?"

"I need you to keep an eye on Lilly and Dieguito for a while." Max was looking at the ground, almost ashamed to have to ask.

"Are you serious?" he asked. "Diego took everything from me." He looked over at the baby and then me. "You want me to take care of his pregnant wife?"

"Yes I do," he continued. "You know, John, you owe me."

"How's that?" he asked. "I'd like to hear this one."

"When Lilly came to us, Diego ignored her completely. I took care of her for you. When the baby was born, I was there, not Diego. I took care of Dieguito, protected them and loved her sincerely."

"Yeah, about that," John said sarcastically. "Thanks for sleeping with my girl."

"I waited four years to sleep with her." Max looked back up at him and made eye contact. "Seriously, John." He paused. "I loved her with everything I had but never touched her."

"Why?" he asked. "Why would you wait? And what made you stop waiting?"

"She wasn't mine to take," He told him. But he did not offer any further information.

"So, you want me to take care of Diego's baby," he said in a disappointed tone. Max and I exchanged glances but it did not go unnoticed by Johnny. "Oh my God!" he shouted in a voice of revelation. "You got your brother's wife pregnant!" He smiled and Max returned his gaze to the floor.

"It wasn't like that," I said. "Diego said he wanted to get me pregnant and I made Max sleep with me without protection before Diego had a chance to do it himself."

"Made him sleep with you," he said sarcastically. "That must have been painful."

"That was our first time," I told him.

"Look man, it was him or me." He paused and took my hands. "We wanted it to be me."

"Does anyone else see the irony in this?" he asked.

"Of course we do," Max answered. "You owe me."

"I do owe you," he agreed. "When the baby's born, can I name it Johnny?"

"I had nothing to do with that," Max replied. "I wish we could change that now, but we can't, it's too late."

"Sorry, a bad attempt at humor." Johnny reached out and stroked Dieguito's hair. "I suppose I can't complain. It'll give me a chance to get to know my… friend and her son again."

"No touching!" Max said and he looked at me.

"It's been five years, Max, I think it's over," he said as he smiled at me. "I am so sorry, Lilly for the last time I saw you." He looked at Max. "I'm sorry about all of it. Getting Lilly shot, trying to kidnap her…" He paused again. "I am clean and sober and I would never hurt her like that again."

"Just so we're clear," Max said. "I love this girl, and I'm trusting you with her life. Don't disappoint me."

"So, give me the story, Max. Where are you going? After Diego, Jorge and Mick?"

"So, you do get to see the news."

"Where's Hector?"

"In the hospital with a gunshot wound," he answered.

"Holy crap!" Johnny said. "What's going on with you guys?"

"My brothers," he started. "They are in a state of unrest." Max laughed a little when he said that.

"Diego thinks the baby is his," Johnny said with a twinge of nervousness in his voice. "Oh, this is bad. He'll try to take her."

"Thus, Hector and the gunshot wound." Max was looking around the house by now. I wasn't sure if he was just nervous or looking for something.

"Sure, I'll take care of them," he answered. "I could use the company. You know Diana didn't come with me."

"I heard," Max replied. "I'm sorry about that."

"Who is she sleeping with now to get the drugs?" he asked.

"Do you want me to tell you?" Max answered. "Really?"

"Are you serious?" Johnny said. It was like they had some kind of language of their own. "She is not sleeping with Ray," he asked in astonishment.

"Sorry man," Max confirmed. "I wish I could tell you no. He's in jail now though if that helps." Johnny got upset and threw a glass across the room. It shattered in the living room.

"Okay, rule number one," Max started. "No touching my girl. Rule number two, no losing your temper."

"I know, I know," he answered. "It won't happen again. This is just the first I'm hearing of it."

"I'd be upset too if I found out Lilly was sleeping with…" He paused. "Let's say YOU!" He pulled out his gun and pointed it at him. John lifted his hands in the air.

"I won't touch her man, I owe you, remember?" Max put the gun away.

"Just checking," he said. He took my face in his hands and kissed me. "I have to run, baby." He went for the door.

"NO!" I yelled and I ran up behind him and grabbed him by the arm. "This is just what happened with Johnny, please don't go."

"What are you talking about?" He turned and faced me.

"When John left, we had only been together a few times. Then I never saw him again. Max…" I put my hands on his face this time. "We've only been together a handful of times. What if this is the last time I see you? What if something happens to you?"

He kissed me tenderly and I kissed him back. We began to feel the heat of our longing when John said, "You know, she's pretty persuasive about the 'one more time' thing, so why don't I take Dieguito to the playground down the street and give you the house to yourself."

Max smiled at me and I turned to John. "Thanks Johnny."

"You can make as much noise as you want," he continued. Max threw a towel at him when he said that. Then Johnny and our son walked out the door.

Max carried me romantically into the guest room. "I have no idea how I am going to get through a day without you," he said to me as he lay me down on the bed beside him. "Lilly, you are my whole world." He kissed me and began to undress me. I got instantly aroused and I could feel him do the same. He brought me to that sacred place over and over again until we both collapsed breathless, two hours after we started. When we walked out of the bedroom, Johnny and Dieguito were on the couch in the living room playing video games.

"You really need to work on that, Lilly," he said.

"I thought you were at the park," I said in response.

"Two hours, man?" John said to Max. "Seriously, two hours?" He laughed as Max's face flushed a little. "What are you made of anyway?" Johnny laughed a little. "No wonder she's so crazy about you. I can't compete with that."

Max laughed and grabbed my hand. "That's good to know." He smiled at John and winked at me.

Just then a man walked through the door. "Max? I'd recognize that Beamer anywhere."

"Hey, Paul!" Max said as he walked over to him and hugged him. "I didn't know you were on Johnny's team."

"Yeah, he's loads of fun." They both laughed. Johnny looked at me and rolled his eyes.

"I'm on my way out, but it's good to see you."

"Oh come on," Paul urged him. "Let me take her for a spin?"

"I think he means the car," John said facetiously.

"I know what he means," Max added, obviously annoyed. He reached into his pocket and tossed him the keys. "Make it quick, man, I have to get back to Arizona."

"Thanks, Max, you're the best." He ran out the door almost dancing with excitement.

"I think he means the car," Max uttered under his breath at Johnny. "What's wrong with you?" They both laughed. We heard the car start and Max's face changed. "Get down!" He yelled it out like it was his last breath. We heard a loud "BANG!" and then an explosion. Before I knew what happened Max was on top of me and John was on Dieguito. The window in the front of the house shattered all over us and I heard John yell, "Max, where's Lilly?"

Max got up when the dust settled and John got up off of little Diego and dusted him off. "Lilly…" Max grabbed my hands to pick me up off of the floor.

"Max," John said. "Oh my God, you took a hit." I looked up and put my hands over my mouth. His whole left side was covered in glass and blood. He had a large piece of glass lodged in his head above his eyebrow. "Are you all right?" John asked me. He looked me up and down and touched my blouse on the side. "Not being fresh," he said. "Looking for glass." He walked over to Max who appeared to be in shock. He grabbed his arm and walked him into the kitchen. "Sit on this stool, Max." Max sat down. "Lilly's fine," he said. "I'm just going to pull that piece of glass out of your face. Grab this towel. He handed him a washcloth. He took some tweezers and pulled the glass out and blood squirted everywhere. Max put the towel on his face. "Push hard," John said. "Come on Max, come back to me."

Two men came running through the door. "What the hell happened, John?"

"Max's car blew up. Paul was in it."

One of the men picked up a phone and called the fire department and the other one called some kind of doctor. "You have to get out here now. Max Montiago is here and covered in blood. His Beamer exploded with Paul inside. The front window blew. Thanks, get here fast." They were all congregated in the kitchen and I was holding Dieguito rocking him in the living room. The fire trucks came and put out the fire. Then some more FBI came inside and said to Max, "He's gone."

"Just think," Johnny said. "If Lilly didn't distract you for two hours…" He stopped himself.

"That should have been me," Max acknowledged.

I ran to his side and grabbed the hand that wasn't injured. "If it was you, I would be sitting here covered in glass and the baby… what about the baby?"

He looked at me as though he was coming back to life. "I really loved that car."

"And… he's back!" Johnny said, laughing to himself. Then he went to Dieguito and said, "How about you and I go play some video games in the bedroom?"

"Okay, Uncle Johnny." I made a face of disapproval when he said the 'uncle' word. They disappeared down the hallway. I was grateful for that.

Max squeezed my hand. "Are you all right?" He looked into my eyes with a sadness I hadn't seen for a while. "John said you are all right."

"I'm fine," I said. "Thanks to you, not a scratch."

"When you're done stitching me up," he looked at the doctor, "I want you to examine her. She's five months pregnant."

"You got it," he said. "Just a precaution," he said to me.

Max looked over at one of the FBI agents. "Why?" He stopped and shook his head. "Why did it explode now and not when I first turned it on before we got here?"

"There was a trigger on it," he told him. "The person who planted it wanted it to go off, after you dropped Lilly off, not before." He looked outside at the smoldering car. "It was set to go off the second time the ignition was triggered."

"So Diego and Jorge knew I was dropping her off somewhere," he said almost in a question.

"They must have figured that you were going to go after them together. John came out of the bedroom. "Turn on the television." He pointed to the television in the living room. One of the agents grabbed the remote.

"BREAKING NEWS," was flashed on the screen.

"This just in from channel 9 in Taos New Mexico. Wife and brother of notorious drug lord Diego Montiago were found dead moments ago in a car bombing.

"What?" Max became alarmed and got up from the stool.

"The two were on their way home back to Las Vegas after visiting Mrs. Montiago's father in Sedona Arizona. Lilly and Maxwell Montiago had the son of known syndicate leader, Diego Montiago in the car with them when the car exploded. Lilly was five months pregnant."

"Hector!" Max cried as he grabbed his cell and started dialing.

"I've been dead twice already," John said. 'It's not so bad."

Max started talking quickly in Spanish to his brother. "We're alive, we're fine and both Dieguito and the baby are fine too," John translated for me.

"A little glass in my face and arm but I'll make it," he translated some more.

"Max!" John yelled. "English is easier to eavesdrop on."

"Oh, sorry," he said to me. "Everything is fine. You're going to have to come and get me when you get out. Man I loved that car."

"Told you," John said. "He's totally fine. "Mr. Two hour man…" he mumbled under his breath.

"You ought to try it sometime," I whispered back.

"Is that an offer?" he asked. "You gonna teach me?"

"Too close," Max said, glaring at Johnny. "Back up now…" John moved away from me slowly.

"No, you idiot!" I said. "I'm just saying that it wouldn't hurt you to give a little more and take a little less once in a while."

"Here's my chance," he said. "I'll try to pay Max back for caring for you all this time." I looked at him suspiciously. "Really," he assured me. "I will keep my distance."

Max came over to us after they finished stitching him up and sent me into the kitchen. I left him and Johnny alone on the couch and Max's face was dangerously close to John's. The doctor looked me over. "Remarkable," he said. "Max was very good at protecting you."

"He always is," I answered. "I'm very lucky."

"It looks like the FBI planted the story to make it look like we were dead to Diego and Jorge. This way, they won't look for you and I will have the element of surprise on my side," Max said to us.

The room cleared and the four of us were left alone in the house. Max took me into his arms and said, "I guess I'm stuck here until Hector comes to get me." He kissed me. "This will give me a chance to evaluate your current relationship with this guy." He leaned his head toward Johnny, and made an unfavorable face.

Dieguito and John were sitting on the couch together. "Uncle Max," Dieguito asked.

"Yes, son…"

"Why are you going to bring daddy home?" Johnny flinched uncomfortably when he referred to Diego as daddy.

"I'm not bringing him home, exactly," he told him. Then he looked at me for some sort of approval. I nodded.

"Your daddy did some bad things and then he ran away." Max knelt down next to him. "I just want to find him and bring him back, so he can pay for his actions."

Dieguito looked at Johnny and whispered, "My daddy is a monster."

"Dieguito!" I said in shock. "Where did you hear that?" Max stood up and walked back over to me.

"Everyone says it," my son continued. "Everyone at the house says he is a monster. That he makes you cry."

"He won't make mommy cry anymore," Max responded.

"Will you hold me like you used to until I fall asleep if he does?" he asked Max.

"Max…" I said in surprise. "What's he talking about?"

"I used to hear you cry at night when you and daddy were in bed." His little eyes got dark and sad. "I would sneak into Uncle Max's room and sleep with him until I fell asleep."

Max picked Dieguito up into his arms and hugged him. "Your daddy isn't a monster." He looked over at Johnny.

"What did you tell him?" I asked Max.

"You were sad because you wanted to be with me," he answered.

"I pray every night that you will want to be my dad," Dieguito said. "Why can't you be my dad?"

"Someday I'll marry your mom and I will be your dad." He kissed his little cheek and put him back down on the sofa beside Johnny. "But I could not love you more if you were my own flesh and blood. To me you are my son."

"You and mommy are together now, right?"

"Yes baby." I grabbed Max's arm and hugged him.

"So when are you going to get married?" he asked anxiously.

"First I have to find your dad," he said. "Then I have to ask your mom to marry me." I smiled and Dieguito smiled an adorable boyish grin. It was funny how he and Max were not related by blood yet he had somehow learned to imitate Max's smile.

"What if daddy finds us before you find him?" He began to sound frightened.

"I'm the best in the business, little guy. No one can beat Uncle Max." He gave him a high five.

"I can sleep with mommy and make sure she is safe," he said. I was charmed by his protectiveness.

"And make sure uncle Johnny isn't keeping mommy company like that, okay?" Johnny laughed at that comment.

"I just got through telling her, I will be a good boy." John reached for Dieguito's hand. "Can I spend a little time with him?" I looked at Max for an answer.

"I guess," Max answered.

"Do you want to try to beat me in a video game?" he asked him.

"Yeah, uncle Johnny, I'm really good ya know." Johnny grinned and I watched them disappear down the hallway.

"I'm glad you're going to be here for a while," I told him. "I will miss you once you're gone."

"And I you," he told me. "My heart will feel empty when I'm unable to hold you."

We lay in each other's arms not saying a word. He put his arms around me and didn't let go. His phone finally rang and it was Hector. He was on his way and would get here by tomorrow. I could feel the panic taking over my body. I began to get confused again.

"I'll see you then," he said. "Sweep the car before you get into it." He hung up and grabbed my chin with the gentlest touch. "I'm not Johnny," he reminded me. "I am not afraid of Diego. I will be back for you." I said nothing but I could feel the tears falling out of my eyes onto his shirt.

I have really come to need you," I said. "Sometimes I feel like I can't breathe when you're gone."

"It is that way for me as well," he said. "I waited all of my life to find the other half of my soul." He kissed me. We sat on the couch kissing for a while. John finally came out of the bedroom. "He's asleep," he said. "I want to tell him."

CHAPTER 22

Who is Diego's real father?

"You're kidding, right?" I asked. "He's not even five yet."

"He's five in a few months," Johnny said. "I've missed all this time." He paused and took a long hard look at Max. "Come on Max, what would you do if you were in my position?"

"I don't want to make this decision for her," he said. "I would never have let this happen, so I am probably not the best person to ask."

"I want to know Max," I said. "Tell me what you think."

"I think you should tell him." He calmly gazed at me with reassuring eyes. "He thinks his father is a monster. Take that burden from him. But John…" he turned his gaze onto Johnny, "you have to step up once he knows. I have raised that boy as though he was my own. You will need to see him, pay for him and spend time with him."

"I think it's about time, don't you?" he answered.

"I don't know," I said.

"Lilly," Max reached for my hand and kissed it, "your son spent night after night listening to you cry after making love with the man he thinks is his father." I looked at the floor ashamed at my weakness. "Don't do that," he said to me. He picked my chin up with his fingers. "I'm not blaming you. You had to do what you had to do to keep the both of you alive." He pulled me onto his lap. "It's time to tell him the truth. Diego will be either dead or in jail for a long, long time, very soon anyway."

"Fine," I said. "We'll tell him tomorrow." Of course I was worried. John dropped me on Diego's doorstep and never came back. What are the chances of him sticking around? However, he's clean now and maybe things are different this time.

"There is something else I have to do," Max said. "I can't believe I am going to have to do this, but…" He took a deep breath and reached into his back pocket. "Johnny is already Tom Smith." Johnny laughed. "You are now Jane Smith and your son," he paused again, "he is Tom Jr."

"Oh no!" I said. "You are going to make me his wife?"

"Believe me, it sickens me to think of you married to yet again… another man who isn't me." He paced a little before handing me the identifications. "But you are pregnant and your son looks exactly like John. We have to be practical."

"Max," I said, feeling defeated, "don't leave me."

"I'm not leaving you," he reassured me. "Listen up, John," he said sternly. "She is only your wife in public. Don't get carried away. You are still really married to Diana."

Johnny made a face. "I get it," he said. "I touch her, you kill me. Pretty clear, Max."

"Good," he said. "Lilly, it is just make-believe. Don't get confused." He returned me to his lap and we sat together a little longer.

Then Hector showed up to take Max away. He looked good as new and I could tell that he and Max were anxious to get out of the house and find the escapees. We had a going away party for Max and Hector. As soon as the party was over Max came to me and whispered in my ear, "Do you want me to be here when you tell him?"

"I'll be fine," I answered. He got up to leave and Hector assured him that he checked the car for explosives. Hector was an expert in this area: Finding things. I stood at the door as he was preparing to leave. Suddenly my heart started to race. I began to feel faint and nervous that he wasn't coming back. Memories of his disappearance in Mexico filled my mind. Johnny's first pretend death came rushing back like floodwater. He kissed my lips and headed out the door. I stood there, empty. Johnny was sitting on the couch with Dieguito behind me. Suddenly something came out of my mouth that I did not plan. It was a piercing scream. It curdled through the air as my knees began to buckle beneath me. "NO!!" was what I heard and I could hear John getting up from the couch to try to catch me before I hit the floor. Max came rushing back in the door and scooped me up like he had done a hundred times before.

"Thanks John, but I've got this one." He carried me to the couch and put me on his lap.

"Mommy?" Dieguito called.

"You know what?" John said. "Why don't you go to your room for a little bit? Let Uncle Max take care of mommy, okay?"

"He always does," he answered, confidently and left us. John got up and went to the kitchen and I could hear the front door open. I could hear Hector ask Johnny what was keeping Max.

"Lilly, what's going on? You can tell daddy," he said with his boyish smile.

"What's happening, Max?" I asked. "I don't understand why you're leaving me again. Did I do something?"

"You know Max," Hector interrupted. "I can take Miguel. You can stay here with her. Everyone thinks you're dead, anyway. Why not stay dead?"

"It's getting harder and harder to tell our friends from our enemies. I can't risk Miguel turning up dirty," he answered. "Just give me a few minutes with her."

"Remember the last time?" he reminded him. "The gun to the head thing?"

Max reached behind him and pulled his gun out of his pants and Hector walked over and gently took it from him. "Thanks," Max said.

"No problem." Hector glanced at Johnny who seemed to be mortified by the whole situation.

"What have we done to her?" Johnny asked Hector.

I could hear Hector and John talking about me like I wasn't in the room. "Let's do a reality check for a minute, okay baby girl?" Max was holding me and trying to get me to look at him.

"Okay," I agreed.

"Who's that ugly guy in the kitchen with the pony tail?" I could see John make a face.

"Johnny," I answered, trying not to smile. "Why am I here with him?"

"Take a deep breath, baby. Relax. You're panicking."

"Why am I here with him?" I began to feel impatient. I could tell I was raising my voice.

"We are here because John is in witness protection and you and your son are going to stay here with him."

"Why?" I asked.

"Johnny is your ex-boyfriend," he added. "You don't sleep with him anymore." I could hear both Hector and John chuckle at that comment.

"I love how he keeps emphasizing that," John said.

"I sleep with you," I said to Max. He smiled and kissed me.

"Yes you do." He smiled and kissed me again. "Who's the other guy in the kitchen?"

"Hector," I said. "I like Hector."

"We've already established that," Max answered. Hector and Johnny seemed to be once again amused.

"Lilly, who is Dieguito's real father?"

"Diego," I said. "No, wait… Johnny."

"Yes, it's Johnny. You are still panicking," he said. "Lilly, I love you. I will be back for you."

"Please, Max." I grabbed his shirt with both hands and pulled at him. "I can't live without you, I don't think you understand."

"Of course I do," he answered. He took my hands and gently unfastened them from his shirt. "Querida, you are my sun, my moon and my sky. There would be no reason for me to draw breath if you were not in my world."

"Oh brother," I heard Johnny say. I saw Hector smack him in the back of the head. I giggled.

"That's why I like Hector," I said.

"One more time," Max said. "Baby girl?"

"Yes daddy," I answered. He gave me a very big smile when I called him that. "Whose baby's in there?" He put his hand on my stomach.

"Yours," I answered. The tears were pouring from my eyes. "Yours, thank God, it's yours."

"What is your relationship with John?"

"Come on, Max," John barked from the kitchen. "Enough already." I could tell he was getting annoyed.

"He's my ex, and Dieguito's father."

He let out a sigh of relief. "No more tears," he said. "Hector and I will find Diego and Jorge and put them away." He kissed me again. "John will take care of you. I told the FBI that you and Dieguito are here, so they will keep an eye on him."

I laughed. "Okay," I said. "I'm all right now."

"I am so proud of how strong you've been through all of this." He smiled. "I was going to wait until I came back, but I want you to be sure of me." I looked at him curiously. "Take off Diego's rings." It was funny how I never thought to do that. I pulled them off of my finger and handed them to Max. He put me on the couch and got on one knee. I could hear Johnny in the background, "Oh my God, no way!"

"Lilly," He pulled a ring out of his jeans pocket. "Will you do me the honor of becoming my wife?"

I started weeping uncontrollably. "Of course I will," I answered. "I love you so much." He put the ring on my finger. I wrapped my arms around his neck and kissed him. "Make sure you give the rings back to Diego when you find him." I added. "Make sure he knows we're done."

"That's what I was planning on doing," he responded. He kissed my lips and got up. "You," he pointed to Johnny, "take care of her." Max's eyes were full of water and I could see how hard it was for him to leave.

"I will guard her with my life," John told him. "I promise, I will return her to you exactly as you left her with me."

Hector and Max headed for the door. Max blew me a kiss as Hector grabbed him from the back of the collar of his shirt and yanked him out the door. I felt cold and empty inside. Dieguito came running out and sat in my lap. "Can I see the ring?" he asked.

"You knew about the ring?" I asked.

"He showed it to me," he said. I showed him my finger and he said, "Yay!" and started clapping. I knew in my heart it was time to tell him. Time to reveal John's true identity in his life. I took his little hand and said, "Dieguito," he sat down, "we need to tell you something."

CHAPTER 23

They say confession is good for the soul

Johnny sat on the other side of Diego. "What is it mommy?" he asked so innocently.

"Remember I told you that John and I were old friends?"

"Yes, I remember."

"We were in love once," I continued.

"You mean like you and Uncle Max?" he asked. I wasn't sure how to answer that.

"Something like that, yes," I answered cautiously. I didn't want him to think that there was ever a love more powerful than what I shared with Max. "When I met your dad… Diego," I corrected myself, "I was already carrying you in my stomach." He looked confused. "Diego told me that John was in a terrible car accident and that I was all alone in the world. So, he offered to take care of you and me. That's how I met your uncle Max."

"So…" he paused, "Diego isn't really my daddy?" he asked. I was impressed at his comprehension.

"The truth is…" I held my breath for a minute, "Johnny and I made you before I even knew Diego. Johnny is your real daddy." I couldn't believe I was hearing that come out of my mouth. Dieguito turned and looked at John. Then he looked back at me.

"I didn't tell you sooner because I wasn't sure you would understand. But Johnny wanted you to know."

"Why didn't you come for us?" he asked John sadly. "Do you know what Diego did to my mother?"

John was distressed. It didn't occur to me that Dieguito might be angry about having to live there. We were very wealthy and he never wanted for anything. But my marriage, especially towards the end, was outwardly painful. I was unaware until that moment how painful it must have been for Dieguito to watch me suffer.

Diego is a powerful man," John answered. "He told me that he would hurt you and your mother if I ever tried to take you." He paused and took his hand. "Not a day went by that I didn't think about you."

"Besides," I cut in. "If he didn't leave us with Diego, I never would have met Uncle Max."

"Are Uncle Max and Uncle Hector still my uncles?" he asked. He looked like he might burst into tears if I gave him the wrong answer.

"Uncle Max and Uncle Hector would be very sad if you stopped calling them uncle. They will always be your uncles, baby." I thought about that for a moment. "Uncle Max has been more like a father to you than anyone else has. He was the only one there the day you were born, you know."

He smiled at me. Then he looked back at Johnny. "I'm glad you're my daddy. My other daddy is not a nice man."

"I know." John looked deeply saddened.

"Should I call you daddy or Uncle Johnny?" I could see how the lines were beginning to blur for him.

"I want you to call me daddy… when you are comfortable doing that." He gave him a big hug. "But until you get to know me better, you can call me whatever you want to."

"Thanks," he said. "Can I go now?"

"Yes," I said. I laughed a little. He ran down the hall on his way to video game heaven.

"Thank you," he said. Johnny put his hands on both sides of my face. I could see he was searching for a trace of a memory somewhere in my eyes. Then he leaned his face in and I pulled back.

"Remember Max's first rule?" I asked. "He's been gone five minutes and you're trying to kiss me. Give me some credit."

"Lilly," he paused and cleared his throat, "you were the love of my life. I've never stopped loving you. Not for one minute."

I stood up right away. "Are you crazy?" I asked. "We are so done. I am beyond madly in love with Max. He is everything I have ever wanted or needed. He is my best friend."

"We were madly in love too… once," he replied. "I know it was a long time ago but…"

I cut him off, "But you couldn't keep the trailer trash out of your bedroom."

"I was using back then, Lilly. If you'd just give me a chance…" He reached for me again and I went into the kitchen. He followed me. "I can try to please you like he does, Lilly."

"I am not having this conversation with you," I told him. "No one is going to get near me like Max does. Max is the best and I saved him for last."

"Fine, I'll let it go for now," he continued. "But you might be here for a while. You could change your mind."

"Whatever," I blurted. And from that moment on I prayed for Max's quick return. But it didn't happen.

Every morning Dieguito and I would wake up to the wonderful smell of gourmet breakfast. Bacon and eggs, waffles, pancakes… you name it, he prepared it. Dieguito slept in the same bed as me apparently due to orders from Max. Max knew that before his footsteps were cold from the bed, Johnny would be trying to keep me warm. He is so intuitive that way. I thought he was being jealous. What did I know? When I came into the kitchen, Johnny was happily singing and preparing food. "You know your mom can't cook," John said to Dieguito. He laughed.

"Uncle Max won't let her in the kitchen," he said.

"I was glad to hear both Max and Diego cook," John said. "At least I knew you'd be eating well. Sit down." He put a plate in front of me and one in front of Dieguito. It was truly amazing.

"You know your daddy used to be a chef in a restaurant back in Arizona," I told him. "Did Pierre ever come back?" I asked John.

"Yes, he did," he answered. "He came back and asked all kinds of questions about you. When he heard your name was Montiago, he stopped asking questions."

"I don't blame him," I answered. "I was just wondering if he ever got his life back."

"Miss him?" he asked.

"As much as I missed you," I answered sarcastically. "And Bobby? What's he up to?" I wasn't sure he would really know.

"Drinking, dancing and partying with young girls." He smiled. "Nothing different than before." We heard a knocking at the door. I went to get it and it was a man and a woman. They showed me their FBI identification.

"You must be Lilly," the woman said. "I'm Miranda. Max assigned me here to help make you more comfortable. This is Steve." She pointed to the man beside her and he shook my hand. "I know how hard it can be to be around all these men all the time. Especially while you're pregnant."

"Leave it to Max to think about that," I said.

"Is there something you need that would make you more comfortable?" she asked me.

I guess, maybe some food for the baby and I could use a few things."

"Make me a list," she said. "You too John," she called over.

"Sit down and have some breakfast," John suggested.

"Thanks," Steve said, "but we actually have some news for you."

"I hope it's good news. What's going on?" I asked.

"They found your father last night," she answered. "He was in Arizona."

"Oh no," I replied. "Diego and Jorge are in Arizona somewhere? Where did they find him?"

She paused. "Lilly, sit down." I sat back down at the kitchen table in front of my breakfast. "He was waiting for Hector in the new house we had settled you all into."

"That means there are still dirty cops out there," I said in disbelief.

"That's why Max insisted on going with Hector himself," she answered.

"Was dad surprised to see Max alive?"

"Apparently so," she answered. "Max shot your dad."

"Oh," was all I could say. "Is he… dead?" I wasn't sure how to react to that.

"Not even close," she answered. "Mick had a gun on Hector. Max was just slowing him down. He's in the hospital and after that he will be sent to prison awaiting trial." She paused. "Max didn't tell you that he replaced your dad in the FBI, did he?"

"He got promoted?" I asked.

"I don't know why he didn't tell you. Maybe he thought it might scare you. Higher risks and all," she laughed. "He gets to give more orders to more people. That's a plus, right?"

"I miss him," I said. "Did dad give up the whereabouts of my husband and Satan?" I asked.

"Not yet, but we expect him to." They started out the door after stealing a few pieces of bacon. "Get me a list, you two," she yelled as she closed the door behind her.

"Wow," John said. "Max shot Mick. That's gotta sting a little, no?"

"He didn't kill him," I said, annoyed at his glee about this whole thing.

"But he still shot daddy," he said.

"That's what mommy calls Max," Dieguito laughed.

"Shhh," I said to him, laughing a little myself.

"Ugly secrets coming to light," Johnny said.

"Thanks for breakfast, Uncle Johnny," Dieguito shouted as he bolted back to his bedroom.

"I don't call him that," I said. I could feel my face flush.

"Yes you do," he argued. "I heard you call him that before he left." He shook his head in disapproval. "You never called me that." He laughed.

"You didn't call me your baby girl either," I answered. We both smiled. I helped him clean up in the kitchen. I could feel the tension between us, as we got closer together. He handed me the last dish to dry. "You really are beautiful," he said. Then he walked out of the kitchen. I felt a little uncomfortable and I was a little embarrassed about it. I glanced over at him in the living room. He smiled a crooked smile at me. My stomach turned as I contemplated what he was probably thinking. I must admit that it made me a little sick. I put the dish away and grabbed my book. Then I sat at the counter in the kitchen and opened it.

"You don't have to hide from me," he said. "We can talk about this."

"There's nothing to talk about," I answered. And I thought I put this conversation to rest.

We began to spend a lot of time at the park. Although it was small, there was a tiny lake where we would let Dieguito feed the ducks some old bread. The challenge was getting Dieguito to actually feed the ducks and not eat the bread himself. It was fun but a little weird. Everyone there thought we were married. I wouldn't let John hold my hand. I felt in some odd way that that would be a betrayal on some level. Months went by. I was nine months pregnant. Max had stopped calling and I became very anxious that something had happened to him. The FBI was very close mouthed and I got little information about his whereabouts. All they told me was that he was deep undercover and was not allowed to make contact.

"It's strange, isn't it?" John asked one day as we sat beside the pond.

"A little," I said. "How long have we been playing house now?" He didn't like my euphemism.

"I think about four months." He reached over and touched my stomach. "At least I get to live through a pregnancy with you. Even if it is not my baby this time."

"Okay," I answered, "it's weird."

"I realize that this is all my fault," he said. "If I had just left you alone…"

"I might be married to Pierre," I interrupted. Then I laughed.

"At least your life wouldn't be in danger," he added.

"You know he raped me," I told him. "Diego beat me and raped me."

He didn't look up. He threw a few pieces of bread in the water. "I should have been stronger," he said. "I remember that night." He looked up at me for a moment and then back at the ground. "It was Jorge, Diego, Felix and me. We were partying in Elena's husband's room. We were… dipping our hands in the candy jar, as Max would say." He looked at me again. "I heard that he hurt you that night. I was sick about it."

"Felix?" I remembered Felix and Miguel guarding our room the night Jorge put a hit on Max and Hector. "Felix was with you?"

"Yes, he liked to party," he answered.

"I guess it's water under the bridge now," I offered. "Max was there. I went to him. I begged him to make love with me but he refused."

"You know, Lilly," he looked almost pensive for a minute, "you did okay with him." He took my hand. "He is a really good man. He could have taken advantage of you a hundred times, but never did. How could he continue to resist you?"

"He was afraid it would confuse me. He didn't want me calling Diego, Max or having to switch back and forth all the time. He said he didn't want our first time to be any way connected to a rape."

"I almost love him myself," he laughed. "Do you know he shot my brother?" he asked. "Did he tell you?"

"No," I said. "Hector did. And while we're on the subject," I started to get angry remembering that he never told me the truth either, "why didn't you tell me Pat was your brother?"

"I didn't like to publicly announce my family connections. Leverage, you know."

"You do know that Pat raped Darla?" I asked.

"Yeah, I heard Max's version. But I don't believe it."

"I heard she was a mess. Wasn't there evidence?" I was confused about his denial.

"They were in love once. How could he have raped her?" He looked at me with total assurance of his convictions.

"Is that what you were thinking when you came after me at Diego's house?"

"It wasn't rape to me," he said. "Not to me." He looked back at the water. I felt badly for him. He lost everything. Just like Jorge… everything.

"I have more bad news for you," I said. I looked down and saw a puddle of water underneath myself. "My water just broke."

There was always FBI following us so Johnny whistled loudly and they came running. "Her water broke. We have to go to the hospital." Johnny ran back to the house for my emergency bag and Dieguito and I were shuffled into an FBI issued car. The five of us drove to the hospital in record time. "Max!" I said to Miranda. "I need Max!"

"I'm sorry," she said. "John is going to have to stand in for him." I was sick to my stomach and when they tried to get me to walk to the room I collapsed onto the floor. I knew I was panicking but couldn't control it. I heard Dieguito crying and Miranda trying to comfort him. John and Steve were trying to pick me up until a doctor and a few nurses rushed over and got me up off of the floor. "We need to get her to a bed right away," they said. "Are you the husband?"

"Yes," John answered reluctantly. But he knew it was time to step up. It was time for him to pay Maxwell back. What a way to do it.

CHAPTER 24

I think we should name him Johnny.

I did what I was told and climbed into the bed. I was tired of being tired and tired of missing Max. John took my hand and leaned into me so that no one else would hear. "I know I'm not him. But I will be here for you just like he was when it was my baby."

"I loved him then," I cried. "Even back then."

"I know," he replied. "Call me Max if you need to. I'll be right here holding your hand."

I smiled. "Like I'm going to call you by his name." He smiled back. "Ever."

"Okay, okay," he said. "I get it. The most important rule." I laughed a little. "A smile?" He put his hand on my cheek. "I always thought you were beautiful when you smiled."

I laid back and he pretended to be my husband. It was hard but the baby came screaming into the world just like Dieguito did. "I think we should name him Johnny," he said. "It's only fair." I laughed. I was exhausted. They put the baby into my arms and I looked at his tiny little blue eyes. He had a full head of golden hair. There was no doubt… he belonged to Max. "Well?" John asked. "What's it gonna be?"

"Max was very specific on not naming the baby after himself. He said it gets too confusing."

"What was Max's father's name?" John asked me. I laughed at that.

"Diego," I answered.

"Next…" he said.

"I would name him Hector but it would still be too confusing, being that we see him all the time," I continued.

"Why don't you put Max in the middle?" he suggested. "Like…" he took a moment to think it through. "Like Michael Maxwell."

"I am not naming the baby after my dad."

"Think about names that you like," he said. "I know this is hard without Maxwell." He paused. "But I'm sure you've been thinking about names for a while now."

"How about Christian Maxwell Montiago?" I said. "We'll call him Chris for short.

"That is a perfect name," he agreed. "May I hold him?" I put the baby in his arms and he smiled at him as though it was his own. The nurse came in and asked if I would like to nurse him. "Yes," I answered. "As soon as possible." John sat in a chair in the side of the room while I was trying to latch the baby's little mouth onto my breast. "Cut that out!" I said to John, watching him watch me.

"I missed it all the first time around," he said. "Please don't take this away from me." So, I didn't say a word and let him watch me nurse Christian. There was a huge hole in my heart as I fed Max's newborn. I didn't know if he was dead or alive and I was desperate for him to see the miniature Max in my arms. "It's weird how much he looks like him," John smiled.

"Dieguito looks very much like you," I replied.

"Not that much," he said. "Diego will know right away that this is not his baby."

"Yes, I supposed he will," I answered. "But they are brothers. There could always be a resemblance." He sat there contently watching me. It felt a little wrong. When the baby fell asleep, John took him and laid him down in the tiny bassinet they had for him while I closed up shop. He was still watching me.

"I am so sorry he's missing this," he said again. "I'm so sorry I missed this the first time." He sat down beside me and took my hand. Then he leaned in and kissed my lips. It was gentle and it was short. "I'm sorry," he said. "I won't do that again." I was too tired to argue. I laid my head on the pillow and the next thing I knew it was morning.

Johnny was running in the room as soon as visiting hours began. He was as excited as if it were Dieguito's birth. He had flowers and a teddy bear. I laughed. "You know this is Max's baby, right?"

"You know you're Jane Smith, right?" was his response. I had forgotten that.

"Just doing a quick reality check," I replied. "I know I need those from time to time."

"I know who's who," he answered. "I can enjoy my time as your husband if I want to."

"I guess you may as well," I answered putting my arms out for the baby. Little Dieguito climbed into the bed with me as I nursed Chris. John finally picked him up and sat him in a chair with a video game. "Making sure your view is not obstructed?" I asked sarcastically.

"Stop being so mean to me," he said. "I'm happy, let me be happy."

"You know they are freeing me today," I said, avoiding the very uncomfortable situation that was happening here. Johnny was falling back in love with me. And I missed Max so much that I couldn't breathe.

"I heard," he said. "I can't wait to get you home so I can pamper you."

"Don't go out of your way, John." I was starting to get a little nervous.

He sat down beside me and took my hand. "I want you to be happy too."

They discharged me and John and Dieguito got me all set up on the couch. The FBI got me a bassinet for the baby with wheels so that he could follow me from room to room. We were the perfect little family except for the fact that we weren't.

Months went by. I had officially been without Maxwell for seven months. I was so lonely. John was happier than I had ever seen him and Dieguito was now calling him daddy. There was still no word from Max or Hector and no sign of life. I was still nursing, much to John's glee and he got up with me every night and every morning to feed the baby. Sometimes he gave him formula just to give me a break. "You know you can stay asleep," I told him. "You don't have to listen for me." He was in the kitchen preparing breakfast for us.

"I wish you'd let me sleep with you," he said. "At least on the floor."

"I don't want to cross any boundaries," I reminded him. He walked over to me. I could feel what his body was trying to say before he even touched me. I put the baby down into his bassinet. He took my face into his hands. Before I knew what had happened he put his lips on mine. He lifted me up off of the couch and pulled my body against his. I tried to stop him then but I was unable to. He moved deeper into me and I couldn't break free and I could feel him getting aroused. I was finally able to free my hand so I pushed him back violently and slapped him as hard as I could across the face. I started wiping my lips to try to remove his kiss. "It's still there," he told me. "I know it's still there."

"Do not tell Max about this," I said. "I mean it, John."

"I don't have a death wish," he assured me. "Besides, I want you to kiss me again sometime."

"I didn't kiss you, let's get that straight. You kissed me."

He smiled and turned the television to the news, searching for information on Diego and Jorge like nothing happened.

"Jorge Montiago has been spotted in the Las Vegas airport by FBI early this morning," the anchorwoman reported. There was a picture on the screen of Hector hand- cuffing him.

"Turn it up, turn it up!" I yelled.

"Police chief Michael O'Hara, who has already been arrested by the FBI months earlier, is believed to be responsible for Jorge and his brother Diego fleeing from the state penitentiary. An FBI agent shot Mr. O'Hara during what appeared to be a break-in a few months ago at the home of the third oldest Montiago brother, Hector Montiago in Sedona, Arizona. No word on what Police chief O'Hara was doing in the home at the time of the break-in. No word on the whereabouts of Diego Montiago at this time. He was not with his brother Jorge at the airport. Any information on this man needs to be reported right away. He is assumed to be armed and dangerous."

"That's not good," John said. "Diego is missing and no word on Max. I don't like it."

I'm glad he still thinks Max is dead."

"Don't count on that," John said. "Mick knows." We were quiet for a few minutes. "If Mick was dirty, who knows who else was," he continued.

"I still can't believe it," I said. "My dad, a dirty cop. I thought that was why Diego married me in the first place, to keep dad in line."

"And it worked quite well," he pointed out. I suppose he was right. Dad did and had continued to do everything that Diego had asked him to do. I was still in shock.

Time went by slowly. We had been living there for too long. The news about Jorge made me think that it wouldn't be long now before Max caught up with him. I hadn't heard Max's deep, Latin, accented voice in so long. I continued to replay it in my head so I wouldn't forget the sound. Johnny cooked all of our meals for us every day and my son continued to keep a close eye on his newly found father. John made no further attempts to get me into bed but he was still watching me ever so closely.

"Still no news?" I asked John and Dieguito as I started yet another new day.

"Nothing," he said. "I could so get used to this." John smiled and passed me some eggs. My phone rang and I looked down at it for the caller ID. It wasn't Max.

"Did you hear about me on TV?" the voice said. "I'm famous now, you know." I didn't say anything. John looked up at me. "Lilly, who is it?"

"I hope you have enjoyed your time screwing my brother," he continued. "I'm on my way to come get you and my baby. He's dead!" and the voice was gone. I dropped the phone and started screaming. Johnny picked up his cell and called the FBI from next door to come over. They raced inside.

"What's going on?" Miranda asked.

"Mommy, mommy!" Dieguito was pulling on my sleeve. All the noise started running together and I couldn't think. John picked me up the way he saw Max do and he put me on the couch. "Lilly, who was on the phone?"

"Is Max dead?" I asked Miranda. "Is he dead?" I demanded an answer. She dialed the phone and said, "You all right?" I waited with my heart beat racing. "He's fine, Lilly."

"Diego," I said. "He called. He said Max was dead and he's coming for me and the baby." I swallowed hard. "For me and his baby."

"Max," she said. "Diego knows you're alive. Mick, you know. Diego called Lilly." She handed me the phone. "He wants to talk with you."

I grabbed the phone from her hand. "Maxwell! You have to come home."

"Baby girl," he said calmly. "Do you trust me?"

"Yes, of course." I answered.

"I'm going to find that dog. You have nothing to fear. He doesn't know where you are. You are covered. I'll ask Miranda and Steve to monitor the house more carefully at night, okay?"

"I'm scared, Max. And I miss you."

"I know," he said. "It's almost over."

"Max?"

"Look at your finger, Lilly." I looked at the diamond on my finger. "Remember that you promised," he said.

"I promised," I agreed.

"I love you. I'm fine and I have not seen Diego. Everything is all right."

"Tell Hector I'm worried about him too," I said.

Max laughed. "Yeah, yeah, I'll tell him. Get Hector out of your mind, got it?" He always made jokes to ease the tension.

"I'm just messing with you," I said.

"I know," he added. "Get Miranda for me," he said. "And Lilly?"

"Yes daddy."

"I love you."

"I love you more," I answered.

"Not possible," he said. I handed the phone to Miranda.

"I told you that I've heard you call him that," Johnny said. He smiled and grabbed my hand. "It's gonna be all right. Max is tough. Iron Man we used to call him. He isn't easy to kill, trust me, I know." I smirked at him.

Miranda hung up the phone. "I'll need to hook your phone up to a trace," she said. "Steve and I are going to intrude for the next 48 hours. Max wants to make sure you stay alive, will you be okay with that?"

I looked at Johnny. I knew he was disappointed. I was thrilled. "Thank you," I replied. "I'm worried, this time." My little boy curled up on my lap. "Uncle Max is the best in the business," he repeated. Something he had heard Max say a hundred times. "He won't let anything happen to us or the baby."

"I know," I said, "I know."

Dieguito finally spent the night in his own bedroom. When I woke the house was aromatic again with breakfast. I had definitely been blessed with men who cook. The FBI agents were eating the breakfast John had prepared. "Wow," I said. "You are totally going to spoil me."

"That's the plan."

"Watch it, John," Miranda warned. "Max told me to keep an eye on you." My phone rang and I looked at Miranda. She and Steve ran into place and she turned on some machine. "Make him think you're worried about him," she said. "Try to remain calm and do not tell him the baby isn't his. That's what is keeping you breathing." She put a set of headphones on and pointed to me. "GO!" she directed. I picked up the phone.

"Have you seen the news?" the voice asked. "I shot your lover."

"Are you all right, Diego?" I asked. I looked at Miranda with worry in my eyes about Max. She shook her head and motioned for me to keep going.

"You don't care if I'm all right," he answered. "You're worried about your boyfriend. My brother."

"I've been thinking about you," I continued. "Can I do anything for you?" Miranda gave me a thumbs-up.

"I wish you could have heard Max beg for mercy. Go ahead and turn on the TV?" Miranda motioned for John to turn the TV on and he did.

"Maxwell Montiago, Lieutenant for the FBI was shot today by notorious gangster Diego Montiago, his half-brother. Maxwell is currently in critical condition. Jorge Montiago, also the half-brother of Maxwell is currently in custody. He was arrested by brother number four; Hector, also an agent for the FBI. Diego Montiago is still at large. Talk about brotherly love."

"It would be a shame for him to die right now, wouldn't it? Never to see my new born baby?" Diego taunted.

"What are you talking about?" I asked.

"I'm sorry Lilly but he's on his way to hell now."

"Diego, it isn't worth it," I said. I could feel my voice start to shake. I was so full of panic, which wasn't my strong suit.

"Sure it is," he said. "I have to make sure Max is dead before I come and get you." There was a short silence.

"Why?" I asked. "Why can't you just leave him alone?" I could feel my cool exterior start to slip.

"Johnny is weak," he went on. "But Max is strong. He won't rest until he finds you. He must be eliminated. Then…" He paused. "Then I will come for you." He hung up the phone.

"NO! No this isn't happening!" I shouted. "Max, critically injured. No, this can't be happening." I put my hands over my ears. I couldn't breathe.

"It's not," Miranda said. "It's a ploy to lull Diego into false security. He was wearing a vest; he's fine. He called last night."

"I want to talk to him," I said. I was growing impatient with all this make-believe.

"She dialed the phone and handed it to me right away this time."

"Max?" I asked.

"I'm fine," he said. "Just trying to throw him off the scent a little."

"How did he get away?" I asked.

"Don't you worry about the details. We got Satan," he reminded me. "Now we just have to get Diego before he finds you," he continued. "Is John behaving?" I paused. "I'll kill that son-of-a-bitch if he touches you," he scolded.

"We're fine," I said. "We've got FBI everywhere, what could happen?"

"I may come home, Lilly," he finally said. "I have a bad feeling that he may have found you."

I was silent. Miranda grabbed the phone. "Sorry Max, but she's just so worried."

"See you soon," and she hung up the phone.

"I'm going to check on the trace. It looks like…" she paused, "he's here."

"What?" I asked. "Here?"

"Stay put!" she ordered. "Lock the door behind me. I'm going next door." The two of them left.

"What's happening?" I asked John.

He quickly got up and reached for my hand. I pulled it away. "We're running out of time," he said. "Max will be back, probably tomorrow. Lilly, we're finally alone."

"Are you kidding me?" I couldn't believe him. I was thankful my son was so addicted to video games.

"Just give me a chance," he said. He pulled me close to him and grabbed my face. He looked at me hoping to see something. He was searching my eyes for the love he had hoped had been re-born. But he found nothing. Then he let me go. "You do love him, don't you?"

"Yes," I conceded. "I'm sorry Johnny, it's just too late."

Just then I heard a gun cock. We both didn't move for a second. I looked up and saw Diego at the back door. He was pointing his gun at me. "Give me your gun, John or I'll spray the walls with her blood." John took out his gun and handed it to him. "I told you he was weak," Diego said to me. "Max has amazing instincts. He would have shot me dead for sure by now."

"Diego," I said calmly. "How did you find us?"

"I told you a long time ago that witness protection was for amateurs." He motioned for me to get closer to him. "Max is dead," he told me. "I had my… connection call the hospital. It looks like I killed your hero." I knew I was supposed to look shocked and angry but I knew he was fine. "In shock, Lilly?" he asked. "He's dead! You're coming with me now and I'll take care of you and the baby." He paused for a minute. I could tell he was getting anxious. "It'll be just like old times, except this time the baby is mine. Where is he? Go get him." I stood there unable to move my legs. "Let's go!" he yelled at me, shaking the gun. I guess I was being defiant by not crying and coming to him.

"Go," John said. "He'll kill you, Lilly."

"No he won't," I argued. "Not until he has my baby." He walked to me and shoved the gun into my temple. "I killed Olivia for less," he shouted. "You will not be any harder to kill." He grabbed my arm and pushed me down the steps that lead to the outside. There were only three steps and I fell down all of them and landed on the ground. My son came running outside, "Mommy, mommy…"

"Go back inside, Dieguito!" I screamed.

"My son," Diego called. "Come to daddy."

"You are not my daddy!" he shouted. Diego's face became enraged.

"You told him?" Diego asked me. "You told him!" He was growing angrier by the minute.

"Calm down," I pleaded. "We can work this out." I pulled my son towards me and crawled as far away from Diego as I could. We heard a loud BANG! Not a sound that was unfamiliar anymore but definitely not something you ever get used to. Diego hit the pavement and John ran outside and grabbed me. I turned around and Max was standing there with the smoking gun. Diego was not dead but he shot him in the thigh and his gun had flown out of his hands. John picked Diego's gun up off of the ground and handed it to Max.

"How did you know?" I asked.

"Querida," he paused and smiled, "I just knew." Hector showed up behind him. I finally realized that it was almost over. Max ran to me and hugged me. "Baby girl!" He kissed me deeply.

I could see Johnny out of my peripheral vision unfavorably watching us. "She kissed me, you know," he said. Max pulled out his gun and pointed it at John. Hector came up behind him and grabbed it. "Not now, Max. Maybe later, but not now." Max kissed me again. "You can tell me all about it later. Right now, I just want to feel you against me."

"Get a room," Hector blurted. Max laughed.

Miranda came up behind him. "Good job Miranda," he said sarcastically. "Where the hell were you?" Hector was handcuffing Diego. Then he slapped handcuffs on Miranda and started reading her rights to her. We could hear an ambulance off in the distance.

"Who's the dirty cop in Arizona?" I asked.

"Felix in Arizona," Max answered reluctantly. "Miranda, right here with you." I couldn't believe how the ones most trusted ended up being the bad guys.

CHAPTER 25

The Boyfriend?

Max and Hector spent the night with us in the safe house. Diego was rushed to the hospital under heavy guard and Max had a few things to say to Johnny. But before any of that there was one very important thing Max wanted to do.

"Please, Lilly let me see our son." Our son. It felt wonderful to hear him say that.

I went into the bedroom and brought him out. Everyone had come back into the house and sat somewhere comfortably in the living room except for Max. He waited impatiently outside the door. He held out his arms and I delicately dropped him into his waiting arms. "Well look at you," he said. He walked over to Hector and Hector grinned.

"Sad, but man he looks just like you." He reached over and touched his tiny cheek.

"I know, it's amazing," Max said. I had never seen such a satisfied smile on his face. He looked up at me with tears in his eyes. "I am so sorry I wasn't here."

"I know," I told him.

"I stepped in," John said. But Max did not like that.

"What's his name?" he asked. "I hope you didn't name him after me."

"Christian Maxwell," I answered.

"Lilly, I wanted him to have his own name." He was still smiling and cooing at the baby.

"He does. He has Christian. We can call him Chris. But there was no way you weren't going to be in there somewhere." John smiled at me. Max handed me the baby. He's sucking on my finger," he said. "I think he's hungry."

"Johnny and I will go… take a walk," Hector said. "You two spend some time together."

"I've seen her nurse," John said. "I'm fine with it."

Max's face seemed to catch fire when he said that. "We'll talk later. Now, go and leave us." The two went outside and I unbuttoned my blouse to feed the baby. "I think I'm a little jealous," Max said with a smile. "Okay, I am definitely jealous. When is it going to be my turn?"

"Hang on," I said. "Let me feed him first. Then it will be your turn." Truth be told, I could hardly wait. It had been almost a year that we hadn't been in each other's arms. I missed him so much. It was like part of me was missing. When I finished feeding him, I laid him in his basinet. Max scooped me up and carried me to my bedroom where he laid me down in the bed. Dieguito came running inside. Max rolled over on his back and started laughing. He jumped on top of Max calling, "Uncle Max, Uncle Max, we really missed you!"

"I really missed you too," he said, rolling back over and tickling Dieguito. "Now, why don't you go play so that mommy can tell Uncle Max how much she missed him."

"Eww!" He got up and ran out. We both laughed.

I got up and locked the door. "Let me show you how much your baby girl missed you." I crawled back into the bed on all fours and jumped on him. He started pulling my clothes off like it had been ten years since he had seen me.

"I couldn't stand it, thinking about you playing house with that guy," he said. "Give me everything, baby girl." I got on top of him and he pulled whatever clothing was left off of my body. He pushed himself inside of me and I let out a cry. He quickly rolled me over and covered my mouth with his. "Don't forget about the boys," he whispered.

"Oh daddy," I cried. He began to kiss every inch of me. My ears, my neck, my leaking breasts and worked his way down to my toes. I don't know how he expects me to be so quiet when he is driving me crazy like that. I whispered his name into his ear and he moaned slightly each time. I was alive. Every inch of me was on fire. We made love until we heard Hector and John come back in. He cried out my name one last time and collapsed beside me. I curled up on his even more muscular chest than I had remembered. He cradled me in his arms. "I so want to do more of that later," he whispered. I kissed his chest a few times. "Stop that," he said. "I have zero will power right now."

Hector knocked on the door. "Hey you guys, are you coming back out?"

"Yeah, yeah, yeah…" Max answered. "Give us a minute." We got dressed and we kissed a little before we walked back into the living room. I set the monitor and he went for the door. Then he took my face and kissed me again. I think we're going to have to talk about the last 8 months." We headed out the door and I dreaded what I knew was going to be the new topic of conversation.

Hector and John were in the kitchen making some dinner. John looked at Max and said, "I meant what I said."

"I heard you the first time," he told him. "You were alone for a long time."

"She kissed me back," he said, smirking at me. I was remembering what he said about a death wish. It didn't take him long to change his mind about that.

"What happened to, 'I owe you?'" Max asked. "Did you think she would leave me for you?"

"I didn't plan it. Here we were, husband and wife having a baby together. I missed the whole first time," he said. He looked down at the potatoes he was cutting and abruptly stopped. "She loved me too once," he continued.

"What happened?" Max asked me. "You don't…" He stopped. He couldn't say it out loud.

"No, no, don't be ridiculous! I love you, daddy, only you." He picked me up and put me on his lap on the couch. Then he kissed me right there in front of God and all His people.

"She kissed me back," he said again. "I may have started it, but she liked it."

"Shut up!" Hector said. "It's over now, he's back."

"You can shut me up if you want to, but she still has feelings for me."

"I don't care," Max replied. "Maybe you just caught her off guard, I don't know. But she doesn't love you. She's been over you for quite some time now. She's mine." He kissed me again.

"Tell him, Lilly. Tell him there's a part of you that still wants me."

"Lilly," Max started, "unless you're planning on leaving me for him, tell me you didn't kiss him back." He grabbed my chin with his hand and made my eyes meet his. "If you are still in love with me, just tell me you did not kiss him back." He looked over at John. "If you want to leave me, tell me you did. But I don't want to hear that you were… I can't hear that, Lilly."

"I didn't kiss him back," I said. "He grabbed my face, kissed me and I smacked him across the face." Max laughed.

"Oh yeah, that's love," Hector blurted. "Let me give it a try."

"Okay, boys that's enough," Max scolded. "No one kisses my girl, but me." John, frustrated, left the room.

"That's all I wanted to know," he resolved. But the elephant in the room was ever present and ever growing. "Whatever happened," he continued, "I know you love me."

I felt so guilty for even having John's lips against mine, even if I didn't want them there. But the man of my dreams was home, safe and that really seemed to be all that mattered.

We were all exhausted and went to bed almost immediately after dinner. We hadn't made any plans yet for tomorrow, but Max and I had a lot of catching up to do. We made love all night; I'm sure to the dismay of Johnny and Hector who had to listen to it. When we woke, the house was full of the smells of breakfast. Only to my surprise it was Hector cooking. "Johnny's pissed," Hector said. "So, I cooked. I hope it's to your liking." He put a plate in front of me and one in front of Max.

"You're the best," I told him.

"You're okay," Max said laughing. "Thanks, man."

"I figured you'd be too tired to cook this morning." Hector winked at me. "So, now that you're nursing, I had better make sure you get some food into your system." I think I saw Max blush. It doesn't happen often, but he was red in the face, a little. "Nursing the baby," Hector laughed. "I think I hit a nerve."

"All right, all right," Max sputtered. "I need to talk to Steve about a lawyer. It's time for Lilly to get a 180 pound Mexican removed from her life."

"A divorce?" I asked.

"First," he continued. "You need to get Johnny to agree to a DNA test with little Diego. I want to be sure we have proof he is not the real father. We don't want his family somehow getting custody."

"I never thought of that. Where's Johnny?" I asked Hector.

"He's outside somewhere. He's still in love with you, Lilly." He sat down and started eating some of his own creation. "You must cast quite a spell."

"I'll go find him," Max said. "He's probably at the park." He grabbed his jacket and blew me a kiss. "Make sure Dieguito eats, Lilly," he reminded me. "Those video games can be addicting." He left and Hector sat there eying me.

"What?" I asked.

"Did you kiss him back?" He sat there waiting for an answer. "Max may not want to know, but I do. He seemed pretty convinced that you wanted him."

I said nothing for a few minutes. Hector continued to wait. "I didn't kiss him. He grabbed me. I didn't like it." He sat there staring at me as though he was sure I was lying. "It's over between us."

"Okay," he said. "I believe you." He continued to stare at me.

"What?" I asked again.

"Why is he so mad?"

"He told me he still loved me," I answered. "I rejected him."

"Okay," he replied.

"Stop that!"

"Stop what?"

"Stop acting like you don't believe me."

He continued to stare at me. "Max loves you, Lilly. You'd better be sure."

"I am sure!" I insisted. "I wouldn't want to breathe if Max wasn't in my life."

As I said that Max and John walked back into the house. "Now, that's what I like to hear." Max smiled and hung up his coat. "I found him. He'll do it."

"Of course I will." John looked over at me. "I still love you and our child. I'll do whatever it takes to keep you both safe." Max glared at him when he said that. But I got up from the table and hugged him. He grabbed my chin and looked into my eyes. I wondered if he doubted me.

"His name is Mark Franklin," Steve said. "He is an FBI attorney. He does all our work for us. Make sure you give him all three paternity tests and… no secrets."

"Thanks Steve," Max responded. He grabbed my hand like a silly little boy and said, "Almost free, baby girl."

Hector stayed home with Dieguito and John came with us to Las Vegas, in case there was some kind of paternity issue. I was still nursing so I had to take Chris with us. I was rolling him around in a baby carriage. When we got to the courthouse Mark was standing outside waiting for us. "Do you have the tests?" he asked us. Max handed them to him. "Before they get here, is there anything else I should know?"

"This is John Malone." John shook his hand. "He is the biological father of the first born."

"That's good that you brought him." He looked at me. "I'm sorry Lilly, but Diego is fighting the divorce. He says you are abandoning him and he still loves you." I looked at Max with an expression of panic.

"Don't worry, baby girl, it'll be all right." He stroked my hair. "Have I ever let you down before?" he asked.

"No," I answered, still in a state of shock.

"Lilly, you must remain calm," Mark warned me. "Even if the opposing council calls you a name, or insults your integrity, remain calm." We walked into the courtroom. Vanessa Hernandez was always Diego's attorney and she was sitting at the opposite table by herself. Mark and I sat together and Max and John sat behind us. We stood up as the judge walked in. She was blond and strikingly attractive. When she sat, we all sat down. She looked up and saw Max and smiled. This made me nervous.

"To what do I owe the pleasure of your company?" she asked. "I believe it is Lieutenant Montiago now."

"Yes, Your Honor." he smiled that boyish grin and she smiled back.

"Max, tell me you are not the Montiago contesting the divorce today." She seemed concerned. "A baby in the picture? You wouldn't do that, right?"

"No ma'am," he answered. "It's my half-brother, Diego."

"Oh, him." she gave Max an unfavorable glare over the top of her glasses. "You're here to speak for him?"

"No, Your Honor."

"Excuse me!" Vanessa interrupted. "I'm sorry but since you seem to have a history with the boyfriend," she became very patronizing, "I would appreciate it if you might consider removing yourself from this case."

"This is not a criminal case, counselor," she answered in a very antagonizing tone. "I am sure I can be impartial in a simple divorce hearing."

She looked back over at Max. "The boyfriend?" She smiled curiously.

"It's exactly as it looks," he said, almost proud of himself.

She looked back at Vanessa. "Mr. Montiago is a high ranking FBI official. I think you will find it hard pressed to locate a judge in this town who does not know him or hasn't heard of his work. I will be the judge on whether or not I can be impartial."

"Yes, Your Honor," she answered reluctantly.

"Since Ms. Hernandez seems to feel I may have trouble being impartial, we will let her go first." She looked at my lawyer and said, "Will that be all right with you counselor?"

"Whatever pleases the court," he answered.

Vanessa started her defense. "My client, Mr. Montiago…"

"This is not a criminal case," The judge interrupted. "I think I already made that clear. Since the husband and the boyfriend," she said boyfriend in a silly voice and looked over at Max, "have the same last name, let's use their first names for this proceeding."

"Yes Your Honor," she continued. "Diego argues that she is abandoning him in his time of need. Diego took Lilly in when she was pregnant with another man's child five years ago. He clothed her, fed her and gave her a place to stay. He paid all her medical bills for the pregnancy and took very good care of them for five years. Diego and Lilly have enjoyed a very physical relationship and as you can see, she just had his child three months ago. He wants her to stay and support him and he feels she owes him that. He has been faithful throughout the marriage and has chosen to forgive her for her indiscretion with his brother. The only thing he is requesting is a restraining order be issued for Maxwell to stay away from his wife."

"Those are some pretty good points, counselor," she added. "Anything else?"

"That is all, Your Honor."

"Okay, Mr. Franklin, what have you got for me?" She looked over her glasses again. "And it better be good."

"Yes, Your Honor," he continued. "My client has suffered sexual abuse and beatings at the hands of Diego Montiago for the past three years of their marriage. They have not enjoyed a sexual relationship, he forced her to have relations with him or he would remove Maxwell from the home, which he did at one time. Maxwell, as you know, is an FBI operative and needed to remain in the house to complete his infiltration of the organization. Mrs. Montiago did what she felt she had to do to keep Max on the property."

"How self-sacrificing of you, Mrs. Montiago," the judge responded in a sarcastic tone. "Go on…"

"The marriage began under false pretenses. Lilly was pregnant with John Malone's baby."

"Is that you?" the judge asked, looking at Johnny.

"Yes, Your Honor," he answered.

"Diego told Lilly that Mr. Malone had been killed in a car crash and threatened Mr. Malone with harm to Lilly and the baby if he ever made it known that he was still alive. Once he married Lilly, he used her as leverage against the police chief in Sedona, to continue his drug trafficking."

"Michael O'Hara?" she asked.

"Yes, Your Honor, her father," he answered. "I have here the paternity test for Johnny's baby, ironically named Diego." He put the papers on the judge's desk. She looked it over.

"Max?" she asked. "The newborn?" He smiled at her. "Yours?"

"Yes, Your Honor." Mark put the test on her desk along with the other.

"As far as Diego being faithful throughout the marriage, this is a paternity test for the baby Olivia Montiago was carrying. She was murdered outside the O'Hara's household, pregnant with Diego Montiago's baby. Olivia was Diego's brother, Jorge's wife."

She began to look through the evidence. "Well Max," she said. "Apparently you and your brother have been busy boys."

"Yes, Your Honor, it looks that way." His dimples seemed to melt her icy façade.

"Diego pretty much ignored Mrs. Montiago for the first two years of the marriage. Although Max will admit to falling hopelessly in love with his brother's wife, he did not initiate an affair until after four years had gone by," Mark explained.

"If you don't mind my asking," she continued, "what changed your mind?"

"May I?" I asked.

"We are not formal here… please Lilly, I would like to hear from you."

"Diego discovered that Max and I were in love and decided to mark his territory, so to speak. He announced that he wanted to win my heart. He told Max to leave me alone so that he could make me fall in love with him. Max was feeling like we missed our opportunity. So we finally gave in. Diego and I had a sexual relationship for two years. I never wanted it." I could see her face, hungry with interest. "After two years of forced sex, something happened to Diego. He promised to stop forcing himself on me and he wanted to have a baby." I took a deep breath and tried to fight the tears welling in my eyes. "I begged Max to make love to me and father my child. He was reluctant at first but I finally convinced him that if I had Diego's baby he would have a permanent claim on me."

"Okay," she continued. "So, he obliged and here we are today."

"Yes, Your Honor, that's the whole story."

"Ms. Hernandez, do you have anything further?"

"I would like to see the tests," she stated.

"I will make them available to you after the hearing," she responded. "I assure you that they are authentic."

"Yes, Your Honor, thank you."

"Anything further, from either side?"

"No Your Honor," Vanessa squeaked out.

"No Your Honor," Mark stated.

"I am going to allow this divorce and dissolve this marriage," she announced. "It is not because I am partial to Mrs. Montiago's boyfriend but because Diego Montiago is a criminal who has kept this poor girl prisoner in his house for too long." She slammed the gavel against the desk. "And besides," she added. "The baby isn't even his. Lilly, you're free."

"With all due respect," Vanessa continued. "Diego really believes that this baby is his."

"Well, it is very clearly not," she continued. Then she peered over at Max. "Maxwell, are you going to marry her?" she asked.

"Yes, ma'am," he answered. "As soon as the ink dries."

"Give the papers a few days to get filed and then…" she paused, "congratulations."

"Thank you, Your Honor."

"Lilly?" she asked. "I see here that you are asking for nothing monetary."

"That is correct, Your Honor."

"Would you like to reconsider?"

"All I want is full custody of my children…" I paused, "and his brother." I laughed.

"Granted!" She said and slammed the gavel back down against the desk. "Case closed. Thank you, counselors, for your service today. Max…" she gave him a flirty smile. "I will see you around, I'm sure."

"Yes, Your Honor," he said and she left the room.

He got up from his chair and jumped over the wall that separated us. "I love you so much, baby girl!" I was so happy that I was sobbing uncontrollably.

"Diego will not be happy." Vanessa walked over to us and grabbed Max by the arm. "There will be repercussions for this decision."

"Are you threatening my client?" Mark passed a glare to her that would have killed if it were loaded.

"Diego might kill me over this, you know." She was so angry that her hands were shaking. "How could you betray me like this?" She slapped Max across the face with full force.

He fell back a little and put his hand over his cheek. "That is so not my problem anymore," he said, trying to regain his balance.

"He might come after you, her or the judge, you know." She was simply not ready to go.

"I'll make a note of it," Mark told her. "I'll also be pressing charges for assault."

"That won't be necessary," Max responded. "She's scared. It's okay."

"I will make sure you pay, Max," she said. "You and your little whore!"

"What am I missing?" I asked. "Why did she slap you?"

"He'll probably put out a hit on her. She and I have known each other a long time. I've saved her butt a time or two. She's scared and rightfully so."

I was not convinced that there wasn't something more. An affair possibly, I wasn't sure. But I was in no position to demand answers.

We all walked out of court that day with hope and excitement. I hugged Mark and Max thanked him over and over. "We still have to get Diego locked up, Max," Mark reminded him. "Let's not get too excited yet. He may get off. It's been known to happen."

CHAPTER 26

You really should have stayed away from their wives.

Mark delivered the divorce papers to us personally. We stayed at Max and Diego's house until the papers were officially filed. It was creepy. When the papers arrived Mark said, "Free at last, free at last!" I grabbed the papers and ripped open the envelope. I jumped up and down and threw my arms around Max. "Are we still getting married?" I asked.

"Are you kidding?" Max said. "I'm going to call Hector and have him fly out here; unless you want to get married in Arizona. Maybe in a little church in the rocks? Baby, I want you to have what you want."

"Fly Hector and Dieguito out here and let's get married!" I was so excited.

"I do have one condition." Max looked serious and it scared me.

"Anything," I said. "What is it?"

"I want to get married on Easter Sunday." He looked at me with the sweetest eyes.

"Are you serious?" I asked. "If we get married on Easter, someone will interrupt the wedding with a machine gun or something. No way!"

"I want Easter to be turned around for you. I want you to remember Easter as being a good day."

"Max, I lost Johnny on Easter. I married Diego a week after Easter. My dad was shot on Easter. My mother's funeral was on Easter and you were shot, almost to death on Easter." I thought about all the sadness I had experienced on such a holy day. "Do you want to have our anniversary so close to my anniversary with Diego?"

"Yes," he answered. "Because you will remember it with love and joy." I thought about his suggestion for a while. Although, I really did think he was crazy, I went along with it.

We decided to hold the ceremony at the Flamingo with Hector as Max's best man and my little son who would stand up for me. I looked at myself in the mirror in my dressing room, thinking about how I hadn't lost all the weight from the pregnancy. John knocked on the door. I opened it and said, "You can only come in if you promise not to kiss me." He laughed, and came inside. "I just wanted to give you one more chance to change your mind."

"I love Maxwell," I told him. I took his hands and kissed his cheek. "I can't thank you enough for all you have done for me. But Maxwell is all I think about. I'm sorry I didn't kiss you back, but I didn't want to lead you on."

"I came on too strong," he admitted. "But I don't regret it."

"Oh and thanks for placing doubt in his head. I needed that," I said sarcastically.

"On some level, you do love me," he said. "And you did kiss me back." He smiled like he knew something I didn't. I shook my head in disapproval.

Just then Hector walked in unannounced. "Get the hell out of here," he said to John.

"I was just wishing the bride a good life," he said and he walked out.

"Any kissing?" Hector asked sarcastically.

"Oh my gosh, no…" I answered. "I love Max, Hector. Only Max."

"Keep that guy at bay," he warned. "I'm not kidding, Lilly. Max won't put up with this."

"I'll tell him he was here," I offered.

"Not today," Hector said. "He is so excited."

"I do not want Johnny," I continued. "I can't help if he still wants me. It's not my fault."

"Be meaner to him," he said laughing. "So, you and Max." He paused. "It's the real deal?"

"Hector, I hope you find it someday." I kissed his cheek. "Yes, it's the real deal."

"That's if you can get over me," he said. I rolled my eyes.

"If I'm going to give you away, we'd better get moving." He started straightening his tie in the mirror. "You know I love you, Lilly. You're like the sister I never had."

"You have Elena," I said laughing.

"You're like the sister I always wished I had," he corrected himself.

I took his arm and he walked me down the aisle. Hector delivered me to Max and took his place beside him. Johnny was an involuntary witness. Our baby was five months old now and Diego was finally five. So much time had gone by and Max and I had never lived a normal life. The preacher looked at Max and said, "You have your own vows you said you would like to recite." I was shocked. He never said anything about it to me.

"Yes, I do." He grabbed my hands and looked into my eyes. I could feel my heart slip into my stomach. My legs got weak and I had to remind myself to remain standing. He kissed my hands, one at a time and searched my eyes for longing. I could tell they were beginning to fill with tears before his musical voice even began to speak.

"Querida," he started. "You are my reason for drawing breath in the morning." His glance never left my eyes. "The first time I saw you, you were like a wounded bird looking for hope. I fell in love with you instantly. My heart aches for you when we are apart and my soul feels incomplete. You make me whole. Together, we can face anything and we will passionately enjoy the journey. Thank you for being my baby girl."

I had no idea how to follow that. He did not warn me, so I had not time to write anything down. "Since you didn't tell me you were going to do this, I am not prepared."

He smiled and said, "Just reach inside your heart."

I took a deep breath and thought about it for a minute. "You are everything to me," I started. You rescued me from my first scary pregnancy and then you rescued me from what had become my life. You are my best friend, an incredible lover and the only part of me that makes any sense." I could hear John snicker a little. "I have never been happier and I pray that you will stay by my side forever. Without you there is no reason for me to go on. I love you so much!" I wanted so desperately to jump into his arms. The preacher continued the ceremony and we exchanged rings. I was crying so hard, I could barely see clearly enough to slip the ring on his finger. When he got to the "kiss the bride," Max pulled me close and kissed me deeply. I was so swept away; he had to hold me up a little.

"We made it," he said to me. "We made it," and he gave me that boyish grin. "It's Easter Sunday and not one got shot." He laughed.

"Just joy and love." He looked over at his brother. "Things are going to be different now." Hector hugged him and then me.

Johnny shook Max's hand and hugged me. Then he whispered in my ear, "If you ever change your mind, I'll be here." Max pulled him away by the back of his collar.

"I don't think you want to mess with me today," he said to Johnny. Johnny looked at him disparagingly.

Hector grabbed John and said, "Where are you going to stay while you wait for the trial. I hear it starts next week."

"I thought you and Max would put me up," he said. "Max and Diego have that huge house." He looked at Max. "Come on, you're married now, I'm no threat."

"You were never a threat," he corrected him. "But you're still hitting on her, I don't want you around."

"Come on Max, we can keep an eye on him this way," Hector said earnestly.

"Lilly?" Max asked. "How do you feel about him staying with us? The trial could go on for months."

"If he becomes a problem, I'll let you know," I answered. "Really, I promise."

"Okay," he said. "But the first time I see you trying to stick your tongue down her throat…" He didn't finish but Johnny got the picture.

As we were heading out the door a man walked over to me with an envelope. "Lilly Montiago?"

Max pushed me behind him and said, "Who wants to know?"

"Is she Lilly?" I began to feel frightened. I knew Easter was a bad idea.

"I'm her husband, what do you want?" He reached around Max and handed me the paper. "You have been served." He turned away and high tailed it down the hall.

"Diego probably had her subpoenaed to testify," Hector assumed. I opened the envelope and looked at Max in surprise. "I don't know anything about Diego's business. What could they possibly want from me?"

"To discredit Max," Johnny answered. "Expose your affair… that kind of thing."

"Crap!" I blurted. "This is just great!"

"It's fine," Max said. "I didn't really hide it from Diego." He paused and smiled for a minute. "Not very well, anyway."

Hector laughed and said, "You think?"

"He knew about it and I never denied it. Besides it took us four years to consummate our relationship. Who waits four years?"

"Like anyone is going to believe that?" Hector mentioned. "I still don't believe that."

"What about you?" Max said to Hector. "You were warming Olivia's bed for years."

"Yeah, we probably should have stayed away from their wives."

"You think?" Johnny said sarcastically, following Hector's lead.

"I'll call the lawyer in the morning. But tonight is our wedding night." He handed the keys to Hector. Go ahead and take everyone home," he suggested. "Lilly and I have to consummate our marriage."

"A little late for that," he said, holding Chris in his arms. "Just kidding, go have fun." Then he put the baby back in the stroller. "I'll take care of Chris for you," he said to me. "He drinks from the bottle now, right?"

"Yes, thanks Hector. There's formula in the diaper bag."

"I'll watch Dieguito," John assured us. "I'm glad to have time with him." They waved and took off down the hall. Little Diego kissed us and helped Hector push the baby carriage down the hallway.

Max and I got our key to our room and he carried me over the threshold.   It was our first night as husband and wife and our last night without any strife. We were going to have to start the trial and I would be seeing Diego every day again. As Maxwell took me into his arms I tried to push back all the craziness that was ahead of us. Max was so romantic and so gentle with me. To him it was like I was the most beautiful woman in the world. We made love all night long. He never tired. By the time we fell asleep it was almost daylight. When he finally woke he put his arms around me and said, "Is it over already?"

"Yes daddy, it is." I turned to look into those ocean blue eyes.

"Do we have to go back?"

"Yes daddy, we do."

"Baby girl..." he whispered. "I'm so in love with you."

"I love you more," I told him.

"That is not possible," he said. And we began to get ready for our day. We had to call Mark and get started on our testimony. But we were finally married. I felt so safe. I was ready.

Mark came over and brought all kinds of papers with him. I guessed they were from Max and Hector's work all those years in the organization. "Lilly," he said, "I understand you have been subpoenaed. Let's talk about your affair with Max." I sighed.

"I know this kind of thing can be embarrassing but no surprises. You need to tell me everything."

"We didn't have a physical relationship for the first four and a half years," I answered. "We only started sleeping together when Diego wanted to get me pregnant."

"No sex?" He looked at Max for confirmation.

"No sex," Max repeated.

"You can't really say you had no physical relationship," Mark continued. "Was there touching?"

"Oh God!" I put my hands over my face.

"I know this is embarrassing, but if you tell me now, I can defend you better." He looked back at Max.

"No, there was no fooling around," Max insisted. We hugged on occasion but that was all. I was too afraid to get her in trouble. I didn't want her to slip and call him by the wrong name. I was worried about her safety."

"Did she ever sleep with you in your bed?" he asked.

"She slept with me one time," he admitted. "There was no sex. Diego raped and beat her at the hotel. She took a cab home and came to me. She asked me to make love with her but I refused. I did ask her to stay with me though, so I could hold her and comfort her."

"Hmmm…." he continued. "Yeah, this is going to be hard to prove. I'm guessing that no one with believe you."

"All I have is the truth," he answered.

"So, you decided to sleep with her because Diego wanted to get her pregnant?" He paused. "That doesn't make any sense."

Max put his hands over his face this time and said, "Oh this is starting to get uncomfortable."

"Take your time," Mark told him.

"Diego asked me to leave her alone so he could…" He paused. "It turns my stomach to think about it," he told him.

"So he could what?" Mark asked.

"Win her heart. He wanted to make her fall in love with him and then get her pregnant. I was sick."

"So, you decided to get her pregnant instead?"

"I just wanted to lay with her; just once before I lost her to him. So, she took me to bed that day." He reached over and stroked my hair. "She asked me to get her pregnant. We had just found out Olivia was pregnant, so I guess the idea was there. She asked me not to use protection."

"I see," he said. "Diego would think it was his baby when actually it would be yours."

"That was the plan. Not a good one, I'll admit, but it was all we had. I knew I'd get her out of there soon, so… well here she is."

"This looks a little premeditated."

"How so?" Max asked.

"You got her pregnant, knowing you were going to help her divorce him and marry her."

"Yeah…" Max said sarcastically.

"You're an FBI agent on a case. You're not supposed to… sleep with your work or should I say…" he started to laugh, "take your work home with you."

"Ha ha ha," Max said. Then he pointed to Hector and just like a little kid said, "He did it too."

"We'll get to him later," he went on. "You did a very unprofessional thing and got personally involved in one of your jobs. That will not look favorable for you."

"Well, I rescued her. She would have been a casualty of war and I didn't want that." He sighed. "Besides, I was already personally involved. Diego's my brother."

"True," he agreed. "And you did know he was using Lilly as leverage. Maybe we can use that. You can say you were trying to keep her safe and you fell in love with her in the process."

"That is what happened," Max answered. "I was her bodyguard."

"Okay," he said. "That shines some light on why you ended up spending so much time with her."

"It was my pleasure." He winked at me.

"Okay, Hector, your turn." He looked over at Hector.

"Yeah, I'm not as moral as my brother," he added. "I slept with Jorge's wife because I could. She wanted me to and I did. The fact that I fell in love with her was a consequence. When Jorge found out she was pregnant he assumed it was mine. It wasn't."

"Yes, I know it was Diego's."

"I thought she would come with me after the arrest but…" He hesitated. "She didn't." He looked quickly at Max and then down at the floor. "So, she used me and I used her. I think that is really all that can be said about that."

"You loved her, Hector, don't cheapen it." Max got up and walked over towards him. Then he put his arm around his shoulder. "You loved her."

"Okay," Mark said. "You fell in love with your brother's wife too. You boys are in big trouble."

"We know," they both said at once.

"Jorge used to beat her and I mean severely. I felt sorry for her and wanted to love on her. Eventually I became possessive of her and before I knew it, I was in love with her. But she obviously did not return those feelings. I think I was her refuge in a storm. Nothing more than that."

"You are only human, after all," Mark answered. "This crime stuff is hard to watch from the sidelines without getting involved in rescuing the casualties." Then he looked at me. "You just tell the truth. Diego ignored you and didn't even want anything to do with you until the night you discovered Johnny was still alive." He was reading some account that Max had written up for him. "You were already in love with Max by that time and it was too late. Tell the jury exactly what you told me. Also tell the jury how Max didn't hide the affair. Diego sent him away to get you pregnant. Tell it exactly the way it happened. Max is a good man. I'm sure it will come across that way. The trial starts tomorrow. Before they begin with Max they will bring you out to make him look bad. Just tell the truth."

"I can do that," I said. "Max saved my life. I owe him."

"Don't say that," Mark continued. "Tell them how much you love him." I laughed and reached for Max. He sat back down next to me and pulled me onto his lap.

"I promise, it will be over soon and you and I will be together in our house with our kids." Johnny winced. I wasn't sure having him around was such a good idea but I did want to make sure he didn't run. I really wanted Diego put away forever.

CHAPTER 27

Always so much drama.

The trial had already been put off twice, which made the baby seven months old. Dieguito's birthday passed with not much more than a kiss. We planned to celebrate his 5th birthday party right after the first day of the trial. Hector and I went out and bought balloons, streamers, a cake and gifts for the birthday boy while Max, John and Mark went over the trial. It was amazing to me how time was flying by and we seemed to have no control over it. I was so mad that I had to testify. I really wanted to put this whole ordeal behind us. We walked to the courtroom and met Mark outside the door. "Diego and Jorge are in there, Lilly. Brace yourself." Hector, Max, Johnny and I all followed Mark into the courtroom. By now we had to hire a nanny to care for the boys. I didn't want them exposed to any of this ugliness. I was glad when I got there, that little Diego was not with me. Diego and Jorge were in shackles at the front table. I imagine there was some fear about their trying something devious, since they had already escaped once. Hector and Max sat with Mark and John and I sat behind them. The judge came in and we all stood. Then she let us all sit back down. Strange custom, I had always thought. Diego's lawyer was Vanessa Hernandez; we knew her well. She represented Diego in the divorce hearing. Diego looked at me and smiled. Then he blew me a kiss. I had forgotten how handsome he was, though the thought of him putting his hands on me was still a repulsive memory. I feared getting called to the stand so much that my stomach was sick.

The first person she called to the stand was Max. The first question was of course the obvious one; "Mr. Montiago, did you have an affair with your brother's wife?"

"Yes," he answered.

"How many times were you with her?"

"Only a handful of times," he answered. "Back then, anyway."

"Did you get her pregnant?"

"Yes," he answered. So far everything was pretty straightforward if not ridiculously obvious.

210

"When did you decide to sleep with her, Mr. Montiago?"

"Please," he said. "Call me Max. There are too many Mr. Montiagos in the room today."

"Max," she continued. "When did you begin the affair?"

"We did not have a sexual relationship for the first four years," he answered. We could hear the spectators in the room gasp in disbelief.

"Why would you wait so long?" she asked.

"I won't lie," he paused and looked at me. "I was madly in love with her from day one. I was afraid for her safety and I didn't want her to get confused."

"Confused, how?"

"I didn't want her calling out my name at inopportune times." The jury giggled.

"Are you sure you weren't worried about her calling out his name in your bed?" I put my hands over my mouth. I couldn't believe she would ask such a question.

"No," he answered. "It wasn't about my ego." He paused and looked at me. "It was her safety with which I was concerned."

"Why would you worry about her safety?"

He put his hands over his face for a minute. I could tell that the memories were painful. "He abused her sexually and physically," he confessed. "I just didn't want to make it worse."

"He abused her, you say?" she asked. I started to panic. "Max, did you ever hear Lilly and Diego making love?" She got a look of superiority and began to pace back and forth. Her tone alluded to the fact that the line of questioning before her was somehow giving her some kind of pay back.

"Oh God," he said weakly and he put his hands back over his face. Then he removed them and looked at Vanessa. "Yes," he answered reluctantly.

"Would you say that Lilly may have enjoyed her sexual relationship with your brother?"

"I don't really know," he answered. "I wasn't in the room."

"I fail to see how a woman screaming out in pleasure is being sexually abused.

No further questions," and she walked off.

"Permission to redirect." Mark stood up.

"Go ahead Mr. Franklin," she said.

"Max, please explain how you know she was being abused."

"At first it was not that way. Lilly and I stayed away from each other and even though Diego suspected that we might be in love, he didn't really know until we did start…" He paused looking for the right words. "It became harder and harder to hide our feelings towards each other as time went on. That's when Diego started the abuse. He was punishing her for it, which is why we waited so long in the first place."

"I would like to submit these pictures taken by Max the night she was beaten and raped by Diego in a hotel room." He handed the judge the pictures. "Max, tell us about the night you took those pictures."

"We were at a territory party." He looked at the jury. "A territory party is when the drug dealers who are in charge of specific areas bring their hit men and their ladies to a cocktail party. A meeting for the men and dinner precedes the party. Diego made her stay with him that night in the hotel."

"Go ahead…"

"I went home, and after a few hours I saw her peek her head in my bedroom door. She was beaten up and told me he had raped her. I photographed her for this reason." He took a breath. "She slept in my arms that night but we did not make love. I didn't want our first time to be soiled by Diego's raping her."

"What was the incident that pushed you and Lilly together physically?" he continued.

"Diego made an announcement that he was going to change. He was going to stop forcing her to…" He paused and took another breath.

"Take your time, Max. I know these memories are hard for you to think about."

"He was going to stop insisting that she be intimate with him every night and give her some space. He said he wanted to win her love and start a family. I was devastated."

"What did you and Lilly decided to do?"

"She asked me to father her child. She didn't want a permanent tie to my brother." He smiled at me. "So, that is why we have a baby together now."

"No further questions," he said smiling. Max sat back down.

Then they called me up there. My hands were shaking and I could feel that my face was already flush. I walked up to the stand and they swore me in. Then I sat down.

"How long were you and Diego married, Mrs. Montiago? I can still call you that, right?" I assumed she knew Max and I were married but maybe not.

"Five long years," I answered.

"What was the condition you were in at the time of the marriage?"

"I was pregnant," I answered. "He took me in and married me."

"That doesn't sound like an abusive man to me, Mrs. Montiago."

"He wasn't in the beginning. He was very kind."

"Kinder than his brother?" she asked.

"Diego pretty much ignored me the first two years. Max was my bodyguard and we got close. Pretty simple," I said, obviously irritated.

"The first time you slept with Diego was two years into the marriage?" I held my breath at this point because I knew what the next question was going to be.

"Yes," I answered and I let my breath out.

"Did you have a pleasurable physical relationship with your husband?"

"Yes." I knew my face had gone passed purple at this point. "He was a very generous lover in the beginning. I had only been with one other person before him, and it wasn't very good." I looked over at Johnny and said, "Sorry Johnny." The jury all looked at him and started whispering. Johnny tried to hide his face.

"This was something you enjoyed then?"

"Only in the beginning," I said. "It was too frequent. It was too much. I started to hate it but he just kept on…" I stopped and started to cry. "Can we talk about something else please?" I could see Max's eyes fill with tears as he remembered our past.

"Where is the relevance in this personal line of questioning, Your Honor?" Mark blurted out.

"I am simply trying to prove that Diego is not the monster they are painting him to be. There was obviously no sexual abuse here.

The incident in the hotel was simply after a heated argument and was an isolated incident." She looked like she was finished but she continued. "I would like to make the jury aware of the fact that there was no police report filed."

"I'll allow it. Please keep it brief," she said.

"Did Diego clothe you and feed you, Mrs. Montiago?"

"Yes," I answered.

"Did he pay for all of your medical expenses?"

"Yes," I answered.

"Did you cheat on him and walk away with his brother?"

"Objection!" Mark shouted.

"No further questions," and she sat down.

Mark stood up. "I have here papers that show that Diego was not faithful to his wife during the marriage."

"Approach the bench," she said.

"These are paternity tests from Jorge's wife's baby. They are both deceased. Diego was the father."

Jorge's face turned green with horror. He was furious. He stood up and started yelling something in Spanish. The judge started hammering the gavel on the desk and the lawyer tried to get them to calm down. Jorge shouted out some kind of order in Spanish and guns started firing. Max jumped over to where I was sitting and pushed me to the floor. He and Hector pulled out their guns and started firing. "Get down!" everyone was yelling. Finally it got quiet. Diego and his unfortunate lawyer had been shot and I could hear ambulances in the background. The rest of us seemed to be unharmed and Jorge was restrained. It appeared that the only casualties were Diego, his lawyer and the shooters. The shooters were wounded lying on the floor by the door of the courtroom. "How the heck did they get their guns in here?" Max asked Hector. Max looked me over and said, "No damage this time?"

"I was still feeling panic but managed to say, "I'm fine Max, go." I knew where he was headed. It blew my mind how he kept saving that satanic sidekick. Hector ran to the shooters and disarmed them. Max ran to Diego, took off his shirt and started applying pressure to Diego's wounds.

"Can you please stop causing trouble long enough for me to put you in jail." Diego laughed and then moaned at the pain. "Quite a few holes this time, bro." He put his hand on Vanessa's neck to check for a pulse. "Not as lucky as you are, today."

"Lilly?" he asked.

"She's fine," Max confirmed.

"No, Lilly…" I could see Diego lift his hand and point to me. Max looked up.

I began to feel a twinge of nausea. The next thing I knew I was laying on the floor and I had hit my head on the table. Before I knew what was happening everyone was standing over me and I was looking up at Hector and Max trying to help me stand.

"Was she hit?" Max asked. "Is she hurt?" Hector gave me the once over.

"I don't see any blood," he said. "Lilly what hurts?" he asked.

"Stop feeling me up, Hector, I'm just feeling a little dizzy," I said. He laughed and winked at me. Max grabbed my shoulders and pulled me away from him.

"It's an inside joke," Hector said to him. "Take it easy."

"You two have too many of those," Max argued.

The ambulance came and they took Diego away. Max insisted that the paramedics check me over but I think I just had a panic attack and I had a small lump on my head from where I fell.

We went to the hospital behind the ambulance to check on Diego. We sat in the waiting room and Max filled out a bunch of paper work on Diego's behalf. "Can't wait for my questions," Hector said sarcastically. "Those weren't embarrassing."

"Tell me about it," Max conceded. "What was that all about anyway?"

"Just trying to make it look like it was a happy marriage that you destroyed." He looked down at me from where he was standing from the side of the room. "Sure glad I told you no," he laughed. Max gave him a disapproving look.

"Hopefully no one ever caught you and Olivia… you know." Max smiled mischievously at Hector.

"Nope, I was careful. Unlike you two exhibitionists." I could see him remembering Jorge, Diego and him catching us by the creek. He smiled. "I never heard them either. She was quiet."

"Not one of my luxuries," Max said. "But I like it when she cries out my name." Hector put his hands over his ears. "Too much information!"

"Maxwell, behave yourself," I said. "It looks like Diego was hurt pretty bad this time." We waited to hear that Diego was going to make it and we went home.

The trial went on without me. The dutiful wife questions were over. My part was simply to discredit Max and make Diego look like the long-suffering husband. The DNA test on Olivia's baby seemed to discredit Diego all by itself and I was off the hook. Diego and Jorge were at odds after that paternity test was discovered. Diego was in the hospital for quite a while and Max was afraid that he was going to try to win immunity by rolling over on Jorge. The FBI called a meeting with Max and Hector to discuss Diego's current condition. We all knew this was a bad sign. I was sure somehow Diego was going to get out of this. Of course our biggest fear was that he would get immunity and come after us. Now there was more than just us to worry about. Chris, who was not his baby, was to be considered. Johnny had already testified. He wanted nothing more to do with the witness protection program and was getting ready to go back to Sedona but not before the birthday party.

The boys left us alone while they went to see the FBI. I sat on the couch completely exhausted. Johnny followed me inside and sat next to me on the couch. He reached out and put one hand on my face. "I know," he said. "Rule number one, no touching."

I took his hand off of my face and took it with both my hands. "Thank you for everything, John."

"I hope they both get put away," he said. "If Diego gets immunity, we could both be in trouble."

"When they get back, we'll talk about the birthday party. I want you to be there," I told him. "I'll never forget how you were there for Chris. I will never forget you."

"Kind of hard with little Diego running around," he said. "Although I am really mad about that name." I laughed, and moved away from him a little on the couch. He was starting to get too close.

He reached for my face again and pulled me close. "I will miss you more than I could ever tell you," he said. "I'm so glad we had some time together, even if it was only brief moments. And the kiss…" He breathed in deeply as though he was taking in my scent. "I will never forget the way you responded to me." I knew I was blushing and that he was delusional.

Max walked in at that moment with Hector behind him. Hector looked at me with disappointment in his eyes. Johnny pulled his hands away quickly and Max said, "What the hell are you doing?" He grabbed John by his ponytail and hoisted him away from me.

"He was just saying goodbye, Max, that's all," I told him.

Max pulled out his gun and pointed it at John. "Do it from here."

"I'm staying for the party," John said. "But after the party, I'll get out of your way. I was just telling Lilly how nice it was to be with them." He sighed. "Max, I hope you will let me see Dieguito when you get back."

"We'll see," he said. Max put the gun away. "I can't leave you alone for one minute without him putting his hands on you."

"It's okay Max, nothing happened."

"What if I was five minutes later? Would you have kissed him?" Hector looked at me as if he too were demanding an answer.

"No, now stop acting all jealous." I could feel the agitation showing on my face. "You are the only one for me. How could you doubt me?"

"You kissed him once, didn't you?"

"He kissed me," I corrected. "Max, I love you, please…"

"He's just mad because Diego got immunity," Hector chimed in. "Now there are all kinds of guys hanging around who you have slept with that he knows about."

"Weren't there girls before me, Max?" I asked. "We never talk about it, but weren't there a few here and there?"

"A few," he said. "I don't like to talk about my indiscretions."

"Well, I don't like to talk about mine!" I was starting to get upset about this unfair treatment.

"You never told her?" Hector blurted. Max gave him a 'shut up look' if I ever saw one.

"Max was a playboy before Darla. Then he quit cold turkey. So, yeah, there've been a few."

"Thanks Hector." He blushed a little. "I'm not proud of my behavior," he said. "But I don't like this whole thing with you and Johnny."

"There's no Johnny and me. Now tell me what happened at the meeting and how much trouble we are all in?"

"I just can't believe five years of torture was all for nothing," he said. "I could have taken you out of there years ago."

"It's not for nothing," Hector said. "Jorge will never see the light of day. The organization will be shut down, and you will get a permanent restraining order on Diego. Diego will spill his guts."

"Oh no," I said. I sat down on the couch so as not to lose my balance. I suddenly felt empty inside. "He's never going to go away. He's never going to leave us alone."

"Yes he will," Max, said. "If I have to kill him myself, he will."

"Everyone take a deep breath. You're going back to Arizona and Diego will go back to Nevada. You will probably never cross paths again."

"What about Dieguito? What if he fights me for custody?"

"That was part of the deal. No custody."

"I don't know Max, I have a bad feeling about this."

"I fought it Lilly, but they had already made up their minds. Diego knows things about Jorge that even we don't know. Where he gets his supplies, his involvement with Olivia's father… all kinds of things. This could be big."

"When is all of this supposed to happen?" I asked.

"We need a few days. Diego has asked to see you, but you don't have to go."

CHAPTER 28

I hated when they did that.

Max came with me, of course. We entered the hospital room where Diego was under heavy guard. Max sat on the chair by the window and I walked over to his bedside. "Where's the baby?" he asked.

"Christian is with his uncle," I answered. "What do you want, Diego?" I was sure my tone was unsettling.

"You look well," he said.

"Thanks." I smiled. "Why did you want to see me?"

"I'm sorry, Lilly." He reached for my hand. I looked at Max first, almost for permission. Max gave me an approving nod and I took his hand. "I'm sorry for everything. I'm sorry for how I hurt you. I'm sorry for keeping you from Max. I'm just sorry."

His face was very sincere. Max held up a Bible he found on the table. "Yours?" he asked Diego.

"Mine," he answered. "And now she's yours. I won't mess with that."

"Took you long enough," Max replied, in his usual humorous way trying to lighten the mood.

"I am especially sorry for those two nights," he said, looking into my eyes for a memory.

"Which two?" I asked. "Really Diego, I have more than just two bad nights tucked away in my memory."

"Of course," he agreed. "The night you discovered John was alive…" He stopped and took a breath like he was in pain. "And the night in the hotel."

My body shuddered when I thought about the last one. "The hotel," I repeated.

"I was using that night. I know, no excuses, but I was. I was just so mad that you didn't love me. I just wanted you to stop seeing him in your head when you were with me."

"I know." I wasn't really sure what to say.

"Remember when we first started making love?" Max shivered a little when he said that. "You seemed to really like it at first. You would lay your head on my chest and I thought it might happen. You might fall in love with me. But the more we were together…" he looked up at Max, "the more you wanted me to be him. I should have let you go then."

"I'm sorry Diego. I spent the whole first two years depending on Max for everything. It was easy to love him."

"Are you happy, Lilly?" He looked up into my eyes.

"Yes, Diego. I've never been happier."

"Good," he said. "Finally, right?"

"How are you feeling?" I asked, trying to change the subject.

"Alive," he said. "A little sore but alive."

"I have to ask," Max started. "Why all the sex questions? Didn't you torture me enough while it was going on?"

"It was just one last dig," he said, trying not to laugh. "I just wanted to try to prove that there were moments of joy for her. Even if they were just fleeting."

"I'll give you fleeting," Max said, still entertaining himself.

"What about Olivia?" I asked Diego. "Were you having an affair?"

He looked disgusted with himself when I asked him that. "You have the right to ask," he said. "No, no affair. She was afraid of me and one night, while I was feeling sorry for myself, I took advantage of that." He took another breath. I wasn't sure if it was pain or shame. "I took her and she let me. It gave me a sense of… I don't know, getting one up on Hector and Jorge at the same time."

"Yuck," Max responded. "So, you were number three then, weren't you," he said it in a statement, not as a question.

"Yeah, I guess," he answered. "She didn't really want me, but she didn't complain either." He smiled, almost proud of himself. "I think she was really too scared to say no."

"Did she plant the cameras?" Max asked.

"Sure did," he told him. "Between Leticia, Olivia and Mick, you were covered."

"The TV?" Max asked.

"My little secret," Diego added, smiling.

"Last question," Max went on. "Why did Olivia tell you she was coming with us?"

"I only heard the part about her and Hector. I was unaware that you were taking my wife at the time."

"Yeah, sorry about that," he said with a wink in my direction.

"Where's Johnny?" he asked. "Living with him has got to be fun."

"Nothing like an old boyfriend hitting on your wife," Max said. "Go ahead and say it… karma."

Diego laughed again. It was weird. They were getting along just like the old days. "You're married now?"

"Yes, finally." Max said it with a huge amount of relief.

"Okay, then," he continued. "Time to move on. What are we going to do about the house?"

"I guess keep it," Max suggested. "It's the only tie we still have to papi." He paused. "I guess you can stay in it, if you want to."

"Yeah, I think I might just do that." He smiled. "If I quit selling, how can I afford a new house?"

"You better quit selling," Max reminded him. "Are you planning on going into witness protection after you testify? Jorge will have you dead in five minutes, if you don't, you know."

"You know better than anyone how easy it is to find someone you want to find," he reminded him.

"Consider it, Diego. I'll hide you somewhere. I did a great job with Johnny, didn't I?"

"I'll give it some thought," he said. His eyes were starting to look sleepy.

"What are you going to do, I mean for work?" Max asked him.

"Maybe I'll become a cop," he said. They both laughed. "I really don't know. I'll be honest with you… it's gonna be hard to walk away."

"I know," he answered. "But you will."

"Lilly, do you forgive me?" he asked. "Please forgive me."

"I don't know Diego," I said. "That's a lot of forgiving."

"I will pray that you change your mind," he said as he squeezed my hand.

"I'll forgive you," I answered. "Just give me a little time." I reached down and gently hugged him.

"Max," he said. "Can I talk to you alone for a minute, before you go?"

"It's okay, Diego, I'll probably tell her anyway." Then he looked at me. "We have no secrets."

"I think you have one," Diego said. I started to panic a little.

"Lilly," Max said. "Can we have a minute?"

"I am so not leaving," I said. "This is obviously about me."

"As you wish," Diego agreed.

His eyes locked with Max's and they started communicating in Spanish. I hated when they did that. I simply must learn that language. They talked for a while and Max was visibly upset. He threw his hands in the air at one point and walked around the room. Then they finally stopped and Max said, "Maybe you will change, after all. Thanks, man. I owe you one."

"She loves you, Max." For some reason, he wanted to make that clear. "Don't blow it. You know between the two of us…" He looked over at me. "She's been emotionally battered. Keep that in mind."

He hugged him. "I won't let her go so easily," he said. "It took me this long to get her."

"Goodbye Lilly," Diego managed.

I walked over to his bedside. I searched his eyes for the story he told Max. "What did you tell him?" I whispered. "Should I hug you or did you just rat me out for something."

"Whatever I told him was for your own good." He reached out his arms and I hugged him. Then we left.

"Wow," he said. "I'm very proud of you."

"Proud? Why?" I asked.

"That's a whole lot of forgiving."

"That's why I said to give me some time." I thought about what he said for a moment. "Do you think he has found God or it's another ploy?"

"I'm not sure. The years ahead will reveal his true thoughts." He stopped walking and took my face in his hands. "But until that time… no touching." I laughed. Like I'd go anywhere near him.

"Max?" I asked. "What did he say to you?"

"I don't want to talk about it here," he said. "We'll talk when we get home." That scared me. It must have been bad for him to want to wait until we were in private.

We drove home in silence. I ran through my head all the different things Diego could have told him. Was it about sex? Was it something I did or said when I was married to him? What could Diego know that Max didn't? We walked in the door and Max sat me down on the couch in the living room. He put his hand on my face and kissed me. But he stopped. Then he picked me up out of the couch and picked up my arms and wrapped them around his neck. I knew I was in trouble. "So it was something like this," he suggested. My stomach started feeling sick. Clearly John had been to see Diego and spilled his guts. Unbelievable. I could see Hector out of the corner of my eye at the top of the stairs watching. Max took my face in his hands and started kissing me. I wasn't sure if I should respond or not. Was this a test? "At first you fought it but he lifted you up out of the couch and pulled your body up against his and …." He paused. "You felt warm inside and did something like this." He kissed me again, harder this time. I couldn't breathe. I saw Hector running down the stairs. "You kissed him back, didn't you?" He pushed me away. "You let him touch you." He started pacing back and forth. "You touched him?" He was undeniably upset and disappointed.

"You're the one who said she shouldn't tell you," Hector reminded him. "Don't go all postal on her now."

"Stay out of this Hector." He was angrier than I had ever seen him. "Did you feel something for John? Are you…?" He turned away from me. "Oh my God, I can't even say it out loud."

"No, no, no… Max!" I panicked. I ran to him and pulled him to look at me. "I didn't kiss him. I swear to you, I didn't kiss him!" He was still pacing. "I love you and only you!"

"What did we walk in on yesterday? What if I was later would you have kissed him again?"

"No, Max, no!" I tried to grab him but he kept pushing me away. "Max!" I grabbed his shirt and pulled him. "Please it was over in a few seconds and I slapped him!"

"I blame myself," he said. "Diego and I… we changed something in you."

"No, nothing has changed!" I started to feel sick and my legs began to give out. I sat back down on the couch and started to cry.

"Max, let it go. It was just a kiss. She's only been with the three of you. Let it go," Hector pleaded.

"It was seven months!" I yelled. "Seven months of playing house with him. He helped me deliver Christian. It's your fault he fell back in love with me. This is your fault!"

"You are going to ruin everything," Hector reminded him. "It was just a kiss."

"Was it?" he asked me. "Was that all it was?"

I grabbed him by the shoulders and looked into his eyes. "Nothing happened." He pushed me aside and I sat back on the couch.

"I promise, Max it was just one time. He kissed me and I slapped him. That's all."

"Max walked over to where I was sitting and got on one knee. He put the back of his fingers against my cheek. "I'm sorry," he said. "I'm getting all Diego on you."

"Kind of," I said, through my ever-growing tears.

"I just love you so much. The thought of another man putting his hands on you…" He stopped for a minute and started drying my tears with his fingers. "It's just unbearable." John walked into the room and Max shot him a look of which I would not want to be on the receiving end.

"I am so sorry you are so upset." I grabbed his hands. "I never wanted to hurt you. I never expected Johnny to go blabbing his fantasies all over town either." I shot John the same kind of look.

"He was trying to drive a wedge between you and it seems to be working pretty well for him," Hector added.

Max laughed. "When you're right, you're right." He got up and pulled me up next to him. Then he kissed me. "I'll let it go. But if he wants to see Dieguito when we move to Arizona… follow the rules." I laughed. I was glad he snapped out of it so quickly. I had never seen his anger directed at me before. I didn't like it. I was so looking forward to the close of the trial so that we could go to Arizona, buy a house and be in love forever. "You!" Max said as he turned and looked in Johnny's direction.

"Don't have a cow, Max." John said. "It's not like I took her to bed."

"No more talk like that. Keep your hands to yourself from now on."

"I would have slept with her. But she wouldn't even let me sleep on her floor."

"Oh my God, he asked you that?" Max asked.

"You know," Hector said. "Let's put this behind us before it gets any worse."

Max took my hand and walked me out of the room. We walked upstairs into his bedroom. The one I only visited a few times before. "Please…" he said. "Tell me you love me."

I reached up and kissed him. He kissed me back. "You are the only one for me," I told him.

Somehow we became a safe house for those who were testifying in the world's scariest trial. Witnesses were dying before they hit the stand, so Max and Hector decided to bring Diego to our house until the trial was over. We all stayed in Diego and Max's house except this time, I was sleeping in Max's room. It was really weird, at least for me. Diego spent many hours reading his bible out by the creek. Hector had his eye on him. Max was oddly comfortable with him. They always had sort of a strangely close, enemy like relationship. They always saved each other when life or death was involved. But this time was different. Diego never touched me or even made a gesture that he wanted to. He was a perfect gentleman at all times and even made breakfast a time or two like Max used to do when things were the other way around. His religious conversion started rubbing off on Max and I found the whole thing disheartening. Max and Diego had heated theological discussions often and I found them reading together like… brothers. Hector was not as biblically moved as Max was and this began to put a little tension in the house.

We finally decided to have the birthday party. It was ridiculously late but it was time: Two dads, two uncles and me. Diego was oddly uncomfortable around Johnny. I had to sit little Diego down and explain Diego's Sr.'s religious conversion. Not an easy story for a five year old. The party went on without a hitch.

When it was finally time for John to go, I overheard him and Diego talking in the kitchen.

"I tried, man. She gave in a little, but not enough to make a difference," Johnny said.

"She would never choose you over him. They're way too close," Diego told him. He was pacing around the kitchen like they were up to something.

"You think you can break through. You're crazy." John laughed a little and threw out the empty beer bottle he had been nursing.

"She is still my wife," Diego said. "I never agreed to that divorce. It was Max's old girlfriend who granted it. Otherwise, she'd still be mine."

All of that freaked me out. Max never talked about his old lovers but I guess Diego would know. "I realize she would rather die than take me back," Diego admitted. "I will ask God for forgiveness. Maybe she will forgive me someday too."

"Don't give me that garbage," Johnny responded. "I don't believe you've found God. Come on…. You're Diego Montiago: Drug Lord."

Diego laughed. "You think what you want." He started cleaning up cake dishes in the sink. "God knows where I stand. I just hope Lilly does too."

I quickly ran off so they wouldn't see me. John came out of the kitchen first. "May I say goodbye to my boy?" he asked.

"Of course," I answered. I went and got Dieguito and called Max over to say goodbye.

"Son," John said. "I love you very much." Dieguito threw his little arms around his neck. Max smiled at me. "Be good for your mommy. I will see you as soon as I can."

"I love you daddy," he said. Johnny's eyes welled up with tears. He hid his face from me for a minute.

"It's okay," Max told him. "Children will do that to you." John bent down and hugged Dieguito. Then he kissed his forehead and stood up. "Look John," Max said. "I don't appreciate your trying to steal my girl but I do understand it." John smiled and looked at me like it was the last time we would see each other. "I owe you for taking care of her and Christian."

"I'd say we're even now, Max. Good luck with Diego hanging around."

"I can't catch a break, can I?" Max observed. They actually hugged each other and John left. "One down," Max said to me. "One to go." We watched John get into his car and drive off. I wondered how long it would be before he caused trouble for us again.

Max, the boys and I went to Sedona often in search of the perfect house. We finally found one on the outskirts of town nestled in the mountainside. We bought it and visited it on weekends when we could. Max had to keep checking on the police department and during the trial that was the only time he had. Our life was sitting there in the hills taunting us as we delayed our fresh start.

Hector and I were hanging out in the kitchen together as we often did since Max and Diego had started to rekindle their relationship. Hector was washing the dishes and I has helping him dry. "What do you think about all the Bible thumping going on around here?" Max and Diego were out at the creek together.

"I'm not sure," I said. "It's a little strange. But you know, Diego did pick up the Bible the first time when he flew Max out here after he was shot."

"I remember," he admitted. "I thought it was a phase."

"What's so bad about a little spirituality?" I asked.

"He goes to that Methodist church around the corner now," he continued. His eyes were wild with distraction. "He goes Wednesdays and Sundays and he helps with the youth. He donates money and gives his time. What the hell?"

I laughed at his blatant disrespect for the subject. "Maybe he is sincere," I said.

"Lilly," he couldn't believe his ears, "you of all people. He raped you. Do you forgive him?"

"I don't know," I admitted. "I'm trying. Maybe he really is sorry."

"Let's not forget what got this ball rolling to begin with." Hector turned away for a minute and then returned his glance. "He and Jorge killed our mother. No amount of religion is going to fix that."

"I think maybe you need to try a little forgiveness."

"You are living with your husband and your ex-husband… a little forgiveness?"

"I know." I looked at him despairingly. "It's weird that Max seems to harbor no hatred for the man who raped his wife."

"Max doesn't know how to hate," he went on. "That's why you love him." He smiled. "Are you okay with seeing his face every day?"

"I'd rather not," I said. "But I don't want him dropping dead before he testifies either."

"Thanks Lilly, that warms my heart." Diego and Max walked into the kitchen where Hector and I were talking. They had their Bibles in their hands.

"Sorry Diego," Hector said. "Didn't mean to cause trouble. I was just checking to see how Lilly was doing with you here. You know after all the… I'm just a little worried about her."

"Perfectly understandable." Diego smiled at me. "Are you all right Lilly, or is my being here making you uncomfortable?"

"I'm fine," I offered. "It's weird, but I'm fine."

He looked me up and down for a moment. "It's weird for me too," he added. "I used to be the one sharing the room with the girl. It feels strange to be all alone again."

"Any time you want to stop picturing yourself with my wife would be great," Max said with a snicker. Diego smiled his charming smile at him. Then Max took my hand and said, "He has to stay here, baby girl, I'm sorry. Our witnesses are dropping like flies. Hector and I will make sure this doesn't happen to him." Hector rolled his eyes and Max laughed. "Come on Hector, it's not so bad."

"Since we don't seem to have a choice, I'll make the best of it."

"Still mad about Olivia? Is that it?"

"You think?" Hector added sarcastically.

"I didn't order the hit. That was Jorge. You know that. I just took the credit for it to make you angry. It wasn't me."

"You slept with her." His voice was being shaken by his anger.

"Once," he said softly. He was obviously remorseful. "Only one time. I don't think she really wanted to be with me." I was surprised at how open he was about it. "I only did it to get to you and Jorge. Max had Lilly's heart so completely…" He paused. "I really am sorry. I never dreamed that she'd get pregnant."

Hector looked over at Max for some kind of approval. Max stared back and nodded at him. Hector put his last dish down and walked out of the room. "He's going to need some time," Max told him. "I ended up with the girl. He ended up with nothing."

Max kissed me on the forehead and headed out after Hector. Diego reached into the fridge and grabbed a beer. "Can I get you something, Lilly?"

"I'll take a soda, thanks." He pulled out a diet soda for me and poured it into a glass before he handed it to me. "I remember you don't like to drink straight from the can."

"Thanks." I smiled. It felt good to be with him like this. "So really…" He gave me that smile again. "How are you? Do you like being a mother a second time?"

"I'm great." I smiled. "Christian and Diego are the sweetest blessings I could ever have asked for. And Max," I could feel my face flush, "I am so happy with Max."

He sat beside me and took my hand. "I wish it was me," he said. "But maybe I'll find my 'baby girl' when this is all over."

"Maybe you really have changed," I said. "I'm not afraid of you anymore."

His face changed. His smile fell and I swear I saw tears fill in his eyes. He squeezed my hands. "I am so sorry, Lilly." He pulled back and turned his face away so I would not see his pain. I could see he was wiping his face. I got up and walked over to where he was sitting. He stood up, and for a moment, a little too close. I backed up. "I'm not afraid of you anymore. That's a good thing."

"What a monster I must have been." I reached up to his face and dried a tear. Then I stopped myself. I backed up quickly and looked around. We were still alone. "I'm not Johnny," he said. And that was all that was said. I sat back in my chair and my legs were shaking. Diego looked at me with a very unfamiliar stare. I put my hands on my face. What was that? I didn't want to mislead him. Then I looked back up at him. "It's fine," he whispered. He squeezed my hand again and let it go quickly. We could both hear Max coming down the stairs.

"What's going on?" he asked. "Did you say something to upset her?"

"She used to be afraid of me," he told him. "It's just hard to hear, that's all."

Max walked around the table and grabbed me. He picked me up into his arms and kissed me. "When was the last time we went out together?"

"I… I can't remember." I said. I was still out of breath.

"Hector said he'd watch the boys and we could go out to dinner. And then later…." He started kissing my neck. Diego rolled his eyes.

"Sounds great," I said. "I'll go change."

"You're totally loving this, aren't you?" Diego laughed.

"You betcha!" Max smiled and said, "Sorry, but I do owe you a little pay back."

"Maybe a little," he admitted. "I wonder what Hector feels he owes me," he continued.

"Right now, don't ask him that question. Give him some time. He'll come around." He followed me upstairs so we could get ready for dinner. I watched Diego watch us leave.

CHAPTER 29

Too Close

Several months had gone by. This was by far the trial from hell. Max had left me alone again, but this time with Diego. It was as if he married me just to make sure no one else could. He was never home and I was lonely most of the time. He left early and came home late. When he came to bed at night I was usually already fast asleep. The only person I spent any time with was Diego, the children and Hector sometimes. This whole situation was terribly reminiscent of my marriage to Diego just the other way around.

I came down the stairs after Max and Hector had left for court. Diego was cooking and it smelled enticing. I was glad to have the company. When I sat down at the counter he put a dish of eggs benedict in front of me. "My favorite," I said as he pulled up a stool next to me.

"I know." He smiled warmly and I felt soothed by it. "It hasn't been that long, you know."

"It's weird," I mentioned. "It's like nothing ever changed. Except you are different somehow." I was eating my breakfast a little self-consciously. He was watching me intently. "So much has happened in this house."

"I know," he replied. "If only the walls could speak." He got up and walked back to the sink. I could see he was uncomfortable. I went to the sink when I finished and handed him my plate. He took it and washed it and handed it back to me to dry. Our hands touched and I dropped the plate. He turned and looked at me. His eyes burned inside of mine. My stomach felt butterflies moving around inside of it. We were frozen for a minute. He reached over with his hand and touched my chin in such a way that my eyes locked on his. He moved closer to me and touched the sides of my face with his hands. I guess this was something that all three of them had figured out by now: My weakness. He kissed me and I melted. It felt so good to be close to someone. To be wanted again. I had no control left in my physical body. He swept me up and carried me to the couch. He laid me down and began to caress my lips with his. I could feel him unbuttoning my blouse and pulling my camisole down. His mouth was slowly moving down my body and I moaned out his name. I felt him pulling up my dress and I panicked. I slid out from under him and landed on the floor. He got up right away and put out his hand to help me to my feet.

"What the hell was that?" I asked, taking his hand and standing up. I started refastening my clothes when we saw a car pull up. We stood motionless looking at each other. He put his finger to his lips and a soft, 'Shhh…' came breathlessly forth. Thankfully it was Hector by himself.

Hector looked at me and touched my face with the back on his fingers. "Lilly, go and throw some cold water on your face." I still stood there, looking at him curiously. "You're flush and I don't know how long Max will be. He can't see you like that." I still said nothing but ran to the bathroom to look at my face. To my surprise he didn't start talking to him in Spanish. I suspect he didn't want me bugging him later about what he said. "How long did it take you to get back in her pants, five minutes?" He was angry.

"It wasn't like that," he said. "She stopped me."

"You had better not have forced her." I could hear his gun cock.

"Hector, please, of course not."

"She's so innocent, Diego. She doesn't understand all this stuff."

"I know; I took advantage. It's not over for me. To me we're still married. I never agreed to give her up."

"You and Max have got to stop playing with each other's stuff!" I came out of the bathroom and the two of them were still arguing. "Did he force himself on you?"

"Put the gun down Hector, it was my fault."

"Did you have sex?" he asked me.

"No, no…" I looked down and noticed that my top was buttoned wrong. "Oh no," I quickly blurted as I turned away and started to fix it.

"You took your clothes off for him…" He was so disappointed in me. "Diego, you had better not say one word to Max. He will not come back from this."

"I'm not Johnny, I won't say a word."

"That's what he said," I remembered.

Diego touched my cheek and looked at me with intense longing. "I won't say a word."

"Get out of here you Bible thumper and let me talk to her alone." Diego grabbed his bible from the end table and walked off.

"Hypocrite," Hector said under his breath as he watched him disappear out the back. "Didn't Max ever have 'the talk' with you, Lilly?"

"You do know I've had two children, right?"

"Lilly, you have only been with three men and they are all intimately connected. You can't really put any of them aside because they're always around. John is Dieguito's father and Diego is Max's brother. You can't even heal with all of this going on."

"Heal?" I asked. "How am I supposed to do that?"

"Once you're intimate with someone, there are always some residual feelings left behind." He brushed my hair out of my tear stained face.

"I don't understand."

"As time goes on the bad stuff fades and you remember the good stuff. You probably let John kiss you because you had a memory of the old days. Probably just idle curiosity. Let's not forget that you were living together for seven months pretending to be husband and wife. He was there when Chris was born…" He paused. "I think that's enough to justify your actions." I rolled my eyes. I could see they were never going to believe I rejected him outright. "Diego," he continued. "Far stronger feelings. He gave you your first…" He looked down. I could tell he was a little embarrassed.

"Yeah, yeah," I said. "I know what he gave me."

"Anyway, you probably remember that fondly. Since he's so different now, you probably are focused on that."

"Hector, I don't know what's wrong with me. I love Max so completely." I looked away. "Damn it, why am I so weak?"

"I'm telling you, you are still very connected to all three of them. It will be hard for you to really separate. Besides, Max is always leaving you alone with them. You don't do alone very well."

I grabbed his hands and started to tear up. "I'm just so lonely. It feels so good to be with a man. To be touched and wanted." I put his hands to my face. "Please, please don't tell Max."

He released my hands and said, "I'll take it to my grave and you do the same. Don't ease your guilt by telling him. He flipped out over a kiss. What do you think he will say about all this?" He motioned with his hand to my top. I turned away out of total humiliation. "Do not have an affair with him, Lilly. You won't be able to come back from that."

"Do you think Diego will…"

He interrupted me, "No, he really doesn't think he did anything wrong. He thinks Max came and took you from him. He still feels like you're his. Besides, it is so cut and dry sibling rivalry. If he tells Max he spoils the game."

"Does Max have residual feelings for his old lovers? Do you?" I didn't know anything about Max's sexual past and that bothered me.

"I know I'll get in trouble for this but look at Max and the judge and Max and Vanessa."

"I knew it!" I said. "I knew Vanessa was that angry because he had a personal relationship with her. And the judge… I had my suspicions."

"Since he blatantly lied to you about it, I'm not going to run to him with this. Plus, you are so naive, I find it hard to blame you." He re-took my hand. "I am a little hurt though."

"Why?" I asked.

"I really thought you'd turn to me before going back to Diego."

"Shut up!" I said. "Give it a rest. I said you had a nice chest, get over it already."

He laughed. "Remember Lilly, he's not the good one here. He's the monster with the fangs that you ran for your life from. Always remember that when he's piling on the charm."

"You didn't finish answering my question."

"Let's walk and talk," he said. "Max will be home soon." He took my hand and we started walking towards the creek. "The judge obviously had fond memories of her affair with Max and if he pursued it, she would probably respond. Sound familiar?" I looked at the ground. "Vanessa was steaming mad that he slept with her and dumped her. That's what he did back then." We could see the creek coming up in the clearing and Diego reading his bible on the rocks. "She was still harboring feelings for him. As for me…" He laughed. "My last lover is dead. I never see the ones I had before her. There are some in Mexico, and some here but I make a point to not keep in touch. It's easier to move on that way."

"Were you a playboy too?" I asked.

He smiled. His face flushed a little. "Not as bad as Max but maybe some. Time to settle down though. Can't be single while Max is all happy and settled. He is happy and settled, right?"

"Oh God yes," I answered. "I have to get control of myself." We were getting closer to Diego. "It's so weird. He looks good and smells so good. I just don't remember all that."

"Lilly, you went from Diego's bed to Max's bed and then back to Diego's again for months. Just like now, your husband worked and the brother stayed home and played house with the wife. For you nothing much has changed. I'm really not very surprised at your behavior. That's kind of why I came home first." Hector approached Diego and he closed his book. "Thou shalt not commit adultery… sound familiar?"

"In my head, she is still my wife." He was very serious about that. "I never agreed to a divorce. It was Max's… friend, who granted it you know. I should appeal it."

"Don't even think about it, Diego. She's happy where she is. You should have explained all this…" he paused searching for the right word, "stuff to her. She doesn't understand. She's only been with the three of you and you all know each other."

"I'm not that innocent Hector. You make me sound so virginal."

"You are to us," Diego agreed. "He's right, I shouldn't touch you like that." When he said that my stomach swooned and my knees went weak and Hector reached out and grabbed me.

"Oh this isn't good." He looked at Diego. In a very soft voice as he looked around he said, "You have to keep this quiet. Please, Diego."

"If I tell him, he'll just take her away. I won't say a word."

"It is so funny how you have switched places. It is even funnier how the two of you say the exact same things in the other's shoes." Diego made a face. "She's young, confused and not quite over you. Let her be, at least for now."

Diego said nothing but looked at me. He reached his hand up and then put it down immediately. We looked up and saw Max approaching. I wondered if he saw that.

"Prayer meeting and I wasn't invited?" he asked in his usual fashion.

"Just taking a walk," Hector lied. "How'd it go?"

"One more day for me, two for you and our Diego is the finale."

"Good, cause I'm sick of keeping an eye on him."

"Come on Hector, I think the new Diego is kind of charming." Max smiled but Hector just passed me a look.

"Max, Lilly was just telling me how much she missed you today."

"Really?" Max asked sarcastically.

"Yes," I quickly agreed. "I really did."

"Well, let me see what I can do about that." He took my hand and we walked away.

"Hector wants to be alone with Diego? Why? What's going on?"

"I don't know," I lied. "You know Hector. He always has his own agendas."

"Something feels weird," he said. "And why are your hands so sweaty?"

"I told you already, I missed you." He stopped walking for a minute and I got scared. He grabbed my face and kissed me. I almost went limp in his arms. "Good," he said. "Just checking."

He was way too instinctive for me to pull anything over on him. I had to make sure I watched my step until Diego was finally gone.

The next day was more of the same: Max and Hector gone, Diego and I alone. I came in for breakfast and he made me scrambled eggs and tortillas. He put them down in front of me and said not a word. We ate in silence, washed dishes together and I left to the back porch as quickly as possible. I took my coffee with me and sat on the swing we had out there. The boys were both still sleeping upstairs. Diego came out and sat beside me. "Are you doing okay this morning?"

"No," I said. "I feel awful for lying to Max like that."

"You can't tell him, he'll go ballistic."

"I know, believe me. He went crazy over Johnny. You… I can't chance it."

"Why Johnny?" he asked. "Why would you kiss him?"

"For the last time, I didn't kiss him!" I shouted. "He kissed me and I slapped him. I love how no one talks about the slap."

"Johnny came to see me to tell me all about it in the hospital. I kind of wish I could give him a call right now."

"Don't you dare," and I slapped him in the shoulder playfully. He laughed.

"I wouldn't. Why should I?"

"Max would leave me for sure," I said. "That's why."

"Hmmm…" he said thoughtfully. "I don't want you that way. I want you to come to me." I rolled my eyes.

"I'm not going to come to you. We can be friends though. You know, that's how Max and I started. We were friends for years before we heated things up."

"I guess you're right," he said. "Besides, Hector thinks I'm taking advantage of your naiveté. If you decide you want me, I don't want there to be any doubts."

"Hector thinks it's some kind of habit or something," I said.

"Probably something like that," he agreed. "More like a familiar body. A familiar place. A familiar touch." He reached for my face and then changed his mind. "What's up with you and Hector, anyway?"

"Hector and me?" I asked in surprise. "Why would you even say that?"

"I don't know. You hold hands a lot, like you used to do inappropriately with Max."

I laughed. "It's not that way."

"He seems very protective."

"Yes, that he is," I answered.

He moved his face closer to mine and I stood up. "What are you doing?" I asked.

"You are still my wife to me," he answered.

"I thought we agreed, Diego," I said. "Friends."

"You can't blame a guy for trying." He smiled and took my hand. I pulled away. He stood up and pulled me close to him. I could feel his breath on my face.

"No, Diego, we can't!" I was starting to get nervous and my stomach started to churn. He let me go and I hurried back into the house. I was breathless by the time I ran into Hector. I smacked right into his chest, without seeing him there, and almost hurt myself.

"Where's the fire?" he asked.

"No fire," I answered. "Just not feeling so well, that's all." I pulled a bottle of water out of the fridge. I was sure my face was flush."

"Pregnant?" he asked. "Do we need another test?"

"No, stop it."

"Max is staying home tomorrow. No more games." He was still scolding me like a little girl caught with her boyfriend in the back seat of daddy's car.

Diego came into the kitchen. "You're really something." Hector eyed him. "I should have shot you when I had the chance."

"I'll be gone in a few days," he said. "Then this will all be over." He laughed.

"What's so funny?" Hector asked.

"I think she kind of likes you." Hector laughed hard.

"We already know she thinks I'm pretty," he continued.

"Would you cut it out," I said. "You're worse than Max sometimes."

I still love her," Diego interrupted. He grabbed my hand and I pulled it away.

"I have to ask." Hector got very stern. "If she does give in," Hector looked at me, "and she won't, are you going to tell Max and leave."

"Stay and fight." he said with brazen authority. "I think I can win this time."

"Damn it Diego, leave her alone." Hector grabbed my arm and walked me out the door. "Walk it off Lilly."

"I don't need to walk anything off," I said in an irritated tone trying to free my arm from his grip.

"Is Max not doing it for you anymore. Because if you're bored, you need to tell him. It won't hurt his feelings, he'll just pick up the pace a little."

"I'm not bored."

"Remember I told you that I was your safest relationship right now?"

"Yes," I answered.

"Don't push it. If I tell him you're fooling around with Diego he will kill one of you. I'm not quite sure which one."

"I'm not fooling around," I insisted. "I resisted this time. I did!"

He smiled. "Okay, I believe you." Then he stopped walking, looked at me thoughtfully and hugged me. "You're very special to me, you know."

"I know," I said. "Hector, I don't know what I would do without you."

"Really girl, behave." I knew he was right. Maybe this was just too familiar. Maybe we needed to move out of here. Why did their father have to leave them this monster of a house? Am I always attracted to the brother I don't have? What was wrong with me?"

He started walking again. "Where are we going?" I asked.

He slowed his pace down. "I was just taking you for a walk. That's all." We got to the creek and he walked me into the bushes where Jorge, Diego and Hector found Max and me making love. "Do you remember this spot?" he asked.

"Of course." I bent down and touched the grass. Then I sat down and he sat down beside me.

"You were desperately clinging to each other. After we caught you, you almost had a nervous breakdown. Max calmed you, do you remember?"

"Yes," I answered. "Is that what's happening now, Lilly? Are we losing you again? Is being here too much for you?"

I started crying and lay down in the grass. Hector lay down next to me and hugged me. "This is the kind of thing I can't tell Max, so I have to try to help you myself. Tell me what to do."

"I can't do this anymore," I said. "You're right. It's too much of the same too soon."

"I'll make you a deal Lilly." He pulled his arms tightly around my waist. "Promise me you will not allow yourself to be alone with Diego. Stay with one of us. Maybe we should tell Max."

"No!" I rolled over and looked him in the face. He looked at me helplessly. "No! He won't forgive me. I know he won't forgive me."

"If I catch you with him again, I have to tell Max." He pulled me close to him again and I put my head on his chest. "I can't watch you have an affair and say nothing."

"I know," I said. We looked up and Max was standing over us. Hector let go quickly and I sat up.

"No way!" he said. "Hector, this is not happening."

"No, it's not," I said. "I was having one of my melt downs. He was trying to calm me like you do, that's all."

"I swear, bro. I would never touch her. Not like that."

"What's going on Lilly? I knew something wasn't right." I swallowed hard. My hands were shaking. I suddenly blanked. My brain went numb. I knew I had lost it all.

"Being here… with him." Hector paused. "It is too much for her, Max. He's constantly hitting on her. Can you make sure you're with her all day tomorrow? Just take a day. I'll testify tomorrow. You and Lilly take a day."

"I can't leave Diego alone. He could bolt."

"I'll take him with me. Just take a day."

He reached for my hand and helped me stand up. "I am so sorry querida. He's so right, I've neglected you."

"Max this is my fault. Everything is all messed up in my head."

"He didn't…" He stopped before he said it. "Did he…?"

"No, no…" I interrupted. "I'm just getting confused again."

He hugged me and kissed my cheek. He looked at Hector and I knew he wasn't going to let it go. Hector stood up. "You believe me, right?"

"Yes," Max said. "I believe that you're not having an affair with my wife."

"She isn't having an affair, Max. She's just uncomfortable."

"Lilly, you need to communicate with me, or I can't help." By this point I was sobbing. Max was holding me and I could feel his eyes on Hector. He pulled me back and put his fingers under my chin. I was facing him, tears and all. "Whatever is happening," he looked over at Hector, "we can get through it. Maybe Hector's right. This is too close to our old life. Too close to the times you broke down before. Too close."

CHAPTER 30

Diego gasped. I don't think he was expecting that.

We got back to the house and Diego was reading in the living room. When he saw Max, he stood up. Max let go of my hand and got right in Diego's face. I looked at Hector with alarm. "Are you sleeping with her?" He pushed Diego in the chest and Diego fell backwards and lost his footing.

"No Max, what's wrong?"

"She's different, there's something wrong. She feels different to me. Is this payback?"

"Nothing is going on, Max. Nothing."

"She's confused," Max continued. "I think on some level she thinks you're me and I'm you." He looked over at me. "When I was where you are she changed when we…" He walked away from Diego. "No…" He began to pace back and forth. "You're having her behind my back." He picked up his gun and pointed it at Diego. Hector ran interference.

"Max, I promise, they're not having an affair." He looked over at me. Max lowered his gun. By this time I was sitting against the wall with my knees pressed up against my chest. "Would you two look at what you're doing to her? She's not made for this. She's too inexperienced for all of this."

Diego and Max both looked over at me. Their anger subsided and one took one arm and one took the other and they helped me up and put me on the couch. "Max," Hector said. "You've been away so much since the two of you have been together. She's losing her attachment to you. The glue isn't as strong. When you were here, you were with her all the time, remember?"

"Lilly, I'm so sorry," Diego said. "I'm so sorry."

"Baby girl," Max put me on his lap. "Whatever it is, I forgive you." He gently wiped the back of his fingers against my cheek. "This is too close, it's my fault. Diego and I… we're both to blame."

"Max…I…." I stopped midsentence and turned away. "I don't deserve you." He looked at Diego at that point with a deafening glare. He pulled me close to his body. "Baby girl," he pulled my chin so that I would be looking at him. "Do you know which one of us you are married to?" 'Here we go again,' I know they were all thinking.

I put my hands over my ears. "Max, the last time you did this I was pregnant. Am I pregnant?"

"I don't know," he said, "Is she pregnant, Diego?" He was furious and desperate.

"Definitely not by me," he confessed. "I told you we never got that far."

"How far did you get?"

"Stop it!" I screamed. I still had my hands over my ears. "Max?"

"No, baby girl. It's just you and me and the boys. No baby."

"Are we sure?"

"We're sure." He looked at Diego.

"We're sure," Diego agreed in a soft voice.

"Lilly, I should never have taken you here. I should never have let him stay. I am so very sorry you are so confused."

"Max, I betrayed you."

"I know, baby girl."

"I'll leave." I said. I tried to get off of his lap. "I'm sorry."

"You're not going anywhere. I should have known that this would break you. I don't know why I thought this would be okay." He pulled me back down into his lap.

"I'm sorry." I put my head on his shoulder and cried.

Hector slowly approached us. I could hear him whisper in Max's ear, "It's not as bad as you're thinking, I promise."

"This is my fault," Max said. "I left her here with him. I went to work; he stayed here, just like I used to do. It's a lot to process. Especially for her. Too many of us." He pulled me closer. "We're going home. Hector, you and Diego will have to finish out the trial without us. Besides it's almost Easter. We have an anniversary to celebrate."

"Stay till the end, Max," Hector argued. "Diego and I will be inseparable until that time. Then we can leave. You might influence the verdict if you disappear."

"I'll be good," Diego said. "For now."

"You have a new best friend until you leave," Hector informed him.

"Okay," Max said. "They cannot be alone anymore."

So we stayed. That night was awful. I lay in bed and cried until I couldn't breathe. Max held me tight. He tried to make love to me but I was too full of guilt to let him touch me. I think he thought I had an insanity gene somewhere. Max treated me like a mental patient for a few days. He was asking me questions about where we were and who was who. It was weird. I couldn't figure out why he forgave me the way he did. No anger seemed to come my way at all. It was like Johnny was a bigger threat or something. Maybe he just felt that he and Diego were more similar and it wasn't as surprising. I couldn't figure it out. The day we knew the trial was finally over the four of us had one last breakfast. I was never happier to see anything come to an end. When we were alone, I finally asked the question. "Max? Why were you so mad about Johnny and so understanding about Diego? What I did with your brother was so much worse."

He smiled and blushed a little. "This is hard for me to think about." He took my hands and looked into my eyes. "You and Diego… again."

"We don't have to talk about it." I started to walk away but he grabbed my waist and pulled me close.

"No, we need to talk more not less." He turned me so that I was looking at him. "You were definitely not confused when John kissed you. He and I are totally different. When you were kissing him, you were kissing him."

"I see," I said, realizing that I would never win this battle. He would never believe me about John.

"Diego is holding onto the details like a dirty little secret. He won't give me anything. Very unlike him. All I know is what Hector told me." I smiled. "See that's what I don't like. You're thinking about him and smiling."

"No, no that's not why I'm smiling. He would never have kept a secret for me before." I still smiled a little. "So, why aren't you angry like you were about John? You should be angry."

"He's a different story than Johnny."

"More like you?"

"Lots of history with the both of us. So much back and forth. And yes, a little more like me. But even more than that, Lilly, whether we like it or not, your memories of me will always be mixed up with him until we get away from here."

"I'm sorry." My eyes welled with tears again. He went to me and cupped my face in his hands.

"I don't like that he touched you that way after you married me. I even hate how he touched you. I think I hate that most of all. But I forgive you. And I feel relief that you stopped it before it got too far." I nodded. "We're okay. I'll make sure he stays away from you. At least until you've had some time to heal."

We smelled the wonderful morning breakfast smells. I love the smile on Max's face when someone cooks for him. We walked into the kitchen and saw Diego and Hector together, like Hector promised, actively preparing food.

"Diego, you cooked?" Max asked. "Will I live long enough to hear the verdict?"

"I cooked," Hector said. "Like I'm going to trust Diego with either one of your meals."

"Cut it out," Diego said. He actually looked a little hurt. "What I did wasn't that bad. Hey, I've improved a lot." He was serious. "I may not be who I want to be but I am definitely not who I was."

"Thank God for small miracles, I suppose," Hector added. Max laughed. I was still a little depressed. Max and I hadn't been together since… that last day. I was too ashamed. I picked at my food while I waited for them to finish. Hector said something to Max in Spanish and Max agreed. I picked up at least that much from the conversation.

"Lilly?" Hector asked. "Would you come with me?"

I didn't respond but I followed. We walked to our usual spot. He sat me down on the rocks by the water. "Why are you punishing Max?"

"I'm not punishing him." I kicked the rocks by my feet into the water.

He put his hands on my legs to make me focus on him. "He isn't even mad," he said in disbelief.

"That's only because he doesn't know what really happened," I answered.

"Yeah, he does." Hector took my hands and looked into my face. "Yeah, he does."

"What happened to 'take it to your grave?'" I asked, a little miffed.

"He heard us talking about an affair when we were lying in the grass. I had to tell him or the pictures in his head would have been much worse."

I put my hands over my face. "He said you told him something, I just wasn't sure how much. I don't understand why he doesn't hate me the way I hate myself." I could feel another wave of misery coming over my body.

A soft voice behind us said, "Maybe I should have been a little more honest with you, as well." I looked up and it was Maxwell.

"My job is done." Hector slapped Max on the back and walked off.

"What a mess, huh?" He sat beside me. "Yes, I slept with Vanessa and Julie." He paused. "Julie is the judge." I looked at him in surprise. "And yes, I know Hector already told you."

"Why would you lie about that?" I asked. "It was before me, right?"

"Oh yes," he answered. "But I still lied about it."

"Why?" I couldn't see how that would be important enough to lie about.

"I'm embarrassed about my past life. I never wanted any of it to touch you."

"Max, before is before. What I did was during. That is much worse."

"Yeah, it is." He agreed a little too easily.

"Hector said he told you."

"Yes, he told me what he thinks happened." I put my face in my hands. He pulled my hands away. "Okay, so you shouldn't have let him get under your blouse."

He continued to look into my eyes. "Look, I don't want to know if it was his lips of his hands." I think my expression gave it away. He suddenly looked mortified and got up and started to pace. This was something he did to try to control his emotions.

"Oh, Max. I do not want to have this conversation."

"I'm pretty sure I can guess." He stopped pacing and looked at me. "I know him pretty well." I said nothing. He paced some more and rubbed his eyes for a minute.

"Just kill me now," I said. He sat back down and grabbed my hands. He pulled them to his face and closed his eyes. "Max," I was at a loss for words, "you are everything to me."

"And you to me." He took a deep breath and appeared suddenly pensive. "We switched roles, it's weird." Still, I saw no anger. "He's very handsome and very charming. Let's not forget that there are no surprises either. You've already been with him. He's changed. Not enough but he is different."

"Why aren't you yelling at me?" I put my hand on his cheek and stroked it. He closed his eyes and purred a little.

"I left you alone too much. Not just anywhere. I left you alone in your previous jail with your previous jailor."

"Shouldn't I be repulsed?"

"That's what I was shooting for, but he has changed. I see it. I'm just thankful that you stopped it before… before we had to take another test."

"I'm sorry, Max." I pulled his face into mine and kissed his very soft lips. He took my hand and brought me back to our spot in the trees. "Now, stop punishing yourself and let me pleasure you."

I smiled. Only Max would see it as I was punishing myself. He laid me down on the grass and unfastened my blouse. I was feeling very uncomfortable and he knew it. He pressed his lips to my neck and I let out a moan. I could feel my body starting to relax. He moved slowly down my body and his lips caressed me slowly. "Oh daddy!" I shouted.

"That's my baby girl," he said. We made love in that same spot and I clung to him like it was our first time. We breathlessly touched and reconnected until there was almost nothing left. When he finished loving me, we headed back to the house. "Are you okay?" he asked me.

I stopped walking and threw my arms around his neck. "Kiss me," I said. He gave me a blank stare. "Kiss me!" He moved his lips onto mine and we inhaled each other so deeply that we almost didn't make it back to the house.

"I think we need to do this more," he smiled. "Keep you busy." I laughed. When we got to the house, the boys were waiting for us.

"Man, for how long can you go?" Hector looked at his watch. "We're almost late." We got in the car and headed for the courthouse.

It had been almost a year before the trial had ended. With my favorite holiday around the corner, the trial coming to a close, we were all ready to go our separate ways. Jorge was finally sentenced. We were all there for the final day. Jorge made sure to stare us down just before the verdict. He was sentenced to the death penalty. Diego gasped. I don't think he was expecting that. When they carried him away he shouted violently to Hector, Max and Diego and laughed like a madman. Of course I had no idea what he was saying but all three of the brothers were motionless. "Clue me in." I leaned into Max's ear.

"I will get you," he whispered. "Traitors, liars and fools. You will all pay. I will hunt you down and…" he stopped. "You get the idea." I was sure he said something about me somewhere. But he was so not going to tell me that. We watched him get dragged off and the hairs on the back of my neck stood up. "I won't forget you Lilly!" were the last words we heard. Max put his arm around my waist and pulled me close, I think it was simply an instinct of protection. History had been made. One of the largest drug cartels had been exposed and somehow I was right smack in the middle of it all.

CHAPTER 31

Home

Diego and Hector were planning to help us move to Sedona after Easter dinner. We were so looking forward to leaving this town and starting over. Diego had refused witness protection after all and Hector was going back to Las Vegas with Diego after our move was complete. Diego insisted that we go to church, so I gathered as many church clothes as I could for all my boys, and that included my husband. Even the baby was wearing a suit. We were all very excited. Okay, I was excited. Three handsome men on my arm, my boys in their good clothes and our first time as a family in church. My dad's hearing was approaching and Max would have to take care of that when the time came, but I wasn't going to accompany him to Las Vegas this time. He decided that I would never step foot in that house again. If we were to see Diego, he was not allowed to be alone with me. It was funny on some level, I'm sure. I was in the living room with the baby. Diego and Max were finishing their morning coffee and Hector asked if he could hold the baby.

"Happy anniversary, you two," Hector said, cuddling the baby.

"Yeah, happy freakin' anniversary," Diego said sarcastically. They all laughed.

"Max, I am so happy for you. This is what I want. A house, children and most of all a beautiful wife who adores me." Hector was letting the baby wrap his fingers around his own much bigger finger.

I sat on Max's lap and he put his coffee down and kissed me. Everything was perfect. "Come on now," Diego said. "There'll be plenty of time for that later. Let's get Dieguito and get out of here. It'll be hard to find parking if we're late."

We started getting ready for church and Diego met me in the kitchen. I was getting the baby's formula ready. "Lilly," he said. "I'm not going away."

"Diego, really." I looked around for Hector. He seemed to be Diego's guard but he wasn't in the room. "We're not supposed to be together."

"If I can touch you for one minute." He looked around as I did. "I'll take the chance." He reached up and touched my face. "I know you love that." I smacked his hand down as Hector came in and put his hands on my shoulders.

"Come on, baby girl," he said. We knew he was trying to make a point. "Time to go see your husband before I call him in here," and he pulled me away from Diego.

We heard a knock at the door and Hector changed gears. He turned back around and Diego grabbed me. Diego pulled out a gun and Hector said, "Watch her." Hector pulled out his gun and I looked up at Diego. "Easter," I said. "Always on Easter."

Diego put me behind him and looked out the kitchen door. We saw a well-dressed woman standing there. She had long dark hair and light skin. Hector was at the door and Max was behind him. As soon as Hector opened the door she put her hands in the air. "My mother is Cammy Malone and she sent me here." Diego put his gun away and we exchanged looks.

"Wait!" I cried. "Let her in." I rushed to the door but Max grabbed me.

"Go ahead and check me," she said. "I'm unarmed."

Max took her purse, "Do you mind?" he asked.

"Go ahead," she said. He looked through it suspiciously.

Hector frisked her and definitely enjoyed it too much. She made a face. "Are you sure you checked every inch of me?" she asked him. "Should I get naked for you?"

Max yanked Hector backwards. "Sorry about that," he said. "My brother is a little… zealous sometimes."

"You must be Maxwell," she said to Hector. Max laughed.

"Hector," Max said. "This is Hector, I am Max, this is Lilly and my other brother Diego."

"Diego and I have already met," she said. "Which one is yours?" she asked me. I hugged Max.

"Good," she said.

"I think I was insulted," Max said in his usual tone.

"I think the zealous one is cute," she continued. Hector grinned.

"Elizabeth, what are you doing here?" Diego asked. He didn't seem happy to see her.

"I was visiting my mom for Easter," she answered. "She told me I have a nephew…" She made a face, "named Diego." She said that in a disapproving tone.

"Yes, you do," he answered. "Lilly is his mother and Max is his step-father. I don't have custody anymore."

"How fitting that she should have taken that from you," she answered.

"Yes, I thought you might feel that way." The animosity between them was pretty serious.

"So, you're the one who killed my brother, Pat?" she asked Max.

"I had my reasons." He began to get a bit defensive.

"I hear you're a hit-man," she continued. "Is that your reason?"

"How does none of your damn business, sound to you?" Max answered.

"Hold on," Hector said. "Everyone take a deep breath." He turned and looked at Elizabeth. "What is it that you want?" He paused for a second. "You must excuse us but we have been through a lot lately. We're slightly paranoid."

"I was just wondering if I could meet him," she asked. "Does he know about John?"

"He knows," Diego answered. "Does he know that you hate his father?"

"I choose not to associate with drug lords," she answered.

"Then what the heck are you doing here?" Max blurted. He and Diego laughed.

"Of course you can see him," I interrupted. "Max?"

"I guess," he reluctantly agreed.

"Look," Hector said. "We're all going to church, why don't you join us."

"I don't know," she said in a hesitant manner.

"After church Max, Diego and I will cook something amazing and you can stay for dinner." Diego and Max exchanged glances. "Please," he continued. "You can get to know your nephew a little better."

"You don't cook?" she asked me. The boys all laughed. "I didn't realize I said something funny."

"I'm only allowed in the kitchen to eat," I answered. She smiled.

Hector put his arm out for her. "Shall we go?" She put her hand on his forearm and we all walked out the door. Max had Chris in his arms and little Diego was glued to my arm. He was uncomfortable with the new person. I couldn't really blame him. All kinds of people have been in and out of his life for months.

The church smelled like a combination of incense and perfume. I never did understand why old ladies had to wear so much perfume to church, when they knew they'd be choking a whole pew of innocent people. Max sat on the end with a sleeping Christian in his lap. Little Diego sat between us. Diego Sr. sat between Hector and me and Hector was chatting it up with our long lost relative. Diego reached over, squeezed my hand and let it go quickly. I looked over at Max but he was too busy being spell bound by our little one. I gave Diego a look. He put his face close to my hair for a second and I could swear he was breathing in my scent. Max looked over when he did that. "Sorry," Diego said, "old habit." Max shook his head.

"Stop that," I said to him in a whisper. "Are you trying to get me in trouble?"

"Yes," he whispered back. "I would so love to get you in trouble."

"Enough chit chat over there," Max scolded. "Behave yourself." He shot a glare at Diego. It was half kidding and half 'don't touch my wife.'

The service was beautiful. We took communion all together at the altar. Diego kneeled beside me and said, "Do you forgive me, Lilly?"

"Forgive you for which time?" I asked sarcastically. I saw Max watching us.

"Do you forgive me?" He paused. "For everything?"

"I forgive you, Diego." I could see tears well up in his eyes. He looked up as if he was talking to God and said, "Thank you." Then he put his hand over mine and said, "Thank you, Lilly. You don't know what that means to me."

"You're a changed man," I said smiling. "Seriously Diego, I see it now." They handed us the wine and the bread and we said a prayer. We put our little cups back on the altar.

When we sat back down Max switched seats with me and winked. Hector and Diego both got a kick out of his actions. I got baby duty. Of course when Chris was in my arms he couldn't keep still. He was crying and moving around. Max was afraid to leave the boys in the nursery. "After all, we are the Montiagos," he said. "There will be too many people there that we don't know." So… I took Chris into the lobby and tried to calm him. Max followed. "What's going on with you two?" he asked.

"He's just a little cranky," I answered.

"I mean you and my brother?"

"He asked me if I have forgiven him yet," I answered. "And I have."

Max shook his head a little. "He's going to fight me for you." He shuddered. "If he was like this before…." He sighed. "Dang it, I just want the world to leave us alone for a while."

"Max," I laughed, "I am madly and completely in love with you."

"That's what you said when you let him…" He paused and picked up Chris to hide the tears I saw developing. "I can't lose you," he continued. "I know I probably deserve it for stealing you away the way I did. But I can't live without you in my life."

"I am so sorry, daddy." He perked up a little. "I will forever be sorry about that day." As soon as he scooped Chris up into his arms Chris calmed right down. "You have a way, don't you."

"It used to work with you," he said. "I see you getting weak around him." He walked around a little and rocked the baby in his arms. "Like you used to get with me."

I walked over to him, and Chris was smiling between us. I stood on my tiptoes and kissed his lips. "You still make my knees weak." He smiled. "Only you." We walked back into the church and sat down.

"Everything all right?" Diego asked.

"Couldn't be better," I answered. Max let me sit back down next to him. I think it was an offer of trust.

We got back to the house and the men took off their jackets and ties as though they were on fire. It was funny to watch. The three of them went into the kitchen and Elizabeth sat down on the couch next to Diego Jr. I sat beside him. "Diego, this is Elizabeth. She is daddy's sister from New York."

"Johnny's sister?" he asked.

"It's confusing for a little guy," I said to her. "Yes, Johnny's sister."

He put out his hand to shake hers. "That makes me your aunt," she said. "Do you have any other aunts?"

"Aunt Elena," he answered. "She's my other daddy's sister."

"I see how this can get confusing." She laughed.

"Why didn't Cammy come with you?" I asked. "I would love to see her."

"She wouldn't love to see Diego," she answered.

"Oh, right." I remembered how he told us John was dead. She thought he killed him.

"They used to sleep together, you know," she added. I made a face and she laughed. "Yes, they all had sex-lives before you came along."

"Why are you so hostile?" I asked. "Have I done something to you?"

"Your family has stolen everything from my family. Diego took you and John's son. Max took Patrick and Patrick's girlfriend. Have they shared the story with you?"

"Yes, of course," I answered.

"You took Diego from my mother." She paused. "Where did Hector come from?" She looked very interested in that piece of information.

"Mexico," I answered. "He used to work for Jorge. He came for a visit and never left."

"Hmmm…" she continued. "Have you had a turn at him yet?" she asked curiously.

"Eww!" I said making a sour face. "He is very much like a brother to me. Nothing more." I thought for a moment. "He's the best brother anyone could ever ask for."

"Was that a 'watch your step' comment?" she asked.

"Could be," I said. I was a little surprised at how protective I was over him.

"You and Diego seem to get along very well." She looked surprised. "I assumed you would hate his guts after taking Johnny away the way he did."

"He's Max's brother," I answered. "It's for the best if we get along."

"Ah…" she continued. "But it is more than that now, isn't it." I think my face flushed at that comment. Thankfully, Hector came out of the kitchen and rescued me.

"Why don't you all join us? I have some snacks out for you before dinner."

"They are wonderful in the kitchen," I added.

"Not just in the kitchen." Hector winked at her with enthusiasm. I almost threw up. She giggled like a little girl and the two of them took off into the kitchen. I followed behind.

Max came over to me and kissed my neck. I got chills and shuddered. "Just checking," he said again.

"Cut that out," I told him. He did it again and pulled me to him. "Did I tell you today how beautiful you are?"

I smiled. Diego was watching us carefully from behind Max. I caught his glance and Max looked behind him. "When are you leaving again?" he asked Diego.

"I'm sorry, I'll behave," he promised. "She just looks so good. You know, Max. Good enough to taste." Max let me go and started towards Diego. Diego didn't flinch. Hector, as usual, got between them.

"Diego stop!" Hector shouted. "If you want her, dream about her. Keep it to yourself. She's Max's now. Leave her alone." Diego continued to chop up vegetables for the stuffing but said nothing.

"Wow," Elizabeth said, looking at me. "I knew I felt some heat between the two of you."

"There is no heat!" I shouted.

"Then why is your face all red?" She had a smug look in her expression like she won the lottery or something.

"I know I'm not perfect," Diego said. "But neither was David and he was a man after God's own heart."

"Who's David?" I asked. I felt foolish asking the question when everyone else seemed to already know.

"David was a king," Max started, "who fell in love with someone else's wife." He turned and looked at Diego.

"We are both guilty of that," Diego reminded him.

"David arranged for the husband of this woman to be away in battle so he could sleep with her. Once he slept with her, she became pregnant." Diego cleared his throat intentionally. "Finally, David tried to have the woman, Bathsheba was her name, sleep with the husband so the husband would think the baby was his." He stopped for a minute and started to pace. "Oh my God, I'm going to hell," Max blurted.

Diego started to laugh. He decided to finish since the similarities were too overwhelming for Max. "Long story short, due to David's orders, Bathsheba's husband was killed in battle. He got her all to himself."

"That's a man after God's own heart?" I asked.

"He repented," Max said, coming back into the conversation. "They got married and had another child."

"So, who looks like David now?" Diego asked.

"Wow," Max said. "A little shocking isn't it?" He took my hand and looked at Diego. "I did try to pass our baby off as yours. I did marry your wife. We did have another child. You probably should hate me."

"But I don't," he said. "I love you. I know you hate that but you are my favorite brother." He looked at Hector and Hector made a face.

"All this brotherly love is making me hungry," Hector said. "So, no more fighting. It's Easter Sunday. It's also Max and Lilly's anniversary and I have a new friend…" He stopped as if in mid-sentence. He put his fingers on her chin and looked at her longingly. Elizabeth smiled. "Let's have some fun." He looked over at Max. "Would you mind if I took her for a walk around the property?"

"Be careful," Max said. "Do you need to stop in my room first?"

Hector smiled. "Got it covered, brother, but thanks for the reminder."

They walked out the back door of the kitchen, obviously heading for the creek. "You guys are disgusting," I said to Max.

"Why? You and Max made love there a thousand times," Diego said sarcastically.

"Twice," I corrected him. Max laughed. "And we knew each other more than five minutes."

"It's been a while for him," Max said. "Cut him some slack." They continued to cook. Diego put on some salsa music and Max and I started to dance. Diego poured us all some wine and they took turns spinning me around the floor. A few hours later Hector and Elizabeth came back covered in leaves and grass. We all started laughing… hard. It was fun to be on the other end of all this. Finally, it wasn't me.

"We sat down for dinner and Diego and Max started bringing the food out. They cooked a turkey this year with all the fixings. They usually cook a ham but they were continuously trying to change our luck on Easter. It looked amazing. I was getting some baby food ready for Chris and Max strapped Dieguito in his booster seat. When I came back out, Elizabeth had secured a chair next to Hector. "Have you seen your brother lately?" I asked.

"Yeah, I was going to get to that," she answered.

"This is the real reason you showed up here on Easter, isn't it?" Hector asked.

"Well, I didn't expect you to be so nice." She took Hector's hand. "Not this nice, anyway." Hector smiled.

"It's okay," Hector said. "I'm a big boy, what's going on?"

"I have three brothers left," she said as she shot a dirty look at Max.

"Rory, and Sean are the other two," Diego interrupted.

"Of course, you'd know that." She was still very angry with him. "They are in Sedona now with John."

Max started to cough. I looked up at him. "Max, what is it?"

"We're talking about an Irish Mafia now, aren't we." He looked over at her angry face and she smirked.

"Well, Ray's in prison and your organization has dried up… for now anyway."

"Please tell me John is not back to using drugs?" I pleaded. "We told Diego the truth." My little son was busily eating as much sweet potato casserole as he could. Covered in marshmallows; he wasn't really paying attention to our conversation.

"Using, dealing… same old, same old." She looked at Hector who was watching her with such intensity that her face began to flush a little. "It's Easter and I've heard all about Easter's Lilly." She looked at me dismissively. "I wanted to make sure Dieguito…" she cleared her throat, "Johnny's son… was still all right."

"Well, as you can see, he's fine," I answered. "But I'd be lying if I didn't think this was going to be a problem."

"See Max," Diego said. "You still need me to stick around." Max looked at him with a serious stare. Not angry, just concerned.

"What do you think, Hector?" Max asked. "Should we all head back to Sedona?"

"As much as I hate to admit it, Diego's right. Egos out of the way and all… there is safety in numbers. We have to think about the children."

"I'm going back there myself," she said. "I want to see Sean and Rory. I want to know what they're up to this time."

"Didn't they used to live in Colorado?" Diego asked. "Why would they go to Arizona of all places?"

"You," she said. "Their nephew is certainly part of it. Let's not forget that John is now the head of his own organization." Then she looked at Max. "You're FBI, right?"

"I guess the news blew my cover," he answered.

"My brothers will certainly be after you." She turned and looked at Hector. "Did you do something to them that I don't know about?"

"I spent most of my time in Mexico," he replied. "I have really only been here for the last year and a half. I barely knew Johnny or Pat for that matter."

"But Jorge," she said thoughtfully. "Won't they hold you responsible for his actions?"

"Possibly," he answered. "I was his hit-man for years."

"Enforcer," Max blurted. "Why can't anyone get that right?" I knew this had to be serious or he wouldn't be making jokes. We were in danger. We had to stick together.

Diego started clearing and I helped him pick up plates. Max, Hector and Elizabeth had their heads together. "I think you're stuck with me for a while." Diego smiled and started taking dishes from my hands.

"I wouldn't say stuck." I smiled at him. "It's okay, I really don't mind." He turned the music back on and started washing dishes. I went out to the dining room and brought in some more dishes for him. I grabbed a towel and started drying the plates.

"You know a small part of you will always love me," he said as I began to start drying.

"Very small," I answered, laughing a little.

"But it's there," he continued. "I can feel it."

"So tell me," I said, changing the subject. "What are you going to do now? Who is going to hire Diego Montiago?"

He smiled for a minute. "Lilly, part of the deal I made with the FBI is I get to keep my money. I knew this would be an issue when I quit the business." He handed me another dish. "I have enough investments that I don't ever have to work again if I don't want to."

"So, you don't want to?" I asked.

"There is something that I want to do but I haven't told anyone yet." He hesitated. "I am certainly not worthy."

I put another dish down. "Tell me," I urged him. "I'd be honored to be your first for something."

He laughed a little. "Wow, you remember that?" he asked.

"Every detail," I answered. "So spill…"

"I think I want to be a preacher," he confessed. I let go of the newest plate that he handed me and he grabbed it just before it fell. "Lilly, you are going to have to stop drawing attention to us when we talk like this." I laughed. "Do you want them to shoot me or something?"

"Of course not," I answered. "I'm sorry, you just took me by surprise, that's all."

"It took me by surprise too," he said. "I get to give a mini sermon every Wednesday night to the youth." He handed me another plate. "Why don't you come and check me out in action?"

"I don't know, Diego." I was starting to feel… weird. "Hearing you preach…" I began to look around the room to see if we were still alone. "It might be too strange."

"Lilly…" He looked off into the living room. He could see Max, Hector and that woman still deep in the throes of conversation. "It is all I can do not to lay you down right now and make love to you."

"Oh my God," I said under my breath. He looked around again and touched my face.

"Admit it, you still want me?" I looked at him and could feel that my face was hot.

"Diego, I never wanted you," I reminded him. "Let's not forget that." He was really pushing me.

"Come and hear me preach," he suggested again. "I promise," he crossed his heart, "best behavior."

"Like you're doing now?" I asked. "Is this best behavior?"

"I'm sorry, I can't help myself." He looked away.

"I'll have to bring Max and Hector, you know." I looked at him for a reaction.

"I would love that," he said. "Really, come."

"Okay, I will ask Max about it later." I looked again for company.

"What are you so nervous about?" he asked.

"Max is insanely jealous of you, you know that," I said, still looking.

"He should be," he answered. "I will not honor this divorce. Not ever."

"Diego, once you become a preacher man," I looked around and then said in a whisper, "you will have to let me go."

"There was a man named Paul." He seemed to be moving away from the subject. "He was just like me. God saw favor in him."

"There is so much I don't know," I told him.

"I can teach you, Lilly. God can use me to teach you." He handed me a glass.

"This is weird," I told him. "You and God. You and me… Who are you?"

"The devil took everything away from me." He made another check for Max. "I am grateful for those bullets. God has given me the chance to redeem myself."

He reached over and handed me another plate. He didn't let go of my hand. "Diego…" I warned.

"Are you saying you don't like it when I touch you?"

"I'm saying that I love my husband, so cut it out!"

"Shhh!" he said. "Remember what I said about that." Max came in at that time. He was watching us innocently wash the dishes.

"Lilly? Is there coffee?"

"There's coffee and Diego's famous flan," I answered. "I will bring them both out to you."

Max got a little closer and put his arms around my waist. "Is he bothering you?" he asked.

"Not at all," I answered. "He was telling me about his work in the church. I think we should go see him Wednesday night. What do you think?"

"I don't know," he looked suspiciously at Diego. "What do you do?"

"It's no big deal," he answered. "I give a mini sermon to the youth."

"I would love to see that," he said with a hint of sarcasm. I hit him gently with the towel. "All right, all right, we'll go." He walked out.

"He's a lucky man," Diego said.

"Reality check." I put up the last plate. "I have a son by John and a son by Max. How would that make you feel? Do you just want me because Max took me from you?"

He looked into the living room and put his hands on my shoulders. He moved us farther from their view. "I know what I lost," he said, almost in a whisper. "I will love and cherish you. I will never raise my hand to you or force you to do something you are not comfortable with again." He looked behind him. We were still alone. "Like I told you before. I will not take you, this time. You will come to me."

I could feel my face getting hot again. He looked behind him and quickly kissed my lips. It was gentle and soft. "Remember," he said. "I'm not Johnny." I pulled away and began to wipe my face furiously. I grabbed the coffee cups and tried to pour the coffee but my hands were shaking. He took my hands and said, "Relax Lilly." He started pouring the coffee for me. "Everything will work out the way God wants it to." I brought the coffee out and Diego was behind me with the flan. We served it and observed a little of the conversation. We cleared the table of the rest of the used dishes and continued to clean.

"You have to stop that," I whispered. "Really, I mean it!" I was still whispering but fiercely.

"As soon as I know you don't like it," he stopped and winked at me, "I'll stop."

"I don't like it, Diego. Really, no more!" I could tell by the look on his face that he didn't believe me. The truth was… I was kind of aroused. We continued to clean up together. I tried to think of something to say but I was way too embarrassed. I could only imagine what Hector would have thought of me if he walked in on us. Max would've shot Diego for sure. I had to make him understand that there would be no romance.

So tell me," he said, trying to change the subject. "When you and Max were alone at the creek, what did you do together before the affair?"

"You really want to know?" I asked. I was pretty sure he didn't.

"I want to know as much about you as I can," he answered. "What kind of things did you do together?"

"Do you like poetry?" I asked him. "He used to read me poetry."

"I am not as educated as my brothers. I was pushed into the cartel at 16 and that was all I knew," he answered. "What else?"

"We shopped together," I answered.

"With my money," he added. I laughed. "I was always happy to see you smile when you bought something new."

"We did everything together, Diego. Everything except for what I was doing with you."

He paused for a minute. He stopped washing and turned to me. "I will forever regret the way I treated you."

"I know," I told him. "If I have forgiven you…" I paused, "and God has forgiven you… don't you think it's time for you to forgive yourself?"

"I suppose you're right," he continued. "If Paul can forgive himself, certainly I can forgive myself."

"Whose Paul?" I asked again.

"A story for another day," he told me. "Let's just say a murderer and a non-believer. Very much like me."

"Like you used to be." I felt that correcting him was the thing to do. I could see he had become very hard on himself. Max finally came in and pulled me away. He brought me into the dining room and placed me on his lap. "I love you, daddy." I kissed his cheek. He smiled and Elizabeth made a face.

"I know," Hector said. "Just imagine living with them."

"I'd better get going, anyway," Elizabeth started. "I don't want to overstay my welcome."

"We're going to church Wednesday night to see… wait for it…" Max was having way too much fun with this, "Diego preach to the youth." Hector laughed out loud.

"Stop it, you two." I had to say something. Someone had to defend him.

"We are so there!" Hector blurted.

"Please join us Elizabeth," Max offered. "You're not in a hurry to get back, are you?"

"You couldn't keep me away," she admitted. She grabbed Hector's hand. "Please, walk me out." She reached over and put her hand on his cheek. She kissed him and we all just watched for some reason. We couldn't look away.

"Thank you for the meal, Maxwell. Lilly," she began. I could tell it was hard for her to say something nice to me. "Thank you for the hospitality."

"Anytime," I said. "I hope you will come back soon."

"We'll pick you up before church," Max added. "Be sure to give Hector your information."

"I'm staying with my mother," she said. Then she opened her purse and took out a card. She grabbed a pen and scribbled something on the back. "This is her address." She held the card up for him to take. "On the other side is my personal information." Hector smiled at us and then took her hand and walked her out. When the front door closed Diego, Max and I, like little children, went running to the window.

"Can you see anything?" Max asked.

"I think they're kissing," Diego answered.

"He's pressing her up against the car," I said. "Okay, we've had our fun. Let's leave him alone." They both stood back. I was pretty sure whatever was happening next out there was something Hector wouldn't want watched. "He's put up with the three of us for years. Let's give him some space." They both laughed a little and we went back into the living room. Hector walked back into the house and glided over to us like he was already in love.

"I don't like it," Diego said. "It's too convenient. What's she doing here anyway?"

"I like her," Hector said.

"We can see that," I added. "Why'd you invite her to the church on Wednesday, Max?"

"Keep your friends close," Diego said.

"Keep your enemies' closer," Max finished. "I don't like it either."

"Max, I expected you to at least be on my side." Hector had real disappointment in his tone.

"Just be careful," he said. "Don't give away too much too soon."

"Too late for that," I said laughing.

"You're loving this, aren't you?" he asked me.

"Yup." I laughed again. "Finally, someone else to talk about." Diego shot me a glance. My stomach sank a little. I think Hector caught it.

"Finally a nice Easter, right Lilly?" Hector asked. "No real drama."

"So far, so good." I told him. "Let's finish cleaning up and get ready for bed. We have to start packing tomorrow if we're planning on leaving by Thursday." We all went our separate ways, except of course for Max and me. We put the boys down together. Diego walked passed the nursery and Max poked his head out to watch him walk to his old bedroom. He came back inside and looked at me. "Do you believe him?" he asked me. "Really?"

"I do," I said. "You should hear the excitement in his voice when he talks about doing work for God. It's spooky."

He laughed and reached for my face. "Do you still melt when I touch you?" He pulled my body into his and my knees almost buckled. He pulled me up. "Glad to see that sometimes." He put his mouth on mine and caressed my lips. I was helplessly under his spell. I was glad to see it too. "Let's go to bed," he suggested. "I think we need each other tonight." We walked hand in hand down the hallway. It felt so right… so very right.

CHAPTER 32

Repent!

We picked up Elizabeth and headed to church. Hector and Max were poking fun at Diego the whole ride over calling him, "preacher man." I tried to hush them but it wasn't easy. We walked into the church and youth started swarming around Diego like mosquitoes to a lake. The ethnicity was diverse among the young people although I would guess that the majority was Latino. They were very excited to see him, especially the little girls. Diego assured me that he never mentioned my name or that the man who is married to his "wife" was his brother when he discussed his testimony. He said he protected our privacy.

The children rushed us and Diego introduced us to them. I felt like I was with Antonio Banderas by the way they were treating him. "Are you his wife, are you his wife?" was bouncing idly through the crowd at me. Max pulled me through the swarms of people, much like the old days. I felt like I had a bodyguard again. Hector and Elizabeth trailed behind. We found some seats up front. We noticed that the front pew was almost always empty. Diego was finally able to get to the pulpit. He was full of self-confidence and pride. Before he got started he said a prayer and asked God to use him to help bring people to Christ. Then he made an embarrassing announcement.

"I would like you all to welcome my family." All heads turned and looked at us as he pointed to our pew. He was so proud that we were there. "They wanted to come visit with us to see what youth night is all about. Please make them feel welcome." They all started to clap and we heard some female voices screaming, "We love you, Diego!" Max looked at me and laughed. Hector poked Max. They were so entertained. "What is he, Ricky Martin?" Hector asked.

"Shhh!" I said. They tried to stop laughing. Diego went on to talk about someone named Paul. I guess he wanted to tell me the story after all. He talked about how God blinded Paul because it was through new eyes that he needed to see. He compared himself to the murderer and it was quite shocking, I thought. I was wondering how he could be so honest without putting himself at legal risk. He talked about the love of his life. He nicknamed her Blanca to "protect her privacy." He said he lost her to his best friend. It was a very sad story. But he went on to say that the best friend was not at fault, and he only wants love and happiness for her. My eyes teared up and I almost started to weep. Max pulled me closer, hoping I wouldn't give myself away with the tears.

"If any of you are struggling with drugs or any other personal issue, I hope you will understand how non-judgmental I will be. If you think what you have done is unforgivable…" He paused. "I have done worse, I assure you. Come to me, and let me share God with you."

He got off of the pulpit and some of the youth got up with a few guitars and started playing music. Diego sat beside Max and Max hugged him and kissed his cheek. "Wow man," he said. "You're really good at that."

"You mean it?" he asked.

"I really do." I was moved. He put his hand to his heart in a joking gesture. "Seriously though," he said. "You had Lilly in tears. You did well."

"Even I thought so," Hector confessed. "Who would've guessed?"

Diego got up and sat beside me. "Tears, really?"

I wrapped my arms around his neck and kissed his cheek, just like Max did. "I stand in awe." He hugged me tight enough to draw attention and then let me go.

"Thanks Lilly, that means a lot to me."

"Don't you mean Blanca?" Max asked in a whisper. Diego put his finger over his lips and let a gentle "Shhh" slip by us.

We headed for the door when it was over. Elizabeth was draping herself all over Hector and he looked as though he was in heaven. Max had little Diego's hand and I had the stroller. As we got closer to the door an old Mexican man grabbed my arm and pulled me towards him. "You'll burn in hell for what you've done!" The crowd began to gasp and accelerate their pace out the door. Max and Diego went into protection mode. Max pulled the man's hand off of my arm and he released his grip. Diego ran up from behind and grabbed the man by the shoulders.

"Who are you, old man?" Diego asked. The man spat in his face. Max pulled his gun out and stuck it in the man's back. People began to scatter. Diego pulled a cloth out of his jacket pocket and wiped his face with it. "That was a mistake," Diego assured him.

"Check his wallet, Diego," Max instructed. Hector was standing behind him with Elizabeth. Diego looked into the man's face as though he needed to see some recognition. He handed the wallet to Max and he grabbed it with his other hand. "Hector Montiago? What?"

"Tio?" Diego asked. "You look like you've aged a hundred years."

"I hope you all burn in hell!" he said again. "How could you betray Jorge like that after all he's done for you? How could you hang around with these half-breeds? And showing up in church with white girls…" He hesitated. "Blasphemy!"

Max handed the wallet back to Diego. "Technically, the white girls are with us," Max said. "So, he's off the hook."

"Shut up you smart ass!" he shouted. Hector and Max laughed. I think they were a little surprised. "I always hated that about you; always a smart ass. The other half-breed too. No respect."

"Do we have an uncle Hector?" Max asked Diego.

"Papi's brother." He paused for a minute. "Polo's dad."

"Polo?" Hector asked. "I remember him. He spent a lot of time at Jorge's house."

Diego suddenly got a disconcerting look on his face. "Hector, sweep the car."

"I thought he was dead?" Max answered.

"In jail somewhere in Mexico," Diego replied. "Boy, no one tells you anything."

"Repent!" he said to me. "Repent before it's too late and you live in Satan's den forever!"

Hector took his jacket off and handed it to Elizabeth. Then he started loosening his tie as he headed for the car. "What's he doing?" she asked. "What does sweep the car mean?"

"That's one of Hector's specialties," Max said rather casually. "He can find a bomb or a bug anywhere." He shot a look at Diego and Diego gave him a half smile. The man stood there with his hands in the air.

"Can't he get blown up like that?" she asked. Hector blew her a kiss before he got under the car.

"BOOM!" The old man shouted as he began to laugh. Max dug the gun into his back. "Shut up moron." Hector stood up and held up what looked like dynamite sticks all wrapped together. Max got on the phone and called the FBI and told them about the bomb. By now the parking lot had pretty much cleared.

"Take Elizabeth into the sanctuary, Lilly." Max looked at me for an obedient answer.

"No, I'm not leaving you here."

"Go Lilly," Diego added. "I won't leave him alone."

"Yes sir," I said angrily. I took the baby, Elizabeth picked up Dieguito and we headed inside. Chris was sleeping soundly and little Diego had his arms spread wide while he pretended to be an airplane flying through the pews. Elizabeth was rocking back and forth in the front pew. She looked like she was in shock. "Are you all right?" I asked.

"This is your life?" she asked. "Every day you worry about one of you getting blown up or shot?"

"This is the way it is," I told her.

"Are they worth it?" she asked. "Is the way you distract yourself from all of this by running back and forth between the two?"

"I am not running back and forth," I answered, uncomfortable with that comment.

"I am in no position to judge," she continued. "I don't know what I would do if I lived with the two of them. Married to one, sleeping with the other and then…" She paused. "Switch."

"I don't understand," I said. "I love my husband."

"I saw you kiss Diego in the kitchen." I could feel the blood rush to my face and I felt a little nauseous. She was not my friend and if she told Max or Hector, Max would not forgive me another indiscretion. "Don't worry, Max didn't see." She looked around. "I won't say anything. I don't know what I would do. They're both beautiful."

"He kissed me. I did not kiss him back," I responded.

"Whatever," she said dismissively. "Can you deny that you are living in a house full of gorgeous men?"

"That's not it," I said.

"It helps," she continued. "Look, you do what you need to do to keep your sanity. I always look out for myself. That's how I got where I am today. Just be careful. They may be playing straight and narrow right now," she looked around again and leaned into me, "but Mob is in their blood. Did you see Diego's face when that old man spit on him? I thought that man signed his own death warrant."

"He may have," I answered. "I'm not really sure."

"Just don't get caught." We saw the boys come back in. She jumped up. "Hector, where's Hector?"

"He's with the bomb squad," Max replied. "They have to make sure the bomb is diffused." She sat back down. "He's really good, don't worry."

"Your uncle?" I asked. "Why would he do something like this?"

"Jorge," Diego and Max both said simultaneously.

"Jorge and Polo have always been close," Diego added.

We got back to the house and Hector insisted that Elizabeth spend the night. I wasn't really sure if he was just trying to get lucky or if he was genuinely worried that she'd be followed. But either way, she agreed. We all decided it was time for bed. It was a long day. It was sad how that old guy ruined our wonderful experience. Diego poured himself a drink in the kitchen and Hector and Elizabeth wasted no time running up the stairs. Max went into the kitchen, I guess to have a word with Diego. I approached cautiously. "Good job, man," Max said. "I do have a question for you, though."

"Go on." I peeked in and could see the exhaustion in Diego's eyes. I know he was not looking forward to being the Hector in the family. He was suddenly the one without the girl.

"When are you going to give up on Lilly and find yourself a girl?"

"Never," he answered. "Sorry, Max but I still need her." He looked around the room but I don't think he saw me.

"Seriously, Diego. You are a good-looking man in your prime. Find a woman for yourself that doesn't belong to me."

"She was mine first," he reminded him. Then he caught my eye from the door and I ducked.

"I just want her to myself for once," Max continued. "I have been suffering forever over the two of you, please just leave her alone."

"You look worried," he said. "Why so worried?"

Max walked around the room for a minute. "I'm going to be honest for a change, okay?" Max looked pretty serious. "I see her weakening. It doesn't matter how good I might be… she's weakening."

Diego smiled. "I want to leave her alone, Max, but you know how it is, better than anyone."

"You can have any woman you want, Diego!" He started getting angry. "Why Lilly?"

"I still love her. I want her back." He never flinched, still as calm as ever.

"We have a baby together." He began to plead. I couldn't watch anymore and I walked into the kitchen.

"Come on, Max," I said. "Let's go to bed." He smiled at me and gave Diego a look of victory. Diego winked at me and Max and I headed upstairs.

When we got inside the bedroom we started to hear sounds. We looked at each other curiously for a minute. He took off his clothes, down to his boxers and got into bed. Then we realized what the noises were. "Oh Hector, oh my God!" Max put his blanket over his face and I giggled. He pulled the blanket back off and said, "Why am I always the one in the room next to the guy doing it with the noisy, white girl?" he asked. I threw a pillow at him. "You don't think Hector's going to start moaning, do you?" he asked. "I'm not sure I can handle that."

"Probably not," I answered. "You're as quiet as a mouse." I took off my clothes and put on a pink, lace nighty. Max's eyes opened wide. "Oh my," he said. "Come to daddy, noisy white girl." I laughed and crawled into bed with him. He reached under my nightgown and shifted me on top of him. This was something Diego used to do a lot. It was strange that I was thinking about that. He put his hands up my dress and slid them up to my panties and gradually slid them down my legs. I moaned a little.

"I love that about you," he said. "It makes it easy to please you when you tell me what you like." He took off what was left of his clothing and secured me on top of him. I let out a moan of ridiculous proportions and he laughed. He put his hands around me and pulled me into him. He reached up and pulled my nighty off over my shoulders. I was thinking about the last time Diego did just that. Being with brothers was complicated sometimes. I actually had both men in my head. I tried to shake it. "Bring them here, he said and I leaned down over him. I ran my fingers through his hair as he caressed my breasts with his lips and tongue. I was crying out, sure the pleasure was more intense than I had ever felt. I gasped when I almost did it… I almost yelled out the wrong name. I stopped myself for a minute and Max stopped dead in his tracks. "What is it?" he asked. "Did I hurt you?"

"No, no," I cried. "Don't stop what you're doing." He resumed and brought me to that place with such intensity that I know I woke the dead. Max grabbed me and rolled me over. "You're a wild woman, tonight." He kissed my neck. "I may take you to church more often."

When I woke I looked over at Max. He was lying in bed with his hands behind his head listening to the moans and cries of Elizabeth as Hector pleasured her over and over again. He looked over and saw me watching him. "This has been going on all morning." I laughed. "Take care of me baby, I'm almost there already." He pulled me close and made love to me like we did last night. He was faster than usual and I was still going crazy with pleasure. When we finally made it downstairs, Diego had cooked a huge breakfast. "You're up early," Max noticed.

"Like I could sleep with all that racket going on," he said. Max kissed me and I put my arms around his neck. Diego shot the water gun from the sink at us just as Hector and Elizabeth made an appearance. "Hey!" we screamed, pulling away from each other, soaking wet. Elizabeth and Hector were laughing.

"Cool down, you two. Have I ever done that to you?" Diego asked.

"I think like a hundred times," Max answered. He turned to me. "You were a wild one last night. I can't keep my hands off of you."

"Oh was she now," Diego commented. Max did not like that.

"What are you trying to say?" Max asked. He began to approach Diego. Hector quickly got between them and ran interference.

"Nothing Max, you're getting way too paranoid."

"Are you trying to say she was thinking about you?"

"He didn't say anything," Hector said. "Not anything, now cool down, Max. What's wrong with you?" Elizabeth sent me a look saying, 'you were thinking of him, weren't you,' but I tried to ignore it.

"I'm sorry Max, really." Diego looked over at me and I looked straight at the floor. I wanted nothing to do with this conversation.

"Maybe I am getting a little paranoid," Max admitted. "Maybe we need to go back to Arizona."

"We'll go back to Arizona, check out what's going on with Johnny and if it appears to be safe, I will come back to Las Vegas and bring the Mexican with me," Hector assured him. Diego's face had no reaction. "You've got a good thing going on here, man. Don't blow it out of unfounded jealousy."

We finished eating and tension was in the air. I had to stop thinking about Diego and I needed Max to trust me again. I really put a wedge between us when I let Diego get too close. Max kissed me and put his cheek on mine. He softly whispered, "I'm sorry, querida. Please forgive me."

"It's my fault you feel like this in the first place," I told him. "Of course I forgive you. Just think about last night. Go to your happy place."

"That is definitely my happy place," he smiled and moved back a little so he could see my face. "Take me back to my happy place." He said it as though he was a little boy begging. It was so cute that I had to oblige.

Hector and Elizabeth looked at us like we were nuts. "Go," Hector said. "But no two hour deal. We have to get moving."

We got up from the table and chased each other up the stairs. I could hear Diego as we left say to Hector, "I swear, I didn't mean anything by it."

CHAPTER 33

The Open Window

"Come with us," Hector asked Elizabeth. "I have to take my car and they're all going together. Keep me company." Elizabeth looked at us thoughtfully.

"Why aren't Max and Lilly taking their own car?" That was a good question.

"Someone very rudely blew mine up a while back," he answered. "I don't have the money Diego used to allow me anymore so… we just haven't bought a new one yet." She made a tense face.

"Okay, Hector, I'll go. Will you take me to my mom's so I can pick up my stuff?"

"And… we're off…" Hector grabbed her and took her out the door.

We packed all our belongings into the car while Hector ran her home to get her things. We finished closing the house up until Diego's return. Max called a meeting, since we were alone. Diego was perfectly comfortable, even though he knew exactly what was coming.

We piled into the living room, since the kitchen was officially closed down. Diego sat across from Max and me. "I need to know if there is anything going on here." Max asked this question with such maturity. I must admit that I was doing a little of my own praying when he said that. "God please don't let Diego give me away."

"We are not having an affair, if that's what you're asking," Diego answered. "We're not even doing whatever it was the two of you were doing when you and Lilly were… well… you and Lilly during my marriage to her."

"I've been in that seat before," Max continued. "Even if you're not having an affair, I know you might be… involved somehow." He turned to look at me but I couldn't look back. I was guilty and his sadness was killing me.

"I'm catching glances and new behavior," he said. Look, if you're falling in love, I need to know." He turned and looked at me. He put his hand on the side of my face with the backs of his fingers.

I looked up at him. "If you don't tell me the truth, I can't fix it." Then he turned to Diego. "I always knew if you brought you're "A" game to the table, I would have some serious competition." He got quiet. Then he continued. "It appears that you may be bringing your "A" game."

Diego laughed. "I can't help how I feel about her."

"If she is falling in love with you, I will not let her go."

"For goodness sakes, Max," Diego said. "You sound just like I used to sound."

"She's my wife, and I will fight for her." Then Max looked at me again. "Oh my God, I do sound like him, don't I?"

"It doesn't matter how you sound, Max. I love you and only you." He smiled a weak smile at me. "If you think something is going on, it's just because it's weird." I looked at Diego. "Come on, back me up, it's weird."

"Yes, I guess so," Diego agreed.

"I do like him now and maybe that freaks you out a bit," I continued. "But I love you. You're just weirded out because we used to sleep together, that's all." I looked at their faces for some kind of reaction but they were both expressionless. "Used to being the operative words. And we have not had sex since we were married."

"Everything she said it true," Diego finished.

"Have you kissed her?" he asked. We both got silent and I know my face gave me away as it always does. "Did you kiss her?" he asked again, a little louder.

"No," he finally lied. "But I really wanted to. And I struggled with it." Max was not convinced but I was not volunteering any information.

"Lilly, he has told me that he intends to win you back. So if I'm paranoid, that's why." He took my hands into his.

"Have a little faith in me," I said as though I deserved any of that. He made a sour face. "Okay so maybe I deserved that," I said.

"Baby girl," he was very calm. "You tend to get weak from time to time. I know you love me. I really do know that. I just worry that emotion carries you away sometimes."

"What about Hector?" Diego asked. "Do you ever worry about him?"

"Hector?" Max asked in an alarming tone.

"Shut up!" I yelled. That just made Max freak out more.

"What about Hector?" he asked again.

"Why is he so protective of her?" he asked. "He's been all over me about staying away from her."

Max appeared to calm right down. "He's just watching my back, that's all," he said. "You scared me for a minute."

"Max, there is nothing to worry about," I reassured him. I grabbed his face with both hands and kissed him. "We are stronger than ever." Hector and Elizabeth walked in just then.

"What did I miss?" he asked.

"Are you sleeping with Lilly?" Diego asked.

"No," he answered in a confused tone.

"Nothing then." Diego got up from the couch. "It's time to go."

Hector grabbed Max by the arm as Max started to get up and said, "Is everything all right?"

"We're good," he said. "I think we're good."

"I know you are," Hector confirmed. "Now put your tremendous ego away for a while and let's get the boys." They all laughed and we headed for the cars. Hector took his and we drove with Diego.

It was a long drive. When we finally got to the house, there was a shiny black BMW in the driveway. It had a giant red bow on the top of the car. "Happy birthday Max!" It was Max's birthday tomorrow. Diego had bought him a car. I don't know if it was out of guilt or out of love but Max got all teary eyed.

"Diego, why?" We got out of the car and Max ran his hand over the outside of the car like it was a woman.

Hector jumped out of his car and did the same. "Diego… I want one, I want one…" Diego laughed.

Max walked over to Diego and hugged him. "Thank you, I can't tell you what this means to me."

"I wanted to thank you." He backed up a little. "It's because of you that I am alive and filled with the Spirit. Thank you, brother."

"Oh, you two make me sick!" Hector said.

"I think it's sweet," Elizabeth added. "That's probably why they share so well." Both Max and Diego gave her an unfavorable glare.

"Well, it's true," she said. Hector hushed her and we all started bringing things into the house.

It was cold and damp inside. It almost smelled a little musty. The house was quite elegant. Not Diego and Max's fortress by any stretch of the imagination but definitely roomy. We already moved the furniture in some time last year, so we just had clothes, food and other odds and ends. I went shopping while the boys and Elizabeth unpacked. I guessed we were putting her up, since Hector seemed to be rather attached to her but she soon put my mind at ease. "I'm going to check on my brothers," she said.

"I wouldn't dream of staying here with all of you. There are enough people here." Hector took her hand and looked sad. "I'll stay with Rory and Sean," she said. "If they are staying with Johnny, I'll call you. I'm not staying in that dump with all those girls he brings around."

"He's married now," Max reminded her. "I think he's still married."

"Divorced," Diego added. "Word on the street, anyway." Max shot him a suspicious look.

"Don't tell me how you know that," Max said with a smile. "Some things are better left a secret." Diego shot me a glance. I could see it out of the corner of my eye but I didn't dare look.

Hector walked Elizabeth out and I unpacked the kitchen. Max came in and grabbed me from behind. "Do you want to break in the house or should I take care of Johnny now?"

I laughed. "I have to put the food away, daddy, go ahead and take care of business."

"I can't take Diego," he said. "So behave!" He said it in a teasing voice but I knew he was dead serious.

"I'll be good," I promised. He walked out of the kitchen and said something in Spanish to Diego as he walked out the door. Diego came in and helped me unpack.

"I've been officially warned," he told me. I smiled. He helped me put the pantry in order and I watched him as I took care of the cold food. I poured him a glass of iced tea that I had just made and then I poured myself one. We sat at the table and he flashed those green eyes at me. "I wish you would let me touch you," he said.

"Cut it out, Romeo," I answered. "It's bad enough that I'm thinking about you when I definitely should not be thinking about you. You cannot touch me like that."

"I knew it!" he blurted. "I knew you were thinking about me last night."

"Egomaniac!" I yelled.

"Why last night?" he asked. "Was he doing something I used to do to you?"

"Stop it!" I said. I could feel the beads of sweat form on my forehead. I got up and stuck my face in the freezer. He laughed. "Let's talk about something else… please…"

"It's just hard for me to watch you with him." He looked away.

"What do you think is going on with John?" I asked in a desperate attempt to change the subject.

"I think he went back to the life," he said, making the transition pretty quickly. I sat back down. "It's hard to walk away. The money…" He paused. "Well, just ask Max about the money."

"I know. He was grateful for the car," I agreed.

"I wouldn't be surprised if Max didn't take another job like that someday. Just for the cash."

"Oh no," I said. "Not with two children and a crazy wife running around, forget it."

He laughed. "I love you so much, Lilly. Just hearing you talk and seeing you smile. It makes my whole body feel alive."

"Thank you, Diego." I smiled and looked away. "Try and look at me as your sister-in-law now."

Max and Hector were back faster than we had expected. So glad I didn't get caught with my hand in the cookie jar. "Back so soon?" I asked.

"Disappointed?" he continued.

"Max, why would you say something like that to me?" I wanted to smack him but Hector hit him in the back of the head for me.

"He wasn't home. But his brothers were both there. They had no answers for us. With no probable cause just yet, there was nothing we could do."

"What's the plan?" Diego asked. "Do you want me to go?"

"Not yet," Hector said. "We really need to see John."

"Let's go check out that bedroom," Max said to me.

Hector looked at him in amazement. "You and Diego are just the same. Leave her alone for five minutes." I laughed.

"I'm going to go check on the boys." I got up from the table and left. They were all muttering something in Spanish as I went to the boys' room. I noticed a breeze, as I got closer to the door and my heart started to race. I quickened my pace and saw Chris sleeping peacefully in his crib. I looked over at Dieguito's bed and he was gone. The window was wide open with the light blue curtains were blowing in the wind. "MAX!" I screamed. "MAXWELL!" All the men came running down the hallway. "He's gone, Dieguito's gone!"

Max and Hector drew their guns and Max said to Diego, "Stay with Lilly and the baby." They ran outside the back door and started chanting his name, "Dieguito, Dieguito…" The sound was deafening.

I knelt down on the ground and grabbed his teddy bear. Whoever took him, left it behind. I put my face against the side of the bed. Diego stoked my hair and then picked me up off the floor and sat with me on little Diego's bed. I put my head on his shoulder as he comforted me. All of a sudden, all the other stuff was no longer important. A little time had passed and Max and Hector returned without my son. Max reached for me and Diego passed me to him like a rag doll. "I called the FBI and the police, baby girl. We'll find him."

"Who?" I asked Max. Then I looked at Hector. "Who would do this?"

"I don't know," Hector said. "Could be Johnny, could be his brothers…"

"Could be Elizabeth," Diego interrupted.

"Let's not rule out Jorge's influence," Max reminded us. "I don't want to speculate. I want to find him. And when I do…"

"We know," Diego said. "No reaction time."

About the Author:

Judy Serrano holds a Master of Arts in English from Texas A&M University, Commerce. She is the owner of Make Cents Editing Service, and was an adjunct professor at a local college. Currently she teaches high school English and is a freelance writer for certain on-line publications. Judy also writes romantic suspense and paranormal romance novels. She is the author of *The Easter's Lilly Series*, *The Linked Series*, and I*vy Vines, Visions*.

Although originally form New York, Judy resides in Texas with her husband, four boys, four dogs and now four cats. She sings and plays guitar when she has time and enjoys singing with her very musical family in church when she is able.

Judy Serrano

Other exciting reads by Judy Serrano:

THE EASTER'S LILLY SERIES

Easter's Lilly – This book

Brother Number 3

Relatively Close

Memoirs of a Mobster

The Lost Years

The Last Fall

THE LINKED SERIES

First Blood

Book 3 coming soon

Scary Reads

Ivy Vines – Visions

Connect with Judy Serrano

http://www.judyserrano.com/

https://www.facebook.com/JudySerranoAuthor/

https://twitter.com/authorjserrano

http://www.judyserranoauthor.com

Judy Serrano

CPSIA information can be obtained
at www.ICGtesting.com
Printed in the USA
LVHW051517110719
623803LV00017B/854